YOURS TO BARE

JESSICA HAWKINS

Editing by Elizabeth London Editing
Proofreading by Underline This Editing
Cover Design © Michele Catalano Creative
Cover Photo © Jade Gabrielle Photography

YOURS TO BARE

ISBN: 099786916X
ISBN-13: 978-0-9978691-6-3

TITLES BY JESSICA HAWKINS

LEARN MORE AT JESSICAHAWKINS.NET/BOOKS

SLIP OF THE TONGUE

THE FIRST TASTE

YOURS TO BARE

THE CITYSCAPE SERIES

COME UNDONE

COME ALIVE

COME TOGETHER

EXPLICITLY YOURS SERIES

POSSESSION

DOMINATION

PROVOCATION

OBSESSION

STRICTLY OFF LIMITS

ONE
finn

If this isn't fate, I don't know what is.

The only coffee shop on Manhattan's east side that serves neither pistachio nor chocolate pastries is two blocks from my apartment. Pistachio's not hard to avoid, but chocolate? Just proves you can find, or not find, anything in this city when you've got fate on your side. Maybe, finally, my luck is changing.

I pay for a coffee and sit at my table by the window. Another reason I was meant to find Lait Noir—my table is almost always available or opening up as I get my drink. That's a certain kind of magic in a café as small as this one. The white walls and floor-to-ceiling windows help to hide how crowded it is, but some tables are crammed with two or more people, and nobody seems to know the person next to them. Every other coffee drinker has a laptop, tablet, or newspaper. Me? I must be old-fashioned. I get out a spiral-bound notebook I've kept in my camera bag since last October.

I blow on my drink. The heater's on, but outside, people bundle under scarves, gloves, and coats. It's the time of year when Macy's bags make it all the way down here, even though the department store is a thirty-minute walk away.

Whenever gigs start to run dry, I go back to page one—a running list of ideas:

Travel the world with a camera, sending award-worthy shots to National Geographic.

Become the go-to photographer for New York's most notable events.

Since neither of those have panned out, I scan to the bottom of the list.

Private Events
Teach a course
Weddings
Back to Wall Street

Returning to finance isn't something I'd even considered a possibility after quitting my job last year. That's how I know I've exhausted every option worth listing. I can't go lower than slinking back to a career that almost suffocated me to death. And I won't. Maybe a year of vainly trying to make a name for myself has been discouraging, but it hasn't killed my hope completely.

I cross it off the list, and weddings too. They remind me of things better left forgotten.

Teaching?

I've taught my daughter a few things throughout her short, eight-year existence. The proper ratio of cereal to milk. How to swap out dopey white shoelaces for neon ones. The most efficient way to locate Waldo. Those are the easy things. I've got my work cut out for me in the more important departments. Can I make her understand that marriage is forever, even though she's just lived through my divorce? That loving someone can never be a mistake, even though I've fucked it up twice?

No, I'm not meant to stand in front of a classroom. I'm not sure I can teach adults how to take pictures anyway. I have a degree in photography, so I've got the technical stuff covered. But art is more than a skill to be acquired—it's communicating emotion, and I'm not equipped to teach anyone how to feel, especially since I've been the opposite of inspired lately. Every time something stirs in me, I'm reminded of how much I risked for inspiration last year. And how wrong I was about Sadie, the woman I thought was my soul mate.

I skip that option but leave it on the list. Some things have to be last resorts.

My phone vibrates.

We're ready for you. Meet me at the listing on 28th & 10th Ave. 15 minutes.

I flip the notebook closed so quickly, my pen rolls off the side of the table. They call, I come. It's my second time working with a realtor. I was referred to her, Liz, by another agent. Getting in the real estate circuit could mean steady work, so I don't delay.

I feel around for the pen, but my hand hits something bigger. Something smooth. Sturdy. I pick up a well-worn, dark-tan leather book secured by long straps tied into a bow. It's a journal, the kind that's twice the size it used to be, pages swollen with life experiences. My ex has a few of these from high school. Boys, summer vacations, unfair-parent rants, and more boys. She'd wanted me to read them, but I'd only managed one flowery, overwritten description of the Trevi Fountain. I never went near them again.

This journal's more substantial, though. The cover has paled and creased where the spine's been bent. These pages have been visited over and over. It almost looks important, as if it doesn't hold mindless streams of consciousness.

I inhale the musky leather before I realize it probably belongs to the girl next to me, and she might not appreciate a stranger smelling her things. Not that she'd notice. She's buried under headphones, her eyes trained on her laptop, her table covered in loose papers. I tap her on the shoulder, and she glares at me. I hold up the book. "Yours?"

She shakes her head and returns to the screen. A few people look over at me. When nobody claims it, I untie the bow. A journal this worn and loved is bound to have a return address printed on the inside. I peel back the cover. The first page makes no introduction, no apology. There's no "dear diary" printed across the top, no "this journal belongs to." Just neat, girlish cursive.

Give me your fuck.
Split me down the middle with it.

My face warms. Without thinking, I read it again. This isn't some banal musing on Italian art. This is intimate. Too intimate for a stranger's eyes. I continue down the page. The beautiful penmanship breaks down quickly, bleeding into barely legible scrawl. Trying to make it out feels even more intrusive, but I can't stop. The leather becomes less pleasant in my hands. Sticky. Hot. I turn the page.

Own me with your fingers. Trace the aches on my chest, touch the words it hurts me to say, press the exposed nerves around my heart until you hear my begging in your dreams.

My throat is thick, as if I've swallowed something I shouldn't have. Beneath the text is a simple sketch of a man's hands holding up a nude, ragdoll-like girl by her waist. Wide-eyed, her lips are parted, her cheeks pink—the only color in the photo.

I was happily yours until you fucked off.

The poetry in her words is gone, but the rawness strikes me in the gut. Just one sentence describes what Sadie left me with a year ago—a loving hate. Sweet, searing memories. The ache of desire mixed with the gut-churn of brutal rejection.

When I slam the book shut, I'm breathing hard. I'm going to be late to meet a client I can't afford to piss off. I stick the journal in my bag and leave the coffee shop. I should turn it in to a barista, but my heart's pounding, palms are sweating—things I haven't felt since Sadie. Fucking her, wanting to fuck her, watching her return to her husband—my reaction was always the same, physical.

I don't exactly enjoy ripping open old wounds, but I need this journal in my possession. Right now, the words inside it belong to me.

I meet my new client at a building between Tenth and Eleventh Avenue. Commercial gigs weren't exactly what I had in mind when I left Wall Street. I'd opted to shoot now and aim later, so to speak. But between child support, alimony, and renting a two-bedroom apartment in the city, I can't be picky.

Liz looks about my age, with dyed red hair and frown lines that give the impression she's permanently stressed. She lets me into the freshly-staged apartment. "You look just like the photo on your website. Most people don't, as if I'd hire or not hire someone just based on their face." She looks at my hair. It gets a lot of female attention, always has. There's a ton of it. "I've got girlfriends who'd kill for that golden color," she says. "What's the name of it?"

Since I moved to the city over a decade ago, I'm always getting weird questions about my hair, like whether it's all my own or where I get it done. My senior year of high school, I was voted best hair. And smile. And biggest flirt. The last one surprised me. I never intended to flirt, but I liked to make girls smile. Growing up, I appreciated when a simple compliment could reverse my mom's mood.

Liz is smiling now, even though I've hardly said a word.

She has me take photos of the kitchen and living areas from every angle. The apartment is a new development in West Chelsea that boasts views of both The Highline and the Hudson. The kind of place I might've come to meet a client when I worked on Wall Street. And here I am, meeting a client.

Eventually, we end up in the master. "Make sure to get the bed," she says, hovering behind me. "They did a good job on it, don't you think?"

"Sure." She sounds excited, so I spend extra time on it.

"People are very particular about where they sleep. I once showed an apartment for two months without so much as a nibble. I change the bedding and *bam*—got an offer the next day."

"Let's get the balcony," I suggest.

"We aren't done in here." She sits on the edge of the mattress, running a manicured hand over the comforter. "Come here."

I wipe my temple on my sleeve. It's stuffy in here and reeks of fresh paint. "I'm working."

She undoes a button at her throat. "Then take my picture."

I've taken many photos the last year, none of which have amounted to anything. I might've lost the ability when I lost Sadie. I remember her eyes, richly purple, when I stepped into the hallway of my new apartment building and met her gaze. The eyes of a woman who'd become much more than a neighbor. Our first night together, we'd gotten caught in the rain. I photographed her in my apartment. Her back arched against my then-wife's green velvet couch. Sadie's wet hair stuck to the cushion as her tits pointed to the ceiling. My lens had loved all of her. I haven't looked at the photos since. She's not mine to look at. That intimacy is reserved for her husband.

Like bullets, the words hurtle through me.

Give me your fuck. Split me down the middle with it.

"I can't," I tell Liz.

She frowns, those lines deepening in her face, signaling her disappointment. Turning her down'll probably cost me future jobs. It's been a while since I've been with anyone, but I crave intimacy over casual sex, I've always needed that with a partner.

I want the weight of those words in my hand again, the stick of good leather.

Back at my apartment, I hang my jacket on a hook by the door without bothering with the entryway light. I drop my camera bag in its usual spot by the couch. Leftovers go in the microwave. Almost thirteen months after moving in here, I'm better at being single. I clean up after myself more, eat vegetables, change the sheets regularly. I at least have to try harder twice a month when I have Marissa. Kendra, my perceptive ex, would find out if I fed Marissa too much junk or had her sleeping in dirty sheets.

Even though the journal's been burning a hole in my bag all day, I haven't opened it again. It's not right to read a stranger on the fly, out in public. But as I sit in front of the TV, shoveling dry chicken in my mouth, my mind wanders. I only read two pages. The journal's huge.

I bring it to the couch and flip through her pages. She shifts abruptly between love and sex, pain and euphoria. It's jarring, no matter how many times she rips me out of one emotion to drown me in another. She's wise, emotional, observant of the human condition, and yet also erratic. Angry. Indecisive. Unreliable. Her drawings are as provocative as they are messy. The beginning of one of the poems makes me stop.

Make me a woman.
Let me be your girl.

It's simple, but I think I get it. I never feel more like a man than when I'm taking care of my girl. This one wants to be adored, to feel worthy. I can see us now, a perfect pair, her arms around my middle as she fits into my side, burrowed against me. Trusting me to read her, let me in, ease her pain. Things I never got to do with Sadie, who kept me at a distance. Or even Kendra. Our intimacy didn't reach that kind of level.

I turn the page.

You throb and throb inside me,
until I'm nothing but a heartbeat.
a bursting beat of heart, coming apart on your cock.

My mouth goes dry. I throw the book aside, shove my hand down my pants, and make myself come in two minutes flat.

Fuck me.

I need to throb so hard inside this woman that she comes apart.

I need to find her, make her mine, and feed her her words until she's swollen with them.

TWO

I have to return it.

I take the journal to the no-pistachio, no-chocolate coffee shop the next day, sit at my usual table, and wait. I set it by my coffee, not too close so I don't spill on it. A safe distance from my cherry Danish so I don't get it sticky.

If the owner doesn't come looking for it, I'll leave it at the counter. It doesn't matter that I feel as though I've opened a window and let some fresh air into my life. It's not mine to keep.

An hour passes while I wonder who she is and how she fucks. If she likes to be slow on top, in control, or if she'd prefer to be put into any position that strikes me. I wonder if she's written something on every page of that fat journal and why I can't stop trying to guess what I'll find next.

I open it—after I've washed my hands—and this time, I begin at the end.

And there it is. A calendar.

This is more than just a journal; it has an agenda in the back. Bare bones—there's only one thing written down for December—but not completely blank.

On the back of the previous page is a drawing of a man and a woman. She's in a chair by an open window, wrapped in blankets. Her feet are propped on the sill, backdropped by a fire escape and falling snow. New York in winter. Behind her, a man lies in bed, watching her stare outside.

I study the drawing. His hair is colored in, but hers isn't. Aside from her feet and face, just one hand sticks out from the blankets, a cigarette dangling between her fingers.

Written next to the bed is a two-sentence love letter.

In my sheets.
In my head.

"Jesus," I murmur.

The only engagement on the calendar is next week.

December 1st—*City Still Life*, 8 P.M.

There she is, clear as day. I don't know what *City Still Life* is, but several Google searches later, I've figured it out. I've found her.

Fate has given me this one chance.

Today was the warmest day of the week, but tonight, my breath fogs like the rainclouds overhead. Exposure Art Gallery has windows all along the front so I can scan the lit room without ever stepping foot in it. Is she dark and sultry or does she look deceptively innocent? Will I recognize her by the poetry in her eyes? By the slender fingers that lend her thoughts a voice?

City Still Life is a photograph exhibit, a collection of work across several artists. The pictures are bland: cityscapes, an empty post office, a fire hydrant nobody ever found worthy of commemorating until now. I prefer people. Every person is worthy. Every person has a story, and even if they won't share it, you can sometimes read it in their eyes.

Especially with a camera.

My attention snags on a white paper cup left on a covered table. Printed on the side is Lait Noir's black logo, the café where I found the journal. It isn't far from here, but it's not the closest café to this gallery.

Someone picks it up. White-blonde, nude-lipped, and dressed in head-to-toe black, her fingers wrap around the thick middle of the cup. She has short, dark nails and milk-white skin. I study her as she studies one of the photographs.

She's put together. Classy. Not the torn-up soul I'd pictured with dark hair and eyebrows to hang over her frown. There's no stoop in her posture from carrying the weight of the world on her shoulders. Maybe it isn't her. I step closer to the window and try to get a better look at her eyes just as she turns them down from the exhibit. She balances her coffee in the crook of her arm and scribbles on a notepad.

She's *writing*.

My body warms, a conditioned response to her pen on paper. I salivate for her words. What about the photograph in front of her is worth noting? Was I wrong to call it bland? I want to know what she thinks.

She travels along the wall, squints, scratches behind her ear. She sips her coffee. People stop her to say something that makes her smile. I don't want to look at her body—it was her words that got me here—but I can't help myself. As she talks, she gestures, and her breasts bounce. They'd be big enough for my hands, and I've been told I have some serious paws. She's got a small waist, great legs, blonde hair that hangs long and layered down her back. I lick my lips.

She flips the notebook shut and shoves it in her purse while nodding at the person speaking. When she shifts, I shift. A man shakes her hand, and she excuses herself. She heads outside, toward me, and before I even know what's happening, she's pushing out the gallery door and standing two feet away. Inhaling deeply, she leans back against a patch of brick wall between the window and the door, just enough to shade her. She turns her eyes to the stars.

"I already checked," I say. "It's too light out."

She flinches, barely glancing over. "You mean too dark?"

"Mmm, no," I say. "If it were pitch dark, you'd be able to see them—the stars. But all this light . . ." I nod through the nearby window. "Enjoying the show?"

She doesn't respond at first, then says, "Yes. Very much. Which one's yours?"

"I'm not one of the artists. Thankfully."

"Oh. I saw your camera and assumed . . ." She finally stands up straight and squints at me. "What do you mean 'thankfully'?"

"I haven't been inside, but they're crap from what I can see."

"*Crap*? That's somebody art in there."

It could easily be my work on those white walls, but if this is my poetess standing in front of me, she writes to move people, and these photos wouldn't budge a feather. "It's just my opinion."

She steps a little closer. "And who are you?"

"Just a passerby," I murmur, feasting on this hard-earned moment of intimacy. She's younger than I thought. All that black clothing and studied posture made her look around my age from a distance, but she's not even thirty. I try to see her eyes again, but again, she's not looking at me.

"I should get back inside," she says.

"No."

"What?"

Shit. I didn't mean it to come out like that. Trying to cover up my command, I sniff. "I mean, weren't you leaving?"

She shakes her head.

"So why'd you come out here?" I ask, hoping conversation is a better tactic for getting her to stay than blurting things out.

"I needed a cigarette."

I remember the December sketch. Colorless hair. Smoker. I'm getting warmer. She makes no move to get a pack out, so I say, "I'm sorry. I don't smoke."

"Me neither."

A smoker without a cigarette, a seemingly nice girl without her naughty journal. Now that I'm closer, I see her better. Her brand of blonde is stark. It almost matches the color of her eyes, a steely shade of gray that might even be ice blue. It's hard to tell in the absence of light. In the shadow she's under, they're just smooth like glass, the calm before a storm.

I've found her. It's her journal I have, her words I possess. I'm the current owner of her thoughts. But what to do with this information?

"So, you're obviously a photographer," she says, glancing at the camera around my neck, which I've taken to keeping close like a security blanket. "Have I seen your work?"

"No. I've never shown anywhere."

"Is it any good?"

I don't know what to say. If you want to be a successful artist, especially in this city, you'd better believe your shit is good. I spent ten months after graduating from NYU trying to make it before my father-in-law shipped me off to business school. That, plus this past year, is the whole of my struggling-artist experience. I haven't managed even a rejection letter from the major galleries. So far, it's been jobs like senior class photos, real estate listings, and Upper East Side dog photography.

Yes, I took headshots of a poodle.

I shrug. "It's my work."

She hands me her coffee and sets her purse on the ground with a *thump*. When she bends over to rummage through it, I look right down her blouse. Her bra is fire-engine red, and a siren call to my dick. That's more what I expected to find in her, some attitude.

It hits me that she's getting out a business card. Good. That's a socially acceptable way to learn more about her.

But when she stands back up, she just has her notepad in hand again. She hoists her bag over her shoulder. "Nice to meet you."

I'm not ready for goodbye—I haven't even said hello. "Wait," I say, but she hasn't made a move to leave. "Can we exchange cards?"

She scratches her elbow. "Um."

No response? I'll take that as a yes. I pull out my card, a little miffed I haven't updated it as I've been meaning to. I don't care about finding work right now, I just want her to reciprocate. I hold it out. "Finn Cohen."

She glances at it before sliding it from my hand. In the next few seconds, she studies my face. "Thanks. I left mine at home. On purpose. Sorry."

Damn. I rub my chin. "How come?"

"People are always trying to use me at these things. Maybe that's what you're doing—"

Use her? I don't even know her. "I'm not."

She pauses. "I believe you. Anyway."

"I didn't catch your name."

"I didn't throw it."

I try to figure out if she's joking or serious. We smile at the same moment. She opens her mouth, but I never get to hear what she says.

"There you are," a man says from the doorway.

She glances over. He's shadowed, but he wears a suit and looks around our age.

"I have to go," she says without looking at me. "Good luck with your stuff."

I go to call her back. With the kind of heart she poured into the pages of her journal, she must miss it. The journal, maybe the heart too. But the man puts his arm around her and takes her back inside.

Forget her, she's not yours, you're not enough.

She isn't who I'd pictured. She's too put together—composed, without scars or mascara streaks or coal-colored hair. I expected storm clouds overhead, fidgeting fingers, lyrics in her movements.

Then again, what the fuck do I know?

I once expected an audible *click* when fate kicked in.

Sparks.

Ignition.

Fireworks.

Like the time I stepped out of my apartment, met eyes with 6B across the hall, and lost my heart to my stomach.

But I'd been wrong about Sadie.

Am I wrong now?

Could I be misreading this girl? On the outside, she's clean lines and smooth curves. But then, the calm before the storm can be more unnerving than the storm itself. Is that who she is?

Or is she red lingerie, ice-gray eyes and fake cigarettes?

I walk away, and she's all I think about on my way home. Whether I was supposed to find her . . . or if fate is warning me to leave it alone. I should listen. Maybe it's best this spark doesn't ignite. Because fireworks can explode in your face—and it fucking hurts.

Even if you're expecting it.

THREE

Six simple words.

Did anyone turn in a journal?

I repeat them to myself as I cross the busy street to Lait Noir. I should've stopped for coffee on my way to get coffee. Situations that make a heart beat this hard should not be tackled without caffeine. Through the café window, I see a woman at the exact table where the book fell out of my bag. I've been back every morning since I lost it, and it isn't there. Which means it's most likely behind the counter. I just have to ask.

Inside the café, I remove my mittens and get in line. There are enough people in front of me to give me time to prepare.

I wasn't going to ask. Once I realized it was gone, I convinced myself it was a good thing. The girl in the journal is dark, depraved, a fraud. She's someone I've worked hard to bury, but for some reason, she continues to come out through my words. Why can't I let this one piece of my former self go?

I move forward in line. Pete throws me a wave from behind the register, and my throat dries. Last night, after the *City Still Life* show, I was restless. Rich noticed, asked if I needed anything.

It might've been my encounter with the handsome, quiet photographer—Finn. He looked at me like he was trying to read my thoughts through my eyes. I'm not used to being seen that way; I wasn't sure how to feel about it. I wanted to stay and find out, but that desire alone made me wary.

Or maybe it finally hit me that my journal was somewhere out there by itself, and that I'd never see years' worth of work again. Bad work, in more ways than one, but still mine. As Rich and I rode away from the show, all I wanted to do was go home, put my feelings on the page as I normally would, and close the book on them.

The customer in front of me steps aside, and suddenly, it's just me and Pete. And the five people in line behind me. And the female barista who only scowls.

"One coffee, black as my heart, coming right up," Pete says with a grin.

I hand him exact change. "Thanks."

"How's your morning, Halston?" he asks, popping open the register.

"Good. Yours?"

"Let's just say my winter-white Tom Ford pants that're as expensive as they sound were not made for this job."

I shake my head. "I've warned you before about wearing designer clothing to work."

"And let Tom Ford waste away in a closet that couldn't house a Chihuahua? Please. Anyway, I hear coffee stains are so trendy, nobody's even talking about them yet."

I smile, but I don't feel at ease. My stomach cramps as I try to force the words to the surface.

Did anyone turn in a journal?

The person behind me sighs.

"So, what's so good about your morning?" Pete asks over his shoulder as he fills my cup.

"What do you mean?"

He turns with the coffee and grabs a lid. "It's just, every day I ask you how it's going, and you always say good, no matter what."

I blink at him. "Doesn't everyone?"

"Most of the time, but not every day. Sometimes there's snow or tourists to battle or some days, people just wake up on the wrong side of the bed. I hear it all. But not you. Do you ever have a bad day?"

I don't know how to answer. Everybody has bad days. I just don't experience them often—or great days, either. Some might call that boring, but it's a form of self-preservation. I don't handle highs and lows like the average person, so I do what I have to do to stay even. "I guess I'm just a generally happy person."

Or, I've gotten help in that department so long, it's basically the truth.

"That's nice," he says, sliding the cup across the counter. "I can't even imagine a day without all hell breaking loose."

I glance at the coffee. This is the perfect job for social Pete. Having gotten to know him through my daily visits the last year, I'm fairly certain he likes some chaos in his life. To me, he's the one who seems happy. I'm just getting by as best I can.

This is the perfect opening to ask about the lost and found. In fact, I do have difficult days, and that's why the journal is necessary. I take a breath. "Pete—"

"Are you two going to chat all morning?" a woman in line asks.

Pete ignores her. "What's up, babe? You finally going to try one of my famous scones? On the house. First hit's free."

I envision the journal sitting right between us, underneath the counter. I doubt Pete'd hesitate to open someone's private diary if it caught his interest. He's nosy like that. What if he was disgusted? Or showed it to perma-scowl and they found it offensively bad? Worse . . . what if they laughed? It wouldn't be the first time. In eighth grade, I wrote and performed a poem for drama and stupidly chose the topic of sex. I could barely hear myself over the snickering. The teacher sent a note home to my parents.

If I ask Pete for my journal and he returns it to me, I have to assume he read it. And perma-scowl too. I could never show my face in here again. I need my journal, but I need this routine too. I pick up my coffee and wait for Pete to finish boasting about his scone recipe. "Not today," I say when he's done. "But thanks anyway."

"See you later for a refill?" he asks.

"Maybe." I wave on my way outside.

Instead of heading down to the subway, I decide to walk to work. I'm not good with nervous energy. I rarely get anxious anymore, my dad has seen to that, but when my regular coping methods aren't enough, I write. I put it all in the journal so I can function properly, do my job, play the roles I'm supposed to and fall asleep at night without dark thoughts creeping in. My words come from a corner of my mind I don't like to shine light on, but sometimes I need to. Not for anyone other than myself to see, though.

I dial the agency to check in with my assistant.

"Halston Fox's line," Benny answers.

"It's me. Is Rich at the office?"

She hums. "Gee, you *could* just call him yourself."

I half roll my eyes. "I want to come in late, but he gets all judgey when I do."

"You can't. Your dad just called a meeting upstairs. That's where Rich is headed, and that's where you need to be in fifteen minutes."

Damn. It doesn't really matter if I'm late—that's one of the advantages to being the boss's daughter—but I don't like to give my dad or Rich excuses for a lecture. "I'll be there in ten."

I hang up, step off the curb, and stick my hand out for a cab. Despite the sun shining bright, it's still a crisp December day. I wedge my coffee in one elbow and dig in my handbag for my mittens. Before I get them, my phone's daily reminder rings. I abandon the gloves and get my meds from the side pocket. I don't normally take them in public, so I hide the bottle in a fist to unscrew the cap.

A taxi swerves over, disturbing a flock of pigeons. When a bird nearly wings me in the face, I throw my arms up, dumping pills all over the street.

Shit shit shit.

"In or out," the cabbie yells.

The alarm continues to ding. A couple people stop on the sidewalk. "Do you need help?" someone asks.

"I'm fine," I say automatically. Little white tablets are scattered on the pavement in a chalky constellation. The only way this moment could get more embarrassing is if I get on my hands and knees to retrieve a bunch of happy pills.

I leave them to hop in the car. "Fourteenth and Fifth," I tell the driver.

Before we've even pulled away from the curb, I touch my fingers to the inked feather behind my ear. My mother's the only person I knew who actually liked pigeons. She insisted birds could love and be loved. For a second, I think I can feel my pulse there, my hammering heart.

Could the birds have been a message from her? If so, what does it mean?

She'd had post-partum depression for a few months after I was born. I hadn't even known until my dad told me following a client meeting where he'd had too many drinks. But once Mom had come out of it, that was it, according to him. Cured. I've wondered many times how she would've felt about the meds. If the birds are any indication, not supportive. But she isn't here, is she? I make a mental note to see if I have a back-up stash at home.

On the top of my purse, sitting precariously close to the edge, is Finn's card. I pick it up, relieved it didn't fall out. Why? I don't intend to do anything with it. Do I? God, he was attractive—taller than anyone I've ever dated, but with an almost gentle demeanor. *Almost.* There was that moment he tried to tell me no. Another where he absentmindedly ran a hand through his golden-brown hair, fisting it with a big, paw-like hand.

And his lips. Rust-colored and a leap beyond kissable. Fuckable? Can lips be fuckable?

That man's could.

I blush, even though I'm alone, and tuck the card

into a side pocket. He's out of my league anyway, and those are the kinds of thoughts reserved for my journal.

Since only some of my coffee spilled out of the top, I drink what's left. My walk might've been cut short, but at least I have my coffee. I calm down as its familiar taste coats my tongue. I have to forget about the journal. It was a way to distract myself when I needed escape, and I have others. I've tried to get rid of them before. Maybe losing that journal is a nudge to move on, another sign from Mom.

It takes a second to register the loss, but when I do, sadness overwhelms me. I let it. I'm alone for the next eight or so minutes, so I can feel whatever I want without judgment. Some days it's as though just having the journal keeps me functioning, but I know that's not true. It takes more than that to maintain my sanity. Not having the journal doesn't change anything. If I won't go outside my comfort zone to find it, it must not be that important, right?

I'll keep telling myself that until it feels true enough.

I have seven more minutes to mourn.

Then it's back to happy as usual.

FOUR

finn

Monday morning, I stake out the coffee shop.

I ignored fickle fate for an entire Friday *and* a weekend—three days, seventy-two hours. It helped that I had my daughter to distract me. But once Kendra picked Marissa up, I was alone with my thoughts again.

Alone with *her* thoughts.

And I just can't let it go.

Finding that journal under *my* table was an accident? An agenda with one entry wasn't supposed to lead me right to her? I can't ignore it. If fate is testing me, I won't fail. I know one thing for sure about the owner—she comes to Lait Noir. So I make sure to get there when the café opens at the break of dawn.

Another thing I know for sure? She fascinates me. She's beautiful in a way that makes her seem untouchable. I don't want to keep my hands to myself, though. I want to feel and make her feel. I want the journal girl I met a week ago to be the one from the gallery.

It's almost nine when I look up from my laptop and spot her across the street, waiting for a break in traffic. Once again, she's in all black. Her white-blonde hair is pulled back except for a few loose strands that float around her face. Pulling her coat closed, she expertly darts through traffic in knee-high leather boots.

I quickly slide my laptop into its case, weave through the tables, and get in line. When I hear her heels clicking behind me, I glance back.

She unfurls a soft-as-fuck-looking gray scarf from around her neck. Her coat is open, her nipples noticeably hard through a dark, sheer blouse.

She clears her throat.

I look up. I've been caught staring.

"Are you following me?" she asks.

"That'd be impressive, considering I'm ahead of you in line."

After a tense silence during which she might be planning to deck me, she smiles. She's messing with me, but like the other night, her sense of humor isn't so obvious. "Finn, right?"

"Good memory."

The man behind the counter calls me forward. I order a black coffee and angle sideways to ask, "Can I get your drink?"

"That's not necessary."

"I insist. How's a latte sound? You like that pumpkin spice stuff?"

The barista laughs. "Yeah, do you like pumpkin spice, babe?"

She smiles—at *him*. That fucker. "Do those even have caffeine?" she asks.

"I got you," he says, looking back at me. "Halston likes it black as the devil's soul. That's why she keeps coming back to me." He winks. "That'll be four-sixty."

I give him my credit card but keep my eyes on her. "Halston. Really made me work for that, didn't you?"

She reaches by me to take her coffee from the counter. All at once, she's in my nostrils, my personal space, blocking anything in my vision that isn't her. She smells like pepper, a hint of masculinity that has me leaning in. Since her hair is pulled back, I see the flash of a tattoo under her ear. I'm keeping tally: secret journal, red bra, fake smoking, strategically placed ink, spicy scent. She hides herself well, and my curiosity's getting the better of me.

"Thanks for the coffee," she says, stepping back before I've had my fill.

"Will you sit for a minute?"

"No tables . . ."

"I know a place." I pick up my coffee, and since I'm headed toward the exit, she has to follow. My predestined table is taken, today of all days, but that's not where I'm taking her. Near the front of the shop is a deep windowsill that'll fit just two ass cheeks—one of hers, one of mine.

She peers outside, and then at me. "Is this about work?"

"No."

Her phone begins to chime. She takes it from her purse. "Don't answer," I say.

She arches an eyebrow at me but silences it. "It's not a call. I only have a minute."

"I'll take it."

She balances on the ledge, facing me. It's cozy, our knees brushing. She doesn't pull hers away, and I'm certainly not about to. "Do you . . . come here a lot?"

I'm about to tease her for what sounds like a pick-up line, but she rubs her elbow in a way that makes me think she might be nervous. I let her off easy. "Best coffee in the neighborhood," I say. "I'd know. I've tried it all."

"It's great," she agrees. "Convenient too."

Convenient. Like me, she must live or work around here. Because it's mid-morning, I doubt her job is a typical nine-to-five. I soak up details like a sponge. "What'd you decide about the show last week?"

"Someone told me it was crap," she says with a shrug. "An eloquent assessment I happen to agree with."

I smile, but the mention of the show takes me back to that night. To the way we left things, her walking away under someone else's arm. Every bone in my body says to leave it alone—because, yes, heartache goes bone deep. The truth hurts. My brain might've been on vacation when I started an affair with Sadie, but it came back the day she left. It's here now, and it knows better. "That man," I say, "was he your boyfriend?"

Watching me, she absentmindedly picks at the sleeve of her coffee cup. "You think that's your business?"

"Yeah I do." I'm bluffing. It's not my business, but I have to know. I can't put myself in the same situation twice. If she says yes, I'll walk away right now and won't look back.

"Not was," she says. "Is."

"Is?"

"He is my boyfriend."

Fuck fuck fuck. I don't even blink. This is a hard limit for me. I'll never get involved with someone like that, someone unavailable, again. I'd thought this was it, though. I really fucking did. I haven't felt anything in a year, not until I opened that journal. It awoke things in me I feared were dead, and I think this girl—Halston—might understand me.

Her forehead wrinkles. "Are you okay?"

"I, uh, yeah." My legs don't move. I'm not walking out the door. I need to, and I will, but first there's the matter of her journal. "It wasn't the answer I expected."

She blushes. Her milky-white skin blooms like a rose. She understands why I bought her coffee and brought her to this tiny windowsill that's currently digging into my ass cheek. There wasn't supposed to be someone else.

"Who is he?" I don't know why I'm asking.

She glances at the nude lipstick stain she's left on her lid. "Are you going to take my coffee back because I have a boyfriend?"

"After you've put your mouth on it?"

She half-gapes. "I . . . I'm going to be late to work."

"I have a confession to make," I say.

"I don't think I should hear it." She puts her purse over her shoulder and goes to stand.

"I found your journal."

She freezes, then slowly lowers back onto the windowsill. "M-my . . ."

"Are you okay?" I ask.

"It wasn't . . . what I expected."

"It's yours, isn't it?" I ask. "I found it here, on the floor. Well, not *here*," I point toward the window, "there, under that table."

She shakes her head. "No."

"I've been reading it. Shitty of me, I know, but I opened it to see if I could find someone to return it to, and your words just fucking gripped me. You write like—"

"It's not mine," she says. "I think you're confused."

I hear her, but the words don't compute. Since the night of the opening, I've grown more and more certain the journal belongs to her. There are some things that don't add up or coincide with how I pictured her, but that's not a bad thing. I'm just as captivated by this complex version of my journal girl.

I memorized some things, so I recite a line for her, one of the many that spoke to me during my past few nights of reading. "'Hot like ice, you melt me down into clean, razor-sharp need.'"

"What?"

"You're telling me you didn't write that?"

She's white as a sheet.

"Because I've been wanting to tell you—I know that feeling. Holding an ice cube against your skin until it burns, but it also kind of numbs . . . which can be nice." I sound like a dumbass. "Sorry. Unlike you, I'm not so great with the words—"

"I don't know what you're talking about," she says under her breath. "People can hear you, you know."

"So?" I continue to push. "If you can be melted, does that mean you're the ice?"

She stands quickly, nearly upending her coffee. "This isn't me. That. That isn't me. It's not my journal or whatever it is you found. I need to go."

And I need to let her. She's spoken for. She's not the girl I thought I'd find, but she wrote those words, I feel it in my gut. She's hurting somewhere, somehow, damaged. Any sane person would walk away. I've done damaged. It didn't work out well. But for fuck's sake, I've never been so baffled by someone I feel might understand me.

She rummages through her bag and pulls out a fiver. "This is for the coffee."

"I told you, it's on me."

Her hand trembles. "Take it."

I shake my head. "Halston—"

She sets the bill on the windowsill and hurries for the exit. She's gone with even less fanfare than she appeared, my hand grazing the weighty leather binding of her concealed thoughts and desires.

I fight the urge to go after her the only way I can, by remembering the look on Sadie's face when she told me she'd chosen him, not me. But the sting isn't as fresh as it was a week ago.

I'm not sure if that's a good or bad thing.

FIVE

I've tracked Halston down twice now.

I can't do it a third time.

Fate may have brought her to me, but at some point, I have to admit it might've actually been fate's asshole cousin *coincidence.* My instincts have been off before—more severely than I'd like to admit. If it weren't for the boyfriend, I'd do it. I'd go after her like the persistent fuck I am when I want something badly enough.

Why does there have to be a boyfriend? How is that I'm torn up thinking about another man's girl, *again*?

I'm on the sunny, open second level of an Upper East Side apartment shooting senior class photos for a group of girls when I get the call that changes everything. It's been over twenty-four hours since I saw Halston in person, but I was with her all night long. As I read more, I felt her with me. I pictured her writing in her journal, fantasizing as her pen moved across the page, then acting out those desires with me.

Pry me apart
Make it slow
Forget my heart
Make it fast
Pry me apart
My thoughts, my thighs
Whatever it takes
Your truths, your lies
Lows and highs
There is no feeling
Like having you inside
When the sky falls through the ceiling—

"Mr. Cohen?"

I start. *Fuck*. I forgot where I was. One of the moms is holding out a coffee. It's not from Lait Noir, but I accept it. That's when I look around and realize I'm sporting a hard-on in a roomful of teenage girls and their moms. I'll be lucky if they don't arrest me. "How do you think it's going?" I ask.

"Oh, I'm sure the photos are *wonderful*," she says. "You seem to know just how to get the girls to liven up . . ."

I stop listening. I could give two shits what they think, it's not exactly my best work, but conversation will distract from my disheveled state. The students chew on ice in a corner. When one of them asked for snacks, they were denied. Anything other than vegetables might make them bloated, and carrots or celery would leave food in their teeth. This is the sort of thing my ex, Kendra, would do—hire a private photographer when the school provides a perfectly good one.

I return my attention to the mother as she speaks. She's not my type with pearls coiled around her neck, and styled, crispy hair. She's also several years my senior, but I catch myself noticing the line of her collarbone, the delicate bracelet on her wrist, the resemblance of her hair color to coffee. I don't want to take measured photos of snotty girls in uniforms. I want to make people feel the way Halston just made me feel without us even being in the same room.

Caught.

Flustered.

Hot.

Guilty.

I haven't been able to do that since Sadie. I've photographed other women for my portfolio, but they might as well be inanimate objects. Sadie continues to fuck me over a year later, stealing not only my future and my family from me, but my art too, the only thing I've ever really wanted to do with my life. Now that Halston's reminded me how it feels to be feverish and consumed by someone, I want to turn my lens on her.

My back pocket vibrates, and I get out my phone. It's an unknown number, which could be new business. "Excuse me," I interrupt the mom, handing her back the coffee. "I have to take this."

Crossing the room for some privacy, I answer the call. "Finn Cohen."

There's silence on the other end. Fucking telemarketers. It always takes them a few seconds to pick up.

"Hi."

I freeze. One word, and I know it's Halston. All the things I want to say come bubbling to the surface. I'm not sure *please don't hang up* is the right choice, so I go with the obvious response. "Hi."

"I'm sorry, I still had your card. I shouldn't have run out on you yesterday. It was a nice thing you did, but I freaked out." She releases a long breath. "This is Halston, by the way. From Lait Noir? Or from the art gallery, I guess."

Even though I believed the journal was hers all along, I'm relieved. I don't know if I can take getting fucked over by fate again. I don't want to convince myself she's the one. I want to feel it in my gut, and my gut is telling me not to blow this. "I know who you are."

"Right. I'm sorry I ran out, except . . . I'm not sure I'm the one who should apologize. You kind of stalked me, showing up at the gallery that way."

"Yeah . . . about that." I glance around to make sure none of the moms are nearby. Between untimely boners and tracking women, I could rack up some serious charges if I'm not careful. I step into the hallway. "The journal seemed valuable. I wanted you to have it back, that's all."

"It is. Valuable. I've tried to stop, but I can't. I've even tried to get rid of them. When I lost it last week, it was . . . I couldn't believe it. I felt so helpless, naked."

I don't know which of the questions running through my head I should start with.

What is she trying to stop? Why get rid of it? *Them*? There are others?

If the journal is so important to her, why deny ownership?

Did she say *naked*?

"Anyway," she says. "Thank you for going through the trouble, and I can pay you for that, but I'd like it back."

"I don't want your money." I scratch the scruff on my jaw. Maybe I should've taken care to shave this morning. "Where are you?"

"Work. Off Fourteenth. I can meet you after."

"I'll send you my address. I live by the coffee shop."

"Should we meet there instead?"

"Nah. I have better coffee at my place." I doubt that's what she's worried about, but I don't want to be in yet another crowded place with her. In public, we're strangers meeting briefly for a benign purpose. I need more of the intimacy I got from her words, even if it can't come close to what I really want. "I have to get back to work," I say, afraid she'll protest, "but I'll text when I'm done." I hang up.

When I get back to my job, the moms don't seem so bad. I have something to look forward to for the first time in a while—since Sadie. And even then, looking forward to Sadie came with a certain sickness in my gut. I never knew when I'd see her. If her husband would appear at my door instead. If the next words out of her mouth would intoxicate or crush. The affair had been exhilarating. Exciting. Stimulating. Everything my marriage wasn't. At the time, I would never have described it as exhausting, but looking back, it almost seems to be the most appropriate of words.

Maybe, just maybe, it was all meant to lead me to Halston. If my instinct is right this time, if she's the one I've been looking for, then the heartbreak, the struggle, the loss—it would be worth it.

SIX

Not much sends my heart racing like a knock at my door. It's a conditioned response to last November, when the person at the door could've been my mistress, her husband, or my wife.

Kendra packed up our house in Connecticut while I got our new apartment here in Gramercy Park ready for her and Marissa. Twice, she came into the city to surprise me, but it only took one fuck-up from me for her to jump to conclusions. She'd accused me of infidelity enough times over our marriage, but the difference was, when she found Sadie's coat in the apartment, that time she was right.

When Halston knocks, I'm instantly tense, even knowing who's on the other side of the door . . . or maybe that knowledge makes it worse. She's early, but I'm ready for her.

She stands on my doorstep, holding her purse in front of her, white-knuckling it with both hands. "I've always loved this neighborhood," she says.

"Don't you live here?"

"No." She gives me a look. "How would you know where I live?"

"Something you said." She'd mentioned Lait Noir was convenient, but really, I'm just looking for more information. I step aside. "Come in."

She cranes her neck, looking around. There isn't anything to see in the enclosed entryway. "Is that coffee I smell?" she asks.

"I just put on a pot."

She won't come in for me, but apparently she will for coffee. Fine. "Can I take your coat?"

She shrugs out of it. Like an old habit, I check her outfit, trying to find a piece of the puzzle I'm creating in my mind. A picture of who she really is. Her top is white but the material is thick enough to hide her bra. With her hair down, her tattoo is hidden. She's wearing black pants and those leather boots again that come up to her knees.

"I told a friend, a man, I'd be here."

I blink from her legs to her face. I'm not sure how to feel about the fact that she needed to tell someone where she is. And to let me know about it. "Do I scare you?"

"No," she says quickly. "This just isn't something I'd normally do. Go to a stranger's apartment by myself."

I turn and lead her into the living room. "What do you think I'm going to do to you?"

She hesitates so long that I glance back at her. "Any number of things," she says softly.

I've seen through her eyes. Maybe if I hadn't peeked inside her mind, I might not understand. I do, though. She lives in vivid fantasies of love, sex, pain, need. Of course, a stranger would slip right into any role she wants—a hero to save her, a villain to be terrorized by. They both make for good fiction. "Don't worry. You're safe with me."

She looks at the only things in the room—the big screen TV, a neutral-colored couch and love seat, an antique wooden coffee table. Books stacked on the window ledge above a vintage record player. My sneakers by the kitchen doorframe. My camera bag on the coffee table. That's all of it.

She touches her neck. It's possible I've made it too warm in here. "How long have you lived here?" she asks.

"Why not your boyfriend?"

She whips her gaze back to me. "What?"

"You said you told a male friend you were here. Why not your boyfriend?"

She swallows. I'd like to feel her skin on mine, the delicate ripple of her throat against my palm. She crosses her arms lightly, as if she needs something to do with her hands.

She looks so uncomfortable, I let her off the hook. "I'll get the coffee," I say, going into the kitchen. "I moved in last November."

"You don't have much furniture."

I pour coffee from the pot into a mug, comforted by the black hole it creates. "I'm in the process of replacing it."

"Bed bugs?"

"What?"

"Is that why you had to get rid of your furniture?"

"Oh." Gross, but I'm not sure if the truth is worse. When I'd rented this apartment, I'd already begun moving things in from our house in Connecticut when Kendra found out about the affair. She'd made me move it all back. Not that I'd been upset to say goodbye to the butt-ugly, green-velvet couch she'd bought without my input, or the kittens-with-babies photographs she'd insisted on hanging in my mature daughter's room.

I guess I should be grateful I got to pick out my own shit for once, but I've never had an eye for interior decorating. I only buy what I need.

I can't begin to think of how to explain all that to Halston without freaking her out. "Sure . . ." I say. "Bed bugs."

I return to the living room with two steaming mugs. She takes one before I even offer it, lifting it to her lips.

"It's hot," I say. "You'll burn—"

She sips and winces, but hums with appreciation. Her eyes are closed, yet I can't take mine off her. I watch her like she's the goddamn Mona Lisa come to life. I want her to hum into my mouth, to melt like that with my tongue between her legs. The way she writes, the way she moves—she's got to be sensuality personified in bed.

My craving for her makes it hard to talk, and even more difficult to control myself. "You shouldn't do that, by the way."

She opens her eyes. "Do what?"

"Go to a stranger's place alone. Drink from a cup without knowing what's in it."

Her lips part for an audible breath. "But you said—"

"You're safe with me. Just don't make it a habit."

She holds the coffee to her chest, right above her breasts, as if I might try to take it back. "It's good. Where's it from?"

This time, it's hard to speak for a different reason. I've had a bag of Quench coffee in the freezer for a year. I couldn't drink it after Sadie left, that shop the coffee came from was something special between us, but I couldn't get myself to throw it out either. Now I realize I've filled the entire apartment with the smell of Sadie but am only now noticing it. I don't want to be thinking about Sadie when I'm here with Halston, so I say, "Quench Coffee, a few blocks over."

"I've been there," she says. "They have a location in Chelsea Market, right?"

I nod. "Best coffee in the city, if you ask me, but like you said, Lait Noir is more convenient."

"Not if you take Lexington. It's probably about the same, distance-wise."

I rub my chest. "I'll go grab your journal."

"Where is it?"

"My bedroom," I say before I realize how it sounds.

"Your bedroom?" she asks.

Shit. It sounds bad, because it is. "I was just, you know, keeping it where I could see it."

"Sure," she says as I turn. "Leave the lotion and tissues, though."

I look back, my eyes wide.

She's busting my balls, and I have no comeback. Just a flushed face. I can slink off, shamed, or I can give it right back to her. "I've made no secret of the fact that your words do something to me. So, yeah, I did something to them. I'm sorry if that's overshare, but why else would I practically hunt you down?"

She bites her bottom lip with all her teeth, hard enough to turn the skin around it red. "Finn . . ."

"Yeah, yeah, I know." *Boyfriend. Fuck off, Finn.* This is dangerous territory. I go into my room and grab the leather book from my nightstand. I should return it to her and ask her to leave. It seems unfair, but as long as there's a third-party, I can't risk getting too close.

She has to go.

When I return from my room, she's sitting on the couch, and I know right away that I don't have what it takes to make her leave. If she does it on her own, it'd be hard not to stop her, but asking her to go? I can't. I've never been able to flip fate the bird, as many times as I probably should have.

To put some distance between us, I take the loveseat. It came with the couch, or I wouldn't know fuck all about loveseats, but now I'm glad for it. As tempted as I am to get physically closer to Halston, distance is my friend right now. Too close, and I might forget how it feels to lose what was never mine to begin with.

To her credit, she holds my gaze, even though I just admitted to jerking it to her words. She's getting braver with me. I can practically feel her *not* looking at the journal until she caves and drops her eyes to my lap. "You read it," she says quietly.

"Not all of it. But yeah. A lot."

"And you can still look me in the eye?"

"I was caught off guard at first." My hand sweats around the leather. "But you're talented. You drew me in and I've been unable to get out since."

I think I see tears in her eyes, but then they're gone. "It's just a bunch of random stuff. I wouldn't have thought anyone would even get it."

I wish I could explain how it felt to read through her pages. Like she'd been inside my head. "I get it."

"Because of the sex?" she asks.

I sit back a little. "It's more than that, you know it is. It's really moving, the way you write." She stares down so hard, I wonder if she's even listening. "I don't understand why you tried to deny it was yours."

"I looked at your website," she says quickly, glancing up again.

"Oh." The subject change leaves me scrambling to shift gears. "My website?"

"It took almost ten seconds to load."

"Yeah, that could be right." I rub the back of my neck. I designed my own website, but I haven't put much effort into making it any good. My technical skills have gotten me as far as I can go on my own, but it's kind of like my apartment. Just the necessities. "It's a work in progress."

"I got bored waiting, so I went to your Instagram instead and looked through everything."

Just like that, she's turned the tables. Now I'm the one naked and on display. Ever since I quit my job, I've desperately wanted people to just *look* at my pictures, hire me for a gig or two. But suddenly, I wish she hadn't. My work is nothing like her words. It isn't worthy of her almost-stormy, definitely-confusing gray eyes.

We stare at each other.

Stalemate.

Neither of us wants to talk about our work. It's too personal. Too raw. I actually care what she thinks, and maybe she feels the same.

"It's good, your stuff," she says finally. "But . . ."

My stomach drops. Well, fuck. I guess we are going to talk about it. "But what?"

"I'm—how do I explain this? One of my responsibilities at work is judging art."

I set her journal on the cushion next to me. "What do you do?"

"Market research for an ad agency. You know how you go into a dentist's office or a chain restaurant or even a clothing store and they have art displayed? Photos on the walls or sculptures out front?" She waits for me to nod. "I help businesses choose art that speaks to their customers. Or in some cases, doesn't."

"Why does a customer care what's on the wall?"

"Because you don't want art that's so good, people get distracted from your product. Or you don't want a patient to see something aggressive while waiting to have their mouth torn apart. Right?"

"I guess. I never really thought about it."

"There's a lot that goes into that." She purses her lips. "I have a team that collects and analyzes data on consumers. We'll run focus groups to see how people interpret certain images or colors, types of clothing, hair color. If you're selling parkas, you don't want people looking at a beach."

I drink from my mug to hide my expression. Is my artwork the beach in this situation? After everything I just confessed this is beginning to feel like a sucker punch.

"That's why I was at the *City Still Life* exhibit," she says. "To network and buy some things for clients."

The coffee tastes stale all of a sudden. "So it wasn't crap then."

"No, it was. I went there for cliché pieces. When I want non-crap, I go elsewhere."

"So you're the final authority on these things?"

"I don't know if I'd say that, but by now, I can almost always predict how a piece will make someone feel."

"Isn't there a word for that, when you see what you want to see? Confirmation bias."

"No, that's not what I mean." She crosses her legs, the leather of her boots creaking. "I've just been doing this a while."

She can't be much older than twenty-five, twenty-six, which seems young for someone to have all the answers. "Not to discredit you, but I'm fairly certain each person would react differently."

"You'd be surprised. And anyway, we're looking at the majority." She says all this straight-faced, like art is akin to science. "I determine what's practical. I'm an objective voice in a largely subjective industry."

"I've never heard of a job like that," I say, mostly because I don't like the idea of it and I'm a little stung that she of all people is implying my work isn't viable.

She flinches. "It's real. It's what I do. Art analyst."

"All right, well." I lean my elbows onto my knees. "Go ahead and say what you were going to say. That stuff you saw—it's not all current. There's a lot more."

"Okay."

She chugs her coffee like it's fucking Gatorade. I should offer her more, but I'm feeling like a giant exposed nerve right now, and I don't really want to move. Maybe it's a good thing if she doesn't like what she saw. I want to move people, not have them treat my work like it's scenery. It's how I connect. It didn't occur to me before Halston that the person I was trying to connect with might reject my art.

"Don't get me wrong, your photographs are nice, but I didn't feel anything."

I glance down at my hands. They're red from gripping the mug. She has balls, I'll give her that.

"Are you mad?" she asks.

A week ago, I might've written off her critique, but when I untied that leather bow and read Halston's words, something in me jarred loose. I was never angry with Sadie. It was the situation, not her, not me. But yes. I am mad. Because Halston's right. I've been looking through the lens, aiming, and hitting a button. Treating the camera like a tool. Forcing it, because I can't not take pictures after I quit my job to do this. I've felt so goddamn numb the last year, though. It's not even that I want to be. It's just how I am now.

"It comes with the territory," Halston says. "If you want to be an artist, you have to be able to take criticism."

"Really?" I look up. "Is that why you hide your work? So you don't have to hear what people think of it?"

"I don't write for anyone but myself."

I should want to crush her like she just did to me. I put everything into this. I gave up a six-figure salary on Wall Street. I disappointed my ex-wife and her overbearing family. I took stability away from my child. For what? To take uninspired junk photos?

I can't do it, though. It'd be a lie to say her work is anything but perfect to me. "You should," I say. "It's a shame to hide it."

"I can see you're good at what you do," she says quickly, scratching the inside of her elbow. "God. I'm such a jerk. I should've started with that."

"You don't have to say that."

"No, I'm serious. You have an eye for this. Maybe it's the models." She fidgets and glances at the journal every few seconds. "Where do you find them?"

"Wherever. Craigslist, art school, the street—"

"Would you photograph me?" she asks.

She's just spoken right to my dick. There might not be any quicker way to get me going. Her question inspires all sorts of reactions in me, like how good it feels to look through a lens at someone you want to fuck and know you're capturing that moment permanently. I'd probably do anything to her she'd allow, but photograph her? I'd give my left arm to have her at my disposal for a few hours—and under my direction.

I don't need any more invitation. I understand what my work is missing. Her. Someone to move me enough to do more than aim. I pick up my camera bag from the coffee table.

"Oh, no," she says. "I wasn't saying . . . I just meant hypothetically."

"No you didn't." I glance up at her. It occurs to me that maybe that's why she's here. Maybe this, coming to a stranger's apartment and having her photo taken, is the red bra. The tattoo. The tell in whatever game she's playing. "You'll be a beautiful model," I reassure her.

"I don't think . . ." She stares while I unpack the bag, like the camera's a surgical instrument I'm about to flay her with. "Why?"

"Why not?" I ask.

"This isn't me." She uncrosses her legs, smoothing her hands over her knees. "I'm no model, obviously."

I can tell by the redness creeping up from her collar that she's nervous. Good. That will come across nicely in the photo, and maybe raw is what I need. "You'd be doing me a favor." For me, this'll be almost as good as sex, getting to look at her as long as I like, position her how I want. Except afterward, I can release her back to her boyfriend without feeling like I've lost so much. "Ever since I read your journal, I've got all this pent-up energy."

Now, she's red all the way to her forehead. She's embarrassed by this, or, maybe she's turned on. I hope it's a little bit of both.

"Okay," she says. "But . . ."

"But?"

"Not my face."

I frown. Without that, she could be anyone, and that's not the point of this. She's the reason I want to take the picture at all. I lower the camera into my lap. "It's all in the eyes, Halston."

She shakes her head. "Doesn't matter."

"Why?"

"I don't want it in the shot. It's better for you anyway. You're selling a fantasy. Men who want one. Women who want to be one. Without my face, the imagination can play."

Call me a greedy bastard, but I want all of her. That's why I sought her out. Why I'm sitting here with her when I shouldn't be. I pick up her journal again and flip through it.

"What are you doing?" she asks.

"I want your face, but if I can't have it, I'll take this instead."

"I don't understand."

I'm careful with the pages, as if I'm handling a relic. I hardly know where to start. I want to take a picture that matches how her words make me feel. Sensual, suggestive, unsettled in a way.

I know the passage when I see it. I spread the book and give it to her. "This one."

"This one what?"

I pick up her coffee mug. It's empty to the last drop, so I take it in the kitchen, refill it, and return to the doorway. Halston traces her fingertip over the open page. Her blonde hair drapes on both sides of her face, hiding her from me. My couch looks bigger than I remember, she's so small in the middle of it.

"Read it to me."

She looks up. "Seriously?"

Steam curls up from the mug. The coffee maker drips behind me. I nod.

"I can't. I never have, not aloud."

"Really?"

"When would I have? Nobody knows it exists, except you."

My lungs inflate. No shit. I'm the first? Not even her boyfriend? I've built the journal up so much in my mind, this is like . . . like watching a flower open or witnessing her first orgasm. It's getting to see something nobody else has, bringing down a wall, and now I want it even more. "Try. Please."

She looks at the coffee in my hand like I'm holding it hostage. I don't give it to her.

Dropping her eyes again, she scans the page a few times and begins. "'Rough me up, dark as . . .'" She reads slowly, her voice raspy. With a short shake of her head, she tries to pass the journal back to me. "I can't. You do it."

I walk by her to the other side of the room. If I stand still, she'll notice how much a single sentence, not even a sentence, affects me. I could've guessed listening to her read would be sexy, but her bashfulness about it is making my pants uncomfortably tight. The girl who wrote these things was supposed to be bold. Daring. Walking sex. Halston is subtle, nuanced. Beautiful, but in a quiet way that draws me in.

"Keep reading," I say, pacing.

She sighs. "'Rough me up, dark as coffee. Burrow deep, make me drip with it, get me so high, I forget how it feels to . . . crash.'"

Neither of us speaks.

"There," she says finally. "Happy?"

Happy? I could eat the words like candy, right off her tongue.

"What's wrong?" she asks. "Did I do it wrong?"

Words aren't my strong suit, and I can't describe how hers make me feel. That's why I have the camera. The mug burns my palm. I offer it to her. "Hold it in your lap."

She looks from me to the coffee, obviously wary. She takes it, lowering it like I told her to, and shifts against the cushion. "It's hot."

I have to bite my tongue to keep from asking how that intense heat feels against the tops of her thighs. I shouldn't be so turned on by someone I can't have, but it's the first time in a year I've needed something more than air. I pick up my camera.

"What do you want me to do?" she asks when I aim it at her.

"Nothing." I study her through the lens a few seconds. I desperately want to capture her confused, timid, curious expression, but I promised—not her face. "Show me your palm, just the right."

She balances the mug with one hand and opens the other.

I slide the coffee table back a few feet to squat in front of her. I fold all her fingers into a fist except for the index and middle ones, and that alone sends my mind to the gutter. They're my two favorite fingers, the same ones I'd use to see how wet she was before I fucked her.

I breathe through my nose to calm myself. This isn't just about me. She has to trust me for this to work. I step back a few paces and perch on the edge of the table. With the camera over one eye, I cut off anything above her lips and say, "Put your fingers in the coffee."

"They'll burn."

"You don't have to keep them there."

She curves both fingers and dips them into the mug, wincing from the sting of heat just as I snap the photo. She pulls them out and sticks them in her mouth but not before a stream of coffee spirals down her forearm.

I capture it all and lower the camera. Normally, it'd take several shots to satisfy me, but that was it. That was the moment.

"That's it?" she asks.

I lean my elbows on my knees and view the first photo. Her fingers are thrust into the mug in her lap like she's going for climax, and one side of her mouth is curled in an ambiguous snarl. It could be pleasure. It could be pain. I show it to her.

She nearly gasps. "It looks like I'm . . ."

"Masturbating."

"But it's a mug of coffee."

"Burrow deep."

We meet eyes, and it clicks for her. "Like what I wrote," she says. "It's just a cup of coffee, but . . ."

"It feels like fucking." I put it out there. "That's *your* talent. I want to do that too, make people feel like that."

"You do," she says, her gaze drifting back to the camera.

Do I? I didn't before, according to her. But her breasts rise and fall a little faster. Her cheeks are still flushed. Is she aroused? I'm tempted to check for myself, test her nipple with the pad of my thumb to see if it's hard.

Swallowing, I go to the next photo. Again, the frame spans mouth to lap. She's sucking her fingers, her lips pink and plump. Coffee drips down the meat of her palm and over her wrist.

She shakes her head. "You made me sexy."

"All I told you to do was put your fingers in the coffee."

"Have you done this before?" she asks. "For your own . . . not for work?"

My mind flashes to Sadie, who, in this same apartment, played for my camera. Different couch, different situation. Since her, it's been nothing but meaningless shit. Until now. "No," I say.

She glances at me from under her lashes, her bottom lip hanging, almost in a pout. "Really? Or are you just saying that?"

"Yes, really." I'm about to ask why she thinks I'd lie, but the hope in her eyes answers the question. She wants to be special. Maybe she doesn't know she already is. Maybe she thinks I do this all the time. Her sudden doubt is stark against the lens-sharpened sensuality I just saw.

"Halston. Look." I move next to her on the couch and flip to the last of the three pictures—the tip of her tongue, pressed to her wrist bone as she catches a drop of coffee. I got her eyes in that one by accident. "You're better than anything I've shot, but you know that."

Almost imperceptibly, her body softens, and she tucks her hair behind her ear. She isn't spice-scented today, more girlish, like a flower. Not as strong as roses. I can't really place it since most flowers smell the same to me. "What are you going to do with them?" she asks.

"Nothing." I flip between the photos. Fuck, they're good. With some editing, they could be great. The composition isn't perfect, but that makes them more real. The day's end offers just enough natural light, and some darkness too. If I faded them with a filter, turned them gray, they'd be eerie, and sexy. "Or, I could post them."

"You think they're good enough?"

"You're the expert," I point out.

"Not when it comes to myself. I think they're, you know . . . I love them. But I'm biased."

"They need . . ."

"What?" She looks me full in the face, and it suddenly occurs to me how close we are. Our outer thighs are pressed together. Lips within kissing distance. Her white skin is pink and patchy from the way we've been talking, and I think I could smooth it all away with my touch. I lean in. I need to take her mouth for my own. Dive into its heat, own her in seconds, claim what I should've days ago.

She exhales a breath I can practically see, and I stop an inch from her mouth.

"What's wrong?" she asks.

So much. So much is wrong with this. Cheating is the one thing I can't do again. I've been scalded, and I'm still one giant scar. I'm vulnerable as fuck to Halston's spell, but I knew that before she walked in the door. I have only myself to blame for feeling helpless. "Nothing," I say, easing back. "It's my issue. Not yours."

"What issue?"

I shouldn't have to tell her she has a fucking boyfriend. Isn't that enough to explain why I won't touch what doesn't belong to me? "What was I saying?"

Her shoulders fall. "That the photos need something. They're not right?"

"Yeah. No. They're right." I rub my jaw. I shaved for her. Did she notice? "I want your words."

She blinks a few times. "My words?"

"As the caption."

"No." Her eyebrows draw in. "No, you can't."

"Why not?"

"I told you, I didn't write that for anyone but myself."

"And I told you, you should. You have a gift. Don't waste it."

"But it's no good. I went to business school." She shifts forward, away from me. "I look at art, I don't create it."

"Then why do you write?"

"To get it out. To feel something."

"Why do you have to write to feel?"

She looks away. "I have a good life. Simple. My dad is conservative, and so are our clients. He'd be embarrassed if anyone in the industry found out. *I* would be embarrassed. I'm past the stage of my life where I need to shock people."

Maybe that's a valid reason, but I recognize her fear. It took me almost ten years to work up the courage to take a second chance on my art, and even now, putting it out there isn't easy. My best work comes from vulnerability, and nobody wants to be judged with their walls down. But I have yet to regret it. "Then nobody has to know," I say. "Just us. I'll make sure you remain anonymous. Promise."

She presses her lips together, suppressing either a smile or a frown, I can't tell. She touches her palm to her chest. "My heart is racing. The thought of someone looking at me like that . . . or reading my stuff. I shouldn't want to do it, should I? I don't know." She takes the camera from me and examines each photo again. "I think I do."

She may not know, but I have some idea. All the hints I've been collecting—the bra, the tattoo, the forbidden thoughts—tell me what I need to know. If she was raised conservatively, then she's probably been burying her sexuality in this journal for a while, hiding it even from herself, and it's seeping out in other ways.

I'm not about to explain it to her, though. I don't want this to stop. "Is that a yes?"

She exchanges the camera for her coffee, and after a pause, looks at me. "That's a lot of trust to put in you."

"I told you earlier—you're safe with me."

"I've critiqued people's work," she says. "Sometimes solicited, sometimes not. If I put something out there . . ."

"You're opening yourself up to criticism. But does it feel less scary if nobody knows who you are?"

Slowly, she nods. "A lot less scary."

I relax. I'm too relieved to get something I didn't know I wanted a few minutes ago. "Then I'll post this picture with your words, and you'll see. People will love it. And if you're still scared after that, I'll take it down."

"And if I'm not?"

I swallow dryly. "Then we can talk about posting the second one."

She nods and finally, a smile breaks through. "I should go. It's getting late, and there's dinner . . ."

"Yeah. Okay." I hold out her journal.

She just looks at it, balling her fists in her lap. "Keep it."

I raise my eyebrows at her. "Yeah?"

"Not forever. Only for a little while. When I take it home, I hide it, and it's sad. Maybe it should be somewhere it can actually breathe."

"Like my nightstand?" I tease.

She maintains eye contact, even as something darker passes over her face—desire? Fear? I'd pay a mint to read her thoughts at the moment. "If that's where you want to keep it . . . I won't stop you."

"I can't be responsible for what it makes me do," I say more gruffly than I mean.

"Then I'll be responsible."

God.

Damn.

This is the ultimate test of willpower. She's flirting with me. She *likes* the idea of me reading her words at night, touching myself, and fuck if it doesn't make me sort of crazy with lust. It's best she leaves now before I make a huge mistake.

I look out the window. Days are getting shorter, and it's already dark. "I'll walk you downstairs," I say. "You should get a car home."

"I'll be fine."

"I insist." I put the journal down. "Come."

I ride down the elevator with her and put her in a taxi. As she's driven away, as my warmth cools, I begin to dread what's ahead of me. Another night alone. I know her now. Her secrets, her small protests against what she thinks she's supposed to be, the bow of her lips.

Being alone when I don't want to be is hard enough.

Knowing everything she is, all that I won't have next to me tonight, will make it worse.

SEVEN
halston

One indication this won't be a normal day is the fact that I'm the one who wakes up first. Seven minutes before Rich's alarm goes off, I'm completely awake, as if I'd only blinked and hadn't actually slept. Maybe I didn't, because I'm still having the same thoughts I was as I'd drifted off last night.

Finn read my journal, and he wasn't repulsed.

He was so un-repulsed, that he masturbated *to it.*

He understood it. He felt inspired. Is there any higher compliment?

Then, he almost kissed me. Finn almost kissed me.

I look over my shoulder. Rich is fast asleep beside me, up to his nose in sheets and blankets despite central heating. I wouldn't have stayed here last night, but I'd already promised him I would. The sheer white curtains glow with morning light, the opposite of Finn's place, which is older than this apartment, more lived in, darker. Finn doesn't have much, but his space seems to expect clutter.

I won't be alone again until Rich leaves for work. That's only an hour away, but I don't want to wait. I take my phone from the nightstand and sit up against the headboard. After pulling my hair back off my face, I check to see if the photos are posted. Finn's username is already in my recent history from after I left his place last night. There's nothing new.

I have four minutes until the alarm, so I search hashtags for erotic photographers. The results are graphic, not artful like Finn's work. I angle my phone completely away from Rich and try *#sexypoetry*. More nudies. Most photos are of actual words typed out or handwritten on scraps of paper. I scroll and scroll and scroll. Some of it isn't bad. Some is even beautiful.

Rich wakes up with his alarm and turns over. "You're already up?"

"I'm checking for an e-mail."

"Yeah? About what?"

I keep my eyes on my phone. "Just a client thing."

"Oh." He throws off the covers, stands, and stretches for the ceiling. Dark hair curls from under the hem of his t-shirt. "Need the shower?"

"Go ahead."

When he's in the bathroom and the water's running, I return to my phone. I check Finn's profile again, and there I am, forty-seven seconds old. At 7:01 A.M., he posted the first photo. Right underneath my coffee-soaked fingers and curled lip are my words.

Rough me up, dark as coffee. Burrow deep, make me drip with it, get me so high,

I forget how it feels to crash.

It has no likes. No comments. Only sixty-one people follow Finn, so that shouldn't bother me. Still, my disappointment surprises me.

I go into the kitchen to start a pot of coffee before heading to the bathroom. Rich holds open the shower door for me, and we switch places. I scrub and shave while he dresses in a suit and tie.

I wrap a towel around my hair and body and return to the kitchen for what's usually the best part of my morning—my first cup of coffee. Today, though, I'm more eager about the photo. Outside of a few speeches and performances in middle school, I've never put myself on display this way. For people to judge. What if they think I'm unattractive? Or my caption is lame? I don't know the first thing about real poetry. I just write what feels right. Somebody could easily call me out for that, and they'd have a point.

Still, even though it makes my stomach churn, I grab my phone and type in my passcode. I can't not check. Finn believes in me. Maybe he's right, and I do have talent. Either way, I have to know.

Before I check, I pour coffee to the brim. Just the smell, the warmth, settles my nerves a bit.

"No e-mail yet?" Rich asks, drying his empty mug.

"Mhm." I refresh Finn's profile. Twenty-four likes and two comments. In forty minutes. It's not a ton, but for the small number of followers he has, it's something. His other photos have much less, even the ones of pretty women.

I hold my breath and read the comments.

Fucking hottt
What's this quote from?

My face warms. Strangers. They're looking at my body and reading my words. My journal entries have always been provocative, but *private.* I'm someone's art. Will Finn post all three? The last photo he took included part of my face.

He has the power to expose me.

A man I met only a week ago.

Goosebumps rise over my skin. Would he do that? Last night I trusted him not to, but things aren't as cut and dry in the light of morning. I should be worried. I'm just tense, though, anticipating, wondering what he'll do next.

"Earth to Halston."

I look up. Rich has his briefcase in hand. His chestnut-colored hair is neatly trimmed and styled. I can never tell when he gets it cut, because it always looks the same. "Sorry. Did you say something?" I ask.

"Did I leave the water too warm? Your face is red."

I'm hot, and I've been hot since I left Finn's last night. Since I arrived there, actually. I touch my throat. "A little."

"Sorry." He checks his watch. The gold glints under the kitchen lights. "When will you be in today?"

"Soon. I'm not ready yet."

"That's okay. I'm a little early, so I'll just see you at the office. Anyway, I was just asking if you're staying here tonight?"

"Oh. No. I haven't been home in a few days."

"But you will tomorrow night, right? We have the Dietrich thing."

"Right." I'd rather have a few days to myself, but I've already committed to the client dinner. Whether it's Rich's account or my dad's, I'm still expected to show. Clients appreciate that we're both a family business and a mid-size agency. The three of us are a package, Rich and I more show ponies at these dinners than valuable team members. "I'll be here."

After Rich leaves, I remove my towel and look myself over in the bathroom mirror. I still haven't gotten used to this body, how my curves are still there, only slighter, or how my smaller waist makes my breasts look larger, even though they've shrunk a bit. My nipples are swollen, as pink as my lips, but Rich and I haven't had sex in weeks. I hadn't noticed until last night. Until golden-haired, tall, muscular, attentive Finn leaned in. Until the way his one hand engulfed my coffee cup when he passed it to me, or until his magnificently green eyes lit up when he asked me to read to him. And his lips—*God*, his lips. They're unreal, so pouty they're almost feminine, except that the rest of his facial features are strong, his jawline sharp. It's the most inviting mouth I've ever had the pleasure of almost kissing.

I'm tempted to ease the ache between my legs, but there's no time. I'm presenting data in a meeting this morning, and final touches still need to be added.

When I'm near work, I stop at Lait Noir. It's crowded, but the black-and-white café is small enough that I can see every table from where I stand in line. People are working, creating, connecting, right in front of me. Three girls share a table, but despite their open laptops, they're all on their phones. Probably checking social media.

My heart skips at the thought of them coming across my photo. They'd never know they were in the same room as the person they were looking at. The author of the words they were reading. That would never happen—what are the odds they'd ever come across such a small, obscure account? But the thought alone excites me.

I take my coffee to go, and two hours later, I'm sitting across from several chuckling men in suits. My dad is always making grown men chuckle, a skill I wasn't blessed with and have made no effort to cultivate.

"Let's move on to campaign idea number three," I suggest, plastering on a smile that'd put a contractor to shame.

"In a minute, Halston," Dad says, tapping the table. "We haven't even gotten to last night's game."

Grayson Dietrich, a CEO client, groans. "What a disgrace."

My assistant and I exchange a look. She knows how my dad's interruptions irritate me. Right about now, steam usually starts billowing from my ears. I'd hoped a promotion to Agency Analyst would stop my dad's routine condescension toward me in front of others, but he's shown no signs of slowing. He doesn't see himself as patronizing. The clients want face time with the founder of The Fox Agency, and that's what he gives them, regardless of how it makes me look to have my daddy sit in on meetings.

I can't say much more about it than I already have, though. When I graduated college and told him I wanted to help artists reach the masses, he created this position for me. Every time we verge on an argument, I remember that and surrender first. He cares about me—I know he does—but when he thinks his way is best, there's no alternative. Even if I want something different, I end up giving in.

My frustration quickly runs cold and soon, my thoughts pick up where they left off earlier. With just his words, his commands, Finn touched me. Having his camera on me was no less intimate than if it'd been his hands. Which isn't a claim I can make yet.

Yet?

I'm as attracted to Finn as I am curious. There's no question. He listens. Watches. I think he even understands me, or else he would've just turned my journal in and walked away. I don't worry that he's at home, flipping through it, laughing at parts. He gives me confidence and at the same time, the thought of seeing him again tightens my insides. He has a distinct pull, and that's dangerous, because I can't do anything about my draw to him.

Can I?

I shudder. Noticeably. The table vibrates. I'm about to blame it on the weather, but nobody's paying attention to me, not even my assistant Benny, who's using her pen to turn Dietrich's logo into a penis. The men are still talking basketball.

I wouldn't normally get out my phone in a meeting, not even during one of my dad's infamous steamrolls, but I'm having trouble following protocol today. Work seems less urgent. My dad is less threatening. I'm running out of meds, so I only took half my dosage. I even skipped my third cup of coffee.

Finn's profile is already open. There's been hardly any activity since I checked this morning. Did he not use enough hashtags? Were we wrong, and the photo sucks? Or the caption? That could be the problem. I tried to warn Finn. It's not like I have any business writing anything. My hand sweats around my phone.

Those comments, though.

Fucking hottt

What's this quote from?

I want more of that. More of Finn and his ideas and his attention—even though I know it's risky. Or *because* it's risky. For so long, I've been moving through days, not rocking the boat, not taking too many chances. Anything more than that can result in mistakes, pain, loss. But maybe taking that photo last night woke up a side of me I put to sleep a long time ago. And maybe I want to do it again.

EIGHT

finn

Less than forty-eight hours after I took her photograph, I wait for Halston under some trees on a park bench. Union Square was my suggestion. It's not only close to her office and the job I had this morning, but it's always busy here. There are crowds, but also privacy, and I think we need both. She seems to be acting out of character around me, and I've already gotten too close. I shouldn't have admitted to jerking off. Between the light stalking, the photos, and that confession, she'll think I'm obsessed. Even if we do have chemistry, I wouldn't blame her for staying away. And if she doesn't . . . she might be just as fucked up as me.

I spot her headed my way. She gnaws her bottom lip and surveys the crowd, holding two coffees and a shopping tote. She's in black tights, a purple scarf, and *click-clack* Mary Janes. I only know what those are because my daughter wears them. When Halston spots me, she walks faster.

"I brought special coffee," she says. She flings her stuff and herself onto the bench before handing me a cup and pastry bag. "Snacks too."

"Thanks." I set them on the other side of me. She takes in the bare branches over our heads, the skateboarders riding from one end of the square to another, the prep school teenagers nibbling on each other's ears. At least, I think that's what she's seeing. I haven't taken my eyes from her profile. Her soft, feminine features are only interrupted by a slight bump to her small nose. There's a dusting of freckles by her hairline, and I get a better view of her tattoo—a small, multi-colored pastel feather that curves behind her ear. She crosses her legs. "This was a nice suggestion."

"I love the parks in this city. I need them. Or rather, I need a break from all the chaos."

"I never thought of it that way. I always saw them as a more scenic route to cross a block." She smiles. "It's nice to see you."

"Anything else nice you want to mention?"

She laughs. "I'm too nervous to think of other adjectives."

"Nervous? You seem like you're in a good mood."

"Do I? I guess I am. I don't mean nervous in a bad way." She cups both hands around her drink. "Coffee just makes me happy."

I arch an eyebrow. She's been drinking coffee since the moment I met her. "Are you sure there's no other reason for your a good mood?"

She suppresses a smile. "No. Yes. I mean, it's just the drink."

"I was glad to hear from you." I'd been home editing photos, wondering when or if she'd tell me whether she'd seen the post, the precise second Outlook had pinged with new mail. "Did you see the photo?"

Her breath fogs between us. "Yes."

"And? Do you want me to take it down?"

"No."

I smooth my hair back. I was worried. The photos are raw. I've grown attached to them, and I want to post the others, but only if she's comfortable. "So it's not as scary as you thought?"

"It's . . . weird. And exciting. Weirdly exciting."

"I've gotten more followers over the last day than I would in a month."

"Really?" she asks excitedly. "It must be the time of year."

"It must be you," I say.

"I don't know about that."

"I do." I get out my phone. "I edited the other two photos just in case you wanted to see them first."

She leans into me, peering over my shoulder, nearly in my lap, smelling like a spicy fall day. Suddenly, I can't remember where the photo app is on my phone. I swipe between screens while she waits. *Fuck*. She'll think I've lost it; I can't even navigate my own phone.

"There it is." She taps my screen and my camera roll pops up.

"I have captions picked out too," I say. "If you agree."

"I'm just not used to this. Seeing myself so . . ." She studies the screen a few seconds. "I used to be fat."

I freeze, stunned by her bluntness. "I-I'm sorry?"

"Not obese or anything. But I just lost thirty pounds. I never considered myself sexy."

I stay frozen. I don't even blink. I was married long enough to know I'm in dangerous territory. Both speaking up and staying silent could be deadly decisions. I swallow. Twice.

"You're turned off, right?" she asks. "It's okay if you are. I don't plan on gaining it back."

"I'm *not* turned off," I say. Wait. *Shit.* I walked right into that one. "I'm not turned on, either, I mean, that's not—fuck. Never mind."

She laughs. "Are you okay?"

I take a breath and start over. "You look great. You're not planning on losing more, though, are you?"

"No. I actually wasn't trying to lose it at first. It just started to come off."

"How?"

"Stuff." She holds her coffee up to her mouth.

"What kind of stuff?"

"Work. Stress, that kind of thing." She takes a sip, returning her attention to my phone. She taps the screen a couple more times, but I keep my eyes on her. I don't know what *stuff* means. I'm not sure we know each other well enough for me to press her, either. She smiles. "You got a couple more followers."

All the times Kendra accused me of hating her body come bubbling to the surface. I was never turned off by my ex-wife physically, especially not post-pregnancy as she'd suspected. I'd found her even more beautiful. No, my disinterest in her all came down to her behavior. It was hard to get excited by someone I'd grown to resent. Kendra knew I was susceptible to guilt. Hell, I married her because of it. The longer we were together, the more she relied on that to get what she wanted. And the more I pulled away.

I give Halston the phone and pick up my coffee and pastry. If she re-opens the topic of weight, having food in my mouth will give me time to think of a potentially lifesaving response.

"I want you to post the second photo," she says.

"Yeah?"

She nods.

I'm glad. Not only do I like seeing her on my account, but since she bruised my ego the other day by implying my earlier photos were boring, her stamp of approval means even more. I tear off some pastry and pop it into my mouth. "Then I'll post it to—" I jerk forward and spit croissant onto the sidewalk. "*Fuck*. Is this . . . it's—"

"Chocolate-pistachio," she says. "Why?"

I widen my eyes and check the coffee cup in my hand. Quench Coffee is printed across the cardboard sleeve, and I can't fucking believe I didn't see it. I've been avoiding the place for over a year.

"You said Quench was your favorite spot," she says hesitantly. "So I decided to surprise you." She gasps. "Are you allergic to nuts?"

"Huh? Nuts? No." I run my tongue over the roof of my mouth, trying to scrape away the taste of chocolate and coffee and *her*.

Sadie.

"The girl said this was their most popular pastry." She takes the bag from me since I'm holding it out like a dirty diaper. "You don't like chocolate?"

I like chocolate as much as the next person, I'd be a freak and a liar if I said I didn't. But I still taste Sadie in it, the chocolate-pistachio croissant she fed me the first time I laid eyes on her and then again outside my apartment door before she went home to her husband. "I had an affair with a married woman while I was married," I say. "I wasn't trying to. It just happened."

Halston pulls away, her eyes trained on my face. "You . . ." As my words process and her expression falls, I realize why she seems different today. She's more expressive. Her eyes are brighter, less clouded. "You were married?" she asks.

I don't think Quench's excellent coffee was the reason for her good mood. I think it was me. I think it was finally freeing words she's been bottling up for who knows how long. And now I've ruined the moment like a fucking asshole. But my relationship with Sadie was based on dishonesty and deception, and I've promised myself I wouldn't go back down that path. "She lives in Connecticut," I say. "My ex-wife."

Halston scratches her eyebrow, leaving a red streak across her forehead. "Um, wow. Did you love her?"

"Kendra? Not how a husband should love a wife."

"I meant the other woman."

"Oh." *Sadie.* She's the physical opposite of Halston, tall and slender with black hair, blue eyes, sharp features. Sadie was confident, professional, unemotional. I think the one thing she had in common with Halston was that she was sad. When I met Sadie, there was pain in her eyes, and over the last year, that's how I've imagined her with *him*. Miserable.

Except that now, sitting next to Halston, I realize I didn't think about Sadie at all yesterday, and I wonder if I still want her to feel those things—regret for the life she gave up with me, despair because she'd made the wrong choice. Maybe I don't need to think of her that way anymore. Maybe I can hope she's happy, even if it's with him. Nathan, that fucker. He hit me, square in the jaw, and I deserved it, but he's still unworthy of her.

"I wanted to love her," I say. "I thought she was so many things, and she was . . . for a while. I was what she needed at the time too."

Halston shifts away from me. "Are you actually divorced? Or 'separated'?" she asks with air quotes.

I'd like to disappear now. I definitely didn't see us having this conversation today, or maybe not ever. It's too much for the little time we've known each other, and it's only half the story. "We're divorced."

"If you didn't love her like a husband, why'd you marry her?"

That question has the most straightforward and complicated answer possible. I got her pregnant. But Halston already looks skeptical. Telling her about Marissa might scare her off, and to be honest, it scares me too. Marissa was a mistake, and a blessing, and as my daughter, she's my weakness. This past year, I haven't been the father I want to be because my affair gave Kendra a reason to skewer me. I can't be this vulnerable with someone who absolutely does not belong to me. "It gets into some personal stuff," I say. "I don't want to lie to you, so let's not talk about it."

"I understand. I have that stuff too." She looks at her hands but nods. "So will it be weird for your ex, what we're doing?"

"What are we doing?"

"The photos. The erotic captions?"

I can't lie. It makes me happy to hear we're doing something together. "They're two separate things. And I've learned a valuable lesson this past year. I'm a better man when I'm not trying to be someone other than myself." I dip my head to catch her gaze, waiting until she looks at me. "It's a lesson I wish I'd learned earlier," I tell her. "Don't hide who you are. It'll come out somehow, some day, and you'll have struggled with it for nothing. Take chances and risks. Make mistakes. Especially now."

"Why would anyone want to make mistakes?" she asks tightly.

"They're necessary. It's how we grow." Having an affair might've been a mistake, but it got me to realize that marrying Kendra out of obligation was the wrong decision. It forced me out on my own. It led me to this bench, and for that, I'm not sorry. At least not at this moment. I like being here with Halston. "If I can help save you from the regrets I have, I want to," I admit. "I know I should leave you alone. But

I've never been good at listening to my head over my heart. It's just who I am."

"Are you saying you won't leave me alone?"

I take a breath. "I can't do it again, the affair. I won't. I never saw Sadie as a fling. I thought she was—the one. I want more in my life than sex." I don't look at Halston when I speak. It's not exactly easy to say. I have feelings for her, but I won't push her. I pushed Sadie and dug my own grave in the process.

"You think being with Rich is a mistake?" she asks. "That's my boyfriend's name—Rich."

I take a sip of the coffee. Damn, it's good. So are croissants filled with chocolate and topped with pistachio. How could chocolate and toasted bread not be good? How could Halston and I not be good? She was literally dropped at my feet. She might be what I've struggled for, the person love and romance and fate came together to give me.

But she's not mine.

I have to believe she never will be, otherwise I'll make all the same mistakes I did with Sadie.

"I wouldn't know," I tell her. "And if I did, it wouldn't be my place to say. How'd you meet him?"

"My dad kind of set us up, I guess."

"That stuff you wrote in the journal . . ." I don't want to know the answer, but maybe if I hear it, it'll make it easier for me to keep my hands to myself. "Was it about him?"

"*What*? God, no." After a second, she laughs. Hard. I don't think I've ever heard such a genuine reaction. "He's not like that. Rich's very even-tempered. Logical. He's attractive, don't get me wrong, but I'm not that attracted *to* him. That's why he's good for me."

My mind reels. It's not about sex. All those things she wrote, the heartache she poured into the pages—it's not for him. I'm not sure I'm relieved, though. If I don't need to worry about Rich, then who else is waiting in the wings? "What do you mean he's good for you?"

"I used to be very emotional. Reckless. But I don't get like that with Rich."

"Okay, but your writing is so passionate, it practically burns up the page." I steel myself for her answer. "Who was it about?"

She gets quiet, picking at the lid of her coffee. Her nose and cheeks are red from the cold.

Somebody hurt her? She must have a Sadie too, and it isn't Rich. I should've guessed. The question is, how deep does the damage run? Has she healed, or does she need more time?

Eventually, I put my hand over hers to stop the scratch of her nail against the plastic. "Tell me. Who was he?"

"Nobody." She looks utterly miserable as she says it. "And I'm not being coy. It's really about nobody. I've never experienced anything like what I've written."

My chest tightens. It's an answer I didn't even think to expect. One I find hard to believe, but one I actually like. "*Never*? Nobody?"

"I guess that makes me weird." She flinches. "Right?"

Halston wants to be consumed. It's there in her words. I could be that for her—I already feel it, and we've barely touched. "Weird? No. Surprising? Yes. I'd have thought you'd have many broken hearts in your wake."

She smiles a little. "Nope. It's just never happened for me, that intensity. I guess that's why I have to write it. I'm not sure I'll ever get it."

I realize I'm still touching her, and I put my hand back in my lap. I chased that passion and took risks—my marriage and Sadie's, my dignity, and, my biggest regret of all, my daughter. Because of my affair and subsequent divorce, I've gone from seeing Marissa every day to twice a month. That's twenty-four times a year and more than I deserve, according to Kendra.

"It's supposed to help your craft, right?" She half-laughs. "Heartache . . . longing."

Supposedly. Not always. My work has apparently suffered since my spirit was crushed. "Seems to work in your favor."

"I want to do it again."

She rushes the words out, but I take a beat to study her. "Do what?"

"The photo."

"We are. I told you I'd post the next one."

"That's not what I mean." She folds a knee under herself and faces me. "For so long, I've been going through the motions. But I've felt like a new person the past couple days. Reinvigorated, or maybe just invigorated for the first time."

I lean my elbows on my knees and massage my face, frustrated. Because I know what she's going to say, and it'll be everything I want to hear.

I want her in front of my camera again.

I've been sleeping for the last year, and she's the only thing that's made me feel awake.

"I want you to take my picture again," she says. "That's why I'm here."

I can't say no to her, and I can't tell her that what I need in order to say yes is *her*. Completely, unequivocally, with no chance of her returning to her boyfriend or anyone else. I need her to be mine before I go down this path again. Halston has to get there on her own, though. I can't, I won't, make her choose me like I tried to with Sadie.

"Did I say something wrong?" she asks.

I look forward. A stoplight changes from red to green. A man steps off the curb, narrowly avoids getting hit by a taxi, and darts through traffic anyway. Are any of us really awake? Are we making decisions about our lives, or just letting things happen to us? Is that why we like art, why Halston needs it, because without it, we'd never feel anything out of the ordinary?

"I don't think it's a good idea."

"Why not?" she asks. "If it's about Rich . . . he won't care. He won't even know."

"That's not why. The affair I had, the husband found out. He hit me."

"Rich wouldn't never—"

"It didn't even hurt, not compared to watching her leave with him." I can't look at Halston or I'll give in. "I *wanted* her, and I *want* you. I *want* to photograph you. That's the problem. When I found the journal, I thought about it for days, and now all I can think about is you. I might be, I don't know, obsessed."

She doesn't respond. I don't blame her. We sit that way a while. Even as skateboards wheel across concrete and down railings, as a woman loudly laments about work into a cell phone, as car horns blare, through all of it, I can hear her breathing.

"Your lunch break is over," I say. I have no idea if it is, but it's been at least an hour since she left her office. "I'll put up the other photos tonight or tomorrow."

"Tonight," she says. "Please? Please."

She gets up but doesn't move right away. I stare at the ground until she leaves. I know when she does because she takes her body warmth with her, and it's just now I realize how cold I am. I look up, and that's when I see it. Today's version of the red bra and hidden tattoo.

Her sheer tights have a thin, solid line running down the middle of the back. It starts somewhere under her skirt and ends inside her sweet, schoolgirl, buckled-up Mary Janes. Maybe the stripe extends along the arches of her feet, to her toes. It wasn't on the front of the tights; I would've noticed when she walked up.

I can't help wondering if she wore them for me . . . and I almost missed them.

NINE

halston

I want to photograph you.

I thought about your journal for days.

All I can think about is you.

I unlock the door to Rich's Tribeca apartment. Finn's definition of obsession has been on repeat in my head since lunch. I've clung to many things in my life for comfort, but never a person. And I've never had anyone cling to me, or ask about my feelings out of simple curiosity, or tell me I'm talented.

And then there's Rich.

"Dinner in an hour," Rich says when I walk into the kitchen. He's fresh from a run, seated on a stool at the island. With his eyes glued to his phone and his ear buds in, I'm not sure how he knows I'm here.

I dump my things on the counter. "Great," I mutter. "I was just wondering the best way to waste a few hours of my life."

He looks up, removing the earphones. "What?"

I begin unbuckling my shoes. "Nothing."

"What's that?" he asks, nodding at my shopping bag.

"Stationery."

His eyes glaze over—as I'd hoped. He knows I have a few 'notebooks,' but they don't mean anything to him. Before meeting Finn this afternoon, I stopped at my favorite local home store for another journal. I've been feeling new things the last couple days, things that deserve their own fresh pages.

"How'd the presentation go yesterday?" Rich asks. "Is it going to be a good dinner?"

"It'll be fine. *Daddy* sat in, so everyone's happy."

"He won't always be around for those meetings," Rich says, sensing my sarcasm, even if it doesn't surface often. "Learn what you can from him."

I look in the fridge and roll my eyes. "Might want to save the extreme sucking up for when my dad's actually in the room."

"I'm not sucking up. I'm trying to get you to see the silver lining. And remind you that he won't be around forever. I wouldn't want you to look back and have any regrets about your relationship."

I grip the door handle. Rich has some goddamn nerve talking to me about *regrets*. I know that feeling better than anyone. I came to the fridge for water, but

I bend over and grab a bottle of Chardonnay I'd shoved into the back corner of the bottom shelf.

Rich eyes me as I uncork it. "I thought I got rid of that."

"I'm glad you didn't."

Wisely, he doesn't respond. "Did you wear those to work?"

"What?" I ask, playing dumb as I pour a glass.

"Those tights."

Rich rarely comments on my wardrobe, but then again, I rarely wear anything other than black, gray or navy. "They're trendy."

"Is trendy right for an office environment?"

"Clients like to know we're cutting edge."

"Our clients are mostly white men over fifty. I guess they'd notice, though . . ."

Just like with my dad, I try not to get into arguments with Rich. Tonight, though, I'm feeling feisty. Blame it on Finn. Or on the fact that I've been halving my pills the last week. Either way, Rich is trying to make me feel bad about the tights, and I'm not going to let him. I sip the wine. "Are you jealous?"

He looks taken aback by my out-of-character question. "I'm just not sure it's appropriate," he says slowly. "Is it Benny? Are you trying to fit in with her?"

"My assistant?"

"She's always wearing stuff that's borderline sexy. She gets away with it, but it's not really appropriate. Maybe she's not the best influence on you."

If he says *appropriate* one more time, I might blow. This is generally the time I start to back down. Admittedly, though, I'm a bit curious what'll happen if I test his limit. "I hadn't really noticed Benny's sexy wardrobe," I say, which is not exactly true. "But I guess you have."

"Are *you* jealous?" he asks. "She has a boyfriend."

"How do you know?"

"I take an interest in the people I work with," he says, tilting his head forward. "Don't you two ever talk about that stuff? You're together all day."

"Not really." Benny may be my assistant, and a very good one, but she's only a year younger than me. She holds me together, rolls her eyes along with me, keeps me on schedule. We get each other, but we're different. Several piercings rim the edge of one of her ears, and her tattoos constantly peek out from her skirts, low-cut blouses, and sleeves. We've hardly spent a minute together past six o'clock. Our personal lives just don't come up. "We gossip sometimes, but just about work."

"That's fine by me. She's not a friend I'd choose for you. Anyway, I really don't think you should wear them to dinner."

"What?

"The tights."

I wasn't going to wear them to dinner, but now I want to, just to piss Rich off. "Why don't you let me choose my own friends and worry about how I come off to clients? Newsflash—I'm not one of those girls looking to date my dad, you should *definitely* know that by now."

"I see. So you're going to turn this argument into another of your dad's faults. All I said was those tights are a bit sexy for work."

After a long, in-your-face gulp of wine, I set down the empty glass and leave.

"Where are you going?" he asks.

I suddenly feel gross and sticky. "Shower."

"I was going to shower," he calls.

"I won't be long."

"We don't have time. We'll have to take one together."

I start stripping in the bathroom. "Fine."

Rich and I didn't sleep together for months after we started dating. I'm not sure it would've happened at all if it weren't for a fifth of tequila. I couldn't even say why we got together. We went to a series of business dinners with my dad, and when clients left, my dad would insist on an after-dinner drink. Then, a few sips in, Dad would make an excuse to go home. Rich and I were each too polite to leave before the other had finished their drink.

One of those nights, when the conversation was good, we ordered a second drink, and then a third.

Tequila happened, and we were a couple. Just like my dad wanted.

After Rich and I shower separately under the same stream of water, I blow dry my hair, glancing at him as he dresses in a suit and tie. Rich is a catch—I know that. He was positioned in front of me for a reason. Smart, thoughtful when he has to be, even-keeled—and all that in a nice package. He takes care of himself, and a solid body and handsome face helps me get in the mood when I need to.

I could cheat on him.

Not with just anyone, but with Finn. Finn does things to me with just a look, and I'm even more tempted by him when he opens his mouth. He read my journal and it didn't scare him off. If it'd been Rich who'd come across it, he'd have put it back where he found it and never mentioned it again.

"Ten minutes," Rich says with a spritz of cologne.

I'm patting on liquid foundation. "Thanks, Dad."

"You've made your point," he says. "I just thought you'd like to know the time since you aren't dressed yet."

"I'll be ready."

"Look," he says.

Great. I know that "*look*." He's going to say something I don't want to hear. "At what?"

He ignores my stunning wit. "You're in a bad mood, I get it. But since that's rare, I have to ask."

My heart leaps into my throat. I should've known this was coming, because Rich is right. I *am* in a bad mood, but I was in a great mood earlier, and any kind of extreme is unusual for me. I'm not temperamental anymore.

I skip ahead to applying eyeliner, the best way I know how to avoid his gaze during this conversation. "Don't start this," I say. "Not right before we walk out the door."

"So I'm right then. Something's changed. Please tell me you haven't stopped taking them completely."

It irritates me that it's been less than a week and Rich has already noticed. Has being on antidepressants changed me so much that the moment I lower my dosage, I become an entirely different person? A person I don't even know, because it's been so long since I've been her? "I'm a grown woman," I say. "I'll decide for myself."

"That's not how it works. We're a team, you and me—"

"*And* my dad, *and* Doctor Dummy."

"It's Doctor *Lumby*." He gets his phone from his pocket. "The car's here. I'll be downstairs, but we can finish this after dinner. And don't forget . . ."

"What?" I prompt just to get him out of here.

"Don't forget your coat. I'm saying that as your boyfriend who doesn't want you to be cold, not as the overbearing father figure you make me out to be."

In the reflection, I watch him disappear. Guilt gnaws at my gut. Despite his faults, Rich does care about me. And he takes care *of* me. Mentally, emotionally, he makes sure I'm okay from day to day. He keeps his distance for the most part, accepting that my decrease in sex drive comes with the territory.

It's a big job, handling me. I should be grateful Rich is up for it. Instead, I've been unnecessarily bitchy to him for no reason.

No, that's not true—there is a reason. He knows it, I know it, my dad knows it.

I knew there would be mood swings, and that they'd eventually give me away to Rich, my dad, or my doctor. It's not as if I was going to keep this from them forever, but they would've talked me out of it. They've done it before.

But it's time. Thanks to a handsy pigeon, I only have a quarter of my prescription left, even though Doctor Lumby thinks I just refilled it. This last week, the air has been colder on my skin. People's features have been sharper. Finn's acceptance of my embarrassing desire for passion makes my heart swell whenever I think of it.

Next month would make ten years of being on antidepressants. I'm determined not to see that anniversary, though. I'll be better this time.

I'll be an improved version of the girl I was before.

TEN

I can't think of much worse than client dinners. At least in meetings, I have work to discuss. At these after-hours engagements, I'm expected to talk about anything *but* work. My dad's method for signing clients is to impress the shit out of them with ideas at the office, then close over expensive food and liquor.

Which is what we're heading into now. The host leads us to our usual table. My dad gets my chair for me. "You look nice tonight," he says.

Not that it's so rare to get compliments from my dad, but I'm immediately suspicious. Did Rich already mention the argument over the tights to my dad? Is this their way of thanking me for not wearing them? I look at Rich, whose nose is buried in the wine menu, pretending he didn't hear.

"Flying solo tonight, George?" Grayson Dietrich asks once we're all seated.

"Unfortunately." Dad unfolds his napkin to put it in his lap. "After my wife passed, I was never quite able to move on."

My throat closes for a few seconds, long enough to suppress my intake of air without killing me. What my dad says is true. He's never even attempted to date since the accident. But I still don't like when he uses my mom's death as an icebreaker, and tonight the sting is especially painful. I've been thinking of her more this past week, ever since the pigeons. I wouldn't call myself a spiritual person, but it's as if she's around.

Mrs. Dietrich touches her collarbone with both hands. "Oh, George. I'm so sorry. When was that?"

He clears his throat. "Almost ten years ago."

"Ten years." She shakes her head at her husband. "Would you go that long without dating if you lost me?"

"Of course, dear."

"And this was your mother, Halston?" she asks.

I try not to fidget. I don't want attention on me. "Yes."

Rich passes me the wine list. "Why don't you pick one out?" He turns to Grayson. "George tells me you're a Knicks fan."

Gratefully, I take the menu. Rich doesn't like me to drink ever since last year's incident, so saving me from this conversation is an olive branch. Suddenly, I'm glad I opted for plain black tights and a more conservative outfit. On some level, I guess I know Rich is usually looking out for me.

I go to squeeze his hand as thanks, but my dad reaches across and snatches the list from me. "Why don't you get yourself a coffee instead?" he asks, halting the table conversation. He turns his glare on Rich. "Don't you think that's best?"

My face warms as I'm reduced to a twelve-year-old in front of a man who's here to decide whether to trust us with his million-dollar-plus advertising budget.

"Yes, sir," Rich says. He smiles uneasily at Grayson, nodding in my direction. "This one drinks coffee like water."

"I used to be that way," Mrs. Dietrich says. "I'm too old to have caffeine this late, though. Let's call the waiter over."

Without my usual armor the antidepressants provide, embarrassment hits me harder than it normally might. It shifts to sadness. For my strained relationship with my dad and Rich. For missing my mom more than usual. For *ten* goddamn years. I put on my best smile. Anything less will irritate my dad. "Excuse me," I say, standing. "Ladies' room."

I sit in a stall and take a deep breath. I don't want to be here. Already, this dinner feels like it's been going on all night. I'm getting restless. I'm anxious that I'm anxious, worried my dad will notice and that Rich will out me. George Fox put me on antidepressants, and he'll decide when I stop taking them. At least, according to him.

I hope that Rich orders me coffee so it's waiting for me when I return. But I need something right now to take the edge off. Something to dispel the gloom creeping in. I get my phone from my handbag and check to see if Finn ever posted the second photo—and to my delight, he has. I'm on the screen, sucking coffee off my two fingers, and it has forty-seven likes—even more than the one before it and in much less time.

I still can't believe he captured that. And took the time to edit it. And post it. With a caption of mine that *he* picked out. Is he looking at the photo right now too? Does it excite him? Is he thinking of me like I am him?

I smile all the way back to the table and through dinner as well—or, at least until Rich makes me switch to decaf.

In the town car on the way home, Rich is quiet. That's not unusual, but tonight he's not volleying e-mails or checking on an international client or tracking his beloved stocks.

"I'm sorry your dad went ballistic about the wine," he says finally.

An apology isn't what I expected, so it takes me a moment to respond. To an onlooker, it would've sounded like a normal exchange, but the three of us know it wasn't. Taking the wine list from me was a reminder that he still doesn't trust me.

"It's all right," I say. "I'm used to it."

"It's been over a year, and you haven't had more than a glass since. I've noticed, Halston, even though you think I give you a hard time. It isn't fair that your dad hasn't let it go yet—and that I haven't, either."

I'm not sure it isn't fair. I *did* fuck up. I disappointed them both. But a reminder isn't helpful. It puts me on edge, and the edge is what I've been trying—what I've been *firmly suggested*—to dull.

"I mean, we should be grateful for coffee, right?" he asks. "It's harmless. Unless you start doing that enema thing." He chuckles. "Have you heard of those? Coffee enemas? I wouldn't be surprised if I caught you hooked up to an espresso IV one day."

It's dark enough that I can't see the nuances of his face. Why is he talking about coffee enemas? "Sure. I guess."

"I'm just a little worried, Halston. If you've changed your dosage without consulting a doctor, well . . ." He blows out a breath and shifts to face me in the seat. "You can't just do that."

I look out the window at all the people having fun on a Thursday night—most of them around my age. I'd like to be out there with them, not trapped in here for a Rich lecture. "I told you, I'm an adult. I can do what I want."

"That doesn't mean you should. I don't think you're ready to go off them—neither does your dad, or Doctor Lumby."

"Doctor Lumby does what he thinks is easiest for all of us, and that's keeping me agreeable."

"What's wrong with easy? Why do you want to make things hard?"

I lace my hands in my lap, squeezing them together. "You're right. Feeling things is hard. Being moody, having PMS, and voicing my opinions, it's a burden for everyone."

"That's not fair."

"If I stop taking meds, I won't be nice, easygoing, doormat Halston."

"I didn't say you have to stay on them, but if you really, honestly feel you need to stop, then at least get professional help."

"I don't trust Doctor Lumby." I never really have, but until my recent perspective shift, it didn't seem to matter. My dad footed the bill, I got to talk to someone candidly a couple times a month, and in exchange, everyone left me alone. Until Finn. He hasn't left me alone. He's dug a little deeper without making me feel like I'm under interrogation. "I missed my appointment last week on purpose," I admit. "It wasn't because of work like I told you."

"Why? He's been your doctor a long time."

"Maybe it's time for a change."

"Then we'll find you someone else." The leather seat groans when Rich moves. "I'm not the bad guy, Halston. I love you, and I want you to be happy."

"How do you know you love me?" I glare at him. "You don't even *know* me."

He blinks a few times, stunned. I don't say things like that. I don't even think them. But it's true that Rich has only ever known this version of me, so how can he actually love me? This is what Finn hinted at this afternoon. It's not healthy to pretend to be someone else to make others happy. And that's exactly what I've been doing since Mom's death. I wear a mask. I keep thoughts and desires and opinions to myself more often than I express them. Rich doesn't get me. If he read what I wrote, if he heard some of my thoughts, he'd think I was sex-crazed. My dad understands me to a certain point. He'd have accepted the quirky tights outside of a work setting. He won't accept, from an employee or a daughter, posting sexy things online for the world to see.

My mom was different. She appreciated art and encouraged me to be creative. Unfortunately, I've ensured I'll never get to share that that understanding with her again.

"How can you say I don't know or love you?" Rich finally asks. "We've been dating almost two years, and I've been a great boyfriend to you."

"I've only ever known you while I was taking antidepressants—"

"They don't change your personality." He furrows his eyebrows. "You know that, right? They clear away the bad shit so you can function how you're supposed to."

"And you would know? Are *you* taking them?" I ask sardonically. "I'm sure my dad convinced you I'm better off."

"He didn't. I've done my research, Halston."

"He never would've let me stop them," I mutter. "He doesn't know how to handle me."

"You're *so* hard on him." He unbuckles his seatbelt to angle his entire body toward me. "Why? He does everything for you. He pays for your treatment. He created a position at the company for you. He doesn't care if you show up late or take a long lunch—"

"That's guilt over how he's treated me the past ten years. It's the only way he knows how to keep me happy and going along with what you guys want. But you never see that, do you? You always side with him."

"I don't, and you *know* that. I genuinely don't believe your dad has wronged you by paying your rent. And it isn't healthy for you to get so worked up over him."

"It *is* healthy. The world won't end if I feel strongly about something."

"Christ," he says, sighing. "What's *wrong*? Why are you suddenly hell-bent on stopping the meds?"

"Nothing's wrong. I'm good." I don't tell him that I'm better than good. Maybe he thinks tonight is going downhill, but for me, I'm finally shedding the past decade of nothingness. Finn has brought a lot to the surface—and I'm surprisingly grateful for it.

"Does it have to do with . . ." Rich's throat sounds raw. I squint to try and read him. "Is it something new?" he asks. "A new . . . pattern? Something really bad this time?"

I nearly laugh. *Pattern* is one of Rich's words for addiction. Other words include *habit*, *routine*, or *weakness*.

"You saw me tonight with the coffee. Do you think I'm doubling up on obsessions now?"

"You know I hate that word."

So does my dad, which is why I chose it over *addiction*. "I guess I forgot. What's wrong with obsession again?"

"Obsessions are for teenage girls."

"Then is it any wonder I'm like this?" I ask, raising my voice. "In a lot of ways, I still *am* a teenage girl. How could I not be?"

He frowns. "What?"

"My dad dopes me up practically *the day* my mom dies. Then terrifies me into staying on them the rest of my life by telling me if I stop, I'll do something destructive and reckless again. How can I *not* be emotionally stunted?"

"I don't know where all this is coming from," Rich says. "I've never heard you talk about this."

"Which is why I said you don't fucking know me."

"Calm down."

"Calm down? You brought this up. You were trying to provoke me, and it worked."

"I was not."

"Yes you were. You brought up the wine, the coffee, the meds, the *patterns*. Why, if not to get under my skin? What do you want from me?"

"Come on, Halston. Look at you. You're acting paranoid and agitated. What could possibly be the reason for that?" he asks wryly. "Gee, let me think."

I curl my hands into fists. It's as if I've been in a box, and I'm pushing the lid open inch by inch. Rich wants it to stay closed, doesn't want to know what's inside in case he doesn't like it. I lean between the two front seats. "Stop the car."

"Do not stop the car," Rich says, then turns back to me. "You're unstable. I'm taking you back to my place."

"I'm getting out whether you stop the car or not," I threaten the driver.

He glances over his shoulder at us. "Uh."

"Then what?" Rich asks. "You're going to walk home?"

"It's not that far."

"It's ten o'clock at night."

You wouldn't know it by the throngs of students and loosened-tie professionals and hip twenty-somethings littering the sidewalk. By the neon *open* signs, the steaming hotdog stands, the endless cars swerving by. "I'm *twenty-five*, not eighty, and it's a Thursday. People our age haven't even gotten started for the night. I'll be fine. Let me out."

"If you want to go out, I'll go with you. Let's just stop by your apartment first. Or mine, even. I think you've got a few pills there, and I really think you should—"

"You don't work for him," I tell the driver, ignoring Rich. "He's *my* dad's employee, and this is *my* dad's company car, and if you don't stop now, I'll call George Fox himself and make him tell you to pull over."

Rich knows my dad would call me unreasonable and hang up, but fortunately, the driver doesn't. I get out.

Rich rolls down the window. "Halston," he calls. "It's freezing."

"I'm fine."

"You're being childish," Rich says as the driver creeps alongside me. I stride down the sidewalk. "Get in the car."

"No."

"Come back with me now, or . . ."

"Or what?" I prompt.

"Or don't come back at all."

Even though there's a definite waver in his voice, my stomach clenches. Is he breaking up with me? Do I care enough to get in the car? In this moment, my answer is no. I don't want to think too hard if that'll be the case tomorrow. "Fine," I say. "I won't."

I turn on my heel and walk in the opposite direction.

"Come on," Rich calls after me. "Seriously?"

I ignore him. This is unlike me, acting on impulse, arguing in front of a stranger, being petulant just to get at Rich.

Or, maybe it *is* me.

Only a couple blocks later, the adrenaline begins to wear off. In the East Village, the bars are packed, the sidewalks livening up with downtowners who remind me of my assistant. Don't I belong here as much as anyone? I consider calling Benny to see if she's around. I think she lives in the area. She's invited me out a few times, but I've always turned her down. We don't have that kind of relationship. But why couldn't we?

I shiver. I've never been much of a partier. I didn't smoke or drink because I liked it. They were just ways to comfort myself. Despite what Rich said, he wouldn't turn me away if I showed up on his doorstep right now. If I did, we'd make up. We'd pretend none of this happened. He'd convince me not to take on my own treatment, and if he couldn't, my dad would. Because Rich *will* tell him all about this. Maybe already has.

I walk toward my apartment, which is a good twenty or more minutes away. It's not where I want to be, though. Rich and my dad have always been more of a team than I have with either of them. I accepted that. But Finn makes me feel important. Heard. *Seen.* We met less than two weeks ago, yet his interest in my journals, his questions, his attention, reminds me of how my mom was with me. When she looked at me, it was as if she couldn't wait to see the person I would become.

Finn does that too, except he knew me before he ever laid eyes on me. It's not supposed to happen that way, as if something greater brought us together.

I already have a missed call from Rich. I clear it. I didn't get out my phone for him. Finn just posted the third photo, but I go right past it to my inbox.

I send Finn a direct message:

Are you home?

ELEVEN

Four minutes have passed since I messaged Finn to see if he was home. He shouldn't be sleeping at ten thirty on a Thursday night, but it's not exactly early either. Now that I've decided I want to see him, it's all I can think about. Just the thought of Rich annoys me.

I'm a couple blocks from his place when his response comes through.

Call me.

His phone number pops up.

I stop in the middle of the sidewalk. My bravery wavers. Finn is a man. He's in his thirties. He won't like being jerked around. If I go up to his apartment this late at night, and he has certain expectations—am I ready to take things to that level?

Breathe. I'm being ridiculous. Jumping to conclusions. I don't even know if Finn will want to see me. Despite the temperature, I begin to sweat. I unwrap my scarf and ball it under my arm before dialing.

Finn picks up after the first ring. “Hey.” His voice is scratchy, even deeper than I remember.

“Were you sleeping?”

“Nah. Just been working all day since I saw you.”

“Oh.” A snowflake lands on my nose as a couple more drift onto my coat. He doesn’t say anything else. “Do you maybe want some company?” I ask.

“Where are you?”

“Close,” I say. “I walked from the East Village, and now I’m by the café.”

He sniffs. “Hmm.”

Clearly, I didn’t think this through. It occurs to me that he might not even be alone. “I mean, if you’re busy, it’s fine, or if you don’t want—”

“I want,” he says so low, I almost miss it. “You know I want.”

This afternoon, he basically admitted to fighting his attraction to me because of Rich. Finn doesn’t want to get hurt. But the way I left things with Rich is as close to breaking up as we’ve ever come “It’s over. We had an argument.” I play with the fringe of my scarf. “So can I come up?”

“I’ll come down.”

I hang up, part triumphant, part scared as shit. I don’t know how to be with someone like Finn. I’ve written about it, I’ve fantasized about it, but what if I can’t actually *be* it?

I need coffee, if only just to smell it, hold it. As fate has it, Lait Noir is only two blocks from Finn's—but I turn the corner to find it closed. I continue toward Finn's, where there's a twenty-four-hour diner across the street. I can be in and out in a minute flat.

I'm about to step into the crosswalk when Finn exits his building a half block away. He comes toward me, passing under yellow streetlights. In sweatpants, sneakers, and a jacket, he's not dressed for snow. He cups his hands over his mouth to warm them and nods at me. "Who do we have here?" he asks as he approaches. "Halston—what's your last name?"

"Fox."

"Fox," he repeats, stopping in front of me. "Are you okay?"

"Yes," I say.

"What was the fight about?"

Sharing the details means getting into some heavy stuff with Finn. It's more than enough to scare him off. I shake my head. "It's complicated."

"In other words, it isn't my business."

"No. I mean yes, it is. Well, it's not, but I can make it your business if you want to know."

He crosses his arms under his pits. "I do."

"I'll tell you more, but can we go to your place?" Maybe if I can get him upstairs, he'll forget all about it. "It's cold."

He tugs my scarf from under my arm and shakes it out. "Tell me now." He wraps it around my neck with extraordinary care, as if he's dressing a queen for her coronation. He wants to know about the fight before he invites me up. It's fair, but the thought of telling Finn the truth has my stomach doing flips, my nose tingling. Unlike Rich, who wanted in good with my dad, Finn has no reason to take on damaged goods.

I glance at the ground a few seconds while the words bubble up—and then fizzle out. "Can we at least go get a coffee?" I ask. "The diner—"

"I'll make you some upstairs." He slips a hand under my hair, freeing it from the scarf, and brushes some flakes away. "Just give me the rundown."

He basically said we're going upstairs no matter what. I might as well get it over with. "You might think less of me."

"I told you I cheated on my wife with someone else's."

I scrape the sole of my boot against the icy sidewalk, carving out a circle in a fine layer of snow. "I just don't want you to see me differently."

"I *want* to see you differently," he says without missing a beat. "As many sides as there are, I want to see them all. I'm sure a week into knowing someone, that'd scare some people. I don't think you're one of those people, though. Are you?"

I smile to myself. Every time I'm with him, I become more confident that he knows me. And he's asking for more. "No," I say, looking up into his eyes. "I'm on antidepressants."

He scans my face. "Okay. That's not so rare these days. Kendra, my ex, went through that phase."

"It's not a phase."

"No, I didn't mean to imply it was. I just meant lots of people take them."

"About a week ago, I decided to stop. I've been weaning myself off them. Rich noticed because my mood's been a little erratic, and he and my dad don't approve."

Finn nods slowly. A strand of his hair falls over his forehead. I have to stop myself from pushing it back into place, from running my hands through his butterscotch-colored locks. "It's not really their decision, is it?" he asks. "It's between you and your psychiatrist."

I wasn't involved in the decision to start treatment. I wouldn't have any say in stopping it. Finn believes I should have that right, though. He's a good man who would see me as a partner, not a puppet. "My psychiatrist listens to my dad. He says our sessions are private, but I don't believe him. They decide together, and I'm supposed to go along with it because he's a doctor."

"Then you need to find someone else. That's a delicate relationship. If you don't trust your doctor, it can't work."

He makes it sound so simple. He almost makes me believe it *is* simple. For that, I want to hug him. "The thing is . . ." I can't believe I'm saying this. It's something I haven't said aloud to anyone other than

Doctor Lumby, a thought I've been trying to avoid. "They're right. After almost ten years, I don't even know who I am without them. I don't know if I can control myself."

Finn's mouth drops open. "Did you say *ten* years? How old are you?"

I look away. It does sound like an alarming length of time, even to my own ears. It just shows how fucked up I am. "Twenty-five."

Finn puts his hands on my shoulders, encompassing them. "Look at me."

He waits until our eyes meet again.

"Taking antidepressants is nothing to be ashamed of. It doesn't change how I feel about you. But why the fuck does a fifteen-year-old need to be medicated?"

"I'm troubled. I make bad decisions." Am I really prepared to go back to that place without any armor on? I've been worried I'd lost myself somewhere in the last decade, but maybe that part of me needs to stay gone. "Without treatment, I make mistakes. I'm dangerous."

"*Dangerous*?" Finn asks. "Let me get this straight. You made a mistake when you were fifteen, and you've been on antidepressants ever since? Do you really think you're the first teenager to make bad choices?"

"It's not that cut and dry."

"It's extreme, Halston." He runs a hand through his hair, moving it off his face. "It doesn't sound right."

After ten years of hearing the opposite, my instinct is to defend my dad. He didn't know what else to do with me. I was reckless. Finn's validation is too heady to resist, though. It was an awful mistake, but maybe I've changed. He's right—I *was* just a kid. "I don't want to keep taking them. I'm just afraid of what'll happen if I don't, and I know Rich is too."

"This is what you fought about?" I nod, and he puts an arm around my shoulders. "Come on. It's cold. Let's go up and you can tell me the rest."

I let him walk me to his building, his body heat warming me instantly like I've taken a pull of strong liquor. I try to inhale him, but it's too cold to smell anything. Even without his scent drawing me in, even with him knowing I'm a head case, even though I'm biting my tongue to keep from insisting we get coffee first, I make a decision—I'm going to sleep with Finn. Rich won't find out. And if he does? I'm not sure I'd feel whatever I'm supposed to. Maybe we really are through. It'd be strange; he's always been reliable. Breaking up with him is like losing a safety net, but maybe that's a good thing. Finn could be my chance at the kind of passion I've only dared to write about.

Finn keeps his arm around me through the lobby, up the elevator, and to his door. He unlocks the apartment, guiding me in with a hand on my middle back. The heat is on. He takes my scarf and coat, shakes off the snowflakes, and hangs my things with his jacket.

"Want something to eat?" he asks.

I unzip my boots and leave them at the door. I'm not very tall, even in heels, so I have to tilt my head back to look up at him. "I'm okay."

"Drink?"

I thought you'd never ask. I nod hard. "Definitely."

I follow him into the kitchen and set my handbag on the counter.

He opens the refrigerator. "I'm a little disappointed you changed out of those tights."

He'd noticed. I've had them in my underwear drawer for years, but today was the first time I pulled them out. "You didn't even get to see all of them," I say.

He closes the fridge and turns slowly. "No?"

Any traces of the wintry night fade. My body warms as Finn's eyes travel downward. "There are little bows at the tops of each leg. Right under my ass."

His expression darkens. I've seen desire in his eyes before—like when our knees touched on the windowsill at Lait Noir or when he *almost* kissed me on the couch. But now he's no longer trying to hide it. "That'd make a good photo."

I haven't stopped wanting Finn's camera lens on me, even though he told me in the park we couldn't do it again. "You posted," I say.

He nods. "A couple hours ago."

"I haven't had a chance to look yet."

He gets his phone from his back pocket and hands it to me. "The code is 2008."

Getting his password to unlock the screen feels like a form of intimacy, but I try not to look too excited about it. I pull up the photo, and my mouth drops open. "You have fifty more followers."

"Are you keeping track, Serenity?"

I blush hearing the handle I use on all my social media, @suhr.enity. In the excitement of wanting to see him, I'd forgotten that we'd never actually connected online outside of e-mail. "How'd you know the message was from me?"

He arches an eyebrow. "Lucky guess. Where does Suhr come from?"

I look at the screen. "My mom's maiden name."

"Did you consider any other 'Suhr' words?"

I glance up. "Like what?"

"Suhr-ender."

My insides tighten. He says it like a command, or an idea he's just had. Is he suggesting I give in to him for a night? How would that feel? "Friends and family follow me on that account."

"And? Surrender's inappropriate?"

Inappropriate. *God.* There's that word again. This time, I'm the one acting like a prude, not Rich. I'm not exactly wild, but have I become boring? No. A boring person wouldn't be here right now.

I return my eyes to the picture. "Nobody commented on the last two posts," I say. "Do you think that means they didn't like what I wrote?"

"No," he says. "In fact, the one with your fingers in your mouth has more likes."

He's right. It does. I hand him back the phone. "Maybe that's because of the photo, not the caption."

"It doesn't mean that," he says. "I got a message just before yours complimenting the captions."

"Seriously?" My face splits with a smile. "From who?"

"Just some random girl."

"What'd you say?"

"I didn't answer, but I updated the description to say 'My model and her words are anonymous.'"

My model. *Mine.*

"Is that all right?" Finn catches my eye. "I know keeping your identity secret is important to you."

I can see the headline in my mind now:

"George Fox's sex-fiend daughter at it again! Poses for racy photos online."

"It's good," I say quickly. "I still want that."

He returns to the fridge. "All right then. I'll leave it." He holds out a water bottle. "Want a tour?"

I don't want to seem like a freak by insisting on the coffee he promised me, it is eleven at night after all, so I take the water. It isn't easy. When I'm uncomfortable, I cling to my *patterns*, as Rich says. Being here is out of character for me. This isn't work or home or my dad's or Rich's place. And Finn certainly isn't Rich.

I follow him down a hall to one of the closed doors. He opens it, gesturing me in before him. It's dark, the lights dimmed just enough to make the room glow. A desk by the window is topped by an enormous computer, both opposite a small couch. Photography equipment is assembled in a corner, including a camera on a tripod. I avoid looking at the prints on the wall because I'll immediately judge them. It's automatic, and I want to think of Finn as the man who made me sexy, not the mediocre, flat photographer I'd thought he was when I'd first looked at his work.

"Should we take another?" he asks.

I spin around. "*Now*?"

"No, not now. Or, maybe now. If inspiration strikes." He half-smiles, almost smirking.

I wonder, if I were wearing the stripe-y tights, would inspiration have struck us down already? Would he have crossed the kitchen, impatient to see the bows? Lifted up my skirt and bent me over the counter for a better look? I curl my hands into balls, an ache forming between my legs. I don't know what I want more, to fuck Finn or pose for him. "*If* you were to feel inspired . . . what might you do?"

"Hmm." He circles me, looking me over. From every angle. I fight the urge to cover myself or hide. Finn hasn't given me any reason to be self-conscious. His perusal is both intoxicating and distressing. I want him to drink me in, but what if he doesn't like how I taste? The hair on my skin prickles as I wait for his assessment. "The white collar of your blouse makes you look so sweet." He says *sweet* with an edge that weakens my knees. "Like a good girl. It makes me want to turn you bad."

My legs are going to give out, and he hasn't even touched me yet, not even close. He's put enough distance between us to ensure I couldn't even reach out and grab him if I wanted.

"You can do that with a photo?" I ask. "Turn me bad?"

"I can certainly try."

I nod breathlessly. I want to say, *"Try! Please try!"* but I don't trust myself to speak without begging.

He stops in front of me and picks up something from his desk. "Do you have words for that?" he asks, holding my journal out to me.

I didn't even notice it before. I take it. The feel of the leather is the only thing that's ever come as close to comforting me like my mother's embrace once had. I open it and flutter the pages, playing the edges like the strings of an instrument. My hands tremble, and I'm certain Finn notices.

I only know what I'm looking for once I find it. "Here," I say, giving it back to him.

He shakes his head. "Read it for me. It sounds so much better from your mouth."

I'm already blushing profusely. I'm sure he notices that too. "I hate reading it aloud."

He grunts. "Then don't, not for anyone but me. Don't read it, don't show it, don't even mention it to anyone else. Just me."

My heart thumps. He wants exclusive access to this part of me. I want to give it to him, but that means stepping outside my comfort zone. Sharing my journal is more baring than his eyes on my body, than having my photo taken. I think I could strip down to nothing with less effort than it takes to read to him.

"Please," he says.

My fear melts, just a little. He wants this, and don't I owe it to him for loving my words enough to want to hear them? Luckily, the passage I chose is short and clean. It's fairly innocuous—until you really start to think about it . . .

"'"Make me a woman,"' I read. '"Let me be your girl."'"

I keep my eyes on the page, but I feel his gaze on me. Is he waiting for me to continue? That's all there is. The meaning isn't obvious at first, but I thought he'd understand. If he doesn't, that choice will sound weird to him. It's not the sexiest line, I admit. And maybe too nuanced for what we're doing.

I open my mouth to tell him I can pick out something else. I don't speak, though. This caption feels right for the moment. I'm not sure if I'm more nervous that I'll have to defend my choice or that he'll like it and want to use it. When it feels as if a full minute has passed, I close the book, squeeze the leather for reassurance, and finally look up.

"Perfect," he says.

"Perfect?"

"It's subtle, like your words, and at the same time, straight up sex."

"You get it?"

"She wants to be handled tenderly, almost like a child. To surrender to someone more powerful than her. And when she does, when he has his way with her, then she'll be a woman."

My heart is in my throat. I shouldn't've doubted that he'd understand. Not everyone would, and maybe that makes it a bad choice for a caption, but Finn does. "I think every woman feels like a girl *and* a woman at some point during sex." I pass the book back to him. "You don't think it's too vague? Or weird?"

"Obviously not."

I don't understand why that's obvious until I drop my eyes to his crotch. I look away just as quickly, but not before I notice the bulge in his sweatpants.

"C'mere," he says.

Butterflies light up my insides, an eruption of fluttering wings, as if I'd spooked a bird sanctuary. *This is it.* I'm going to do this. Finn will be the fourth man I've ever slept with, and I don't want to mess this up. I want it to be right, to be good, better than good.

I walk to him, closing the space between us. He reaches up and moves my hair over my shoulder, resting it against my back. He looks at the neckline of my blouse, his eyes trailing the curve of my neck up to my mouth. He never meets my gaze, but circles around me, so he's at my back. "It'll be simple," he says. "Just undo the top button of your blouse."

He leaves me where I am. I look over my shoulder. He turns the camera equipment around. My thoughts jumble. I don't understand what he means. Or what he's doing. Or why I don't go stand in front of the camera instead of him moving everything to face me.

I look forward again and my eyes land on the couch. The *couch*? He's aiming the camera there? If he thinks he's going to record us having sex, he's delusional. He saw how hesitant I was about taking photos while fully dressed, does he think I'd let him video us while he strips me, lays me down, kisses me?

It occurs to me—I don't know. I have no idea what he expects, because I don't actually know him at all.

I asked to come up here. I read to him from my journal. Maybe I've made him think I'm looking for danger, thrills, sex. Aren't I, though? Isn't that what it would be to record something so intimate? Dangerously thrilling, taboo, wrong?

I inhale sharply as I imagine performing for the camera—and then him watching me after I've left.

"Doing okay?" he asks.

I look back at him. "Are you . . . are you going to record it?"

"Record what?"

"Us?"

He stops fiddling with the camera to stare at a spot on the floor. He seems to think hard about his next move, then comes over and looks me straight in the eye. "Halston?"

I try not to fidget. "Y-yes?"

"We're never going to do anything—*anything*—that makes you uncomfortable. I wouldn't record something like that without talking to you first. To be honest, it never crossed my mind."

I exhale a long breath, relieved. Or am I? A small part of me likes the idea of Finn savoring this later. "Good," I say.

"And another thing." He looks me over. "We're not going to sleep together."

This time, I know exactly what I feel. Disappointment. "We're not?"

"No."

I try to pinpoint what might've happened the last few minutes to extinguish his desire, but my mind is reeling too fast. It wasn't easy for me to decide to do this. Did I imagine his interest, from the earlier fire in his eyes to the bulge in his pants? "Why not?" I ask.

Even though I'm already looking at him, he lifts my chin slightly with his knuckle. "Don't lie to me. Ever. I've had enough secrets and sneaking around for one lifetime."

"When did I lie?" I ask. "Everything I told you was true."

"You didn't break up with him."

"We . . . we're as good as—"

"That's not enough. That affair I had was a nightmare. I won't do it again."

"Then why'd you bring me up here?" I ask, embarrassment igniting my temper. I'm already as uncomfortable as I've been in a while. I don't need to be spurned after I've put myself so far out there.

He sighs. "I believe you if you say you're not in love with him—"

"I'm not."

"But on this one thing, I won't budge. I will not sleep with you unless I know you're mine. Really and truly mine, until there's no chance you'll ever go back to him. Until he knows it's over too."

My entire being aches for Finn, as if I've been holding off my need since the night I met him on the sidewalk, and just now let it flood me. Only to be rejected by him. "I want to be yours. Isn't that enough for tonight?"

He takes a few steps back, rounds the camera, and looks through the viewfinder. "Come closer."

My pulse beats at the base of my throat. I walk toward him until he holds up his hand, until I'm close enough that my face won't be in the photo. I take the hem of the V-neck sweater I'm wearing over my blouse and pull it off. I look slimmer without it. My hair frizzes with static, so I smooth it back in place. I drop my sweater at my feet.

"Just the top button," he says.

My nails are bare, like a good girl's would be. I unbutton the collar while he photographs me. I watch his hands around the camera, big, strong, skillful. I raise my chin to expose my neck and continue down the middle of the blouse, all without instruction.

When I reach the button between my breasts, he stops me. "That's good enough. Do it up again."

I would've kept going. I've never considered myself a seductress, but maybe it's just been hiding under the surface. I do up all the buttons and go to pick up my sweater.

"Hang on." He pulls back from the camera. "Hmm."

"What is it?"

"They're not right. Better in theory than reality."

It took hardly any effort to get the first three photos. Maybe I'm trying *too* hard. I touch my face. "Is it me?"

"No. It just doesn't say what the coffee pictures do."

God, I need some of that right now—a mug to hold, something to sip when doubt rears its head. "Maybe it would work better with the caption?" I suggest.

"They should work separately and together, your words and my pictures, don't you think?"

It makes sense. I've attempted to paint a picture with one line. He wants his photo to tell a story. "What I wrote isn't about a girl undressing herself," I say. "You should do it."

"Do what?"

"Unbutton my blouse. That would be more accurate."

He blinks down to the floor, then back up. "I want to be the one to take the photo."

"Put it on a timer. If you set up the shot, it's still yours."

He considers this and returns to playing with the camera. "Take a small step back. Show me your throat, like you did before."

My insides quiver. His commands are serious, businesslike, but he wants people to look at these photos and think of sex, and how can that not turn me on?

When he seems satisfied, he looks up. "Ready for me?"

I nod. "I think so."

"Don't move. Let me do the moving."

That's harder than it sounds. I'm already trying not to squirm. He presses a button. Comes to me. Gets close. Moves behind me, even closer, until his front warms my back. He can't be more than inch from me. "I'm going to touch you now."

My skin is like one giant exposed nerve anticipating his hands. He doesn't touch me, though, not really. He hums in my ear, "Count to three."

"One."

He raises his hands, and they hover at my throat.

"Two."

His stubble ghosts against my cheek, giving me goosebumps.

"Three."

He undoes the first button, barely even touching the fabric, as the camera snaps. Despite that, or maybe because of it, I shiver. His lips brush the side of my head, his breath in my hair, as he continues down. "I don't want to stop," he whispers.

"Then don't."

"I have to."

He stops opening my blouse. I hold his wrists to keep him there, and he steps into me, his hardness pressing into my lower back. When I exhale, it comes out as a pained, unnatural sound. "Please," I say.

"Please what? What are you asking for?"

"Anything. I-I want this."

He pulls his hands from mine, and slides one down the front of me. He grips me between the legs and backs me against him, reminding me with his intimidating length that he wants me too. "I already told you why I can't, but when you beg . . ."

My heart beats in my stomach. I need relief. To feel good. I move against him, pleading with my hips. "Is that what you need?" I ask. "For me to beg?"

"I need you to *not* beg."

I'm overcome, and it's a first for me. Everything over the last week has been foreplay, leading to this moment. If he pulls away for good, I'll be forced back into a restricted state of arousal. "What if I do it?" I ask.

"Do what?"

I push his hand away and slip mine down the front of my skirt, into the elastic of my tights. "It's not cheating if I do it to myself."

"You wouldn't."

He's right—I wouldn't. Not normally. But I am, that's how desperate he makes me. I slide a finger along the damp seat of my thong. Surprised by how wet I am, I envision Finn easily slipping into me and moan.

"You're not fighting fair."

"I'm not the one fighting." His erection alone assures me he wants this too. Emboldened by that knowledge, I go out on a limb to hopefully persuade him. "I want this, Finn. Tell me what I have to do to get it. What do you need?"

When he answers, he pronounces each word, as if it's taking all his concentration to speak. "It can't be about what I need."

"*I* need it."

His ensuing silence isn't a no, and it's the permission I need. I've been circling the idea since I met Finn, but now I can leap knowing Finn will catch me—and that he *wants* to. "I'll end it with Rich right now. My phone's in the kitchen."

"No." He puts a hand around my bicep, keeping me where I am. "You shouldn't decide like this."

I cling to the hesitation in his voice. "It's already over for me. I just have to make sure he knows so you'll believe me."

"Halston."

He could be warning or pleading with me, but either way, his resolve is weakening. I can sense it. If I leave the room, I might break the spell, so I pull my hand out of my skirt and feel behind us for his back pocket. I slip his phone out. My fingers shake as I try to correctly type in the passcode.

"You need a clear head for this," he says. "We both do."

"It's not as impulsive as it seems." I dial Rich's number and hold my breath. It rings twice before going to voicemail. I need to tell Rich we're over—for all of our sakes. Rich deserves that before anything happens. So does Finn.

"Rich, it's me," I start.

"*Halston*, please," Finn whispers.

With just my name, I understand what he's trying to tell me. This is wrong. No matter how badly I want this, I can't break up with Rich over a message. Reluctantly, I say, "Call me when you get this. We need to talk."

Finn takes the phone from my hand, hangs up, and puts it away. "There's no rush." He's still pressed against me. I'm not sure how he's restraining himself when I've told him how badly I want this.

"I'm going to end things with him. You believe me, don't you?"

"Yes."

"So what does it matter if I do it tonight or tomorrow? It's over."

"Once I start thinking of you as mine, that changes everything." There's undeniable need in his voice—sadness too. "I can't let myself believe you're mine if you're not. I'm the one who'll get hurt."

He must not realize that the idea of staking his claim only makes me want this more. I gyrate against him. "I'm not going to hurt you."

"You don't know that."

"I want to be yours."

He grabs my hip, his fingers digging into my skin, trying to still me. "You have to slow down."

"I don't want to with you. Everyone else tells me to calm down or take it easy or go slow. I want to be myself with you, Finn. I want to be allowed to want you this way."

He drops his face into the crook of my neck and sighs deeply. One arm wraps around me from behind and then his other. I continue to move against him and eventually, he answers, syncing his thrusts with mine. "Christ, Halston," he mutters. "You're killing me here."

"Then stop fighting me."

He walks us forward a few steps. We reach a wall. I put my hands on it and push back against him. Momentarily, I think I've won. He's going to rip off his pants and fuck me. But he just touches me through my clothing, circling his fingers over my clit quickly, as if our time together could end any second.

I curl my hands into fists, scraping the wall with my fingernails. He secures my back to his front as he slides his shaft up and down the crack of my ass. Even with layers of clothing separating us, he's growing bigger, harder, engorged—or maybe that's just what I believe because *I'm* seconds from falling apart. Even though I'd rather wait to climax with him, his hand feels so good that I end up humping it.

"You're going to make me come in my fucking pants," he says.

He's losing control. Knowing I have that power over him makes me crumble. I orgasm with Finn's hand between my legs while he grinds into me and *doesn't* fuck me. He takes my hips and thrusts against me more furiously, burying his face in my hair and groaning until he finishes.

If my heart pounds any harder, it'll burst through my chest. Finn shudders behind me. "Fuck," he says. "I had one rule."

One rule—and he bent it for me. Maybe I should be sorry. I don't want him to regret anything when it comes to us. But being simultaneously coveted and owned is addicting, a high I've never felt, one I couldn't fight in the moment. And we haven't even been skin to skin yet.

"Technically, we didn't break it," I say breathlessly.

He releases my hips. "I think the line is too thin to say."

I turn around. Concern is etched into his features. I want to erase all his doubts, comfort him. "It's over with him. Completely. Trust me."

My phone rings from the kitchen. Finn and I look at each other. "It's him," I say.

"I'm going to clean myself up." Finn walks away but pauses in the doorway. "Whatever happens, don't go to his place. At least not tonight. I can't stand the thought of it."

He leaves the studio. With his final plea, I understand his fears run deeper than just the injustice of cheating on Rich.

If Finn is worried about what'll happen if I don't end things at all, maybe he already thinks of me as his.

TWELVE

I make it to Finn's kitchen right before Rich's call goes to voicemail. "Hey," I answer.

"Sorry I missed you earlier," he says. "I was on the other line, and I didn't recognize the number."

"With who?" I ask. "It's the middle of the night."

His silence answers my question.

I scoff. "You couldn't even wait until tomorrow to call my dad? Did you give him every last detail of our fight, or just the gist?"

"I was worried. You took off."

"I'm not a child, even if you guys treat me like one."

"Being concerned about your wellbeing is not belittling you. Where are you?"

My legs are weak from the intensity of the orgasm I had not five minutes ago, so I turn to rest my back against the kitchen counter. Finn is leaning in the doorway, his arms crossed. This is a private conversation, and Finn has no business listening, but the fact that he's doing it anyway turns me on a little. As if he's too impatient to do anything other than hear me end it. "I'm at my apartment."

"No you're not. I called your doorman when you didn't answer your cell, before I got your message. Whose number was that?"

"We need to talk."

"I know, but I have to be up in five hours," he says. "Can you at least tell me where you are so I know you're okay?"

"What I meant was *I* need to talk. You can listen."

He starts to remind me of an important meeting in the morning he can't afford to doze off in. I don't want to hurt Rich; I'd rather let him down gently. But he can't even give me a minute to break up with him, so I rip off the Band-Aid. "We're over, Rich."

He pauses. "You know I didn't mean what I said earlier about you not coming over anymore. I was mad."

"It's not about that."

"We fought, Halston. I know we rarely do it, but it's normal. It's probably even good for us. Couples fight."

I shake my head, looking outside to avoid Finn's gaze. "The fight was nothing. It just opened my eyes."

"To?"

"We aren't right for each other. I don't think we need to get into the nitty-gritty details, because you know it's true."

It's so silent, I can almost hear the flakes of snow brushing against the window. "All right, Halston. You want to split? Sure. Let's do that."

I'd like to thank him and hang up, but I get the feeling the conversation isn't over.

"I mean," he continues wryly, "calling me in the middle of the night to end a two-year relationship is completely rational. I'm sure it has nothing to do with the fact that you've stopped seeing your doctor and taken your treatment into your own hands. The two aren't related *at all.*"

I feel Finn's eyes on me. The apartment is deadly quiet. I turn my face and whisper, "It's not about that."

"No?" he asks. "And I'm a Russian spy. Obviously, messing with your dosage is your reason for storming off and then calling me like this. We've been good up until a few days ago."

"No we haven't," I say more heatedly. "I've wanted this for a long time, I just didn't know it."

Shit. I didn't mean for it to come out that way. I'm not even sure if I mean it. If I backtrack, though, what will Finn think?

"Is that true?" Rich asks.

"Yes. No. I don't know." I haven't really thought of leaving Rich in the active sense. Once in a while, I wonder if there's more out there for me or if it matters that something between us has always felt off. He's the first man to love me, though. Finn is the first to pursue me.

"If you're not sure, why the hurry?" he asks. "Go home. Sleep. We can talk at work tomorrow. I'll even cancel my second meeting."

Finn watches me. With him, there are no guarantees. Is my urge to take that risk a red flag? Or an inner push toward something better? If I want Finn, there can't be any in between or uncertainty; he's made that clear. Maybe he's the wrong choice. Maybe he'll hurt me. At least I'll feel something, though, and that's more than I can say for Rich. "There's nothing to talk about aside from logistics," I tell Rich. "I love you as a friend, but as a partner—"

"We can pick this up tomorrow," he repeats.

"There is no tomorrow."

"Yes there *is*. At the office. Where you and I will both be. And your dad, who won't be on board with this."

"I'll handle my dad," I say, even though I'd rather elope with Finn than stay and deal with my dad's disappointment. "Please box up my things and—"

"Have you been drinking?" he asks.

My face warms. I'm not sure if Finn can hear. "No. Have the boxes sent to my apartment. Charge it to Dad's delivery service."

"Is it something else?" he presses. "Something worse to cope with everything?"

"Everything?"

"I know this time of year is hard for you."

Terrified he'll bring up my mother and make this night even more uncomfortable, I shake my head. "I have to go. Please just tell me you get that we're breaking up."

"Fine," he says. "Take the time you need. I hope I'll still be here when you realize your mistake."

Mistake. I have no doubt he intentionally chose that word to drill home the point that without my meds, I can't make rational decisions. "Goodn—"

He hangs up. I check the screen. Three minutes, eleven seconds. That's how long it took to extricate myself from Rich. Appropriate, I guess, considering this relationship often felt half-assed. Two years lost, just like that. It's angering in a way. Years of my youth have been spent bending to other people's wills. The worst part is, it's my own fault. It was easier to accept what I had than convince myself I was worth more.

"Hey," Finn says from above me. I didn't even hear him approach.

I look up and realize my vision is blurred. "Hey."

He frowns. "I'm sorry."

I shake my head, and a few tears fall onto my cheeks. "I'm not crying over him."

He wipes under my eye with his thumb. "It's okay if you are. You're allowed."

"I just feel like I'm waking up from a long sleep. Not even a restful one." I could be referring to the break up or my meds. Both, I guess. "I've wasted so much time."

"We'll make up for it," he murmurs.

"Was that enough?" I ask. "Are you satisfied?"

He pulls me against his chest, tightening his arms around me. "Don't worry about me right now."

"But—"

"Will you let me hold you?"

I'm stiff as a board with my hands at my sides. I force myself to relax against his body, hug his middle, and rest my chin on his chest. "Better?" I whisper.

"Yeah." He searches my eyes a few silent seconds before bending his head. My mouth opens for his like we've done this a million times, but I've never been struck by lightning, and that's how his kiss feels—electric, exceptional, and bigger than us. His lips are as soft and full as they look, but more firm, more certain, than I'm used to. They're made to kiss away my tears while inciting a fire in me. I could fall in love this second or fuck him until one of us goes blind.

He cradles my face in his hands.

Fall in love.

Then slides them down my back to grip my ass.

Fuck him blind.

"I want you as mine," he growls.

"I want to be yours."

He hooks a finger into the waistband of my skirt. "Say that again."

We breathe into each other's mouths. It's too soon to tell him I think I already *am* his. So I untie his sweatpants instead. "Let me show you how badly I want it."

He stills my hands. "It's too soon. You're vulnerable."

I haven't thought of much else in a week. Just him. *Finn Finn Finn.* Seeing him. Fucking him. Posing for him. I've already forgotten about Rich, and right now, I can't even remember a life outside this apartment. "I'm ready," I say.

"You're not. It's been a rough day."

"That's why I need this." I move even closer. He releases my hands, and I slide them up his chest, around his neck. "Please," I murmur, rising onto the balls of my feet to nuzzle his neck. I can smell him now, woodsy hints mixed with sweat and brine. He only came in his pants a few minutes ago, and I can almost convince myself I can smell that too. "I have to feel good." I beg for a kiss and he gives me one. "I haven't felt good in so long."

He rests his forehead against mine. "We can't."

"We couldn't ten minutes ago. Now we can. We *so* can."

"No, I mean, we actually can't." He takes my shoulders but seems to brace me instead of pull me off. "I don't have any condoms. I wasn't expecting . . ."

Score. The red light is actually green. I smile as I suck the skin right underneath his jaw, leaning my weight on him. He's unmistakably hard against my belly. "I'm on birth control."

His head falls back. "Doesn't matter. I won't."

I might be insulted at his insinuation if I weren't so eager to move this along. "I'm clean. Rich and I haven't even been intimate in a month. Are you?"

"Yes, but . . ." He finally succeeds in detaching my mouth from him. "But I just can't. It's not a conversation for the heat of the moment."

The last thing I want to do is get into another deep conversation.

"I'll go get condoms," he says. "Make coffee while you wait. That'll give us each time to think this through."

I was wrong. Talking isn't the last thing I want to do. The last fucking thing I want to do is *think*. I'm not worried I'll change my mind, or that I need time to get over Rich. It's that I've fantasized about this so long—urgent need, hunger, a real *man*. After years of dulling everything around me, including sex, I want to be devoured by Finn. I don't want to talk or think because I'm so hot for him, I'm about to strap on a harness and climb him like the mountain he is.

If he won't fuck me, there are other ways to get close to him.

I drop to my knees on the kitchen tile.

"Halston." I hear the warning in his voice.

"You don't have to do anything," I coo, blinking up at him. "Just stand here."

His eyes darken. "I'm bigger than you're used to." Another warning.

"How do you know?"

"I just do."

I pull his pants down his thighs. His heather-gray boxer-briefs outline every ridge and vein of him. He's right. He's not like any of the other three men I've been with, but at least I'm not intimidated.

"I'm not as hard since I just came," he says. "I will be once you touch me."

Oh.

He's not completely hard yet?

Fuck.

He pinches my chin and turns my face up to him. "You have nothing to prove. We can go lie down until we fall asleep. I just want to be with you."

"I haven't done this much," I say, determined. Rich was the only man I felt comfortable enough to blow. He liked it at the start of the relationship, but we fell into a routine that didn't include it unless he asked. Which he didn't. "You might have to sort of, you know, coach me."

He shakes his head in disbelief. "I stand corrected. You didn't even have to touch me to get me fully hard."

I blush. "You like the idea of me being your student?"

"Let's take it one step at a time, all right? I can't manage roleplaying on top of this."

"So that's a yes?" I run my hands up his thighs.

"I don't want to take advantage of you."

"You already said that. But if you don't, how else will I earn my 'A'?"

His nostrils flare. With his eyes on me, he pulls himself out. I glance down, and my heart skips. *Now* I'm intimidated. I can't handle all that, especially with my lack of experience. What if I don't do a good job? What if after all this build up, I'm just okay? We've based important decisions on our chemistry, and if it isn't there, where does that leave us?

I glance up at him. Finn's been respectful so far, but now I wonder if I pushed too hard. There's an edge to him that both thrills and unnerves me.

"I love when you look at me like that," he says. "So innocent, and yet so far from it at the same time."

I put my hand around his shaft, test him with my tongue, and meet his eyes. I've heard men like that, and he just told me as much. I open my mouth, determined to take all of him, but I only get halfway before I have to pull back. I play it off like I wasn't even trying. He's sticky and salty from earlier, and the thought dampens my underwear.

I run the tip of my tongue around his crown. "Tell me what to do."

With a moan, he runs his fingers through my hair and takes my roots in a light fist. "You're perfect."

"Tell me."

"Suck," he says. I put my mouth on him and pull, bobbing my head back and forth. I do it until my jaw aches and he says, "Yeah. Like that. Deeper."

I inhale through my nose and take as much of him as I can, and then even more. My mouth is crammed with him when I go too far and gag. I jerk back. My throat constricts as I gasp for air. "I'm sorry," I wheeze.

"That my cock's too big for your mouth?" he asks, gravel in his voice. "I'm not. And you won't be later, either."

I wipe saliva from my chin. "What?"

His grin borders on sinister as he takes my upper arm. "Come up here."

"Am I that bad?" I ask, standing.

"No. I'm stopping you so I don't come now and end the night early." He takes my face in his hands and leans in.

I pull away. "I just gave you a blowjob."

"And?" He holds me in place and kisses me full on the mouth. "You better get un-squeamish, Hals." He lowers his voice, trailing kisses down my neck. "So I can kiss you when I want. Touch you where I want. Fuck you how I want. You can always say no, but just assume I want all of it."

Hals. Nobody's ever called me that before. I raise my chin toward the ceiling, exposing my neck for him. I think I was going to ask him what "all" he's referring to, but I'm quickly losing my train of thought.

Finn embraces my waist and lifts me, walking me backward. He sits me on a surface. "The kitchen table?" I ask.

"Of course. This is where I eat all my meals."

Before I can ask what he means, Finn attaches his lips to mine like he needs my breath to keep him upright. He tugs my blouse from my skirt, separating from me only long enough to pull it over my head.

Planting a paw-like hand on each side of me, he traps me where I am. "Let me see you."

I sit up straight. Our mouths almost touch. Sucking in my tummy, I reach back and unclasp my bra. My breasts are one area I've never had complaints, but when I lost weight, they got a little smaller. Rich and I slept together less and less over the past few months, even though he made sure I knew how much better I looked thinner.

Finn nods once, urging me on, and I slide both straps down my shoulders.

He stares while I try not to look at his cock, hard and reaching between us. "What the fuck'd I do to deserve these?" he asks, thumbing one of my hardening nipples. "You've got the tits of a . . . I don't even know. A chick with great tits."

I can't really blame him for going dumb. I did too a couple minutes ago. I'm more concerned with what he thinks of the rest of me. Finn's the most attractive man I've ever been with.

The elastic of my skirt and tights creates a roll of fat. Like my breasts, it's smaller than it used to be, but Finn doesn't know that. "Finn?"

"Hmm?" Without looking away from my breasts, he runs a hand under my skirt and licks his lips. "Can

I just . . . taste you everywhere and all at once?" he asks.

I smile shyly, and finally, he looks back into my eyes. "You like it?" I ask.

"Like what?"

"All of it. Some of it?"

He squints at me. "You're asking if I find you attractive?"

My chest tightens. If he says no, I don't trust myself not to react badly. I shouldn't've asked when tonight's been going so well. "You don't have to answer."

Propping himself up with one arm, he scoops his other around my waist and hauls me to the edge of the table. My legs open wider, automatically wrapping around him as he pushes his cock right up against me. I gasp louder than I mean to.

"It likes you," he says. "*I* like you."

"Yes, but—"

"It wants to be inside you. I want to be inside you."

"Okay." I blush. "I get it."

He moves against me slowly, every nuance of his shaft sliding between my legs, over my silky tights. "It wants to make you feel so good, you're *ruined.* Right here, right now. I won't let it, not tonight anyway, but that's what it wants."

I begin to quiver. The table is cold, even through my stockings. He's all man, bordering on

Neanderthal, and I'm certain sex with him will be unlike anything I've ever experienced.

"Are you afraid?" he asks.

"A little."

"Good. You should be. This is scary. Are you good with that?"

His words have the opposite effect they should. They're more calming than troubling. He recognizes this is more than just sex. If he means to ruin me, I don't have the desire to stop him. "Yes."

He holds me in place by my lower back. "I don't want casual sex, I never have. I want you to come knowing *I'm* doing this to you. *I'm* giving you this and taking what I need from you. *I'm* watching you. That's why I couldn't do this before. I have to know you're not holding back a single fucking thing from me."

If I let him in the way he's asking . . . what if I have to one day rid myself of him? I won't be able to. This feels permanent. Being ruined takes on a new meaning.

He skates his hand up my spine, to the center of my back, and applies pressure until I arch into him. My nipples graze his chest. "Does that answer your question?" he asks.

"What was my question?"

He smirks and lowers his mouth to suck the skin between my breasts. I gulp air and let my head drop back. My nipples are painfully erect when he draws one between his teeth.

"Oh, God, Finn." He tugs. Sucks it hard. Lets it go with a *pop*. "God. Please." I pray for relief. It's too much. It's not enough.

"You like that?" he asks. "Because I'm about to do the same thing to your clit."

When I squirm, I'm reminded my legs are still open. Suddenly, I want to get my tights the fuck off. I want for him to tease me, sliding, filling, slamming until I feel nothing else.

Finn lays me on my back. "Shut your eyes," he says. "Just focus on what I'm doing."

My lids are already heavy, so I give in. He urges my hips up to undo my skirt. The zipper ends right at my tailbone, eliciting a shudder from me. He pulls the waistband of my tights down around my thighs and leaves them there, cutting into my skin. "Do you have the kind of tights that stop halfway up your thighs?" he asks.

"Stockings? I can get some."

"Get some." He removes them. "Cheap ones."

"Why do they need to be cheap . . .?"

"They'll only last a night."

My mushy brain doesn't even know where to start with that. He's not only going to ruin me, but my clothing too, and it's going to be in the future. We haven't even done this yet, and we're making plans to do it again. I feel my breath moving through me, my blood circulating through my veins.

With my eyes closed, I reach out for him. He complies, covering my body with his, and kisses me good and thorough. His fingers between my legs test me without entering. I groan and moan, arch and writhe, wanting him inside me any way I can get him. I don't even know how it's possible that I could climax already. He kisses his way down my sternum and parts my knees. I'm already at the edge, but he grabs me under the ass and pulls me onto his mouth so I'm practically hanging off the table.

I put my feet on his shoulders. His appreciative groans vibrate against my pussy. My hips buck as he licks and tastes. He puts one hand on my stomach to pin me down, then grabs my knee with the other. Pushing my leg up, he bares me to him even more. After plunging his tongue in me a few times, he makes good on his promise to love my clit.

As good as it feels, nothing sounds better than connecting with him in the most intimate way. I want to feel him, look into his eyes, come with him. "Please, Finn . . ." I beg.

"I know what you want, but we can't. You can orgasm like this."

"But you didn't."

"You first."

I don't know whether to cry or come. It wouldn't be the first time tonight I did either. His ministrations continue until my thighs shake around his head and my back arches off his kitchen table, and *oh yes*, finally I understand his joke about eating his meals here. *I'm* dinner.

"Now," he says, muffled by my thighs.

Now? Now what?

He digs his fingers into my skin and gorges on me. Aha—*come*. Now. That's what I've been ordered to do. And like the good girl I am, I do, right in his mouth. He laps me up until I'm finished.

When I come to, he's standing over me. "You good?" he asks.

My breasts rise and fall. "Amazing."

He picks me up from the table to cradle me in his arms. "It's only fair you taste yourself since I did."

Another first for me, kissing a mouth covered in *me*. Finn somehow makes it sexy. "This is just the start," he says.

"I think we've gotten as creative as it gets without a condom."

"I look forward to proving you wrong. But right now, we should sleep."

Even when I messaged Finn, I never dreamed I'd be spending the night with him. I nuzzle into his chest. "Here?"

"Yes. Well, not in the kitchen." I hear the smile in his voice. "How's my bed sound?"

My skin prickles. I hope he can't feel my goosebumps, how excited just the idea of *his* bed makes me. I try to play it cool. "That would be fine."

He carries me down the hall to his bedroom. It's dark, but the open shades provide some moonlight. He lays me on the mattress and disappears. Either he's only gone a few seconds, or I fall asleep, because next thing I know, he's wrapping himself around me from behind. He squeezes me to him until I'm perfectly puzzled into his body. "You'll be able to sleep with me crushing you like this, right?" he teases.

I wear a smile on my face I doubt even the deepest sleep could erase. "I'll manage."

"There's so much I want to know about you," he says, his mouth at my ear. "Earlier, when I said this was the start, I meant of us."

Us. How is it possible to make it all the way to twenty-five without ever having felt like part of an *us*? "You know more than you think," I confess. "You probably know more than anyone else."

"Because of the journal?" he asks softly. "Are there others?"

I don't answer. I've bared enough of myself for one night. I've gotten the intimacy I wanted, and being with him has been just right. I don't want to risk going any deeper.

He seems to understand my silence, letting the question hang as we drift to sleep.

THIRTEEN

Finn's bed is white. Snowy pillows and sheets match the frost forming on the glass. An indigo dawn yawns through the window. He's no longer curled around me, but the mattress dips with his weight.

I look over my shoulder. His face is shadowed, his silhouetted profile strong and square against the linens as he stares up at the ceiling. I want to go to him, but I'm warm and heavy where I am, glutted with him.

"Hey." My voice cracks.

He turns his head. "Hey. Didn't mean to wake you."

"It's okay."

"I'm going to take a quick shower," he says. "Go back to sleep."

I check the clock on his nightstand. "Do you always get up at five?"

"I'll come back to bed when I'm done."

"You want company? I should shower before work."

"No."

I'm not entirely awake, but his rejection is harsh enough to sting. I turn back to my side of the bed. "Oh-*kay*."

He laughs and squeezes my shoulder. "I didn't mean it like that. The thing is, I'm kind of dying over here."

"Dying?"

"I want to fuck you so bad, Halston. More than I've ever wanted to do anything. I can't believe I'm the idiot without a condom."

"You could've just gone downstairs to get one."

"Then I'd have to leave you. Anyway, I'm hot and hard and it's not going so well for me. That's why I just need to take a cold shower. Alone."

I bite my lip to keep from smiling over his discomfort. "But it's like forty degrees outside."

"Yeah. I realize I sound like a sex addict. I should keep my mouth shut."

"I like it open," I say, my voice raspy. "Your mouth."

"Yeah?" He kisses me on the back of the head. "I promise, I'll do nothing other than buy condoms today. All day long. Or at least until you can get back here. When do you get off work?"

Work. *Shit.* It's warm and perfect in here, cold, crowded and loud out there. I have to see Rich. And my dad. Maybe I can avoid them . . . the arguing . . . the attempts to change my mind . . . and come back here.

My new happy place.

Finn's warm, soft bed.

"What?" Did he ask me something? Oh, yes. Work. "I'm done at six . . . ish."

"How about five-ish?"

"Hmm?"

"Four?" His laugh sounds distant. "Sleep. I'll be right back."

I nuzzle into my pillow, but just as I'm drifting into a dream, I'm jolted back to reality. I have to see Rich today. And no, there's no avoiding him *or* my father. They'll want answers. Rich will blame the break-up on my change in treatment. I'm not even sure I can defend myself. The two things may be linked some way or another.

I'm wide awake now, and the sky is bleeding into sapphire. A wispy layer of snow fleeces some bare branches outside. Work problems aside, there's romance in the air. I'm supposed to leave Finn alone, but I think it's because he's so turned on, he can't sleep. He didn't come a second time last night, and after the way he ate me to orgasm, I owe him. I salivate just remembering him in my mouth. Maybe I'd be welcome if I showed up to finish what I started.

I sit up in bed and rub my eyes. The cold wood floor has me scurrying to his bathroom. The door is cracked, and I push it open just enough to see his reflection in the mirror. His back is turned to me, his ass firm and delicious enough to take a bite out of.

Leaning one hand against the tile wall, the muscles of his other arm bulge.

He's touching himself.

No, he's *jerking off.*

His arm moves faster. He drops his head back, then turns slightly to grab the showerhead. He repositions it to beat right on his hair. Since there's no steam at all, he must not've been exaggerating—the water's cold.

I should return to bed, but I'm riveted and aroused by his grunts. The pained expression on his face. The tightening of his back muscles. His broad shoulders. My eyes travel down his body. His *cock*. It's at least twice the length of his massive fist. He pumps his hand back and forth as water slicks his hair back from his face, its golden color turning his wet skin bronze. He takes his bottom lip between his teeth and visibly holds in a groan, probably so he won't wake me.

I could help him. Get down on my knees in front of him and offer hands and a mouth. I've never swallowed a man's cum, but I'd do it, I would. I don't move, though. I watch until the end. Until he curls one hand into a ball and paints the tile in front of him.

As turned on as I am, I hope this is the last time I see this. I want to be that hand, that lip, even that wall. I'd let him come in my mouth, but also on my back, my tits, my face—wherever he wanted.

My throat goes dry when a chilling realization hits me.

Maybe *I'm* the sex addict in this relationship.

I love the office break room. My assistant could easily help maintain the steady stream of coffee into my mouth, but I look forward to my morning, late-morning, afternoon, and late-afternoon trips from my office to the break room. I mean, for God's sake, it's a no-work zone that's lousy with my absolute favorite smell. *Yep*. Coffee.

Rich never comes to the break room, so my first mistake is assuming I'm safe there.

When he walks in, he glances at the mug in my hands. "Can you excuse us?" he asks Benny.

She grabs an apple. "I'll be at my desk."

I wait until she's left the room to address Rich. "She doesn't know. Nobody does. I don't want to do this here."

"Your dad wants to see us in his office."

"Is it about business?"

"It's going to happen, you know it is. Unless you change your mind about us, your dad's going to get his two cents in."

I put my mug down and walk past him. "It doesn't help your case when you run to him first chance you get. This isn't *Three's Company*."

We walk through the maze of desks. "I was worried," he says in a hushed tone.

I don't respond. Already, people at this company are too invested in my personal life since I'm the daughter of the founder and the girlfriend of the top-performing account manager.

In the elevator, Rich hands me the mug I just put down. "You'll want this."

I cross my arms to prove I don't need looking after, but my rebellion only lasts one floor. I take the coffee and mutter, "Thanks."

The doors open to the executive floor. My dad's office is front and center. His secretary glances up as we approach. "He's expecting you."

My dad's on the phone, pacing the length of the window in his office. He takes his eyes from Fifth Avenue to watch us enter. "The bottom line is, never date a woman who knows what you drive before she meets you, and a mouse in a cheese commercial will kill your brand, so forget about the rodent, would you?" he asks, completely serious, as if those are two perfectly normal statements to string together. I sit in a chair across from him, and Rich follows suit. "Uh-huh. Sure." Dad laughs. "We're happy to make that contribution, Bob. See you next week."

Dad flings the phone aside as his smile flips upside down. That doesn't tell me anything. His bullshit always clears the room as soon as we're alone.

"He won't give up the mouse," I say. "We've all tried."

"Sure he will. It's all about approach with a man like that." He sits forward and plants his elbows on the desk. "What's going on between you two?"

"We broke up," I say.

"*She* broke up," Rich corrects. "I haven't agreed to it."

I shoot him a glare, the brown-noser. "That isn't how breakups work, Rich."

"No need for the sarcastic tone," my dad says to me. "We can do this like civilized adults. What's the problem, honey? Is he working too much? I can arrange to cut back on his hours."

"I don't want that, sir," Rich says. "I love my job, and I want to do my part."

"I know. Believe me, I know, Rich. Nobody's as dedicated as you." He steeples his fingers and looks at me. "But relationships are work, and you guys are getting to the point where you either commit or move on, and I'd hate to see you end this over something that could be fixed."

"It's already ended, Dad," I say. "Moving on is my choice."

"Let's not be rash," he reasons. "This isn't something you just decide overnight."

"It wasn't *overnight*." Maybe a little. Was it really less than twelve hours ago that Finn nearly fucked me fully clothed? Pushing me up against the wall, unable to keep his hands to himself? I suck in a breath and try to push the scorching memory out of my mind.

"It was . . . I . . ." I try to remember the point I was about to make.

Dad and Rich exchange a look. "Rich, will you give us a second?"

Rich hesitates but stands. "Sure."

When we're alone, my dad looks suddenly tired. "Why are you doing this to me, Banana? Why now? You know how December is."

As if I need a reminder of the time of year. Using that in combination with the nickname given to me as a yellow-haired toddler is enough to make my throat thick. "I admit, it isn't ideal timing."

He rubs his eyes with the heels of his hands. "I've lost three clients since summer, and the ones I have are twice as demanding around the holidays. I can't be worried about you on top of work."

And work comes first. That isn't anything new, but it never feels good to hear, even if he doesn't mean to hurt my feelings. "I thought things were going well," I say.

"They are, and if anyone around the office asks, even Rich, business is great. But the economy's unstable with this political climate, and clients are hesitant to pay for premium work. It'll pass, it always does, I just don't need more stress."

"You don't have to worry about me. I'm fine."

"Rich says you've stopped seeing Doctor Lumby and you're taking on your own treatment. I don't believe him."

I close my eyes. I knew this conversation would come, but I'm not feeling as bold as I was last night. "It's time, Dad. It's been ten years—"

"Ten years." He looks at the desk. "Don't I know it."

I allow us a moment of silence. "I'm sorry, but wouldn't you rather I figure this out now instead of later, when we're all more invested?"

"Figure what out?"

"That I don't *love* him. If it hasn't happened by now, it's not going to."

"That's because you don't understand the definition of love. Your generation thinks everything's easy. Love is commitment. It doesn't come like that." He snaps. "It's an investment of time and energy."

"Is that how you felt about Mom?"

"Damn right it is. We worked on our marriage every day and to let her go at any point would've been like tanking a business I'd spent years investing in."

Even though my dad refers to my mom as an investment, I know he means it as a compliment. He was even more dedicated to her than this company. "Not every business can survive," I say.

"You don't think we had our problems in the beginning? Two years in? Ten years in? Shit, twenty years? Of course we did."

Guilt weighs on my shoulders. If not for my mistakes, he'd have been able to say thirty years soon. "But Rich and I aren't married."

"You could be. Do you know what a weight it would lift off my shoulders to know you were happy and taken care of?"

"How can I be happy with something I don't want?"

"You work at it. That's what I'm telling you." He stands and comes around the desk to perch on the edge in front of me. "What's wrong with this picture?"

I blink at him. "What?"

"I'm asking *you*," he says. "What's wrong with it? What haven't I done for you? You don't have to struggle like I did. I've kept you safe, and I've tried to make you happy. Rich is a nice, smart young man, and he's on track to take over for me when I step down."

"Because he's good at what he does," I say.

"No, Halston. Rich is a good kid. Hardworking. But he's not a natural businessman. I can get him there, to a place where he'll be the right man for my position. It's an investment I'm willing to make. For you."

He has it all figured out. I could walk out the door back to Rich, ask for a ring, stand by his side as he moves up in the company, raise his children. I have stability at my fingertips. And maybe with a little more effort, I *could* fall in love with him.

The room feels suddenly smaller. I close my eyes and think of Finn, of being comfortable in his white bedroom and his arms. "No."

"No what?"

"You're manipulating me. This is what you and Rich do."

"If trying to give you a good life is wrong," he raises his palms, "guilty."

"A good life would be *my* life. Not the one you decide for me."

"Do you know what I would've given to have all this handed to me?" he asks. "Or to even get my good life back?"

I hear what he doesn't say: the good life *I* took from him. I've never stopped feeling guilty for my role in my mom's death, but it's especially sharp now, when the anniversary of it is around the corner. When my dad and I are on opposite sides. I see the pain in his face. Sometimes I forget it's there until something makes him genuinely smile or laugh. To others, it looks like stress or anger. Dad doesn't show weakness. Except to me, because we've seen each other at our worst.

What do I do? Give him the peace and reassurance he wants so he can rest a little easier? Or fight this battle for myself and for a man I just met?

"I can't stay on these drugs," I say. "I just can't. It's not fair to ask me to just because you don't want to deal with me. You don't even know what I'm like without them."

His face darkens. "Yes I do."

"That was *ten* years ago. Isn't it possible I've changed? Matured? Are you the man you were ten years ago?"

"What do you fucking think?"

I sit back. My dad rarely curses at me. It makes me want to slink off to my room, especially because he's right. Why would he be the same after losing the love of his life? "I'm sorry," I say. "Of course you're not."

"If you stop your meds, then what? You'll be fine? Do you honestly believe that?"

I open my mouth to argue. I'm tired of them doubting me and pointing out my shortcomings at every turn. *Yes*, I believe I'll be fine.

Won't I?

You're troubled. You make bad decisions.

I've heard it since I was fifteen.

The truth is, I don't know if it's wrong. It could be right.

"I'll worry about you more than I already do," Dad says. "At least with Rich, I know someone else is looking out for you. With Christmas coming up, and—and the anniversary—if you're off your treatment and alone . . . I don't know that I can take it."

My chest hurts. I can't do this to him. His vulnerability is hard-earned, a privilege, and I can't just turn a blind eye to it. But I can't give myself up, either, or say goodbye to Finn knowing how good it is with him. "I'm stopping the drugs," I say firmly. "It's time."

He sighs. "That alone is enough for you to handle. You don't need a stressful breakup on top of that. Who knows? Maybe this will be the thing that changes your feelings about Rich."

It's the only option if I want to give my dad some relief during the hardest time of the year. Not just any year. The tenth year.

"Will you try to make it work with him *one* more time, Banana? For me?"

How can I say no?

FOURTEEN

After an unsettling conversation with my dad about resuscitating my dead relationship, Rich is the last person I want to see. But there he is when I leave Dad's office, perched on the secretary's desk, talking to her.

He looks up. "Should I go back in?"

I start for the elevator. "No."

"What happened?" he asks, catching up with me as the doors open.

I wait until we're alone to speak. "You and I are getting back together—"

"We are?" Rich raises his eyebrows. "Talk about finding the right approach. Your dad's even smoother than I thought."

"It's only as far as my dad knows."

"What?"

"We're not *really* getting back together. This is an awful time of year for my dad and me. I don't have to tell you that. My dad feels better when you're looking after me, so we're going to let him believe you are."

"I'm not comfortable with that."

The elevator stops on our floor. "It's not up for negotiation."

"Why can't I just take care of you for real? Have I not done a good job of that?"

"You have," I say, "but I—I want more. I want to . . ."

"What?" he asks.

Saying what I want aloud isn't easy. It's not only hurtful to Rich, but it's embarrassing to admit, even though I doubt he'd mock me. The doors close. "I want to be in love."

He frowns but takes my hand. "I know we don't have the most affectionate relationship, but I thought that worked for us."

"It does. It *did*."

"I'll try harder to show I care."

I shake my head. "I want to feel more than just contentment about my life. This works out for both of us, Rich." I hit the button for our floor to get the doors to open again. "I get to keep my dad happy through the holidays, and you remain in good standing with him. I suggest you use this time to make yourself indispensable—some other way than through me."

"So that's it?" The doors start to close, but he catches them. A few people in the office look up. Rich lowers his voice. "I don't want to lie to him."

"You will if you want all three of us to get through—" Pain shoots through my head. I grab the rail as sudden pressure weighs on the bridge of my nose.

"Are you okay?" Rich asks.

I swallow a few times, and the stabbing pain subsides, disappearing as quickly as it came on. "I'm fine."

"You don't look it."

I'd read that there'd be some physical side effects to lowering my dosage. I wanted to rip the Band-Aid off, though. Ten years is coming up soon, and I can't be a person who's been medicated an entire decade. At this rate, I can ring in the new year feeling like a new person.

I push past Rich and get off the damn elevator. My temples throb with the start of a headache, so I go to my office and shut the door. I turn out the glaring lights and open the blinds instead.

Once I'm in my desk chair, I close my eyes. My dad's disappointment is tangible. He's right to be upset. I've broken an unspoken agreement. He gives me money, a stable future, my choice of job, and in return, I'm a good daughter who doesn't make waves. It's a cycle I'm not sure should continue, but the thought of breaking it makes my scalp hot. It could be the best decision I've made in years—or the worst.

I need something to calm myself down. I go to buzz Benny, but a knock at my door comes first.

"Go away, Rich."

"But I have coffee," Benny says in a deep voice, a horrible attempt to impersonate Rich. She laughs. "Rich said I should bring you some."

Damn it. He knew what I'd need. Why can't he just get angry with me like a normal ex? Why does he have to be kind while I'm trying to abandon him? "Bring the whole pot. No—get the entire machine."

My chin trembles. I don't know why doing what's best for myself means I need to be a bad daughter and ex-girlfriend. I don't normally seek comfort in Rich when I'm upset, or anyone really since my mom. My dad's too practical. He only wants to hear enough to fix the problem. In a way, my journals have been my confidantes, even when I only write a line or two. Now, someone else has read them. Someone else has seen me, stuck around, and wants to *know* me.

I get my phone from my handbag. I don't need to spill my sorrows to Finn. We aren't at that place yet. But just saying hi, just knowing I'll see him tonight, will be enough for now. I press the Home button. I have five new texts from Finn in the last two hours, and I can't help the grin that overtakes my face. I type in my passcode and start with the first message.

Haven't stopped thinking about last night since . . . last night.

You coming here straight from work? Or wanna get dinner first?

We could also order in. I've taken all the necessary "precautions" for a night in.

I smile. He got the condoms. Oh, the delicious positions he had me in last night—against his studio wall, on my knees for him, spread out on his kitchen table. I bite my bottom lip against the assault of flashbacks. I'm not sure if I'm more aroused by the ways he made me come, or by watching him furiously get himself off in the shower this morning when he thought I was asleep.

I scroll down, hoping for more of what we'll do when I walk through his door.

I have to cancel tonight. I'm sorry. Don't come.

Halston? I need to know you saw my last message. Please don't come by my place. K?

My heart drops. What happened within an hour that made him change his mind? I re-read all the texts. Is it because I took so long to respond? Is he having second thoughts?

My eyes well with a fresh round of tears.

I can't do this. I can't be so attached to Finn already that his rejection is like a knife between the ribs. I tap out a response I can't even read through my blurry vision.

I saw

I lay my head on my forearms and give in to my sobs. I don't understand what changed. His words were so short. Cold. As if me not going over there is more important than how he's just made me feel.

When my phone buzzes again, I'm torn between snapping it up to read his response and pushing it over the side of the desk into the garbage. I can't handle any other response than "just kidding."

A knock on the door momentarily decides for me. I stand up to cross the office. Thank God for coffee—it's never let me down. Well, except the time a barista served me decaf by accident, and I spent the following hours confused and lonely before I realized what'd happened. And yes, liquids can let a person down. Wine has. Wine has fucked me over in the past, but rarely coffee.

I open the door just enough for Benny to pass the decanter and machine through. "I'll set it up for you," she says instead.

"I can handle it."

She purses her lips. "You look like you're about to jump out your window. I'm coming in, or the coffee goes bye-bye."

I roll my eyes and step aside. She sets the coffee maker on my desk and plugs it in.

"Wow," I say. "I'm glad you were here. How would I have managed without you?"

She smirks. "Damn. I forgot a mug."

I pull out two from a bottom desk drawer.

"I should've known," she says.

"Yep. You should have," I tease, passing them to her.

"So, what'd your dad say?" she asks as she pours the coffee. "I've never seen you cry."

"I'm not crying."

"Sorry. You're right. I've never *heard* you cry. What'd he say to you?"

I take a comforting sip. "Can you keep a secret? Like, this isn't office gossip, not even my dad can find out."

She nods. "Hit me."

"Rich and I broke up," I say.

"*Seriously*?"

"Yes. Seriously." She gapes at me. Am I the only one who sees Rich and I aren't actually that good together? "I mean, I know Rich is great and all, but I don't think he and I—"

She waves a hand at me. "No, it's not that. I just can't believe he's why you're bawling. Your relationship seems so cut and dry."

"Oh." I sit back against the lip of the desk. "So you're not surprised it's over?"

She looks into her mug. "Should I not have said that? Since you're my boss?"

"No, it's . . . it's okay. It's good. I was worried for a minute that everyone would think this was a mistake but me."

She shrugs. "If you're not into it, why does it matter what anyone else says?"

For a split second, I consider telling her about Finn. It's not really the kind of relationship she and I have, and I'm not even sure how she'd respond, but it would be nice to let my hair down and bitch. To share how completely blindsided I feel by his sudden flip in personality.

I pick up my phone and read his message.

I'm sorry. I'll explain next time I see you.

Next time I see you? Is he implying maybe he'll see me, maybe not? This is a complete one-eighty from this morning. I didn't peg Finn to be the one-night stand type. We didn't even have sex.

"So how long's it been since you were single?" Benny asks.

I've had my fill of men for today. I put the phone down and return my attention to Benny. "Do you want to grab a drink?"

The bartender sets three martinis on the bar, one in front of each of us. "Extra dirty," he says. "From the dude in the suit."

"Which dude?" Benny asks. "They're all in suits."

I slow-blink at the bartender, pointing at my half-empty drink. "But I haven't even finished this one."

He shrugs as Benny laughs. "If I finished all the drinks men bought me, I'd never be upright."

"I think that's the point . . .?" Cara says.

Benny elbows her. "You know what I mean."

I could get used to this girlfriend thing. I'm on my third cocktail of the night, and each one has been paid for by a different guy. Benny has serious flirtation skills. It could also be the slight Latin accent that flavors her words. Or her long, richly brown hair.

"Cara's sleeping with her manager," Benny explains, "otherwise she'd be more fun tonight."

"At the firm?" I ask.

"No, I work nights at a restaurant in Meatpacking. I'd never sleep with the misogynistic asshole lawyers I work for. Dan's a misogynistic asshole, but at least he's not a lawyer."

"She's exaggerating," Benny says. "Dan's sweet, she just doesn't like people to know it."

"Where's your boyfriend?" I ask Benny.

"Pssh. What boyfriend? I've been playing the field since college."

"Oh. Rich mentioned one."

Benny frowns and puts a hand on my shoulder. "He flirted with me once while he was waiting for you to come back from a meeting. It was harmless, but I said I had a boyfriend just to make things easy."

Rich hit on her? He rarely even attempts to flirt with me. "I'm sorry," I tell her. "That must've been awkward, getting seduced by boss's boyfriend. You should've told me."

She waves me off. "I handled it fine."

"Who's Rich?" Cara asks. "The guy you just broke up with?"

Benny nods. "Her dad likes him."

Cara cringes.

"That's supposed to be a good thing," I point out.

"Not in your twenties. Now's the time to get back at dad for all the ways he fucked you up, and the men you date are your best weapons."

"Huh." I pick up my fresh martini. "I never thought of it that way."

"So our mission is to find you a guy Mr. Fox would hate," Benny says.

I've already accomplished that. Finn's several years older than me and a struggling artist with an ex-wife. He also doesn't put me in a box. Nothing about that would appeal to my dad. I shift on the barstool.

"Or maybe she's already found one?" Cara asks, eyeing me.

I smile into my drink for a full second before I remember how Finn blew me off. "Actually . . ." I look up. "I need advice."

"You *already* met someone?" Benny gasps. "You were fooling around on Rich! And that's why you broke up. Did he catch you in the act? Were you buck naked, sprawled out on some burgundy leather couch I'm sure Rich has in his apartment—"

"No, no, no," I sputter, trying not to laugh. I'm supposed to be pissed at the men in my life, but Benny's right—Rich *does* love burgundy leather. "I didn't cheat on him." For the first time, I'm glad Finn had the sense to stop me so I wouldn't have to lie about it. "This guy's been pursuing me, but—"

"Sleep with him," Benny says. "Those rules about waiting are bull."

"I would," I say. "In fact, we . . . we had this amazing night last night."

"You whore," Cara cries.

Benny shoves her so hard, she almost topples off the stool. "You don't know her well enough to call her a whore, and by the way, she's my boss."

I force a smile. I think Cara's teasing me—she's laughing. But nobody's ever called me a whore, joking or otherwise. "It's fine. I can take it."

"So, you banged," Benny urges me on. "Then what?"

"I stayed over, but we didn't bang. We just had a great night, like really *really* great."

Cara nods knowingly. "Good call. Keep him on his toes."

"Was it, though?" I ask. "We made plans for this weekend, but he just canceled on me out of the blue."

Cara and Benny exchange a look. "Are you *sure* you didn't sleep with him?"

I scoff-laugh. "Of course I'm sure. I think I'd know."

"Hmm." Cara plants her elbow on the bar and her chin in her hand. "Does he have a girlfriend?"

"No. He's very anti-cheating, which is one reason we haven't slept together. Because of Rich. He has an . . . ex-wife."

"*Damn*," Benny says. "He's older?"

I nod. "Early thirties, I think."

Cara rubs her palms together. "Now we're talking. Older men are fucking awesome. Chances are, he isn't dicking you around. Did he say why he had to cancel?"

"No."

"So it wasn't a girlfriend," Benny tells Cara, squinting as if she's scheming.

Cara shakes her head. "Most likely not a blow off, either, since he didn't even get laid yet."

I take a long pull from my straw before I point out, "Not afraid of commitment. He's been married."

"This is going to bother me," Cara says. "Let's get a second opinion."

"Good idea." Benny sits up on her stool, scans the crowd, and waves at a pair of men. They come right over.

"Hi," Benny says. "This is Cara, Halston, and I'm Benny."

"Nice to meet you," says the dark-haired one. "I'm Jude, and this is Matt. Are you ladies—"

"How old are you guys?" Cara asks.

Matt rubs the back of his neck. "Uh . . . don't worry, we're legal."

Cara smirks. "We're conducting research, and we're looking for men in their thirties."

"You're in luck," Jude says, raising his glass. "We're both thirty."

"Excellent. My friend here," Cara gestures at me, "had a great date with a guy in his thirties, didn't sleep with him, and made plans for a second date, but he canceled last minute."

The guys shrug. "Something probably came up."

"And?" Benny asks.

"And what?" Matt turns to me. "Have you asked him?"

Everyone else turns to me.

I stir my drink. "It didn't really seem like he was open to talking about it."

"Then he has a girlfriend," Matt says.

"He's divorced." Benny shakes her head. "*Unless*—maybe he was burned by his ex, and he freaked out."

"Yes," Cara shouts. "That's it. He's not ready to jump into the next relationship. Right, guys?"

Matt and Jude exchange a look. "*Maybe*," Jude says. "I wouldn't say I've freaked out before, but I have skipped a date with a girl I knew was looking for commitment."

Finn *had* shut the marriage topic down when I'd asked for details. He said he hadn't loved her like a husband, but was he trying to play it down so I wouldn't know I was a rebound? I nod a little too hard, my head swimming from the alcohol. "That makes sense. His texts were so schizo."

"Texts?" Benny asks. "No way. You need to talk to him face to face, or at least on the phone. Texts are too ambiguous."

"They were really sweet at first," I say, "and then when I didn't respond, he got weird."

"So you rejected him," Jude says.

"No I didn't, I was just busy at work—"

"Did you tell him that?"

"Well, no. I didn't really say anything. I was upset."

Matt makes a face. "When was his divorce?"

"Recently, I think."

"My older brother was traumatized after his divorce," he says. "It's been three years and he still hasn't been on a date."

"So basically," Cara says, "this guy's trying to get back out there after a devastating divorce, and you go and blow him off."

"*I* blow *him* off?" I think back to his six text messages—and my single two-word response. Do I have this all wrong? Was *I* the jerk? "Oh my God. Do you really think that's what happened?"

Jude nods. "Definitely. Girls think we have it so easy, but the truth is, getting shot down by someone you really like fucking sucks."

A wave of guilt—or gin, more likely—courses through me. *I* had burst into tears when I thought Finn had rejected me just a few hours ago, so of course I can understand why he'd be hurt. "What do I do?" I ask. "Call him?"

"No. You bruised his ego. You need a grand gesture." Cara points at me. "You should go over to his place."

"But he told me not to come."

"Of course he did." Benny nods. "He's proud. You have to prove you're really interested and not planning to screw him over."

"Just planning to screw him," Cara chirps.

"If a hot chick showed up on my doorstep to screw in the middle of the night," Matt says, "I'd think I'd died and gone to heaven."

"Really?" I ask.

Jude puts his hand on the back of my stool, his fingers mere inches from my ass. "If he doesn't invite you in, he's a loser. Better to find out he's a loser now rather than later."

I take another generous sip of my drink, feeling suddenly warm. I want to remove my sweater like I had last night for Finn's camera. For Finn. And having Jude's hand near me is reminding me of Finn's, all the things they did to me . . . and to himself.

Did I make a mistake assuming he was no longer interested? I have limited experience with men as it is—I know virtually nothing about divorce. I should've been more sensitive. I slide off my stool. "I'm going over there."

The four of them applaud. "Good girl," Cara says. "If he turns you down, come right back here. We'll be waiting."

If he turns me down, I'm certain I won't be going anywhere but right to bed so I can crawl under the covers for the rest of the weekend and drown myself in tears.

FIFTEEN

Outside, the cool air is refreshing, but not jarring enough to kill my buzz. I don't even put on my coat, just wave down a passing cab and give him Finn's address. On the ride over, I lower the window, unusually warm from the alcohol. I take off my mittens. I ask the driver where he's from. When I've exhausted all the ways to distract myself from what I'm doing, I get out my phone. Looking at Finn's photos of me makes me feel close to him. They have more likes and follows, but no comments.

As we get closer, my confidence wavers. Finn specifically told me not to come. If it was because I hurt him, I want to show him he has nothing to worry about. It could be something else, though. Something he doesn't want to share. The only thing he's been secretive about is his divorce—could this have to do with his ex?

The cabbie looks at me in the rearview mirror. "Well?"

We're at the curb in front of Finn's. I pay and get out of the car. The building has a keypad. I debate whether to wait for someone to come in or out. Buzzing his apartment seems almost more intrusive than just knocking on his door.

I'm not experienced in showing up unannounced. I've been on the receiving end of it, though. Just this afternoon, I talked to my dad about not respecting my wishes, yet here I am, doing the same thing to Finn.

This feels wrong. I open my messages and pull up our conversation from earlier.

I'm downstairs. I'll go if you want, I just wanted to see you. And talk.

I don't know how long I want to wait for a response. He might be asleep. Or worse, out. My Uber app tells me there's a car two minutes away. As I'm trying to decide a reasonable time limit for my desperation, a bubble pops up to indicate he's typing. I hold my breath until his message comes through.

You're here? At my place?

I don't know what to think. He doesn't seem happy, and this is starting to feel less "grand gesture" and more "desperate stalker."

I'm sorry. I can go. I've been drinking & my friends said all these things & now I'm here.

I've barely hit send when his response comes through.

Come upstairs

I don't know what to think. He doesn't seem happy, and this is starting to feel less "grand gesture" and more "desperate stalker." It's too late now, though, because the door to the building clicks as he unlocks it from his apartment. Inside, I ride the elevator up to the sixth floor. Right as I approach apartment 6A, the door opens, and Finn steps out in only sweatpants. I have to swallow to keep saliva in my mouth. His abs are in full effect tonight, and they're even better than I remember.

He runs a hand through his hair, pulls the door almost closed behind him, and whispers, "Hey."

"Oh my God. You were sleeping." This just keeps getting worse. "It's late."

He smiles a little. "It's barely eleven, but, yeah. I was out like a light."

I shake my head. "I'm sorry to show up like this, I just, I was confused, and your texts were so—"

"It's fine. You've been drinking?"

"I don't normally drink, not like this. I just had a really bad day—"

"I told you not to come." He glances behind him. "But if you're drunk and alone, I'm not going to send you away."

I'm an idiot. This is why I don't drink—my judgment sucks. I'm about to apologize when I realize Finn is whispering. "You're trying to be quiet," I say, my remorse fading. "Why?"

He looks down the hall, his eyes distant. "Listen, I . . . I have to tell you something."

My heart stops. I really *am* an idiot—a blind, trusting, rash idiot. "You're not alone."

"No."

My stomach revolts. My martinis are about to get way dirtier. "Shit. I . . . I can't believe I came here."

"Let me explain—"

I can *only* see this situation getting worse, and I don't want to stick around to watch it crash and burn. I step back.

"Stop." He lunges for my arm but misses while trying to keep his apartment door from shutting. "It's not what you think. Come inside, and I'll explain everything."

I freeze out of pure shock. "Have you lost your mind? You want me to come in where she is?"

"No." He rubs an eye with the heel of his hand. "Look. Fuck. I didn't want to do it this way. It's so damn complicated."

"Do what?"

"It's my daughter. She's inside. Sleeping."

"Your . . . *what*?" I'm not breathing. My brain, fuzzy from the alcohol, takes a few seconds to catch up. "You have a daughter?"

"Yes, and I'm sorry I didn't tell you, but she's in my life, and I was afraid you'd freak out. I planned to say something eventually, but that *plus* an ex-wife? I didn't think you were ready for all that." He pinches the bridge of his nose. "Fuck, that's a lie. I'm the one who wasn't ready."

I go to him. "Oh, God. I-I'm sorry. We've only known each other a couple weeks, of course I don't expect you to spill your life story right away."

His forehead wrinkles, his eyes darting over my face. "Really?"

"Yes, really. God. I'm so embarrassed."

He half smiles, the lines in his face easing, a dimple denting his cheek. "I wasn't going to tell you over a text. Plus, I felt like a huge ass because I forgot I had Marissa tonight. What kind of dad does that?"

"Marissa?" I ask.

He nods. "She's eight. It's not my usual weekend with her, but my ex went to a concert in the city, so I said I'd watch her tonight. It slipped my mind because . . . well, you know."

"I do?"

"You," he says. "You've stolen all my sense since I met you. You've dominated my thoughts."

I melt a little. He must notice, because he slips an arm around my waist to pull me against his body. "You look good tonight."

"I'm wearing practically the same outfit I was last night."

"That's why I like it." He runs the tip of his nose along the bridge of mine. "I can't let the door shut. It locks automatically. Come in."

As good as it feels to be back in his embrace, he was right when he said his personal life is complicated. This is the last thing I expected to find tonight. "I should've respected what you said. I thought—I don't know what I thought. My friends convinced me to come here."

"Who are these friends?" he asks. "You haven't mentioned any yet."

"Oh, they're not really friends. It's just Benny, my assistant, and a friend of hers."

"Well, I'm glad that—Benny?"

"Short for Benedicta."

"I'm glad *Benny* talked you into it. I really did want to see you, I just didn't think it'd be a good idea to explain things like this."

"I understand." I tilt my head up, angling for a goodbye kiss I probably don't deserve. "I'll let you get back to her."

He just tucks some of my hair behind my ear, distinctly *not* kissing me. "Kendra's picking Marissa up first thing in the morning. God forbid she lets me have her for longer than twelve hours during *her* weekend."

I'm not sure how to respond. "I'm sorry."

"Not your fault. Stay tonight. You can sleep late while I hang with Marissa. She'll be gone by the time you get up."

"No. I'm not here to butt into your life."

He looks at me thoughtfully. "I think I like your butt in my life."

"I can't—"

"I insist."

I chew the inside of my cheek. It's tempting, and thankfully, I know how persistent he can be. Otherwise we wouldn't be standing here. "Are you sure?"

He nods. "It's probably too soon for . . . all of this. But you're here, and I don't want you to leave."

Crossing paths with Marissa sounds terrifying—for all of us—but I showed up because I wanted to spend time with Finn. That hasn't changed. I smile. "All right. I'll stay."

He glances over his shoulder. "She's asleep."

"I'll be quiet."

He takes my hand and leads me through the apartment. It's dark and still, as if they've been snoozing a while. Jenga blocks are scattered on the coffee table. We pass through the hallway and I remember the other closed door that isn't his studio or his bedroom. It must be hers.

When we're in the master, he gently closes the door behind us. "You're probably not even tired."

"I'll be fine. I'm a good sleeper."

"I know you are." He grins, walking over to his dresser. "You wear a men's large, right?"

"Excuse me?"

He laughs, holding up a gray t-shirt. It's several sizes too big, but he tosses it to me. "It's all I got."

I sneak a sniff while his back is turned. Freshly-laundered Finn. "Can I, um . . . use your bathroom?"

"I've seen you naked," he teases. "Not a fraction of the times I plan to, but still."

Sure, right after I'd gotten him good and horny with my mouth. Now, we're just standing here in the moonlight, and I'm supposed to get naked without any reservations? "I'm still a little shy."

He gestures for me. "Come here."

Gripping the t-shirt, I close the small space between us.

"I like you shy. And not shy." He drops a smooth, lingering kiss on my lips. "And everything else you are or are not."

I smile against his mouth. "For a photographer, you're not half bad with the words."

"I'm not half good, either. I'll leave that to you." He turns me by my shoulders to the bathroom. As if I could forget where the shower is after this morning's peep show.

I change quickly, folding my clothes on the counter. I fix my hair and squeeze his toothpaste onto my finger before running it through my mouth. Instead of drinks with Benny, I'd been planning to run home and grab some things before coming here for the night. Change of plans, though.

A daughter. An *eight-year-old* daughter. Finn must've had her young. Younger than I am now. By my age, he would've had a toddler at home. I widen my eyes at myself in the mirror. A toddler!

I'm not sure how I feel about the fact that he's a dad. He's had a history, a marriage, and a baby with another woman. It's too soon for me to decide if it means anything to me, which is just as well. I don't have time to process it now.

I come out of the bathroom in nothing but Finn's t-shirt and a thong. I'm glad the hem sits well down my thighs. If I'd known I'd be here tonight, I would've worn booty shorts to hide the dimples in my ass.

Finn is splayed on the mattress, his arm behind his head. He takes one look at me, rolls his eyes, and looks away.

"What's wrong?" I ask, stopping at the foot of his bed.

"That's the kind of thing you'd wear right after we'd, you know. So it makes me think of . . ." He turns on his side, away from me. "I don't want to have sex while she's in the apartment."

"No, of course not," I say quickly. "I didn't expect that. At all."

"Good." He doesn't look back at me. "Get under the covers and pull them up to your chin."

I laugh.

"I'm not joking. If I see a sliver of skin, I can't be held responsible for breaking my own rules. Again."

With what's beginning to feel like a permanent smile on my face, I pull back the bedspread. Finn shifts over until there's enough space to fit Canada between us.

"Are you decent?" he asks.

"Not yet." I tent the covers over us and mirror his position, folding my arm under my head as I turn onto my side. Except that I can actually see him.

Finn's still in his sweatpants.

Still shirtless.

There's an adorably sexy smattering of freckles on his shoulders. I trace some with my finger, skimming my hand across his back and then down toward his waistband. "My mom used to do this when I couldn't sleep," I tell the space between us.

He doesn't respond, but I hear him breathing. A car passes outside.

I graze my nails up and down his skin. "I never told Rich that. Or anyone, I guess."

"You've never mentioned her."

My instinct is to shut down the topic, but Finn shared with me tonight. Now it's my turn. What's more—I *want* him to know. This is an enormous part of who I am. "She died when I was fifteen."

"That's when you went on the antidepressants?"

"Yes."

When I graze his shoulder again, Finn reaches back and scoops my hand into his. He brings it to his mouth, kisses my palm, and releases it. "I'm sorry."

"Thank you."

"Is that what your tattoo means?"

My ears warm. "Yes. I wanted to memorialize her life, not her death. She loved birds."

"Is it a certain kind of feather?"

"No—that's the thing. She had birds growing up, all different kinds. She named them after colors. Baby Blue, Pink Polly, Lily Lavender. That's why the feather's colored in pastels. But she didn't care about species or even their actual colors—she just loved them all."

I resume scratching his back. I can't believe I'm going here with him. I don't like talking about it for a number of reasons, and I usually only do it when I have to. I could blame the alcohol for my loose lips, but I've already lost my buzz.

"She must've been young," he says. "Was she sick?"

"Car accident." I swallow. "I was in the car."

"Fuck. Were you hurt?"

"The other car. Not hers." My heart pounds. I'm sure Finn can hear it in the silence that follows.

He turns around to face me. "What?"

"We can stop here," I warn. "It's not exactly my finest moment."

"Were you . . ."

"I wasn't driving. Thankfully, I guess, although it doesn't change the outcome. My, I don't know what he was, my short-lived boyfriend, I guess—he was."

"Drinking?" Finn asks.

"Yes." It pains me to say it. I could've stopped Bobby from having even one beer. I could've spoken up after his second, or when he got his car keys from his pocket. I didn't want him to see me as childish, though. "I wasn't that kind of kid," I say. "I really was good until I wasn't."

"I believe you," he says. "What happened?"

I go back to the beginning. "I grew up in Westchester, where my dad still lives. My parents had high expectations, but I always met them. Usually at the expense of a social life." That's putting it mildly, but Finn doesn't need to know just how unpopular I was. Growing up attending Broadway shows, I'd had it in my head I wanted to be a famous playwright like Samuel Beckett, so I joined the drama club. It was the only hobby my parents hadn't forced on me, and through middle school, I took it seriously. I wrote plays and practiced my lines alone in the cafeteria at lunch, not caring that people snickered and called me a freak behind my back. "Like I told you, I was a little overweight, and I only had a couple friends. I never got asked out. And then Bobby came along."

"The driver," Finn says.

I nod. "He was the ultimate bad boy. Every girl in school wanted him, but oh my God, when he asked me to the winter formal—*me*—nobody could believe it, least of all me."

"I find that hard to believe," Finn says. "I'll bet you were the perfect package and never knew it."

"I wasn't. I was an outcast, Finn. Bobby was the first guy to take me out. We dated a short time before the dance. I even cut one of my semester finals. I didn't care, but my parents did, and they banned me from the dance. So I snuck out, and Bobby picked me up down the street. It was the craziest night I'd ever had. I lost my virginity to him."

"While he was drunk?"

"Yes."

Finn watches me closely. He inches closer until we're almost touching. "He sounds like a piece of shit."

"In hindsight, he was. Anyway, he drove me home later that night, or by that time, it was early morning, three thirty-seven to be exact. My mom had found me missing from my room. My dad called the cops and she got in the car to look for me. She was less than a mile from the house when . . ." A lump forms in my throat, and I try to breathe through it. I've told the story enough times—to my psychiatrist, Dad, Rich, law enforcement—that I can do it without getting emotional. Just the facts. But it isn't working at the moment. "Less than a mile when . . ."

"You don't have to say it."

"I killed her."

"You didn't kill her."

"I'm the reason she's dead. Same thing."

He cups my face. I think I hear a lump in his throat when he says, "You made a mistake. You were a kid."

I cry. I haven't cried for my mom in a long time. Too long. I'm not even sure it's her loss I'm mourning.

Finn strokes my hair. "That's it. Let it out."

"It happened the weekend before Christmas. Bobby's dad was a politician and my parents had been regulars on the social scene. They tried to keep it quiet, but it was too juicy. Some local tabloids picked up the story. They claimed I was an out-of-control, sex-crazed teenager who'd seduced the senator's son and disgraced her poor, widowed father. That's part of why I'm adamant about staying anonymous." My classmates were sensitive to my mom's death until a certain point. Many of them also believed what they read, as if I'd led some kind of secret life that'd killed my mother and made Bobby into a real live bad boy. "I was institutionalized for depression by mid-January."

Finn stops playing with my hair. "Like a psych ward? Jesus."

"My dad had to carry me to the car and then into the facility because I couldn't get out of bed. I was there less than a month, even though I wanted to leave from the moment I stepped in the door. He told everyone I went to stay with relatives."

"That's wrong, Halston. You were grieving, not mentally unstable."

At the time, they were one in the same. At least, that's how it was put to me. I didn't get to grieve as hard as my dad, because I'd caused it. Nobody at the institution was compassionate toward me about the accident after they'd heard how I'd been involved.

"My dad didn't know what to do with me." I shrug one shoulder, and more wetness leaks from my eyes. "Still doesn't."

Finn wipes it from my cheeks with his thumb. "I know what to do with you."

I can't help smiling a little. When I look up at him, moonlight and tears make little crystals in my vision. "You do?"

"Mhm." He pulls the hem of my t-shirt up my belly, just under my breasts. "Turn over and take this off." Then he adds, sternly, "In that order. Whatever you do, don't flash me."

I switch sides so I'm facing his bedroom door, and together, we get the shirt over my head. He smooths my hair out of the way, then begins scratching my back as I'd done for him.

I close my eyes and shudder as I release a few silent sobs. "That feels nice."

"Just relax," he murmurs.

I haven't been touched so lovingly in over ten years.

After what I just confessed, it's not the reaction I might've expected from him.

It confirms what I think we both suspect.

Finn was meant to find that journal. To find me. To be a salve for, and perhaps even heal, a heart I'd worried was destined to ache forever.

SIXTEEN

finn

While I scramble eggs, Marissa makes a case for owning a horse. Thing is, it's not so far-fetched. She has friends with them. Kendra had one growing up. One of the many reasons I had to get out of that family—horses shouldn't be standard pets.

"Do you need one to be happy?" I ask her.

"No, Dad, and I knew you'd say that. But a horse would make me *more* happy."

"How?"

"I'd get to ride it. You're always telling me to go outside more. And some girls are so good, they'll go to college free."

"Is that so." I scrape some eggs from the pan to a dish and try not to think about Halston sleeping down the hall. I want to focus on my time with Marissa. "Where are you going to keep this horse?"

"At grandma and grandpa's."

I serve Marissa her breakfast. Without my prompting, she's already packed, dressed in jeans and a sweater with her blonde hair in a neat ponytail. Sometimes I think she's got it together better than her mother or me. "Look, you know I'd buy you a pony if I thought it was a good idea."

"Not a pony, Dad. I'm not five years old."

"Sorry. My mistake." I turn back to the stove to make myself a plate. "Pets require a lot of upkeep. Are you going to go straight to Gran's every day, right after school, to take care of the horse? Then go home *and* do your homework? You won't have time for friends or fun or anything else."

"It won't be that hard if we're living there," she says.

I set my plate on the table and sit across from her. "Where?"

She chews, shrugging. "Gran's."

"Why would you be living with your grandparents?"

"Mom said maybe. She hates the apartment."

I shouldn't be surprised. It's not news to me that Kendra thinks she's too good for the place I helped her pick out earlier this year. Moving in with her parents, though? Kendra's beyond help, but Marissa still has a shot at growing up well-rounded and cultured—not sheltered and spoiled like her mom.

And since Kendra's family is loaded, any job Kendra's ever had has been for pleasure. I never cared what Kendra did with her days until the divorce went through and left me paying alimony and child support to a woman who has over a million dollars in her trust fund. Marissa needs a dose of reality, and Kendra obviously isn't going to give that to her. That's why I wanted to bring her to the city in the first place. But that was before the divorce.

I pour us each a glass of orange juice as I formulate my argument. "Horses cost money," I say. "A lot of money."

She picks up a piece of bacon. "Never mind. I'll just ask Gran."

"Why?"

"She has money. You're broke."

I slow-blink, sliding her juice across the table to her. "Why do you think that?"

"Mom and Gran. I heard them talking."

I rub my jaw. I can sugarcoat the truth for Marissa like Kendra does, like I used to. Or I can be honest and teach her a valuable lesson she's never had to learn—money doesn't appear from thin air. It has to be earned. "Marissa, I don't want you to worry about me. I'm not broke." Not yet anyway. "I will always take care of you."

"And Mom?" she asks, peeking up at me.

"And Mom," I agree. "At least as long as it's court mandated."

"What?"

"Never mind. My point is this: Gran and Grandpa have money because Grandpa worked very hard to earn it. He was good at what he did and he went to work every morning until nighttime." I have to pause to keep from gritting my teeth. It's all true, but I have little respect for Kendra's father, who reminds me of my old boss when I worked on Wall Street. Anything for a buck, no matter who it affected. "So," I continue, "that hard work made him money, and that's why Gran and Gramps are rich."

"You work hard," she says. "I know you do. I saw you go to work every day when you lived at home and it was always nighttime when you got back."

I put my elbows on the table. "Yeah, but I didn't like my job. For most people, that's okay, but I want to love what I do. So I started over, which means it'll take me longer to get back to making money."

"I'm sorry," she says.

I smile. "You're not in trouble. I'm just trying to explain to you about money. You've always had it because of Gran and Grandpa, and I know your friends have it too. But not everyone does, babe. Some kids, *most* kids, would never even dream of owning a horse. When I was your age, I had to mow lawns in my neighborhood and give my parents the money I made to buy groceries."

She widens her eyes. "You didn't have food?"

"We did," I say. "Because your Grandpa Frank had a steady job, and I pitched in." Marissa doesn't see Kendra working, and Marissa's grandpa is recently retired. I pinch her nose with my bacon-greasy fingers to ease the wrinkles in her forehead. "Don't worry. I promise, we're all going to be fine. I just want you to go home and think really hard about whether or not you need that horse, and if you can't live without it . . ."

She bounces in her seat. I guess she knew I'd give in one way or another.

"Ask Gran for one for Christmas."

She giggles. "All right."

Once Marissa's fed, I put her in front of Netflix. "I'm going to make sure all your stuff's packed," I tell her.

"It is," she says, eyes glued to *Fuller House*.

I head down the hall to my room and knock softly before opening the door. Halston is seated on the edge of the bed, her knees drawn up to her chin. Thankfully, she's pulled my t-shirt over her legs, blocking anything of interest, or I'd be in trouble.

"You're awake," I say. "How do you feel?"

"A little hungover." She glances behind me. "I was going to shower, but I didn't want to make noise."

"Kendra'll be here any minute, so I'm going to get Marissa's things and take her downstairs. Get some water from the fridge. You know where the shower is."

She smiles with closed lips. "Is it still okay that I'm here? Or do you want me to go?"

I close the door behind me and walk over to her. When her text woke me last night, I'd panicked. I was sure she'd come in here, find Marissa, and run for the hills. Halston is only twenty-five. She doesn't need to get involved with a man who has an eight-year-old kid. But, selfishly, I didn't want to turn her away. Luckily, her drunkenness had given me an excuse to make her stay.

"The weekend's just starting," I say. "If you go now, I'll be extremely upset."

She bites her bottom lip. "*Extremely*?"

"I've slept next to you twice and kept my hands to myself." Lifting her chin with my knuckle, I free her lip with my thumb to lean in and kiss her. "I don't want to keep my hands to myself anymore. When I get back up here, be ready."

She shivers, actually shivers, and grips the hem of the t-shirt in two fists. "I'll be waiting."

Her words go directly to my cock, her gaze even dropping for a split second. I leave the room to avoid a boner that'll make my encounter with Kendra very awkward.

With her overnight bag in tow, I take Marissa out front. A shiny, black Audi S3 idles at the curb. Kendra gets out of the passenger's side. I give Kendra's boyfriend a cursory wave. He's been a source of contention between us since Kendra introduced him to Marissa five weeks after their first date. Seemed to me Marissa shouldn't've been meeting anyone I hadn't met. But I have no problem with him as a person.

"How was the show?" I ask.

She takes Marissa's bag. "Fine. I just can't believe you forgot."

"Oh, okay. We're still on this." I squat down to Marissa's level. "Thanks for coming over, sweetie. I'll see you in a couple weeks?"

She frowns. "*Did* you forget, Dad?"

"Of course not." I glare daggers up at Kendra. "Mom's just teasing. Go get in the car." I kiss her on the forehead.

When she turns and walks away, I stand. "I'm not naïve enough to think you don't make me the bad guy when I'm not around, but don't ever do that to me while she's standing here."

"I show up at your door last night, and you look completely shocked. What father forgets one out of the four nights a month he gets with his daughter?"

"Five nights," I correct.

"No. Last night counted as one of your days."

"When you asked for this favor, you called it an extra night."

"That was when I thought I was doing *you* a favor by giving you more time with your daughter. Apparently, I was just shitting on your weekend plans—"

"That's bull."

"So I changed my mind."

"Come on, Kendra." I rub my temples with one hand. I don't need this headache right before I spend my first weekend with Halston. "You're going to make me split up my weekend with her? You're turning me into a deadbeat dad against my will."

"Don't start that shit again. I'm not the reason we got divorced. This victim act is getting old."

"I'm just saying, you're punishing me for wanting to spend time with my daughter. That's not fair."

"And you're the authority on fair, Mr. *Fucking* Adultery?"

I take a step back. Kendra has too much control over this situation, and engaging her in an argument can only hurt me. "I'm not going to fight with you again. I'll see you next time."

I head back into the building. Kendra just wants to hurt me, but Marissa suffers too. If Kendra really thought I didn't want time with Marissa, she'd probably have Marissa here every weekend. If I hadn't worried how the judge might take it, I'd have considered asking for no time at all to get the reaction I wanted from Kendra.

I left that Connecticut life behind because I felt helpless going to a job I hated every day and returning to a wife I didn't love. But I'm just as helpless now. I don't have a steady income or much say in how my daughter's raised. When I tried to tell Kendra it was too early to introduce Marissa to her boyfriend, she threw Sadie in my face. Marissa met Sadie *once* in the hallway between our apartments. Kendra was there;

she knows it was an accident and that Marissa had no idea who Sadie was.

The sliver of light in all of this is Halston. It's the first time I've had someone to revive me after one of Kendra's soul-sucking sessions. Halston doesn't treat me like a pawn or an ATM. The way she looked up at me from the bed moments ago, eyes wide, cheeks pink, lips parted, is what it means to be a man. Her man. She's a girl I want to turn into a woman, and I want to start now. I've been aching for this since I opened her journal.

I burst into the apartment and head straight for my bedroom. The shower is on. *Perfect*, since I plan on doing dirty things to her.

I stop at my nightstand for a condom, nearly breaking off the handle when I yank the drawer open. I peel off my t-shirt and step out of my sweats before entering the bathroom.

Halston turns quickly, covering her breasts. "Finn? What—"

I tear the condom packet open with my teeth. "I told you to be ready."

She keeps her hands where they are. "I'll only be another minute."

"I can't wait that long." I strip off my underwear and start rolling on the condom.

"I'm not ready," she says. "I thought you'd be longer."

I open the door, and she backs into a corner.

"I have no makeup on, my hair's all tangled—"

I step into the shower, shaking out my mop when water beats it down, and close in. "This is exactly how I want you," I say when I'm standing over her. "Stripped down to nothing. Nowhere to hide."

Her smooth, white throat ripples when she swallows. Her eyes are huge and gray. Any fog from the night I met her is gone. She's open right now. For so long, I've just wanted to connect with someone. Not someone—*the* one. And now, she's here—soaking wet, looking a bit petrified—but here. I forget about the last ten minutes downstairs. Those minutes, months, years of making mistakes? They were leading me to this, my girl. I can't be mad about that. I can only be happy and grateful to finally have her. Not to mention horny as fuck to finally *claim* her. "I want you raw. Just you and me, Halston. Nothing else."

She drops her hands, and I take her face in mine. I kiss her so hard, she squeaks. Her back is glued to the tile, but I can't seem to slow down. I grope her breasts, squeeze her ass to bring her even closer. I shouldn't fuck her right off the bat. I shouldn't. I can't wait, though. I'll take my time later. I hook my hand under her left knee and lift her leg until her thigh is pressed against her breast. Reluctantly, I stop kissing her, but I don't move a millimeter from her mouth. "Want me to slow down?"

"No."

I line my dick up with her opening and thrust halfway in. She sucks in a breath. "How about now?" I ask.

She squeezes her eyes shut and shakes her head. I need to be all the way in, rooted to the base of my cock. But I enlist all my patience and stay where I am while she adjusts to my size. I'm big, and I might've guessed she'd be this tight. "Look at me."

She opens her eyes, and they're full of fire. "Do it," she says.

"Do what?" I urge. I want to hear her.

Her voice wavers adorably when she says it, even though I can tell she's trying to sound confident. "Fuck me."

I squeeze her leg, lifting it even higher so she inhales sharply. "I changed my mind," I say, easing into her inch by inch. "I want you to feel as tortured as I am."

"I do," she rushes out. "I've wanted this as much as you. More."

"I don't believe you. When we met outside that gallery, you barely noticed me."

"That's not true," she says. "I thought you were sexy. I didn't think . . . someone like you'd be interested in me."

"And now?" I ask, licking my lips. When I've sunk as deep as I can get, I thrust my hips once, ramming her against the wall. "Think I'm interested now?"

She can't even respond, just breathes through her mouth. She's hot and soft around my dick, but I wish like fuck I could lose the condom, the last barrier between us. I draw back and push in again, watching her expression like she holds the answer to every question I've ever wondered.

Her face screws up.

"Am I hurting you?" I ask.

"No."

She drops her head back on the tile as I let her have it. Her moans echo through the bathroom, stealing the last of my control. I've wanted this too long. I'm going to come already, and she's not there yet. I fuck her until I'm right at the edge, then pinch the base of the condom to keep it in place as I slide out of her.

She doesn't move a muscle. I lower her leg and rest it on the ledge of the tub.

"Wha . . ." she mumbles. "What are you . . ."

I get to my knees while she tries to form a sentence. I lick her long and hard, and her body shudders. I take my two favorite fingers and slip them up inside her, fucking her with them until she pulls my hair hard enough to make me growl. I work her clit with my mouth, but to make her feel better than she ever has before, I have to make this a full-body experience. I turn her by her hips so she's facing the tile. "Support yourself with the wall," I say.

She leans her forearms onto the tile and juts her ass out. I grip her cheeks and lick her pussy front to back. So far back that the tip of my tongue teases her anus.

She wiggles, reaching back to try and push my face away. "*Finn*," she gasps.

"Save the squirming for when my tongue's actually inside you," I suggest. I pin her wrists to her hips and spread her ass cheeks with my thumbs. I rim her asshole good and fast as she writhes. I don't know if she's fighting me, but I *do* know she's enjoying my mouth in the one place it shouldn't be, whether she admits it or not.

I massage her clit until her legs give out, and she drops to her knees. I wrap an arm around her shoulders, pulling her back to my front, and finger-fuck her from behind until she comes, crying out to the ceiling.

I stand, pick her up by her waist, and put her over my shoulder. She might be spent, nothing more than a bag of bones, but I'm still painfully hard and swollen. I shut off the water, step carefully out of the tub, and carry her into my room. After tossing her onto her back, I grab the comforter in my fists and yank her to the edge of the bed.

"You can't do that," she wheezes, her chest rising and falling.

I half smile. "Already did, Hals. Don't worry. I won't tell anyone you enjoyed it." I part her knees and run my hands up her inner thighs. "I won't tell anyone you're just as kinky as me. That your pussy's better than heaven. That you kissed me after I ate your ass."

"I didn't—"

I bend over her, and she whips her head side to side, her lips sealed. I can't help it. I start to laugh. I don't care about kissing her with my dirty mouth, but I don't want to traumatize her. I right myself, grabbing a pillow to elevate her hips, putting her in a position I think will be comfortable enough for me to take her good and hard.

She watches me and breathes. Just breathes. She might've short-circuited with that orgasm, and I plan to give her another one.

When she's ready, I put my hands under her ass and pull her hips up to meet mine. I keep her in that position while I slide into her and get to work making a pretty good case for her second orgasm. She reaches above her. Her tits go high and bouncy while she grabs at nothing, as if trying to hold on. I drop her back on the pillow, fold over her, and angle deeper. I pin one of her flailing arms by her head, then do the same with the other. I restrain her and fuck her and have my fill of her and I'm just lost enough that I'm not sure if she comes, but I think she does, so I finally release, exploding like a volcano that's been stopped up for centuries.

Either she's shaking, or I am, or we both are. Water drips from my hair to her chest. It could be sweat. My arms feel weak, so I drop onto my elbows and finally rest my body on top of hers. I'm sure I'm crushing her, but she wraps one arm around my back.

With that one gesture, I feel a wave of guilt for how I just handled her.

"I'm sorry," I say.

"For what?"

"I don't know." I've been told by some of my partners that I can be dominant in the bedroom, but that I'm a lover first. I'm worried that right now, I got so carried away, I didn't take good enough care of her. I try to get up, but my muscles are liquid. "It was too much."

"It was perfect," she says.

I sigh, too beat to argue over something I want to be wrong about. "Good."

After a few seconds, I'm able to move off of her. I stand, but she stays splayed out on the bed, sunken into the mattress. "Did you come again?" I ask.

She just nods.

"Can you move?"

She shakes her head.

I smile. "All right. You don't have to. How about if I bring you some coffee?"

She sighs deeply, her eyes closed. "Sure. Whatever."

My eyes nearly pop out of my head. Here, I've been worried she might prefer coffee to anything else, even sex. Even me. And she feels *whatever* about it? She must really be out of it. I need something to do with myself until the next round, so I trash the condom in the bathroom, pull on my boxer briefs, and head into the kitchen. I start a pot of Quench coffee. It no longer belongs to Sadie. It's post-fucking-Halston coffee now, and it'll taste even better. Because Halston and I are better. I might've elbowed my way into her life, but Halston hasn't held back with me. She was completely present just now. Sadie often went somewhere else in our most intimate moments—to Nathan, I guess. I could tell, even when she denied it.

Not Halston, though. She gave me all of herself, and all I had to do was ask.

As soon as the pot drips its last drop, Halston shuffles into the kitchen, blonde hair damp and tousled, wearing just my t-shirt. It swings around her bare thighs. I'd bet a million bucks she's got no panties on under there. That's enough to get me half hard again. "Hey."

She grins like a junkie who just raided her stash. "Hi."

"Sit. I've got your coffee coming right up. Strong as an ox."

She scrapes a chair out from under the kitchen table and plops onto it. "That was . . ."

"Shitty?" I ask.

Her cheeks burn red. "That's not funny. I can't believe you did that."

"I told you to get un-squeamish. At least we were in the shower." I get two mugs from a cupboard as she scoffs. I look back at her. "Listen, in the bedroom, if it feels good for both of us, it's fair game. That's all I'm saying."

She narrows her eyes, shaking her head with a small smile. "You're unlike anyone I've ever . . ." She looks down at her lap and goes completely still. "Um. Finn?"

"Yeah, babe." I set her coffee down and sit across from her.

"The condom."

"I know." I plant my elbows on the table and run both hands through my hair. "It fucking sucks we have to use one, but I've got issues about it."

She looks up at me, her bottom lip between her teeth. "Issues . . .?"

I massage my jaw. It's not something I enjoy talking about, but I feel close to Halston right now. And I plan to get even chummier, so she needs to know. I'm comfortable enough to go where I'd rather not. "Kendra and I dated when I was just out of college, for about a year, and then I ended things. But she was used to getting what she wanted, and she wanted me."

She knits her eyebrows. "What's that have to do with condoms?"

"She came by one night. We had break-up sex. No big deal, lots of couples do it, but it didn't change my feelings for her. We were completely over. Unfortunately, she didn't tell me she'd stopped taking birth control. That's how Marissa was conceived."

Halston looks horrified. "Oh my God."

I sip my drink and Halston does the same. The mug's the same cool gray as her eyes. "Yeah. It started this whole downward spiral of stuff. I felt responsible, so I married her. Her parents were devastated. They thought I was a bum. At the time, I'd been trying to make it as a photographer, but I was barely getting by. Her dad got me admitted into business school without asking me, and I went. Not for him or for Kendra, but for Marissa. I knew, even if I tripled the work I was doing as a photographer, there was no supporting a child on what I'd be making."

"She manipulated you."

"And she's been doing it ever since. The affair was the catalyst for the divorce, so she brings it up any chance she gets. She uses Marissa against me at every turn. It's not ideal, but it's my life."

Halston doesn't respond. At first, I think she's shocked, but then I realize she's gulping air fast—*too* fast to let any out. "I-I . . ."

I stand, pushing my chair back. "What's wrong?" She turns sheet-white and begins to wheeze. I kneel in front of her. "Are you having a panic attack?"

Distantly, she looks down and grabs the edge of her t-shirt. Awful scenarios filter through my head. Did I hurt her? Is she bleeding? Did the Kendra stuff scare her? She lifts the hem, but there's nothing there.

"Halston, talk to me. What is it?"

"I think the condom broke." She touches herself between the legs, and her fingers come back slick.

"I'm so sorry. I didn't know. I swear, I didn't do it on purpose."

I sit back on my heels. My relief eases slightly, but not completely. *Fuck.* I didn't check the condom before I tossed it. It definitely wasn't empty, but maybe it wasn't full, either. I cover her hand with mine. "Are you on birth control?"

"*Yes.* I swear, I would never, ever lie about that, no matter how upset . . . no matter how much I wanted . . ."

I kiss her hand. "I believe you. I do. It's not—I mean, if I have any doubt, it's because of Kendra, not you."

"You have some doubt, though?" she asks, her voice small.

I wish I could say *no, babe, of course not,* like a normal boyfriend would. It's just that Kendra blindsided me so bad, I still haven't recovered. I was in shock until well after I'd made an honest woman of her and Marissa was born. Not even Sadie shook that distrust in me. She might've eventually, but I made sure we used a condom every time we were together. "I don't doubt you," I say. "But it goes deep. I don't even have the faith I should in condoms or birth control. When it comes to this, I don't entirely trust anything I can't see with my own eyes."

"I can show you my pack," she says and goes to stand. "It's in my—"

I push her back into the seat. "It's okay."

"No it's not. I don't want you to think I . . . that it was intentional or—"

I smile a little, and she stops, clearly confused. It's just fucking cute that she's so worried about it, and for some reason, it makes me less worried. "I know you didn't."

Finally, she deflates into the chair. "I promise."

I chuckle. "I hear you."

She looks out the window over the kitchen sink. "Okay. Good."

"Yes, good," I repeat, trying to catch her eyes, because she doesn't sound at ease. Once again, I've gone and spoiled her mood. Fuck me. "Shit, if it's anyone's fault the condom broke, it's mine," I say, attempting to cheer her up. "I'm the one who bought them. And it was my bright idea to fuck in the shower. You have every right to be suspicious *I* plotted to get *you* pregnant."

She whips her head around, her expression pure shock.

I grin. "If you don't shut that mouth," I warn, "I *will* kiss you."

She covers her lips and says through her hand, "Please go clean it."

I laugh, standing. I'd like to kiss her at some point today, so I go into the bathroom and brush my teeth. The condom's on top of the trash, full of my jizz. It doesn't look broken from here. I'm good. I should be totally good. Condoms break all the time. The chances of pregnancy *without* a condom or birth control are relatively low. And I barely came in her. We'll be fine.

Belatedly, though, I think about what I just said to tease her. *Me*, plotting to get *her* pregnant. It's the last thing I want, and maybe that's the reason it turns me on to think about. Coming inside her. Claiming her permanently. I never had that urge with Kendra. Before our split, I'd been adamant about not having another baby. With Sadie, I thought about our future a lot, but a family would've been a concession on my part to win her.

On my way out of the bathroom, I stop at my nightstand for another condom. They might be crap, but they're all I've got and I'm not about to get dressed and go downstairs to find more. I start to shut the drawer when I catch sight of Halston's journal. God, just a couple weeks ago, I was jerking it to her words. I would've given anything to have her.

Now I do.

I pick up the warm, weighty leather with respect and gratitude and bring it with me to the kitchen. She has her hands curled around the fog-colored mug, her cheeks pink from hot coffee and hotter sex.

"Hey," I say, passing through as I head to the living room. "Come with me."

I go to the couch, lie on my back, and open an arm to her.

"What's that?" she asks from the doorway.

"You know very well what it is."

She half rolls her eyes but comes to me. As she settles in, I take a moment to appreciate how her skin warms against mine. How she fits herself to my side. Her silky blonde hair tickles my bicep as she runs her fingers up my middle, abs to chest. I won't last like this very long, so I open the journal. "Read to me. Will you?"

She takes a few moments to answer. "I don't know."

I turn on my side, encircling her from behind, and flip through the book so we both can see. She stops me by touching one of the pages. "This one."

I nuzzle her ear and whisper the first line to her. "'I have a thirst I can't deny.'"

"'I try, baby, do I try,'" she says. "'But I want to be drunk down like you do a handle, taste me better than your first-love liquor, your fingers tightening around my whiskey-bottle neck.'"

I'm harder than hard against the cushion of her ass. I let go of one side of the journal and gently take her throat in my hand. When she lifts her chin, I angle over her to capture her mouth. I accidentally drop the book but leave it. Her words are sex, and I need to feel her now. Shoving down my underwear, I push into her from behind.

"Oh my God," she groans. "Oh, fuck. But the condom."

"Just for a second," I say. I trust myself, and only myself, not to go too far. "I just want to feel you."

She's nice and wet, accepting my length easier this time. Her warmth soothes me. Skin on skin is magic. Maybe I'm wrong to think I can stop. Maybe I should not have fucking done this. I'm not sure how I'll be able to go back to having a layer of latex between us.

My hand is still around her throat. She wants things she can't ask for. That's why they go in the journal. I can give her all of it, but not without talking to her first. And now is not the time for talking. Still, her words live inside me, and I only know one way to get them out.

Without releasing her neck, I lean over the side of the couch and feel around for my bag. When I find it, I dig out my camera.

Her eyes follow until it's outside her frame of vision. I get it. She's been unsure about the camera from the start, and now she's naked, exposed—not just her body but her face, her emotions.

"Do you trust me?" I ask.

She swallows against the palm of my hand before nodding.

It's not the most comfortable position for me, and since I know the photo won't turn out perfectly, I use that to my advantage. While I'm inside her, I get up on my elbow and take a picture of my hand around her throat. I keep anything above her lips or below her collarbone out of the frame. But her open mouth and splotchy skin add a level of perfection to the image that should be captured. Anyone who wants to see it, will—she's getting fucked in this photo.

When I have what I want, I put the camera down and bury my face in her sweet-smelling hair. I move a hand to her tits and fuck her that way for a few silent, fire-burning seconds and then reluctantly put on a condom to finish both of us off.

I begin to drift, still inside her, my arms around her, my camera and her journal tossed aside together. Her breathing softens, evening out.

The clouds break and sunlight comes through the window, jarring me back to consciousness. My first thought is that I can't wait to have her again. My next is that I'm a fucking idiot, putting my dick anywhere without a condom. But I settle down quickly when the truth hits me in the chest like a bag full of beautiful bricks.

It's been a perfect day. Time with my daughter, then with the girl I've been waiting for a long time. Fucking perfect.

SEVENTEEN

halston

As soon as I step out of the elevator onto the yellow-lighted sixth floor and see Finn waiting in his doorway, I forget that my new heels have been pinching my feet since this morning. That my shoulders ache from three hours in a qualitative analysis seminar.

He follows me with his green, adoring eyes. He's in slacks, a tie, and a button-down because he wore a suit to a meeting with a prospective client. I watched him shave earlier, but now golden stubble shades his jaw. I forget how to speak. I've stayed here every night since Friday, and each time I see him, he gets better. Sexier, because I know what he's capable of.

Those hands. That mouth. It goes beyond touch and caress. His words alone can leave my knees shaking.

"Mmm," he says when I approach. "Take off your clothes."

"Here in the hallway?" I ask.

"Would you?"

I tilt my chin down, keeping my eyes on his. Is he serious? By his silence, I think so. He seems to think I'd do what he says. I glance down the hall, even though we're alone. Maybe I would. Apparently, I trust him already. I don't believe he'd hurt me. Unlike the other men in my life, Finn doesn't pretend to know what's best for me. For that reason, I almost trust him more than them.

"Yes," I say.

He cocks an eyebrow, looking pleased. "Good girl. I won't make you. Not tonight."

I'm relieved, but only slightly. I'm also curious how Finn's face would look as I undressed for him here, on display for his neighbors. Not that I'm bold enough to take that kind of initiative. "You look good in the suit. Uncomfortable . . . but good."

"I used to wear one every day. I wish I could say this is the first I've put it on since I quit the nine-to-five, but it isn't."

Finn in front of a computer all day, adjusting his tie, retiring to the break room, eating lunch in his office? I can't picture it. He needs to be free of a cage. It's suddenly clear how well—and how little—I know him. "What'd you do before this?"

"Wall Street."

I start to laugh but stop when he doesn't. He isn't joking. He mentioned business school, but Wall Street is a whole new ballgame. "Seriously?"

"It was all wrong for me."

"I never would've guessed."

"It was what I had to do for my baby." He shrugs dejectedly. "Anyway, I thought being an artist would mean I never had to answer to anyone, but first impressions matter. In a suit, clients treat me more like a businessman than the dreamer I am."

I smile. "Dreamer, huh?"

"You should know that about me," he says seriously. "That stuff in the past with Kendra and Sadie—it's been hard, but I'm still a romantic guy. I'm even glad for it if it brought me to you."

He says it simply, as if it isn't a powerful declaration about our relationship. He'd be grateful for his failed marriage, devastating affair, and broken heart . . . because of *me*? Someone he's known two weeks? I don't doubt my feelings for him, but it's a lot for me to live up to.

"Kendra teased me about being so idealistic all the time," he continues. "She's no-nonsense." He glances down the hall, specifically at 6B. Is it a habit? He did it the first time I came to his apartment, and this morning while we were leaving. "I don't even think Sadie liked that about me."

The admission makes me want to hug him. I do like it about him. Even if it comes with some pressure, being the center of Finn's attention is heady, intoxicating. "Well, I love it," I say. "Rich and I were missing that in our relationship—" I pause. Finn might've brought up his exes, but they're much further in the past compared to mine. I don't want him to worry I'm still hung up on Rich. "Is it okay to talk about him?"

"As long as you know I'm taking notes."

I smile a little and touch his tie, admiring how the hallway's buttery lighting turns silver to gold. "I'm a closet romantic, Finn. That's my dirty secret. My journals, yes, they're sexy, but they're really about love."

"I know."

"What I'm trying to say is, I like that you're so passionate and creative." I tug on his tie. "But I don't mind this, either."

"Yeah?" He grins. "Suits do it for you? To me, it still feels like armor before battle."

I work around men in suits every day, but none of them look like Finn does now. He's in charge, and surprisingly, I'm comfortable with that. I've been fighting to regain control from Rich and my dad, yet I'm almost willing to hand it over to Finn. And the suit? It just highlights that. It's his command over me personified. "Even right now?" I ask, with a few bats of my eyelashes.

He slips his arm around my waist and leans in for a kiss.

"Wait." I push his chest. "You haven't eaten anyone's ass today, have you?"

He laughs. "Just yours. While you were sleeping. You thought that was a wet dream, didn't you?"

I squirm in his grip. I'm still not ready to admit I enjoyed what he did in the shower the other day. It wasn't just the sensation of being licked there, but the knowledge that what he was doing was *beyond* wrong. Dirty. Forbidden. Probably illegal in some states. And also . . . I think it was what ultimately impelled me into an orgasm. I can't imagine anyone in my life who'd ever do that or want it done. Except Finn.

I let him kiss me.

As if I could help myself.

I *melt* for his kisses, and he knows it. I've gone to work the past few days and thought about his tongue down my throat, his hands gripping me anywhere and everywhere he can reach, his cock bulging all the fucking time. Two days in a row, I've locked my office door and shut my blinds to get myself off.

Which reminds me.

"You're not going to post that picture I sent you, are you?" I tease when he comes up for air.

He just grunts, pulling me against his erection.

"Does that mean you liked it?" I ask.

"Why do you think I'm practically on top of you in the doorway?" he asks. "Why do you think I texted back nothing but gibberish and emoji?"

I smile and let him pull me into the apartment. The photo wasn't much—a close-up of my lips, blowing him a kiss—but it's out of character for me to send an unsolicited picture.

"I should probably thank you for the lady giving me the job today." He puts my handbag aside and removes my scarf and coat. "I had a boner during the interview thanks to your picture."

I cover my mouth. "Is that true?"

"Yeah, Hals. You can't just send me that shit without warning. Your juicy, pink lips, knowing all the places they've been on my body? My eyes nearly popped out of my skull in the waiting room."

I can't help giggling at his earnest expression. "I'm sorry. Really." I remove my heels. *Sweet relief.* "I won't send anything like that again."

He gives me a look. "Naked. Now."

"But *you're* dressed."

He undoes a button at his collar. "Then we'll both get naked. How was work?"

I sigh, following him into the living room. I flop onto the couch while he sorts through his mail. "Blah."

"Why?"

"Just one of those days where whenever I got a minute, something else popped up."

He flips an envelope over before tossing it on the coffee table. "You eat lunch?"

"Benny brought me something but honestly, I couldn't tell you what it was. It's probably still on my desk behind a stack of papers." I'm exaggerating. Most of what I do is digital, and food doesn't exactly interest me these days anyway. I've been battling bouts of nausea. As far as withdrawal goes, I've mostly gotten off easy with a few random headaches and an uneasy stomach. There's no use worrying Finn, so I skip over that. "And to make matters worse, Rich and I can't avoid each other, so he was in my office being annoying."

Finn looks up. "What?"

"What what?" I ask.

"Why's Rich at your office?"

I sit up a little. "He works there. For my dad. You knew that."

"No I didn't." He drops the rest of his mail on the table. "You told me your dad founded the agency, and that your dad introduced you to Rich. That's all."

"Oh. Well." He's right. It hasn't come up. I didn't intentionally omit it, but . . . maybe out of subconscious self-preservation. I *have* been avoiding talking about Rich's job. "He works on my floor, but his office is all the way—"

"Halston."

I cross my legs underneath myself. "I guess I should've told you."

Finn sits on the coffee table in front of me. "Does he bother you?"

"Just about work stuff. *Mostly* about work stuff." So far, I've managed to avoid being in the same room with Rich and my dad since deciding to keep the relationship charade going. But Rich is being his usual ostrich self about this break-up, pretending everything's normal between us, even when we're alone. Once in a while, he even surprises me with a sweet comment or gesture. "We have projects together, you know?"

"No, I don't know. Tell me."

My hair is suddenly scratchy on the back of my neck. I twist it up into a makeshift bun as I talk. "He's an account manager. A liaison between the client and the agency team. Sometimes we have to work together on things."

He leans his elbows onto his knees. "I'd think you would've mentioned seeing your ex every day. Is there a reason you didn't? Do you still have feelings for him?"

I stop messing with my hair, taken aback by his bluntness. "Not romantic feelings, no."

"But other kinds?" he asks. "Because people look for all kinds of things from a relationship, and if he gave you something I don't—"

"No," I say. "It's not that. Not at all." Knowing Finn's sensitivity to cheating, I should've been more upfront. I can't fault him for being a little paranoid considering his history. "I didn't keep it from you for that reason. If anything, it was something else." Finn values honesty. He won't be mad, as long as I tell him the truth. I think. I look at my hands. "I guess on some level, I was afraid if I told you we worked together, you'd ask about Rich's job. And Rich . . . he has a lot of sway in his position."

"Meaning?" Finn asks.

"He can make changes or decisions about lots of things if he wants, including creative. In some cases, he'll hire or recommend people for jobs. Like photographers for print or digital campaigns."

He sits back. "Oh."

"I could've given him your card when I met you. Or any time since then. But I haven't. I feel weird about that."

"You didn't like my portfolio. Why should you recommend me?"

I open my mouth. "That's not what I meant."

"It's true, though, Halston. You implied my older stuff was boring."

"It isn't *boring.*" I hold his gaze so he knows I'm telling the truth. "I said it lacked something, but the photos you took of me? They're everything, Finn. They don't lack a single thing. If I showed him your work, we'd probably hire you, but . . ."

"I get it," he says when I don't continue.

"It's selfish. I want you all to myself. If Rich hires you, it changes things. That first time you took my picture—it never would've happened if you were working for my boyfriend."

"I understand." He runs a hand through his hair, leaving it sticking up like straw. "I mean, fuck. I just had no idea you'd even seen him since that phone call. It's going to take me awhile to get used to that. Hasn't that been weird?"

"Very." He looks concerned, so I add, "It's nothing I can't handle. It's amazing how little I feel for someone I spent two years with. Because with you—it . . . it's the opposite. If you walked out of my life tomorrow, I'd be," I swallow thickly, "I wouldn't even go to work. I'd be in bed for a week. I'd be—" Oh my *God.* It's the truth, and it makes me sick to my stomach. Two weeks in, I'm already in too deep. But shouldn't I have seen this coming? Finn told me he might be obsessed early on, and given my history to nearly smother what gives me comfort, his admission gave me an excuse to obsess back. Now that we've been fucking morning and night, how could we not be here, sunk into each other like we're bodies of quicksand? "I'd be heartbroken."

Finn covers my hands with his. "I'm not going anywhere. And I'm not mad. But I am a little, I don't know, jealous. I told you I have issues with that shit."

My palms get clammy. There is one more detail I haven't mentioned—my dad still believes Rich and I are together. It isn't true, though, and it has no effect on my relationship with Finn. Once the holidays are over and my dad is feeling normal again, that will end. I could see how Finn'd take it the wrong way if I told him now. If it comes up later, maybe then. "You've talked about the affair, but help me understand the issue," I say. "If you're the one who cheated on your wife, why are you so worried about it? Aside from the obvious reasons."

He rubs his jaw. The scrape of fingers over stubble reminds me of his scratchiness on my cheek. If this weren't a serious conversation, I'd interrupt it with a kiss. "It's not the physical cheating per se. The affair only lasted a month or so. It started when I moved in here a year ago. She was my neighbor."

Neighbor. That's why he always looks across the hall when he opens the door. "6B?" I ask.

He nods. "I was in a bad place. I felt strangled where I was, so I got an apartment in the city and gave Kendra an unfair ultimatum: move with me, or we're done. Sadie, she was unhappy. I just had this draw to make her smile or laugh or drop her guard for a few minutes. I chose her over Kendra. I made promises. I gave her everything I could in a short amount of time because I wanted to win her." He loosens his tie. I just process it all. It isn't easy to hear that he recently offered someone else his love, but I doubt it's half as hard as having to admit that to me. I keep listening. "I'd actually met Sadie once in college and she'd left an impact on me. So when I moved in across the hall from her, I thought it was destiny. That's why I went all in without a safety net. I thought fate was on my side, and I could blame everything on that, including hurting Kendra."

I knew Finn was a believer in fate, especially considering his comment earlier about past heartache being worth it to meet me, but it runs deep for him. He's truly invested in the concept. Finding my journal, and then me, must mean a lot to him. I'm glad. I also think it was more than chance. "What happened?" I ask.

"In the end, Sadie chose her husband over me. It hurt. I could've lived with her staying with him out of obligation, but the truth is, she wanted him."

Finn thinks he wasn't enough for her. Maybe it's because I'm not part of the situation, but I know instinctively that isn't true. Whatever reasons Sadie had for choosing her husband didn't have anything to do with Finn not being good enough. "I'm not going to choose Rich over you," I say slowly. "By leaving Rich, I'm choosing myself. He—that life—wasn't right for me."

"You say that now, but things change. I didn't choose Kendra because I loved her. I did it for Marissa, to feel good about myself, to please Kendra's family. It's not always about love."

"That's not how I see it. There's love in all those decisions you made, if not for Kendra, then for your unborn child."

"It was a complicated situation, just like yours."

Rich offered me things I thought I wanted—security, love, and, in some ways, understanding. Even if he liked me best in a box, and noticed me because of my dad, Rich wasn't a bad boyfriend. He could have had his pick of women when I met him, but even though I was heavier and being treated for depression, he'd still chosen me.

"Did she—Sadie—ever say she'd leave her husband for you?"

"Not until the end. I assumed a lot of things would happen that didn't. So I'm trying not to do that with you, but I'm not doing a great job of it."

As far as I can tell, he hasn't held back yet, and I don't want him to start. "I've trusted you with a lot, Finn. My body, my words, my secrets. You could hurt me with everything you know."

"I wouldn't," he says. "And I love what we're creating. I wouldn't destroy that."

What we're creating. Finn took my photo mid-fuck on Saturday and posted it. Every time I see it, I get a thrill. All his photos of me are beautiful and never explicit. His hand around my throat is just that, but his gentle hold juxtaposed with the obvious power he has makes it erotic. More so with my journal entry as the caption. Only he and I know the truth behind it.

Now that he's brought it up, I get a craving to see the photo again. Has anybody commented or liked it since I looked this morning?

As of my train ride to work, Finn has posted nine of our photos, including one today.

That amounts to four hundred seventeen followers. Finn's meticulous about lighting and uses the same settings to give each photo a faded, gray-ish quality that enhances the details.

I've kept a running tally of likes per photo. My fingers dipped in a mug? Fifty-nine. Sucking coffee off them? A hundred and ten—our most popular photo until today's, which has a hundred and seventeen. It's my hands splayed over my bare knees, my thumbs pressing into the skin of my inner thighs. Not even our best one, but with each post, our reach grows. As do likes and fans.

Comments too.

Fucking hottt

What's this quote from?

Sexy account

No tits???

This ones kinky, love it

There are even more, mostly people tagging other users. The first two still make my stomach flip.

"Speaking of, I have something to show you," Finn says, calling my attention back. He gets his cell from the pocket of his slacks. "A couple hours ago, this really big account shared our last photo."

My heart skips. I try to see upside down as he navigates to the app. "Seriously?"

"Yeah." He finds the account and passes me the phone. "Look."

I take it, and when I see the number of likes, my jaw hits the floor.

One-thousand, two-hundred-fifty.

Holy *shit.*

Make that fifty-one.

Fifty-two.

I cover my mouth. My words are there too, for everyone to read. There are over thirty comments. "When did this happen?"

"A few hours ago. It's an account featuring up-and-coming artists. Photographers, writers, painters.

But really good, progressive work. I've been getting a ton of new followers from it."

"How'd they find us?"

"Someone tagged them in a comment on our photo. I did a little research. Accounts like this one get a lot of followers *just* from reposting other people's photos. They're called feature accounts."

"Did you read the comments?"

"Yeah." He closes his knees around mine, pressing my legs together. "They're all good. Really good, Hals. It's all you. Your words."

I'm grinning like an idiot, but I can't help it. People are looking at his photograph. My caption. My body. "It's us," I say.

"It's you." He runs his hands up my thighs. "You and your fucking amazingness."

I go through the last few photos featured on the account. "None of these have even a thousand likes," I say.

"Ours *is* the sexiest one on there. Maybe even of their entire account." He slides a finger under the hem of my dress. "Or all time."

I look at Finn. A few weeks ago, I would've burned my journals before letting anybody near them. And just because I've lost weight doesn't mean I'm not self-conscious about my body. This photo is validation I might be doing something right. People other than Finn and myself are connecting with what I wrote. They *get* me. Finn did this for me. This project is ours, but he's given me confidence. He wants to make me happy, and I am—without medication. "I love—this." I choke on *this* and cough to cover my blunder. I almost said *you.* Almost. Out of habit. I don't mean it. I feel love, not for Finn yet, it's too soon, but I feel it. I never expected, when I agreed to do this with Finn, that anyone would really care what I had to say. Not like this.

"I love this too," he says. "And I love being able to turn your day around."

I drop my eyes to his lips, the most kissable lips on the planet, I'm fairly sure. "Technically it's night," I say softly.

"Technically, you're wearing too much clothing." He stretches forward to kiss me. His warm mouth gives me permission to melt. Without disconnecting from me, he gets up, planting his hands at my sides on the cushions. I bend my head all the way back to meet his kisses.

He reaches one hand under my dress and pauses. "Halston?"

"Mmm?"

"Is this what I think it is?"

I pull up the hem and show him my black thigh-high stockings. "As requested."

He blinks at them. "You weren't wearing these when you left this morning."

"I bought them on my lunch break. Just for you."

He grunts, fingering the lace trim. That's all it takes. He kicks the coffee table out of the way, pushes my dress up around my hips, and drops to his knees. I drop my head against the back of the couch when he buries his face between my thighs. I run my hands through his thick, honey-colored hair. It sprouts soft and silky from my fingers.

He squeezes his hands under my ass and picks me up to get even more of me in his mouth. I steady myself on the couch cushions, grasping them when he spears his tongue inside me. "Imagine if someone took our photo like this," I say.

He stands, mouth glistening. He drags me down the couch by my hips, licking his lips like I'm a meal he hunted, slaughtered, and refuses to give up. He props me up on the arm, slides down his zipper, and pulls out his cock without even undoing his belt. He takes it in his hand and skims it through my wetness. "Fucking condom." He groans. "It's a hassle."

"Forget it," I say. "I'm on birth control. You've seen me take it the past few days."

He furrows his eyebrows, then looks between us as he teases my entrance. "You wet, Hals? You look good and wet."

I inhale sharply. "Mostly from your mouth."

He sinks into me, and *I* sink into the couch. Into him. I bliss out while he pulls me onto him harder with every thrust. "Don't come," he says.

I lift my head to look at him. He's golden and sexy, but there's an edge of darkness in his eyes. Just watching him handle my body makes me hot. "Why not?"

"I don't know. I like the idea of keeping you on the edge while I come. Of you dying for me to take you again."

I look up at the ceiling. *Don't* climax. *Don't* think of Finn toying with me until he's ready to fuck me later. Submitting to his demands excites me, the opposite of what I need to be happening. I close my eyes as he takes me, willing myself to stay in control of my orgasm. Perhaps seeing the frustration on my face, Finn doesn't torture me long. He pulls out, dropping me back onto the couch. I open my eyes just in time to watch him pump his fist and come on the couch cushion.

He still doesn't trust me. If I didn't know his story, I'd be worried, but it's less about me than him.

He looks down at me, his chest heaving. "I almost came on you."

The ache between my legs, tender and swollen, flutters at his admission. "Why didn't you?"

"I . . ." He cocks his head, studying me. I don't think it's the question he expected. "Next time."

I should argue. I can't imagine any other man telling me he'll come on me and getting away with it. I'm helpless to Finn's command, though, as his model, his girl, his doll. Maybe because I'm used to being under others' control. But with Finn, I want to be.

He tugs my dress back into place before tucking himself in his pants. There's a wet spot on his trousers from my pussy. If I didn't want to come already, that makes me pant for it.

He holds out his hand to hoist me to my feet. "How do you feel about showing some leg?"

I glance down at myself. Somehow, without explanation, I understand he means for the camera. I look back at him, at his soiled suit. "It doesn't always have to be me, you know. I could write something for you."

"Nobody wants to look at me."

I grin and pull him close by his button-down. "Wrong. Some women like a man in a suit."

"Are you one of them?"

I nod my head all the way up and then down. "Right now I am."

"I like to be behind the camera."

"Just this once?" I begin to unknot his tie. "I already have an idea. You can show me what to do."

He stands tall and solid as I undo him. "I'm not a teacher."

"Not even for me?" I ask.

He looks down his nose at me. "If you'll give me your legs, you have a deal."

I slip his tie off. "Deal."

Finn leads me into the studio and unpacks his bag while I slide his silky fabric through my hands. It's just a tie, but it has so many potential uses.

"Come here," Finn says.

I hang the tie around my neck and take the camera when he holds it out to me. It's heavier than I thought, colder too, so I use both hands to inspect it. "I can see why you like this. It feels sturdy. Professional."

"It is. Expensive too." He smiles but says through his teeth, "Don't drop it."

I laugh. "Never."

"You want to keep it steady." He moves behind me to nudge my feet shoulder-width apart. "Easier said than done, but balance helps."

"Do I look through the viewfinder?"

"Nah, we'll use the display." From behind, he cups his hand around mine, lifting the camera to my face. "Fill the screen as much as possible with your subject."

"You."

"Yes, me." His tone is serious, authoritative. "Touch the shutter button, but don't push it."

I do, and he rests his index finger over mine.

"If you press it halfway," he says, demonstrating, "it'll focus your shot. You know what you want me to do?"

"Yes. Take the tie."

As he pulls it from my neck, it slithers over my breasts. My hairs stand on end. "You ready?" he asks in my ear.

My goosebumps get goosebumps. I shiver with a nod.

"You're shaking a little," he says. "That's normal, especially with a piece of equipment half your size." He flattens a hand on my stomach and splays his fingers. "Before you take the picture, suck in a deep breath and hold it. It'll help."

His touch is seventy-five percent comforting, twenty-five arousing. "You're a better teacher than you think," I say because it's true, but also hoping to tempt him into another round. I haven't forgotten his comment about roleplaying.

"We'll see, won't we?" He stands in front of the camera. "Where do you want me?"

I bite the inside of my cheek, looking him over. Since his face won't be in it, I need details. "Roll up your sleeves."

He undoes each cuff, folding them up while his eyes stay on me. "Next?"

"Wrap each end of your tie around your hands." I frame the picture from his shirt pocket to under his belt buckle. He fists the tie as if he's about to blindfold me or tie me up, then pulls it taut. The strength in his forearms is evident. They're bronze and veiny, just as I knew they'd be. I make sure to get them in the shot. When I press the button gently, the lens focuses, and I snap the picture. I take a few more for good measure, then lower the camera. "Got it."

He half smiles, takes the camera from me, and checks my work. "Only one is blurry. Good job."

I straighten my back with his feedback. "Thanks."

"Your turn." We trade places. "Show me everything and nothing, Hals."

Standing before him, I lift my dress by the hem, positioning both hands in the middle to keep anything good hidden. I stop above the tops of my stockings.

"You take direction better than I give it," Finn murmurs. He squats in front of me, inches from my pussy. Inches from the dull ache he promised to satisfy.

My heart beats in my stomach. It was all fun and games a minute ago, but now I'm reminded Finn has suspended me in a state of arousal. Suddenly, nothing seems more important than relief. "Finn?"

"I know, just a couple more," he says from behind the camera. "I'm coming."

"I'm *not*."

He shows his face to smirk at me. "I'm going to upload these. Go wait for me in the bedroom."

I pout. "Upload me first. Do them later."

With a laugh, he turns me by my shoulders toward the door. "I'm paranoid about these things. I'd hate to lose your masterpiece." He pats my ass. "Go, take off everything. Except the stockings. Leave those on."

With an exaggerated huff to make my impatience known, I go to his room. As I reach back for my zipper, I catch sight of myself in his full-length mirror. I stand in front of it and let the dress fall around my feet. I turn to the side in just my bra, stockings, and cheekies. I only lost thirty pounds, maybe even a couple more since my appetite vanished a few days ago, but my body could belong to someone else. I've never looked better, despite faint stretch marks, a fat roll from my underwear elastic, and my shrunken boobs. I wonder if I'll gain it back once I completely stop the antidepressants. Even though I'm not sure I want evidence of myself this exposed, I consider asking Finn to take my picture nude in case my weight fluctuates again.

Finn makes a noise from the doorway. "I'm glad I'm not the only one who gets caught staring at you."

By habit, I cover my tummy. All the lights are on, and he's looking right at me. "I was just . . . making sure everything is in the right place."

He smiles and walks around me. We look at my reflection together. "I probably haven't told you enough how incredibly sexy you are." He removes my hands from my stomach and scans me head to toe. "You know you are, right?"

I blink from his face to my body. I've never been overly confident, not even now. I know I look good, but those insecurities don't go away overnight. "I think so."

"I need you to *know* so."

I look up again at the intensity in his voice. "I'm not going to gain it back," I promise him. "The photos—"

"Fuck the photos," he says gently. "Kendra was always worried about staying thin. She got that from her mom. They talked about it way too much—the latest diet or exercise fad, whether or not they'd lost or gained a pound, like it was a competition."

"That's not me," I say. "When I was heavier, it didn't bother me enough to interfere with my life."

"I'm not saying you are, but I don't want it to ever be an issue between us. If Kendra gained even a few pounds, she'd get depressed and refuse to have sex because of how she looked. And when we *did*, she didn't enjoy it, because she was worried about lighting and angles and stupid shit like that. You think that was fun for me?"

I hazard a small smile. I'm actually enjoying his lecture on body image. "I'm guessing no."

"I'd rather see cellulite than worry that you're worried about how I think you look. You look perfect because you look like you, and believe me, that's the most I'm thinking when I'm hard and you're naked." For emphasis, he steps into me. He's not talking hypothetically. "There's not much else happening in my head. Well, the head on top, anyway."

I face him, even though the light will show my upper-thigh dimples in the mirror. I've exposed myself in terrifying ways to Finn, and he's still here. There are no words to thank him for that, but I try. "I know it's only been a little while, but I just, I feel like you know me better than anyone in my life."

"I might," he agrees. "And I know there's more. Much more. I intend to keep peeling away your layers, Halston. You won't try to stop me, will you?"

He knew me before I even met him. My desires, my insecurities, my aches. I don't think I could stop him now if I wanted to.

EIGHTEEN

finn

While the last few weeks have sped by in a blur of camera flashes and ruined lingerie and soul-searching, two nights away from Halston have felt like a fucking lifetime. I check the time on my phone again, convinced it must be wrong. I should be grateful for this job shooting promotional images at a rural Vermont bed and breakfast. They're paying me well *and* putting me up in their coziest room. But since Halston had to stay home and work, being away from her has me questioning whether the money's worth it.

It's a troubling thought. Between sporadic work the last year, alimony, child support, and living in the most expensive city in the world, my savings account is headed into dangerous territory. I need to work, but no need feels more essential than being with Halston.

She feels the same. I heard it in her voice this morning, her cheerfulness a thin veneer for the frustration my absence is causing. Knowing her like I do, I worry what loneliness is like for her.

That's why I've prepared this love letter for her. While the owners try to get their chickens and goats to cooperate for me, I check my post one last time before I hit share. I don't have to tell her to check for it. We're posting daily now. Every image brings more followers. More followers make Halston happy—and me too. It's validation that giving up a stable, mediocre life for my art wasn't completely insane. Even if I haven't sold anything or scored work yet, over a thousand people have decided my photography is worth a spot on their feed.

I don't hear from Halston the rest of the day. With the year-end around the corner, she's been working late a lot to prepare. I hate the idea of her working after dark with a scorned ex-boyfriend, but I don't have much say in the matter.

Tonight, I walk through my door at seven in the evening, and her things are in the foyer. I'm filled with a sense of calm I've been missing the last couple days. I dump my bags on the ground and look for her. "Halston?"

She doesn't respond, but I find her in my studio, looking out the window.

"I'm so damn happy to see you," I say, stepping into the room. "I was worried you'd be working." When she doesn't turn around, I repeat a little louder, "Halston?"

She startles, spinning toward me. "Oh my God." She covers her heart. "I didn't hear you come in."

"Apparently not. Are you okay?"

"There was a bird on the windowsill—a sparrow, I think. But they aren't nocturnal. Isn't that weird?" She glances outside once more, then turns back to me. "How was the trip?"

The dark circles under her eyes are hard to miss. I haven't been away from her since the first night she slept in my bed. She's a little thinner than she was when we met. "Awful. I missed you."

"I missed you too." There's so much emotion in her voice, I'm overwhelmed by the urge to wrap her up in my arms.

"Then let's try this again," I say. "Get over here and say hello for real."

She hurries across the studio. When her arms circle my neck, I lift her by the waist. "Don't leave me again," she says, nuzzling me.

I'd like to bottle up those words and keep them close. It's something Sadie never asked of me. And when I spent too many hours in the office, Kendra used my time away from home as a weapon. Halston actually missed me, and the evidence is right in front of me. "What's wrong?" I ask.

"It scares me how hard it was to be away from you."

I rub her back. It doesn't scare as much as worry me. Halston's mood has been relatively good since we met three weeks ago, but the day before I left was the anniversary of her mom's death. It was important to her that she end her meds that day so she could feel everything. And something about not wanting to hit the ten-year mark. I held her as she cried and reminisced. I listened. What I didn't do was tell her it might not be the best time to stop. She's mentioned enough times how Rich and her dad try to control her treatment.

"Did you try writing?" I ask. "Doesn't that help?"

"I started to. It was the first time I've written since we met, but then . . ."

"What?"

She hesitates. "It's stupid."

"Of course it's not." I scoop an arm under her knees and carry her to the studio's small sofa. I sit her across my lap. "If it's something I did, you can tell me."

"No, it's not that."

I set my jaw. There's only one other explanation. She admitted recently that Rich's still sniffing around, trying to change her mind about their break-up. I don't need that. One of the worst things about my affair with Sadie was being kept in the dark about her marriage. I could never be exactly sure where we stood, because I only ever heard her side. I might need to step in with Rich before things get more complicated. “Is it Rich? Did he bother you while I was gone?”

“No. I mean, yes, he did, but I don’t care about him. It’s . . .”

I bend my head to try and get her to look at me. “What?”

She plays with a button on my chest and I temporarily forget that I’ve wanted to get out of this stiff shirt since the moment I put it on. “That photo you posted yesterday . . .”

I think back to the photo. We’d shot it a few days earlier. She’d dropped a glass in the kitchen in the middle of the night while getting water. I found her on her hands and knees cleaning it up. “You’ll cut yourself,” I’d said, pulling her up by her bicep. “Leave it. I’ll get it in the morning.”

I’d turned out the light, and the glare of a nearly full moon silhouetted her, her red slip the only color in the dark. She’d started to apologize, but I’d cut her off to get my camera. I slid down the strap of her negligee, positioned her sleep-disheveled hair over her shoulders, and shot her in the dark. Since we were apart yesterday, I’d posted it without her permission, but her face was shadowed. She hadn’t told me not to as she’d watched me edit it.

“What about it?” I ask.

“Did you see the comments?”

“I don’t think so. What’d they say?”

"Someone called the caption weird."

I'm a toy.
Come, wind me up,
Play with me.

Her voice cracks. "They said it was *sick*. Do people think that?"

"Person, not people, and no, they don't think that. How many other comments were there?"

"I don't know." She shrugs. "There were four more."

"And?"

"They were good."

"So it's one person, and clearly, this kind of stuff isn't for her."

"Him," she corrects. "I looked at his account. It's private, but there's a bible verse in the description."

"It's one comment out of many from someone who obviously came across the photo by accident." I kiss her temple. "Don't let it get to you."

She flattens her hand on my chest. "It just made me think. I *am* weird. How come I can't just keep these thoughts to myself like a normal person? Why did I write them down? Why would I *want* people to read them?"

I study her face, the way her nose slopes to a perfect little point. Bible thumper or not, I'll knock out any motherfucker who makes her feel ashamed. Her words come from deep inside her. They can never be bad, because they're honest. "If either of us was a normal person, I wouldn't have met you," I tell her. "I wouldn't have gone out of my way to find you, and," I pause, my heart thumping, "I wouldn't be falling in love with you."

She blinks up at me, a tear dripping off her eyelash. A megawatt smile spreads across her face. "What?"

"You heard me." I can't help mirroring her grin. "This has been the best month of my life. I'm falling in love with you, Halston. I think I'm already there, but I don't want to scare you off, so consider this a warning—it's happening."

"It's happening for me too."

"I figured."

She laughs and jolts me with a quick kiss on the lips. "I'm falling in love with you."

Her eyes sparkle, partly from the tears, but I hope from what I just admitted. Fate finally took pity on me. It dropped her most intimate thoughts and feelings right at my feet and said, *This is it, you poor schmuck. Here you go, now leave me alone.* I knew then, I needed this in my life. Once Rich was out of the picture, there was no reason for me not to love her.

"What about my post from today?" I thumb the hollow of her cheek. "It wasn't for them. It was for you."

"I didn't see it. After I spent too long trying and failing to stalk that man who commented, I deleted the app from my phone."

I raise my eyebrows. I wouldn't be surprised if she checked it ten times a day. "Seriously?"

"I overreacted. I'll restore it." She tries to get my phone from my pocket, squirming in my lap as she feels around. So help me God, I've got the patience of a saint. I've held out over forty-eight hours and now she's tempting the beast. She finds what she's looking for and goes to the post.

In the photo, she's asleep. Her body is outlined by my white sheet, her legs scissored across the mattress.

In my sheets.
In my head.

"When did you take this?" she asks.

"Sunday morning, before I woke you to say goodbye."

"I love it. You're so talented." She widens her eyes. "Four-hundred-likes talented. Wow."

I smile. I haven't read the comments. I don't normally. Maybe I should start, though. I don't like seeing her this upset over something a stranger said, and I won't be able to wipe it away with *I love you* every time. I have to start watching for these things.

I tilt her head up and touch her bottom lip. "I only care about one like."

She catches my thumb between her teeth, then licks it. "You have it."

"I might need some convincing. I haven't been inside you in three days, and you're not all over me like I'd hoped."

"It was *two* days," she says. "We had sex before you left."

"Oh yeah," I say, nodding. "I woke you up to say bye, and I was almost out the door when you jumped me."

"I promised I'd be fast, and I was. Have *you* ever gotten a condom on in two seconds? Maybe I should be in charge of that from now on."

I squeeze the side of her ass, adjusting her so she can feel what her words do to me. "I don't remember it being *that* fast. I might need to see it again." I rake a hand through her hair and hold her in place for a kiss. She was crying only a couple minutes ago, and I should restrain myself, but I've been suffering without this. I put my hand up her skirt and find a treat. "Are these for me?" I ask, unhooking one of her garters.

She responds with a hip-swivel so skilled, I almost lose my eyeballs to the back of my head. "Fuck, Halston. Touch me. Don't make me wait."

She opens the button of my jeans and squeezes her hand inside. Her cold skin jolts me, but she warms up quickly, stroking me long and hard. "Like this? Or . . ." She looks me in the eye as she thumbs my crown, spreading precum over it. "That?"

I fist her elastic band. "How important are these tights to you? I'm either going to rip or come on them."

"You said that last time, and you did neither."

A challenge? I stand, nearly upending her onto the ground, but I catch her at the last second. "Bend over the couch."

When she does, her skirt rides up the backs of her thighs, exposing more garter clips. I unzip my pants all the way. I haven't had her from behind often, mainly because I like to watch her face as she comes. No time like the present. She's just as pretty from this angle and appetizing as fuck.

I slip my hands under her blouse to grasp her breasts. She prepared for me. The scrape of her lace bra is welcome against my palms. She shivers when I caress her lower back, goosebumps pebbling her skin. Slipping a finger into the elastic crotch of her panties, I say, "Next time wear white, so I can see how wet you are."

"White is for virgins," she says, backing onto my hand.

"There are still so many things I haven't done to you," I murmur, admiring her smooth apple of an ass. "You practically *are* a virgin."

"Tell me what things," she says. "It's only fair. You've read most of my dirty thoughts."

"Most?" My cock strains against the confines of my underwear. I pull my shirt over my head before removing my pants.

"You think I could fit everything in one journal?" she asks.

I stroke myself and look up at the ceiling. Lord, help me. This woman is figuring out just what it takes to ruin me, and I'm not even going to try and stop her. "All right. I'll tell you. We've fucked, we've made love," I say. "We've even dry humped."

She drops her forehead onto a cushion. "What else is there?"

I can't go much longer like this. I'm so hard, it hurts. My balls actually pulse. "I haven't fucked your mouth."

"I've given you a blowjob."

"I'm not talking about that." I yank her underwear down around her thighs and suck on my two favorite fingers. "I'm talking about fucking your mouth."

Her legs are already shaking, and I've barely touched her. I tease her entrance to get her as wet as possible.

"What else?" she asks.

She wants to hear more. I've eaten her dirty secrets like candy, and now she's the hungry one. Maybe it's not my hands making her wet, but the admission of what I want. Exposing myself through the ways I want to own her. "Your ass," I say. "I'll get that too, but later. There's enough time for me to explore, lick, suck, and fuck every hole on your body. You can be my student, my patient, my submissive, my toy. Even my teacher. If you want those things."

Her back expands with a deep inhale. "What else?"

Greedy, just like me. I curl my fingers inside her and massage. "Mmm. In public. Side of the road, friendly skies, beach—whatever does it for you."

She groans. "Don't stop."

When I first saw Halston through the window, there's no doubt I was attracted to her. But now that she's bared herself to me, she's walking sex. It isn't just physical. It's the way she's let me in so deep, so fast. I've submerged myself in her, or she's done it for me. "I want to fuck you as a bride," I say, pushing the limits of the conversation as I finger her to the edge. "In a wedding dress so white, any stain would show."

"Oh my God," she says, writhing on my hand. "Keep talking."

"I want to come inside you so bad. Make you mine. I want you so many ways, and one day, as the mother of my child. If you want those things."

"Why?" she asks. "Why do you want to ruin me?"

"Just in case any other fucker tries to come along," I say. Her pussy flutters around me. With my fingers inside her, I bear down and line my cock up to her entrance. It takes me a few seconds to get just my head into such a tight space. "To me, you'll never be ruined, Halston. You'll always be perfect. Am I hurting you?"

She fists the cushion and shakes her head. "Are you going to do it like that?"

I slide out a little and push deeper, the ridges of my shaft rubbing against my knuckles. "If I last long enough, yeah. Does it feel good?"

"I feel . . . tight."

"So goddamn tight." I flatten my other hand on her lower back and pump my hips a few times. When she moans, I flick my fingers inside her and fuck her for real. She's shuddering in no time, making noises so foreign, I have to check to make sure she isn't crying. She's in the throes of an intense orgasm. Her cum, or maybe mine, seeps onto my balls, over my hand. My body reacts to the sight of it. Mid-thrust, I yank out of her and erupt all over her back, thighs, dress, stockings.

Fuck.

My legs buckle, and I steady myself on the back of the couch. By the time I'm finished, cum drips down her skin.

I'm breathless. She's so still, for a second, I'm worried she passed out. Or that I fucked up by thinking it was okay to come on her. I massage her ass cheeks, her lower back. She moans, turning her head to the side. Hair sticks to her temple. "Finn."

I don't have to ask what she needs.

I tug her up by her arm, and she stands, her back to my front. I turn her face to give me access to her mouth. I kiss her for the way I just took her, feed her love so she knows how I worship her body even when I'm rough.

"You can come inside me," she whispers.

"I know."

She liquefies against me. I love it. I love her.

I'm the lucky bastard who gets to hold her against me, making sure she doesn't fall. The one who can chase her sadness away.

I hope I'm always the one to do it. And that I'm always able to.

NINETEEN

Around the corner from Halston's office, I browse a selection of flowers outside a bodega. They're nothing extraordinary, overshadowed by miniature Christmas trees, metallic ribbons, and potted poinsettias. But they're here now. If time and money were no object, I might aim for something nicer.

It's no coincidence that I'm here, but I'm not about to admit that to her.

I choose red roses. Red says romance. It's the color of love and sex.

It also means stop, for anyone who might need to hear it.

I hand over some cash and once I have the bouquet in hand, I call Halston.

"I was just thinking about you," she answers.

"You must've sensed me nearby."

"What?" Her voice pitches. "You're here?"

"Downstairs." I grin. "I had a thing in the area. Let's go for lunch."

"Really?" I hear the smile in her voice. "All right. I just have to finish up a few e-mails. I'll be right down."

"There's no rush. I'll come up."

"No, no, don't bother. I can meet you in the lobby."

Halston has a whole other life I'm not part of, and that's been fine up until now. But I've told her I'm falling for her. I'm not going anywhere. I just want to make sure that message is clear. "And miss the opportunity to finally see where you spend your days?" I ask. "Fourth floor, right?"

"Well—"

I hang up and cross 14th Street. On the ride up the elevator, I smooth my hair and scruff into place. I decided not to shave the stubble I already had this morning, but maybe I should've. Maybe it's more "wandering vagrant" than "intimidating boyfriend." The doors open to a white-tiled, gray-walled lobby with black and white print ads on the walls. I wonder if Halston chose which ones to feature.

Halston comes around a corner and smiles. "Are those for me?"

I look at the roses. "Oh. I hadn't thought of that. Sure."

She laughs and takes them. I lean in, but she pulls away before I can kiss her. "I'm sorry. I can't."

"Why not?" I ask. "Are we doing something wrong?"

She twists her lips and turns away. "I'll show you my office."

I place my hand on the small of her back and walk with her. She doesn't seem to mind that. As she points out the different departments, I look around the office. It's a big floor. Rich works on the opposite side, but apparently that doesn't keep him away. I don't know what he looks like, but I think I'll know him if I see him. In case there's any question the roses are from me, I keep my hand where it is. If he's not here to see it, maybe someone will deliver the message.

Halston stops at a desk where a girl around her age is working on a computer. "Benny, this is Finn."

Benny arches her eyebrows, looking between us. "*Finn*? The guy who . . . the one—"

"The very same," I say. "I think I have you to thank for sending her to my doorstep that night."

Benny's cheeks redden. "It was my friend, Cara. She's loony."

I kiss the side of Halston's head. "Thank her for me, Benny."

Benny and Halston exchange a look that makes me wonder what I'm missing. "Dad?" Halston asks.

"Across town," Benny says.

Halston exhales a breath and finally takes my hand. She pulls me into her office, shuts the door, and leans back against it. "I know why you're here."

"You do?"

"My office is on your fuck-et list."

I straighten up. "My *what*?"

"Your bucket list for fucking. You said you wanted to do it in a car, on a plane, on a train, riding a bicycle, during a game of tennis—"

I laugh. "I did *not* list all those, and that's not why I'm here. Swear. I think about you when we're apart, and I never know exactly where to picture you." I glance around the office. There's nothing on the walls, a couple second-hand-looking chairs, and a messy desk. "Now I know."

"I've never gotten around to decorating." She nods at a small couch against the wall behind me. "Just some pillows."

"Now you'll have flowers too." I walk over and take the roses from her, pricking myself with a thorn. *Damn it.* "I think you should display them on Benny's desk so everyone can enjoy them."

"By everyone, do you mean Rich?" she asks.

Busted. "Nah. You look beautiful, by the way."

She rolls her eyes. "I told you I'd handle him."

"I know. I'm just checking on things like a good boyfriend."

Halston scratches the inside of her elbow, absentmindedly, sluggishly, as if she's thinking. I didn't think she'd like me checking up on her, it sounds like a Dad move, but I'm willing to take the heat if it means getting Rich off her back. She sighs.

"Look. My dad doesn't know about us. He's protective. I'll tell him when the time's right."

I kiss her on the forehead, no small feat since she's in flats today and barely comes up to my chest. I get it. I'm a dad myself. And if he cares about his daughter the way I do mine, the way I care about *Halston*, I'd feel the same. "Don't worry about it. You said you had some e-mails to send?"

"I can do it later."

"It's fine. I'll use the restroom while you finish up."

"Okay." She gives me directions, but I'm not listening. I turn to leave her office. "You're taking the roses?" she asks.

"You ever been in a men's bathroom?" I ask. "I need somewhere to stick my face. The smell alone—"

"Yuck." She waves her hands. "I don't need details."

I exit her office, close the door behind me, and walk no more than five steps. "What's the deal?" I ask Benny.

She looks up at me and blinks. "Sorry?"

"With Rich. Is he causing problems for her?"

"I don't . . . I'm not—"

"What are those?" I ask, walking around her desk. On the corner is a vase with—that fucker—vibrant purple and white roses complemented by baby's breath and lavender.

"They're mine," she says.

I read the card. "This says *Love, Rich*."

"We're in love," she says and then shudders. "Nope. I can't even say it without getting the creeps."

I ball my fist into my other hand. "Call him."

"What?"

"Rich. Call him down here. Tell him it's important." I'm not sure how Halston will react to me confronting Rich, but at the moment, I don't care. I was blindsided when Sadie chose Nathan, and this time, I intend to know what I'm up against.

I can see Benny doesn't want to make the call, but she does. After she hangs up, she says, "He's coming."

"Don't mention it to Halston." I pick up Rich's vase and hand it to her. "Trash these flowers. We need the vase for mine."

She gets up slowly, glancing at Halston's office door. "Oh-kay . . ."

"I'll hang onto this," I say about my bouquet.

I settle against the edge of Benny's desk, cross my arms, and wait. I trust Halston. I don't trust this guy. I'm not even sure how I feel about her dad from what I've heard. Halston is with me now, and I'm not going to sit back while Rich tries to sneak back in.

I spot him weaving through the cubicles. I know it's him. He looks younger than me—that's a point in my column as far as I'm concerned. Halston isn't just any girl. She's a lot to handle and worth the effort. Her dad couldn't do it, so he put her on drugs. Rich couldn't do it, so he convinced her to stay on them.

He slows down when he sees me, his eyes darting between my face and the roses.

"Rich?" I ask in case he's thinking of retreating.

He frowns. "Yeah? Who are you?"

I set the bouquet on the desk beside me. They've served their purpose. I wait until he's close enough that we won't make a scene. "I'm Finn. Halston's boyfriend."

"She doesn't have a boyfriend," he says right away. "Well, she did, and still kind of does, and it's me."

"Kind of?" I have to take a deep breath to keep from raising my voice. This guy needs to get a clue, and I guess I'll have to give it to him. "What exactly does that mean? Be precise. Does she know she's your girlfriend?"

"Yes."

I shake my head. "Try again."

He stands up straighter. "Look, I don't know who you are—"

"I'm Finn."

"Okay, but—"

"Listen, I don't have a lot of time." I scratch my jaw, fucking itchy stubble. "Halston tells me you've been coming around lately, trying to talk your way back into her life, bringing her shitty flowers. That stops here. Today."

"Does she know you're talking to me?"

"Not your business. Your business is this." I hold up a finger and count off. "One—she's not with you anymore. Two—she's with me. Three—it's over between you."

He narrows his eyes. "You don't know shit about my relationship."

"Oh, hang on. There's another." I put up a fourth finger. "Stay the fuck away from her." I stand, and he seems about half my size. "If she tells me again that you bothered her about anything not work related, I'll come back, and I won't be so pleasant. See, I'm in a pretty great mood at the moment, because I've got the prettiest fucking girl around on my arm. But if you try to take her from me, my mood will change."

"Do I want her back?" he asks. "Yes. But that's the only part of the story you have right. As far as anyone in this office knows, as far as anyone *in her life* knows, I'm her boyfriend. Ask her. Her dad wants us together, and he always gets what he wants."

"Bullshit."

"Are you coming to her house for Christmas?" he asks.

I close my mouth. Christmas is four days away. I've avoided the topic, which has been easy since she hasn't brought it up, either.

"I didn't think so," he says. "Because I'll be there."

Frustration tightens my muscles. He's just trying to get under my skin. There's no way Halston's spending Christmas with her ex. "I didn't call you here to make holiday plans. I'm telling you to back off."

"But—"

"You should go. Now."

He looks behind me at Halston's office. "We just want what's best for her."

By we, I think he's lumping himself in with her dad. It might take some effort to win her father over, but I'm up for the task. Rich, though? He's gotta go. "So do I," I say with a dismissive nod.

He leaves. I wait until he's out of sight, stand, and return to Halston. She's putting on her coat, so I help her into it. "Benny's taking care of the roses."

She rises onto the balls of her feet, and I bend my head to kiss her. "Thank you," she says. "The red ones are my favorite."

I win. Lavender-boy loses. On some level, I must've known that. Red roses lure you in with beauty and passion, which is why they suit Halston so well. Can they hurt you? Yes. If you don't know how to handle them.

Beautiful things should be that way, difficult to get to, to touch.

Otherwise, people would destroy them.

I've sprouted a human vine. I'm sprawled out on the mattress, Halston intertwined with me. Her leg must be double-jointed or something, because it seems to wrap around mine twice. Her head rests on my arm, so I do a bicep curl that brings her mouth to mine. "You good?" I ask.

She nods breathlessly. "So good."

Sex is a drug for us, plain and simple. It's true for me, and it's definitely true for her. Over the last few weeks she's stopped drinking so much coffee. I'll put a mug in front of her, and she'll barely look up from her phone. Or she'll take a sip, straddle my lap at the kitchen table, and forget all about it.

I stroke her hair off her face until her panting subsides. It's only ten o'clock at night. Before her, I read every night before bed, or my mind would keep me up into early morning hours. Luckily, great sex and great books have the same soothing effect.

She runs a hand through my chest hair. "This is nice."

"What would you normally be doing now?" I ask. "If you were at your apartment. Before me."

"Hmm. I can't remember a time before you."

I chuckle. "Twenty-five years, wiped out just like that."

She gets up on an elbow to look down at me. "I seriously can't remember. My apartment feels like another planet right now. I guess I'd probably be watching Netflix or playing with my phone."

"Do you like to read?"

"Depends. I kept books at Rich's. When I stayed there, he usually read before bed." She grimaces. "Sorry if that's weird."

I shake my head, trying to be cool. It's good for me to hear about Rich. Know your enemy and all that. I haven't decided if I should bring up my conversation with him yesterday. There wasn't even supposed to be a conversation. If it weren't for his last comment about Christmas, I'd leave it. "What's he like? Rich?"

She flops down onto her back. "He's, I don't know. Even-tempered. Hard-working. A little insecure. His dad ignored him a lot."

"Why? Lots of siblings?"

"He's an only child, but his dad's a big shot lawyer in Chicago who worked long hours. His mom had a prescription drug problem, still does, so his nanny did most of the heavy lifting."

I look up at the ceiling. An almost imperceptible crack runs along one side. My dad broke his back working long hours too, but it was out of necessity. He was away a lot, doing overtime at the factory where he worked. He was the opposite of a deadbeat dad—so much so that I rarely saw him. So, I was the man of the house. That's what my parents told me, at least. I didn't take that responsibility lightly, but no matter how hard I tried, I wasn't man enough. I couldn't keep my mom from spiraling downward, even though I rarely left her side. "Maybe Rich and I aren't so different," I say.

"You feel different." She curls back into me. Her lashes brush my chest when she looks up. "You never talk about your parents. All I know is you're an only child."

"My pops passed a few years ago. My mom has . . ." Halston shifts against me, and I wrap my arm around her shoulder, pulling her closer. "She's got something like Alzheimer's. Brain damage from drinking so much. She stopped drinking when my dad died, but it was too late. She's in a home now."

"I'm sorry." Halston's gray eyes get cloudy, but not the way they were when we met. I bring her hand to my mouth and kiss it, accepting her sympathy. "Was she an alcoholic when you were younger?" she asks.

"Yeah. I didn't understand that back then, and we didn't call it that. But she was. She functioned all right. She'd get up, send me off to school with lunch, promise me it would be a good day, and sometimes it was."

"And the bad days?" Halston asks.

"At school, I'd think of things we could do when I got home, like garden or sit at the dog park or rent a movie. On grocery days, I made up games to get all the items on the list."

She grins. "Sounds like fun."

"I guess I thought if I kept her busy enough, if I gave her a reason to be happy, she wouldn't drink. I didn't understand alcohol, but I knew when she went to this specific cupboard in the house, she'd turn into a different person. Once, we were in the middle of planting flowers in the front yard, and I was telling her about my day, and she just got up in the middle of it to pour herself a drink. You don't forget that feeling." My throat thickens. Am I blind to trust Halston to stick around when others haven't? "Every day I tried to get her to choose me over that cupboard, but she chose the alcohol more often than not."

My watch on the nightstand ticks, the only noise for a while.

"It wasn't you," Halston says gently. "She had an addiction."

"I know."

"I choose you every day."

I look down at her. "What do you mean?"

"I'm like her," she says. "I get like that, where I need something or I don't feel right."

"You're not like her," I say. "Are you talking about the coffee?"

She frowns. "You knew?"

"Knew what?"

"I tried stopping antidepressants about a year and half ago. I was doing well with Rich, and it'd been eight years since my mom's death, so I wanted to see how it'd go. Doctor Lumby lowered my dosage, and I was fine for a few days, but then I started to get antsy."

"Did Rich know?"

"I sat down with him and my dad and told them my decision. They weren't thrilled, but they said they'd help." She rolls onto her back, away from me.

"Anyway, one night I was on my own and had a big meeting the next day, one of the most important of my career. I was anxious, so I had a glass of wine. Then another. I felt calmer and I pulled off the presentation so I celebrated."

"With wine?" I guess.

She nods. "Nobody noticed how much I was drinking until I made a scene at a client dinner and got us kicked out of the restaurant. Of course, my dad and Rich were horrified and made me go back to my psychiatrist to tell him I needed the meds. And truthfully, I agreed. I'd never acted like that. Except once, when my recklessness—" She squints at the ceiling. "I would've started treatment again whether the three of them had made me or not."

My heart begins to race. Coffee, I can handle. Antidepressants too. But alcohol? I don't know. I've been down that path once and have no interest in ever returning. When Halston showed up drunk at my place that night, I figured it was a one-time thing. "Do you still drink?"

"Occasionally, but not like that. We upped my dosage, but for whatever reason, my *patterns*, as Rich calls them, stuck."

"Patterns?"

"I weaned myself off wine with cigarettes, which is when I lost weight. But I hated the stink of smoke, so I started running and when I got bored with that, I went shopping. A lot. I had this incredible new body to show off, after all. My dad put an end to that when he saw my credit card bills, so I moved on to coffee."

"That explains why the first few times I saw you, you were never without your cup."

"For a while, I was drinking it all day—black coffee, lattes, cold brew, however I could get it."

My mind reels to catch up. I'd suspected something with the coffee, but that was only the tip of the iceberg. What does it mean that she's nearly stopped drinking it since we met? Could something else have replaced it? *Me*, even? "Huh," is all I can think to say.

"Yeah." She swallows audibly. "The writing too. I've kept a journal compulsively since I left the psych ward. My counselor there got me to start it. It's just the past few weeks I haven't been doing it. I'm sorry."

She tacks the apology on so quickly, I almost miss it. "Sorry? For what?"

"I'm not what you thought. I didn't know about your mom. If I had, I might've told you all this sooner. Or not. I would've been afraid to freak you out."

"Ah," I say. "Tell me, what would've happened if I'd freaked out?"

"You'd have left," she says. "I wouldn't have blamed you. But now that you love me, well . . ." She looks over at me. "Maybe you're more open to accepting my weird behaviors."

I bring her back into my chest. "None of it sounds weird to me."

"How does it sound?"

"Like you went through something traumatic, and nobody really took care of you after." Any concern I just felt vanishes. At her core, she's still the fifteen-year-old girl who blames herself for her mom's death. I doubt anyone tried to convince her otherwise. She's not obsessed with the photos or me or sex—not that I'd mind since I can't get enough of her, either. She just stopped drinking coffee because I'm here now, and she doesn't need it. I satisfy her in ways nobody else has been able. Like she said—she chooses me.

"I'm going to take care of you now," I say. "I promise."

"You already have. With you, I'm . . . I'm happier than I've ever been. Even when I was taking drugs specifically to be happy."

We both laugh softly, and I kiss the top of her head. I'm even more confident now that yesterday's chat with Rich was necessary. Maybe he's not bad for her, but he's not right for her. She needs a man strong enough to carry some of her burden, committed enough not to drop it when it's too heavy. He isn't that. He couldn't keep the *patterns* at bay like I do. He didn't protect her. "Speaking of happy stuff," I say, "we haven't talked about Sunday."

"I know. I've been afraid to bring it up."

"Me too." As if on cue, we both sit up. She gets my t-shirt from the end of the bed. I can't stand that she still isn't comfortable enough to be naked with me when we aren't in the heat of the moment, but I'll keep working on that. She crosses her legs, and I get a peek under the shirt right before she pulls it over her crotch. We just made love, but my cock stirs. When she tries to hide herself, I'm even more tempted by her.

"Christmas," she says seriously.

"Yeah. I want to spend it with you."

She brightens. "I want to spend it with you too."

I take her hand. "But I can't. I've thought about it from every angle, and I just can't make it work."

"Oh." Her posture droops. "I figured."

"Kendra's boyfriend talked her into giving me three days at her parents', which is why I haven't had Marissa since earlier this month. It's the only way I'll get to watch Marissa open her presents. I didn't get to spend last Christmas with her, so . . ."

"Then you have to go." Halston nods. "My dad's expecting me anyway. I wasn't sure of your plans, so I didn't tell him otherwise."

"If I could bring you, I would." I can't. Kendra will never let me forget how I admonished her for introducing her five-week-long boyfriend to Marissa. I've known Halston less time than that. "It's complicated."

"It's okay." She smiles. "I should be with my dad. It's a difficult time of year for him because of the accident."

I squeeze her hand. "It's difficult for *both* of you. Last year was hard for me too. Kendra had just learned about the affair."

"You're lucky she came around."

"Yeah. Her boyfriend's going to be good for her, I think." This is as good an opening as I'm going to get. "So it'll just be the two of you?"

She opens her mouth but just looks at me.

"Let me put it this way," I say. "If I didn't have Marissa to see, would you be bringing me home to meet the dad?"

"No." She plays with the hem of the shirt. "It wouldn't be a good time. What with my mom's stuff and all."

A movement outside catches my eye. The people in the apartment across the street have their curtains open and lights on. So do we. I wonder if they saw what we just did, if they notice us verging on an argument. "So that's the only reason?" I ask, returning my attention to her.

"No."

My throat gets dry. She's obviously circumventing the truth, hiding something. "You promised me honesty, Halston."

She sucks in a breath and spits it out. "Rich will be at the house. His parents too."

I press my lips into a line. Rich was right, and I must've looked like a complete ass yesterday, peacocking around like I knew what was what. "Were you going to tell me?"

"Yes."

"When?"

She frowns. "When I was ready. You don't corner the market on complicated."

"I know, so I'm asking you to explain."

She rubs the tip of her nose. A light goes off in the apartment across the street. "He still thinks Rich and I are a couple," she says. "Everyone does. His parents, our colleagues. Except Benny. She knows."

My face warms. A couple. With Rich. I flex my hands in and out of fists. "Why?"

"It's a hard time of year for Dad. He's under a lot of pressure with it being the end of the last quarter, and dealing with the anniversary of Mom's death—"

"How is that different from every other year?"

"It's not, but . . ." She crosses her legs more tightly. "I mean it is, because it's ten years now. That's big."

"I get that, I do. But there'll always be something. At some point, you have to stop giving your dad the excuse to run your life."

"I tried. I told him I was ending it with Rich and stopping the meds, but it's too much right now. I could see how stressed he was. It could only be one or the other, and I knew I could lie to him about Rich, but not about my treatment."

She's not hearing me. I have to wonder if she's making excuses so she doesn't have to cut off her dad's power over her. Either she's afraid of him, or she's gotten so used to it, she doesn't really want the freedom she says she does. "It's not healthy, Hals. You've got to come clean with him. You don't owe him your life because of a mistake you made years ago."

"I'm not going to kick him when he's down. When I'm medicated and being looked after, he doesn't worry about me as much. I couldn't take both those things out of the equation and expect him to be okay with that."

"He doesn't have to be okay with it. You're a grown woman."

"He's my dad." She frowns. "I'm only talking about a few weeks. I'll tell him after December. Why does it have to be now?"

"Because I get the feeling you've been making excuses for him for a while. Is that why you never broke up with Rich?"

Her posture slumps a little. "It's not that black and white."

That answer's as good as yes. It *is* the reason. She was willing to stay with Rich to make her dad happy. Would she go back to him for that reason? Her dad introduced them after all. "Is that why you got together with him in the first place? For your dad?"

"Would it make you feel better if I did?"

People stay in relationships for all kinds of reasons that have nothing to do with love—including not believing they deserve better. "It makes me think if push comes to shove, you'd put your dad before yourself. And that could be bad for us."

Her expression softens. "You still think I might go back to Rich."

"If your dad's been controlling you this long, what happens if he doesn't accept your breakup?"

She shakes her head. "I don't know how else to tell you it's over."

"Does Rich know that?"

"God, Finn, you have to understand—it means absolutely nothing. It's just a show for my dad. Rich wants me back, but that's his issue."

I lean my back against the headboard. "I'm asking you to tell your dad now. Before Rich's family comes over."

"I can't. It's Christmas. It'll ruin everyone's holiday." She looks at her hands. "I'm sorry. We'll all spend a polite weekend together, and then I'll come home to you."

"Weekend?"

"I'm going to take the train to Westchester tomorrow after work. My mom baked on the twenty-fourth, and I think my dad would really like if I started that tradition again."

I look out the window. Dinner with the ex and his family isn't how I want my girlfriend spending her holiday weekend, but I'm doing the exact same thing. I'm not sure how else to tell her what I want. "Let's forget about it for now," I say. "We'll spend a few days apart, make our families happy, and before we know it, we'll be back in bed, fucking in the new year."

She launches herself at me. "Best idea I've heard all day."

I catch her and lie us back on the mattress. "But what'll we do until then?"

She straddles me. "I can think of a few things."

"You know people can see us?"

She looks sidelong out the window. "Does it bother you?"

I lift her t-shirt to steal a peek at her breasts, appreciating their round fullness, the pretty pink peaks. *My* pretty pink peaks. "A little."

"Aw." She reaches between to touch me. She's not as timid as she was when we started sleeping together. I liked her timid sometimes, but I also like her bold if it's because I've made her comfortable. She sinks down on me. "You're jealous?"

"You would be too if—" I groan as she swivels her hips. "If you had someone others could only dream of having."

She drops her forehead to mine, looks me in the eye, and says, "I do."

I try to focus on how her warmth envelops me.

I try not to wonder what Christmas at the Fox's is like.

Or if I mistakenly worried about Rich when it's becoming clear Halston's dad is the one pulling the strings.

TWENTY

halston

I wake up early to pack for Westchester so I can spend the morning with Finn. It occurs to me as I bag up tampons that I've hardly been to my apartment the last few weeks. I'm not bringing much, most of what I'd need is already at my dad's, but it's still strange to pack here rather than at home.

I put my overnight bag by the front door and take my phone into the kitchen. I check inside the refrigerator. I haven't ever made Finn breakfast, but that's usually because he's up before me. I get out some eggs and find bacon in the freezer. While I wait for it to defrost in the microwave, I check our latest post. Only thirty-two photos in and we're nearing three thousand followers. It's incredible. I have friends who've been using the app for years and can't crack a thousand. I've started tracking the number of followers we get a day. If the photos are good, we can double our numbers by posting twice in twenty-four hours. We can quadruple them or more if a bigger account shares our work.

Not every photo works. I've inspected the ones that don't—the angle, my pose, my words—to see what's missing. I don't have enough data to identify any patterns yet, but the sexier the photo, the more attention it gets. The peek at the tops of my stockings has been one of the most successful ones, but one of just my hair and bra strap fell flat.

I put the phone away to search for a frying pan and bump the coffee maker with my hand.

I forgot.

About *coffee*.

It's not the first time this has happened. One day last week, I didn't think about it until three in the afternoon, and that point, I didn't feel like making any. Even before I drank it like water, I still had a cup a day.

This must be what it feels like to be satisfied. Happy. I stopped the antidepressants on the seventeenth—the anniversary of my mom's death—and I can't help but think it was the right choice. Aside from some headaches, mood swings, and minor anxiety, I've handled the transition well.

I get a pot going. I'm scrambling eggs when Finn zombie-walks into the kitchen wearing only boxer-briefs. His burnt-butter hair sticks up on one side, and his eyes are heavy with sleep. He yawns. "Eight solid hours, and I still feel like I was knocked out with a two-by-four."

"That's the power of good pussy."

"The power of *your* pussy." He grins. "What's all this?"

"What's it look like?"

His smile falters a little as he takes in the open cupboards, pan, orange juice on the counter. The energy in the room changes as his eyes land on the eggs. "Breakfast."

"Is that okay?" I asked. "I wanted to do something nice for you."

He blinks a few times and looks back at me. "Yes. God, yes. Thank you. I'm not sure if I've ever mentioned how much I love breakfast food."

I laugh. "Good to know you can still surprise me after all this time."

"Yes, all—what's it been, twenty days?"

"Twenty-three. We met on the first."

"*You* met *me* on the first. I like to think I knew you those few days I had your journal."

I fluff the eggs with my spatula as Finn's words fluff my heart. He's more of a man than anyone I've been with, and yet so sweetly sensitive. When I look back, he's leaning against the doorframe. "Sadie helped me unpack the kitchen," he says. "And we had an inside joke about breakfast."

"Oh." I turn back to the pan before he can see the disappointment on my face. Finn's never made me feel unwelcome here, but now I know—the kitchen belongs to them. I guess *she* woke up early enough to surprise him. "Sorry."

"No, I'm not upset," he says. "I'm really fucking happy."

I glance over my shoulder. "Happy . . .?"

"I just realized when I walked in here—I haven't thought about Sadie in days. Not that I'd been thinking about her with you, but little things over the past year have reminded me of her each day, whether I like it or not. So to go without that . . ." He crosses his arms. "It's a relief."

I'm not sure if I should feel as excited about that as he does, but I do. It isn't easy to get over someone. I can't fault him for being hung up on her after the way she hurt him. "I love you," I tell him. I'm still testing out the words. They're a little foreign.

He also looks a bit startled. "I have a Christmas present for you."

My heart falls. It's not the response a girl wants to hear to a declaration like that. I try not to deflate, though. Last night's argument was foreign territory for us, and I don't want to return there. I didn't like having to stand up to Finn, but there are some things I can't budge on. This time of year, I owe my dad my compassion.

"A present?" I ask with a smile, trying for optimistic. "What is it?"

He goes into the hall closet and returns with a small rectangular box wrapped in gold and green paper. The shape gives it away, and I wonder what kind of jewelry it is—bracelet or necklace. I don't care. Either would be nice, although jewelry is the kind of thing Rich always bought because he didn't know what else to get me.

Finn hands me the present. "Open it."

"Now?"

He nods, so I untie the metallic ribbon and carefully unfold the paper so I don't look as eager as I feel. The box is smooth black leather, somewhat untraditional for jewelry, but then I see Mont Blanc printed across the top. The top creaks open to reveal a slim, rose gold ballpoint pen. "Wow."

"I thought that pink color would match the leather nicely. Of your journals."

"It's beautiful. I love it." I look up at him. This wasn't picked out by a sales associate. Finn really thought about what I'd like. But my dad has a couple of these pens—they aren't cheap. "You shouldn't be spending money on me."

"I want to." He cups my face, brushing his index finger over the tattoo behind my ear. "I love you too, by the way."

The gesture warms my skin—and my soul. Acknowledging my tattoo when he says he loves me is accepting that my pain is part of me, and it doesn't scare him. "I also have something for you."

"I don't need anything more than this," he says and kisses me.

"Be that as it may, I already paid for it, and it's non-refundable." I wiggle my eyebrows. "It doesn't come in a box, and it can't be wrapped, but it'll be delivered next week. Aren't you curious?"

He narrows his eyes playfully. "All right. What is it?"

I grin. "A new website."

"A *what*?" He shakes his head in disbelief. "No way. Can't be."

Finn's website needed work. The photos took forever to load, and it was minimalistic, but not in a good way. The only thing worth keeping was his bio and the photo he posted with it. He told me it'd been taken at sunset on a family vacation to the beach. His bronze skin turns his enormous smile blindingly white. His hair is lightened from the sun, his eyes so green they're almost gold. He's male model material anyway, but in that photo, he's Greek god status. "I hired one of the designers we use at the agency. He has a six-month waiting list, but I sweet-talked him into a rush job."

"Okay, I lied earlier. I do need some things, and a decent website is one of them." He laughs. "Thank you, Hals."

We eat breakfast at the kitchen table with my feet in his lap. A few inches to the left, and I'd wake the beast—then *I'd* be Finn's breakfast. But I'm already pushing it. I have to be at work soon, and I still haven't showered.

Finn massages the arch of my foot with one hand and shovels eggs into his mouth with the other. "I'll miss you," he says.

I melt a little. "At least I start my period today. I can already feel it. So you won't be missing much."

He grunts. "I like you for more than what you've got going between your legs," he says. "But don't be naïve enough to think I won't fuck you on your period. It's called a shower."

I half roll my eyes. "God forbid you go a few days without sex."

"Yeah? And you weren't all over me last night?" he asks. "Sitting on my cock while the neighbors watched."

My heart skips with his sudden dirty talk. It feels extra filthy in the daylight over eggs and bacon. Lying by his side last night had been like floating on a cloud. Sheets so soft, my body calm and sated. Heaven. "Amen."

"Hmm?" he asks.

"Nothing." I arch my foot in his hand. "You'll text me, right?"

"All day long."

"Will you post?"

He nods as he chews. "I have some great ones from earlier this week." He winks. "And the one with the red bow."

I blush. We had fun with that ribbon, tying it on all sort of body parts.

Finn looks at me from the foot of the bed, camera in hand. "Spread out. Arms above your head."

I do as he says, my insides clenching at his command. I'm naked and turned on enough not to worry how my tits or stomach look. He's in work mode and fully-clothed, but once he gets his shot, he'll fuck me.

When I'm in position, he trades his camera for a fat, satin, cranberry-red ribbon we purchased at a giftwrapping kiosk. His eyebrows cinch as he secures my wrists together, tightening the bow just enough to pinch. "I wouldn't mind finding you like this under my tree," he says, getting onto the mattress.

I bite my bottom lip. "Maybe you will."

He takes the photo, a bow vibrantly red against my pale forearms, the ghost-white sheet.

Posing for him is an unrivaled sort of foreplay.

"You'll send me a caption for that today or tomorrow?" he asks. "I want to post it on Christmas."

I put my fork down. Finn's been taking passages from my journal for most of our photos, but he wants something special for that one. An 'enchanting' caption he said. I've been trying, but I haven't written anything decent since those couple days we were apart. The more I want to get it right, the harder it seems to be. "Sure," I say. "I'll give it some thought. Has anyone reposted since yesterday morning?"

"I haven't checked." He nods at my phone. "Why don't you? Sign into my account."

It takes me a moment to register his words. I try not to get too excited in case he's teasing me. "Really?"

"My password is your name and December, all lowercase. Halston December."

I try unsuccessfully to hold back a smile. "My name?"

"Yep. I changed it. Easier for both of us to remember."

I push my plate away and pick up my cell, suddenly giddy. "You're sure you don't mind?"

"Why would I? I meant to give it to you a while ago. You going to finish your breakfast?"

I sign out of my own account and type Finn's username into the login page.

"Hals?"

"Huh?"

"You should eat more."

I try the password. It works. My palms sweat around the phone, my heart racing even faster than it did while I opened my present. "I'm full."

"All right." He slides my plate over and gets to work on it.

A little red bubble pops up with Finn's notifications.

Holy shit.

Hundreds of likes, some comments, and a few tags. This truly is the perfect gift, and one that'll keep me occupied while I'm avoiding Rich and his family this weekend. I scroll through the alerts until I can't anymore, and I only make it through this morning. "How often do you check this?"

"Couple times a day. Once to post, once to see how it's doing."

"Wow." I wiggle my feet in his lap. "It's way more exciting when you get to see that bubble pop up with—" My jaw drops when I navigate to his profile. "*Finn.*"

"What?"

"You have DMs. So many!"

"DMs?"

I widen my eyes at him. "You've never checked your messages?"

"I didn't even know you could get them."

I browse his inbox. There are too many for me to get through now, so I read the first couple. A request from a half-naked girl to post her photo. *Shit.* Maybe it's best he doesn't read these. The next one mentions the captions, and I smile to myself. Whenever I start to wonder if Finn even needs me for this project, I read comments that make me think my poetry is a big part of the reason we're doing so well.

I open one with simple black and white logo as its profile picture—two B's back to back. They've sent more than one message, so I start at the beginning.

Hello Mr. Cohen,

My name is Kelly, and I'm the marketing director here at Butter Boudoir. We're huge fans of your work and we'd love to talk with you about partnership opportunities.

Underneath her unanswered message is another, sent a week later.

Hello again. I know you must be inundated with requests, but I hope you had a chance to consider my previous message. Can we send you some complimentary lingerie for your photo shoots? Or, if you're willing to act as an ambassador and promote our brand, we can offer $1000 in exchange for 10 posts. Thanks for your consideration and we look forward to hearing from you.

Kelly

"Oh my God."

"What?" Finn asks.

I look up, grinning. "There's a message here from a lingerie company. They want us—me—to model and post their stuff. They'd *pay* us."

Finn snorts. "Scam."

"No, it isn't." I click on the profile photo. There are photos of women in Butter Boudoir's pieces, but nothing nearly as stunning as the work Finn does. I should know, I'm an expert at analyzing art for its market. The description has a website, so I browse their shop. "It's totally legit."

"Well, if it is, doesn't matter. I'm not posting photos of you in lingerie."

I raise my eyebrows. "What about the stockings?"

"That was a one-time thing, and you were completely covered."

"But—"

"Halston." He gives me a look. "I don't want my fucking girlfriend naked on the Internet."

I sit back, surprised by his obstinacy. "First of all, nobody would know it was me. Second, what do you think we've been doing? It's the same thing."

"No it isn't. Every photo we've taken has been painstakingly presented to be suggestive, not explicit. They're erotic, not pornographic. That's a line I don't want to cross."

"You were literally inside me during one of the photos," I shoot back. "Like, we were having sex when you took it."

He thins his lips into an angry line, and I feel immediately scolded. "You don't *see* that in the photo."

"But it's implied."

"That's why it's sexy. If I posted a picture of us fucking, that'd be porn."

I look back at the screen. *That sucks.* The garments are beautiful and tasteful. Black and white lace. Little pink bows. I'd love to own some, see how they'd look in a photo, and I think Finn could use the money. I haven't told him, but I eavesdropped on some of his conversation with Marissa the morning she was here. I couldn't resist poking my head out.

When I'd heard how cute he was with her, I hadn't wanted to stop. Then, she'd called him broke, and my heart had dropped. It shouldn't have surprised me. Finn never acts as though money's an issue, but he hasn't had much work in the last year.

I clear my throat. "They'll pay us," I say. "A grand."

He looks at his plate. "Just to post some pictures?"

I nod. "We can make money at this, Finn. I know you'd hoped to get some commissions out of what we're doing, but that's only one way to do it. People will pay us to post, and the more followers we get, the more money they'll offer."

Finn reaches out and takes my hand, lacing our fingers together. "Then another offer will come along. Something that works for us. This . . . *you*, out there, I'm not comfortable with it. Maybe I'm a greedy bastard, but I want you all to myself, Hals."

I should be swooning. Grateful to have someone who cares enough to keep me safe. But I can't ignore the tug of disappointment. I'd look good in that lingerie, and based on previous, sexier posts, I know it'd get us a lot of attention. "Okay," I say. "We'll just ignore it."

"Yeah." He nods at the phone. "Anything else good in there?"

"I'll look while I'm at work. If something else comes up, you'll consider it?"

"If it makes sense for us. Would I like to get more work, or maybe even sell some of the stuff on my website? Yes. But not at the cost of our art. Or our relationship."

The sincerity in his green eyes is overwhelming. I almost can't believe I'm not dreaming. Maybe I am. I don't know what I did to deserve Finn. I get up and go sit in his lap. "I don't want to go to work." I kiss him lightly on the lips but pull back when he goes in for more. "Let me stay here. We'll take photos all day and figure out how to make lots of money so I never have to go back to that stupid office."

"Mmm." He squeezes my hip, chasing me down for a kiss. "I wish you could."

"I can. I will. Screw my job. This can work, Finn. We just need a business plan. We can do this."

He smiles and runs his hands up under my tank top, exploring, like it's his first time touching me, but also navigating my body like a map he's memorized. "You're so smart," he says. "I've got lots of business experience, but you're a natural. I just want to take pictures and for people to pay me to do it."

"You can get there," I say. "But you have to start somewhere. Working artists have to make sacrifices. Just little ones." I peck my way around his mouth. He has the most intoxicating lips—inviting, soft, full, wet.

Agreeable, even. Maybe I can kiss my way to getting a *yes*.

Because this is my venture too, and I don't see why we both shouldn't get what we want.

TWENTY-ONE

At the sound of a car engine, I walk to the dining room window and pull the drapes aside. Rich waves. He and his parents are bundled head to toe. "They're here," I say, turning away.

Dad sets his prized honey-baked ham on the table. Candles on the banquet warm the room with a glow. In a pullover and gray slacks, after a couple spiked eggnogs, Dad looks relaxed. He comes over and takes my shoulders, kissing me on the forehead. "Thank you for today. If they hadn't come all the way from Chicago, I might've canceled on the Halperns just to spend more time alone."

All day, he's been easygoing. We've come a long way. Ten years ago, around this time, in this room, we had our worst fight to date. I decided last minute not to attend my mom's funeral, but he wouldn't hear of it. I smile. "Really?"

He shrugs. "Despite the mess, and a few bad batches, baking with you was fun. The sugar cookies were . . . they tasted just like your mom's."

A lump forms in my throat. Dean Martin Christmas music plays in the background. For the second time today, I'm tempted to tell him about Finn. I'm afraid of turning the warmth cold, though. "It was a nice day," I say as the Halperns knock.

He leaves to get the door. I chose the black tulip dress I'm wearing for its pockets. I pull my phone out of one and text Finn.

They're here.

He writes back immediately.

Good luck. Just arrived in Greenwich. Call if you need anything.

I take a deep breath. The light bourbon buzz I had going fades when I hear Rich in the foyer. It's my fault he's here, but I'm not in the mood to play future daughter-in-law tonight. Rich's parents prefer denial to reality. If they sense anything off tonight, they won't mention it. I don't know whether to feel sad or happy that I'd probably be standing in this same spot living that same life if it weren't for Finn.

Finn. Naked and tangled in his buttery sheets. Eating ice cream out of a shared cup as we walk home from a show in forty-degree weather. Reading softly to him from my journal in the twenty-four-hour diner, the hairs on the back of my neck standing up because the people in the booth behind us can surely hear. I'm not the sweet, quiet girl our families want me to be. I like sex and black coffee and knowing I've made someone *feel* something. Even if they're feeling it in a plastic-covered booth.

Glasses clink from the family room. Pre-dinner cocktails. I should join them, but to put it off a little longer, I resume my project of sorting Finn's direct messages. Between yesterday being the last business day of the year for our office, and the time I spent with Dad today, I've been too busy to get through them all. I open them one by one.

You work is amazing. We've featured you on our account today.

Who do we contact to license your photography?

We're writing an article about boudoir photography. Can we mention you?

I move down to the next message, but the preview makes me stop.

Do us all a favor and

I shouldn't open it. I'm about to have a potentially stressful dinner of make-believe stories about how great Rich and I are doing. I don't need anything to upset me, especially without Finn here to comfort me.

It's a troll trying to get a reaction, Finn would say, and he'd be right. It's stupid. I lock my phone.

Laughter comes from the next room. My dad will come get me any minute.

Whether I read the message or not, I'll think about it all during dinner. Wondering if it's bad. Or legitimate. Or justified. I can't expect everyone to like what I write. Even the greats have critics.

I type in my passcode and pull up Finn's inbox again.

Do us all a favor and stop posting this CRAP, you slut.

My throat closes. *Crap. Slut.* I don't recognize the sender. But why would I? I read it again. I shouldn't have opened it. The backs of my eyes begin to ache. Obviously, she doesn't get what we're doing. She doesn't understand my poetry, not like the thousands of other people who follow our account. Why would I care what she thinks?

I hit reply to tell her that in so many words, to suggest she find someone a little less complex to follow. She's too simple for us. My fingers shake so much that I type gibberish. I backspace to start over, but I just stare at the screen.

I hear Finn's voice. *Leave it. She's not worth it. You're the expert.*

Some people will think my work is crap. It's inevitable. And why shouldn't they? I have no real experience. No degree in literature or journalism. I'm not a model. I can't really take offense to somebody pointing out the truth: in many ways, I'm a fraud.

But what happens if Finn figures that out? If he realizes my journals are nothing more than the desperate words of a teenage girl in a woman's body?

"Halston?" Rich asks from the doorway.

I swallow down the urge to cry and turn. "What?"

"George sent me to get you." He puts his hands in his trouser pockets. His chocolate-colored hair is a little longer than normal, curling around his ears. "Are you okay?" he asks.

I put my phone in my pocket. "I'm fine."

"Look . . ." Rich walks farther into the room, out of hearing distance of our parents. "For what it's worth, I didn't really want to do this, either."

"Really? It seems to me like you'd enjoy the fact that I'm obligated to play along for a whole weekend."

"Not really. It actually feels pretty shitty pretending everything's great when I know we might be over soon."

I blink away. I don't want to make him feel that way, but I also can't have any ambiguity between us. Finn's made it clear he wouldn't appreciate that. "It *is* over, Rich. I won't change my mind."

"It's hard to believe you're so certain when we were fine just a month ago."

"We weren't fine. I mean, we were, but we've never been a good match. My dad just needed someone to pawn me off on. With your upstanding family and career track, you were the guy for the job."

"I still am. Why is it bad that I'm a good boyfriend to you?"

Rich looks handsome in the yellow light. Dean Martin croons about a marshmallow world. Rich *is* attractive and won't have trouble finding a girl who's gaga for him. "I'm not looking for a handler. I want a partner."

"I can be that. Give me another chance. If not for me, then for yourself."

"What does that even mean?"

He toes nothing on the ground. Just when I think he won't respond, he says, "Look at you. I can see right now, and sometimes at work, that you're sad. You were late yesterday for the third time this month."

Finn and I had post-breakfast sex in the shower. "So?"

"So I'm worried."

"Why?"

"Obviously, because I still love you. I'm not the one who ended this." He sighs. "He's not good for you."

My dad? Well, that's a plot twist I didn't see coming. Rich has always been my dad's champion, taking his side over mine nine times out of ten. Maybe some distance has made him see if he wants me, he has to support me. At least more than a ninth of the time. "We have our issues, but I wouldn't say he's bad for me."

"No? If you ask me, that guy's trouble."

That guy?

"It concerns me whether or not you're my girlfriend. I think I have that right since we were together two years."

Rich sounds almost jealous—of my dad? There are a lot of words to describe George Fox, but trouble isn't one of them. If he's not referring to my dad, then who?

"How long have you been seeing him?" Rich asks.

Finn. Our private little world cracks open. It's too soon for Rich to know about Finn, for my dad to come in and make changes. I curl my hands into fists and take a few steps toward Rich, my pumps solid on the wood floor. "You've been spying on me?"

His eyebrows meet in the middle of his forehead. "No. If anything, it's the other way around."

"Excuse me?"

"He's the one who hunted me down. He brought me into this."

"Finn?" I ask. "How? When?"

"At the office Wednesday." Rich's expression eases. "He didn't tell you?"

What the . . .? Finn *was* at my office on Wednesday. But so was I. We were together the entire twenty minutes he was there . . . except when Finn went to the bathroom. "What'd he say to you?"

"He nearly threatened me, Halston."

"Over what?"

"To stay away. He said he was your boyfriend."

I told Finn I'd handle Rich. That was my way of saying butt out. This is the kind of thing my dad would do, talking on my behalf, trying to protect me from things that *could* or *might* happen instead of letting me handle it on my own. Finn abused my trust, at my office of all places, when he's the one who's encouraged me to take back control over my life. I try to muster the anger I should feel, but I'm just as annoyed with Rich, and he's here. "He is my boyfriend," I say.

"How can that be?" Rich asks. "We just barely split up."

This explains the roses and Finn's surprise visit to my office. He has a possessive streak. I don't know what to think about the fact that I'm not angry with him. I've proven the last few weeks—I'm not all that unhappy about being possessed by him. "When you know, you know."

"How can you know anything? You're not yourself right now."

"Maybe I am." I touch my chest. "I need to figure out who I am without my meds. You obviously can't respect that, but you don't have to."

"It's not about respect. I don't want you to do something you'll regret, to make a . . ."

"Mistake?" I finish.

Rich closes his mouth. He looks surprised by what he just said, but I'm not.

"You don't have to bite your tongue around me anymore," I say. "You can blame me. My dad does."

His face falls. "Jesus, Halston. You act like you and I are on different sides. What you can't seem to understand is that I care about you. That's why I want you to be well."

"You want me to be easy. Calm. That's what you care about."

"Is that so bad? Being stable? Not drinking too much wine or beating yourself up over what happened ten years ago or making bad decisions."

Bad decisions. Rich would think this life I'm building with Finn is bad. Posing half-nude for a man I met earlier less than a month ago and putting the pictures online—it sounds bad, but it doesn't feel that way. "You have no idea what I'm like without them. *I* don't know what I'm like without them. I've never had the chance to find out."

"Yes you did, and to be blunt, Halston, it was a shit-show. Do I have to remind you how we nearly lost a big account because of that dinner?"

I cross my arms. I'm ready to be done with this conversation. "No."

"You can be reckless, which is why someone has to look out for you. Someone who knows your past."

He runs a hand over his face. "Why do you think your dad has done all this? It's for your mom."

"I don't want to talk about this."

"Maybe it bothers you that we didn't meet some other way. Or that I'm not some bad boy who wants to help you over the edge. But I'm good for you, and I can give you a good life. That's what your dad wants, if you not himself or you, then for her . . ."

I stop listening. My dad orchestrated all this for her. Setting me up with Rich, letting me create my own position at work, handing us the reins. Maybe it was a conscious choice, maybe it wasn't, but he's trying to give me a life that would've made my mom happy. And I'm rejecting it.

On some level, I suppose I knew. I played along, because it meant we could keep sweeping things under the rug. It meant neither of us had to say what we truly believed.

If it weren't for me, she'd still be alive.

And if she were, what would she think of the choices I've been making?

Would she be proud that I'm taking back the reins? Or, like Rich, would she think I'm in the midst of another giant mistake?

TWENTY-TWO

I dash down the hall to Finn's room, squealing as champagne erupts from the bottle in my hands. "It's spilling everywhere," I cry over my shoulder.

"That's because you're running," he calls after me.

I get to his bathroom sink, holding it over the drain. "Bring the glasses."

"Got 'em." He comes in behind me and takes the bottle. Once he pours two glasses, he kisses me on the mouth. "Drink up. It's almost midnight."

"Should we have stayed at the bar?" I ask, pouting. "Are we old farts for coming home before the ball dropped?"

"I don't know about you, but I had my fill of twenty-dollar cocktails and sweaty bodies. You are, without a doubt, the only person I'd brave New Year's Eve in the city for."

"Aww." I rise to the tips of my toes for another kiss, but I sway and spill champagne down the front of my multi-colored sequined dress.

"Perfect. I've been looking for an excuse to get you out of that," Finn says, laughing. "Did you I tell you how jaw-droppingly beautiful you looked tonight?"

"You might have." I hold onto his arm for support as he lifts my dress by its hem. "I'm very sparkly."

"Yes, you are." Sequins scrape my tummy as he pulls it over my head. "And very beautiful."

"You said that already." I wrinkle my nose with a smile. "You're drunk."

"I might've had a couple tumblers of Scotch. It is a special occasion."

"New Year's."

"New Year's with you." My dress is flimsy in his hands, no more than a scrap of fabric. He takes it with him. "Bring the glasses."

In my bra, panties, and heels, I follow him to the studio with the drinks. "Are we taking a picture?"

"Yep. A New Year's post." He lays the dress on the ground, shifting it around. He points to a spot right next to it. "Heels. Take them off here. One standing, the other on its side."

I do as he says without question. He's in work mode, and his serious side turns me on. "What else?"

"Champagne flutes. Fill them up and set them on the corner of my desk." He looks back. "Actually, take a sip from one and leave a lipstick mark."

"Yes, sir." I get to work, leaving my lips on the glass before pouring the champagne so it'll be nice and bubbly for the picture. "Now what?"

"Panties."

I peel off my black lace thong, hand it over, and sit in his desk chair. He repositions the articles of clothing. I'm getting wet just watching him. On the leather. But I'm certain Finn will be more interested in my arousal than the condition of his chair.

I rest my elbow on the desk and bump the computer mouse. The screen wakes up to reveal Finn's inbox. "Is this your work e-mail?" I ask.

"Yep."

He doesn't say anything else, so I nose around a little, reading the subject lines. Since my work is his work, it should be our account anyway. "What's this one about an article?" I ask.

"That came in this afternoon. A reporter from Gotham magazine asking if he could include us in an online feature."

"Really?" I ask. "Why didn't you tell me?"

"I didn't want to get your hopes up." He looks back at me. "I responded to ask if you can remain anonymous. Otherwise we aren't interested. Read it."

I open the e-mail. Finn's right. The reporter mentions Finn's photos and my captions. A real, legitimate publication. I pitter-patter my feet on the carpet, bouncing in the chair. "I can't believe it."

"I can." He's smiling, I can tell, even though he's turned away from me.

"Did you know we have over six thousand followers now?" I ask. "The Christmas post was such a hit. How long do you think it'll take us to get to ten?"

Finn comes over to the chair and squats, aiming his iPhone at the clothing. He usually uses his camera, but I think the alcohol's made his head as fuzzy as mine since he rarely drinks. "Probably much faster than it took us to get to six."

"I looked into sponsored posts a little. That offer from Butter Boudoir was pretty high."

He checks his work, swiping through photos.

"Finn?"

"Hmm?"

"I said that offer we got—it was sort of out of the ordinary."

"The article?"

"No, the lingerie."

He frowns at me. "I thought we decided against that."

We did. Well, he did. I don't want to tell him that in my head, I've fantasized about accepting their offer, slipping into their beautiful things, playing for Finn and his camera. I just know he'd made me look good; he always does. And we'd get even more followers, both from the nature of the pictures and from Butter Boudoir themselves. Nobody's ever made me an offer like that. I've hardly ever been noticed like that, not by anyone but Finn. But I don't want to ruin our night, so I just say, "I was using them as an example. If we can get a few more thousand followers, offers like that would be standard." I bring my knees up under my chin. "I think we should try to hit ten by mid-January."

He returns to his session. "Sounds good to me."

I swivel back to the inbox. The browser refreshes and bolded e-mails from the past few hours appear. The subject line on top snags my attention.

The stockings

I move closer to the screen. Stockings? My stockings? The sender's name is Jack Guthrie. Doesn't sound familiar.

"Got it," Finn says as I'm about to click on the e-mail. "I'm just going to run it through an editing app instead of doing the whole thing. It's almost midnight."

"You should share it at midnight on the dot."

"But that's when I'm supposed to kiss you." He winks, thumbing around his screen.

"Post it, then kiss me."

"Too late." He shows me the photo, two champagne glasses in the foreground, a trail of my out-of-focus clothing behind them. It's muted, the sequins as matte as the gold fizz. My lipstick stain is a deep, sultry crimson because of the low-contrast filter. "What do you think?"

It's the first time he's ever not asked me for a caption, but when I see why, I smile. He's turned it into a joke, also a first. "From us to you," I read. "Make your New Year's extra special—the poor bastard only comes once a year."

He hands me my glass and holds out his, but before we can cheers, there's commotion in the street. People yell out the countdown. "Twenty . . . nineteen . . ."

"Shit." Finn puts down the champagne and tosses me my underwear. "Come on. We're going to miss it."

I look back at the e-mail, my fizzing drink in one hand, a ball of black lace in the other. I have fifteen seconds, which means I either open it or go to Finn. I should do the latter. But if I don't read it, I'll be wondering what it says while the ball drops, and that's no way to bring in the new year, wondering about another man. I click on it.

I can't stop looking at them. Where are they from so I can buy my girlfriend a pair.

I swallow. He's just admitted to staring at my crotch. A man named Jack is looking at me, fantasizing. And he has a girlfriend. He has a real live woman, but I'm the one he's thinking about. It seems so wrong, and yet . . .

"Halston!" Finn calls. "You're missing it."

"Ten . . . nine . . . eight . . ."

I hit reply.

Intermix on 5th & 19th

In case he thinks I'm Finn, I also sign the e-mail.

—Anonymous.

"Four . . . three . . ."

I hit send and abandon the drink and underwear to sprint into the living room. Horns blare in the street. The TV is a blur of confetti and beaming B-list celebrities with microphones. Finn turns and laughs at me in just my bra. He grabs a cream, faux fur throw we picked out together and opens it to me. "Happy New Year, babe," he says, wrapping me up and tying me off with a kiss. "So far, it's turning out to be pretty great."

I smile against his mouth. "It's only been five seconds."

"And isn't it pretty great?"

I nod. "Extremely. We forgot our drinks."

He rubs my back. "I'm good."

"I'll get mine, then." I pull out of his embrace and return to the studio. Before I even reach the computer, I see the subject line bolded at the top. It's 12:01 and Jack already responded.

I lean over the chair and open his reply.

Are you wearing them now?

My face flushes. I don't know if I should respond—or how. I test out responses in my head.

No, you pervert.

No, my boyfriend already took them off.

No, I'm naked under here.

"What's that?" Finn asks from behind me.

My heart jumps into my throat. Fuck. Now I look guilty. I stand up straight. "Some guy e-mailed you asking about the photo of me in the stockings. I replied to be nice, but . . . his answer was . . ."

Finn hugs me from behind and reads over my shoulder. He chuckles. "Pervert."

"Exactly my thought."

"Can I blame him? Nobody likes those tights as much as I do." Finn nibbles my ear. "Fuck, this blanket is soft. I just want to rub my dick on it."

I smile. "What's stopping you?"

"Good point." He keeps one arm around me while presumably removing his underwear. Next thing I feel is his length through the throw as he slides up and down the crack of my ass.

"Please don't ruin it, though," I add.

He clears some of my hair from my shoulder and kisses my neck. "I wouldn't waste a good load on a blanket."

My stomach clenches remembering how Finn came all over my backside. It was a first for me, and a power play that I surprisingly loved. He's done it once more on my stomach. "For a man who wouldn't get within five feet of me without a condom on, you've really come around to not using one."

"Because I love to feel you," he whispers in my ear. "Reminds me that you're mine."

Goosebumps rise over my skin. I have nowhere to look but at the computer, so I notice right away when a small box pops up in the corner of the screen.

Jack has invited you to chat

"Huh."

"What?" Finn asks.

"Look. That guy wants to talk to me."

"Wonder what he could possibly want to say."

So do I. Maybe he's going to ask about another picture. I wiggle an arm free and bend forward to accept his invitation.

Jack: If I promise not to ruin them, will you leave them on?

"I was being facetious," Finn says. He stops touching me. "What's he talking about?"

"The stockings."

"Oh. Yeah."

I get the chills. A total stranger wants to fuck me. Right? Why else would he send a message like that? I realize that in all likelihood, there might be several strangers who feel that way.

Finn runs his hand down my front, parts the blanket, and feels me. "You're wet."

"I am?"

"Your face is red."

"I'm sorry."

"Why? You're turned on by this?"

Am I? It's not the worst feeling to be wanted by men, even if they might be creeps. I'm not used to that kind of attention, at least not more than the average girl gets. "I guess I kind of am."

"Hmm." He runs a finger along my slit but doesn't enter me. "Do you want to respond?"

I bite my bottom lip. "Can I?"

He hesitates. "What makes you think I'd let you? You know I'm not keen on sharing."

"It isn't really sharing," I point out. "You're here. You're in charge. He's not."

He inhales sharply in my ear, teasing my entrance with his finger. "I like the sound of that. Go ahead, if you're comfortable with it."

I swallow. I don't know what to say to Jack's question. Finn pulls the blanket from my shoulders so my hands are free. I lean toward the computer and re-read his message.

Jack: If I promise not to ruin them, will you leave them on?

Me: No. They were expensive. You might tear them.

I hit send a get a rush of adrenaline. I never tell Finn no. I don't want to. But Jack isn't Finn. Jack has zero power over me.

Jack: Then I'll take them off. Slowly.

Jack: I'll start with your right leg, peel them from thigh to ankle. What color are your toenails?

Finn pulls out the leather desk chair and sits down. Just as I think he's about to shut this down, he pats the seat. "Come."

I sit between his legs. With his hands resting on my thighs, he sticks his chin on my shoulder. "Tell him."

Me: Red.

Jack: You're my dream girl.

Jack: Sorry if that's too romantic. I'm a writer too. Like you.

The air around us gets tense. His comment is personal, as if he knows me. I guess, in a way, he does. He's read my innermost thoughts without ever having met me . . . just like Finn did. The clock in the top corner of the computer changes to 12:08 A.M.

"What should I say?" I ask.

Finn rubs my leg. "Tell him he can't have you."

Me: I have a boyfriend.

Jack: Of course you do. I won't try to romance you, then.

A nugget of disappointment forms in my stomach. I wanted to see where this would go. I never did things like this in my past life. It's exciting, dangerous, but since Finn is here, it's also safe. To my relief, the computer dings again.

Jack: Let's not stop at the stockings. I want to see all of you. Take off your dress.

I wait for Finn to stop me. I don't want him too, but I don't want to make him mad.

"It's off," Finn whispers in my ear, making me shiver.

Me: It's off.
Jack: Now everything else.

Finn gathers my hair in a loose ponytail and hangs it over my shoulder. He opens the clasp of my bra and gently drags the straps over my shoulders. I'm so wet already, I feel it on the leather underneath me. And it's not just me. Finn is rigid against me, and I swear I feel his moisture on my back.

Jack: Are you naked?
Me: Yes.
Jack: Good girl. Since I don't have to worry about the stockings, I don't need to be careful with you. Do I?

Finn reaches around me to respond.

Me: No.

A few seconds go by without a response. Finn runs his big, impatient hands down my arms to my wrists, then up my knees, along the insides of my thighs. My heart beats so hard, I feel it at the base of my neck.

Jack: Here's what I'd do if I were there. I'd make you spread your legs open so I could see how wet you are. Do you need a little help getting wet?

Me: Yes.

Jack: My pleasure. How many fingers do you want?

"Sick fuck," Finn breathes onto my neck. But he parts my thighs as far as they'll go, which isn't much since he's boxing me in, and slides two fingers inside me. I drop my head back on his shoulder. "More."

Finn shows me his glistening hand. "One or two?"

Four fingers scares the crap out of me. "One."

Finn types for me.

Me: Three.

He resumes fingering me, stretching me with more of his hand than I'm used to.

Jack: Three is a good warm up. I'm pretty big. Maybe too big.

Me: I can handle it.

Me: My boyfriend is huge.

Jack: Bigger than seven?

Finn grunts and pulls one of my feet onto the chair. He finger-fucks me a little harder. "Yes."

Me: Bigger.

Jack: Then I don't need to be gentle. I'll finger you almost as hard as I'll fuck you. Until you're close.

I can't respond. I hold onto the arm of the chair with one hand, gripping Finn's wrist with the other. I'm not sure if I'm trying to slow him down or keep him there. He feels so good. Too good.

I let go of Finn to type with one hand. I'm shaky, so it takes me a couple tries.

Me: Kiss

Me: me.

I turn my head and Finn latches his mouth on mine, swallowing my moans as I approach the edge. When I begin to contract around him, Finn pulls out. "Not yet."

"But—"

"Shh." He soothes me, petting my hair. "Tell him you're coming."

Me: I'm going to come.

Jack: Don't.

Me: Why not?

Jack: I'm not touching you anymore. I'm taking off my pants. Bend over and show me your pussy.

Finn lifts me up by my waist. "Stand."

I get up, and Finn thumbs my ass cheeks apart, working his fingertips down to open my folds. "It's beautiful," he says.

I'm at an awkward angle, but I type.

Me: beautiful, isn't it?

Jack: The most. I can't restrain myself any longer. I'm ready to feel you.

"Come back here," Finn says.

I sit on his lap. With his palm on my upper back, he pushes me down until my chest rests on the keyboard. He enters me from behind, a new angle for us. My face is practically pressed up against the computer screen. Finn yanks my hips down, filling me all at once, and I cry out before he slams into me again.

Jack: How does it feel?

Finn pulls my arms behind me, grabs my biceps, and thrusts up into me. My tits bounce against the keyboard.

Me: dfioweh9834h3ibvdlap

Jack: You feel so good. God, you're tight. I'm a little too big for you, but we'll make it work. I'm sorry if it's too fast. I've just been thinking about this so long.

I come. Jack's words. Finn's huge cock. The most forbidden sex I've ever had. My eyes cross as my body sucks Finn deeper.

Jack: Tell me before you come.

Finn shoves the computer screen away so it's facing a wall. He stands, sliding me forward. The keyboard clatters at our feet. He puts his hands on both sides of me, trapping me on the desk while he nails me to it, so long and so hard, he has time to work my clit and bring me to climax again.

My skin burns hot, my pussy slickens, accepting all of him with each plunge. We're connected on so many levels, Finn and me. We have been since the start, but our bond just gets deeper, stronger. "Come inside me," I say.

"I—"

"Please."

He slams me with three punishing thrusts. "Turn around. Quick."

It's just like Finn to want to look me in the eye the first time he does this. I turn and sit on the desk, spreading my legs.

"Give me your mouth."

It takes me a second to realize what he's asking. I've gotten to know his tells over the past month, and I know he's about to explode. Unsure of what else to do, I get on my knees.

He holds my chin. "Open."

I take him in my mouth. He pushes to the back of my throat a few times, cramming my mouth until I gag. "I'm gonna come. Where?"

I look up at him. I guess my options are anywhere but where I asked. I want to be claimed once and for all, owned, but it won't happen tonight. I nod as best as I can, and that's all it takes. He grips my hair, groans up at the ceiling, and spills into my mouth.

TWENTY-THREE

When Finn calls my name, it echoes through the nearly empty museum. I blink out of my daze, and just like that, I've lost a staring contest I didn't know I was having—against an Indian rhinoceros.

Finn is a few taxidermied species ahead, but he comes back to get me. "Are you sure you're feeling all right?" He presses the back of his hand to my cheek. "You seem out of it."

I lean into his touch. "I'm fine."

"You can tell me if you're bored."

"I'm not." Well, not *that* bored. "Just a slow reader."

He brightens. "I'm glad you're interested."

Finn's been giving me a tour of the American Museum of Natural History for the past hour. He couldn't believe I grew up outside the city and still had never been. He brought Marissa for the *third* time last weekend while I moped at my apartment for two days, but he still seems fascinated by every stop.

He takes my hand and leads me to the next diorama, making a point to stop in front of the plaque. All right, so I wasn't reading about rhinos. I was thinking about the article for Gotham's digital magazine again, but I don't want Finn to know that. We already toasted each other, went to dinner, and discussed it at length, so there's nothing really left to say.

Except . . . I can't get one particular detail out of my head.

What do I have to celebrate, when nobody knows who I am?

It came out nine days ago, the middle of January, Friday the thirteenth of all days. Finn was lauded as an up-and-comer in innovative, modern boudoir photography. The kind of *evocative* art you'd hang in your entryway rather than hide away in the master bathroom. *Provocative* images of Finn's *seductive* model to stimulate your guests. And Finn, my love, my rock—he credited his model as his muse—not for her body, but for her words. He was very clear about that. Nobody who read the article would doubt I had as much to do with his success as he did.

Anonymous.

There are theories. Celebrities, socialites, and professional models have been named as Anonymous. Boyfriends tag girlfriends in the photos, teasingly accusing them of keeping secrets. People care who I am, but they *know* who Finn is. He's begun getting inquiries about commissions. Where does that leave me? It's not as if I can come along.

We blew past ten thousand followers before my target date.

Finn has been leading me around, and suddenly I realize we're in the Hall of North American Birds. A dead, stuffed falcon is mid-flight. Inside a glass case, ten, fifteen owls watch me walk by. My scalp prickles. I wore an Angora sweater because Finn likes how soft it is, but the museum's heat is on and now I just feel suffocated. While Finn's back is turned, I check my phone. A notification alerts me to a message from Butter Boudoir. Again? This'll be the third message from them to go unanswered. I want to check it, but just two days ago, Finn told me I spend too much time on my phone when we're together. I'm trying to be more conscious about it.

Last week, we accepted two-hundred-fifty dollars from a jewelry company who'd read about us online. I wore a thin, silver bracelet for one shot. They had more followers than us, but they were looking to target a more niche audience. I'd suggested Finn and I use the money to splurge on a nice dinner, but he wanted to put it in the bank. After the conversation I'd overheard with Marissa, I didn't try to talk him out of it. Instead, I made him a special meal at the apartment. It ended with lovemaking that involved an oven mitt, spatula, and a creative use of linguine.

At the elevator, Finn turns to me. "The dinosaurs are on the fourth floor. Want to see or have you hit your limit?"

It's my stomach that answers him. Saved by the grumble. "I think my limit's hit."

He slings an arm around my shoulders. "Let's get you fed."

We return to the main entrance to retrieve our things from the coat check. While Finn uses the restroom, I step outside. I put on my *fingerless* gloves, which I bought specifically for occasions like this, where it's freezing outside but I want to use my phone. Since I have a couple minutes to myself, I check our inbox.

Mr. Cohen,

Congratulations on seventeen thousand followers. I'm sorry we haven't heard back from you yet. I know sometimes communication gets lost in the shuffle. Consider this our last and best offer.

Valentine's Day is around the corner, and we're making a huge push to reach new customers. We'd love to gift you some pieces from our V-Day collection as well as $5,000 to feature them in a 10-photo series. Again, we're big fans of your work, and our appreciation has grown even more the last few weeks as the posts just get better. I'm sure twenty thousand followers is just around the corner.

Thank you for your consideration,

Kelly

"I know a burger place nearby," Finn says behind me.

I turn and nearly knock him down. I open my mouth to tell him.

Five.

Thousand.

Dollars.

I can't even get the number out, as if saying it aloud will make it disappear. This is a sign. We can't turn this down. "You—I . . . we—"

"What's wrong?" He rubs my upper arms. "Christ, Halston. Are you shaking? Maybe we should get you home—"

"Five grand," I say. "That's what the lingerie company wants give us."

"What lingerie co—" He glances from my face to the phone in my hands. "You're still talking to them?"

"No. I never responded to their last message. But they just wrote and upped their offer because of a Valentine's Day campaign."

He squints behind me. "We already decided against this."

We didn't, but I'm trying to convince him, not anger him, so I keep that to myself. "We decided against a grand. This is *five times* that. I think that merits re-opening the discussion."

"I admit, it's tempting," he says, "but it isn't worth it."

"Why not?"

"Because it's not what we do. You're my girlfriend." He drops his gaze to mine again. "I'm supposed to protect you, not put you on display for a little extra cash."

"A *little* extra cash? This would cover your rent for two months."

He tilts his head and stops trying to warm me. "Why are you worried about my rent?"

"Because you're *not*." As soon as I say the words, I wish I could take them back. This is an area of our relationship we haven't yet broached. We didn't talk about money in my household. My dad still pays my rent. Rich came from wealth. I'm finding that I don't like feeling so uncertain about the future, but since it's Finn's problem, shouldn't he have been the one to bring it up?

He stares at me, his breath fogging in front of his face. "You're worried?" he asks. "About my finances?"

"Well, no. But . . ." I shift on my feet. Two joggers weave through the crowd. A blue jay hops along a bare tree branch, and I'm beyond grateful for a real, living bird. Absentmindedly, I touch my feather. "I mean, you only work two or three jobs a month, but you live in a two-bed apartment in a very expensive neighborhood." I look back at him. "How long can you keep that up?"

"You and I haven't discussed money," he says slowly. "You don't know the first thing about my bank account."

"I heard you talking to your daughter that morning after I spent the night." A chill runs down my spine, and I blow hot air into my mittens. "It wasn't on purpose, I just overheard. She said you were broke."

"Well, if an eight-year-old says it, it must be true."

"Is it?"

"I made serious Wall Street money up until last year. I managed to save a good chunk of it. And I trade stock on the side. You didn't know that, did you?"

"How would I?" I ask. "You never tell me anything about that part of your life. I know nothing about your finances or your ex-wife or even Marissa."

"And *you* won't tell your dad you've broken things off with Rich. You promised you would after the holidays, and it's January twenty-second."

My face warms. He's right. I don't talk about work or my dad with him anymore. I don't want Finn asking about Rich. Every time I work up the courage to tell my dad the truth, I lose my nerve. He'll accuse me of making bad decisions without the drugs. I just want to be stable, happy, and sorted with Finn so I can show my dad that I'm able to do it on my own.

"One fight at a time, okay?" Finn crosses his arms. "No, I'm not broke. I'm good with money, but I am moving through my savings faster than I'd like. I've stashed some in my retirement accounts, but I don't really want to touch those."

"Then let's do this." I pull on his forearm, trying to get him to uncross his arms. He doesn't budge. "It's a lot of money. And it fits our brand—"

"No."

Why *wouldn't* we say yes? We get to do what we're already doing, but better, and for money. Not only can I earn us more of an audience, which in turn commands us a higher price tag, but I can also take some of the financial pressure off Finn's shoulders. All with a few risqué shots. "The pieces are tasteful, Finn. They're sexy lace and sheer—"

"*Sheer?*"

"But in a tasteful way—"

"No." He steps back. "I said no, end of discussion. I'm not going to share you."

"You mean again," I say. "You aren't going to share me *again*."

"What the hell does that mean?"

"We had online sex with a stranger," I say. Some people look over, so I lower my voice. "I've used the word *fuck* in our captions, and you've been inside me during a photo shoot. Sex is our brand whether you like it or not."

"That doesn't mean I'm going to pimp out my girlfriend—"

"I'm not your girlfriend right now. I'm your business partner."

"Not in this case," he says. "You come before business. Our relationship comes before business."

"But you're not 'pimping me out.' I *want* to do this."

"Why?" he asks.

"Because it makes me feel good," I yell. "It makes me feel *wanted*."

"It's not enough that *I* want you? You need to know creepy men are looking at you in sheer underwear? Why does talking to a stranger online, or people looking through our windows, get you off?"

My lungs empty like I've been sucker punched. Finn's never made me feel anything other than confident, smart, desired. Until now. Throwing all that in my face as if he wasn't there every step of the way. "Are you saying none of that turned you on?"

"Exposing my girlfriend to other men? No, it doesn't. On New Year's, it was fun, and kinky, and I was drunk. A one-time thing, not a recurring show. You're *my* girl. At least with your journals, I'm the only one getting access to you, no matter how sexy or sweet or weird your entries might be—"

Of course. I thought I was safe with him, but maybe that was a dangerous assumption. Maybe Finn's finally beginning to see the truth. My journals aren't sexy or provocative. They're just weird. *I'm* weird. "Why don't you just come out and say what you really mean?" I ask. "You think I'm a freak."

He looks taken aback. "I didn't say that. This behavior does alarm me a little, but—"

I take a step back, stunned when my dad's face flashes through my mind as he tells me the exact same thing when I was fifteen. And then all the ways I've failed to cope. Now it's Finn telling me I can't make decisions about my own body, that I can't earn money how I want. "Excuse me for wanting something for myself."

I can't do this. I can't be with someone who thinks I'm strange, especially Finn, because Finn has seen the deepest, darkest corners of my mind. And if he thinks that about me, then it must be true. I turn and head for—I don't know where. Not here. The opposite direction of his place.

"Halston." Finn chases me down and grabs my arm. "Wait. That came out wrong."

I whirl around. This is why I hide. I'd rather have people judge my façade than my true self. In this moment, I can't remember why I thought it was a good idea to stop my treatment. At least then, I could blame anything on the pills, even on my mom's death. But without that crutch, I'm just me. "You're the one who pushed me to put myself out there. You said I was good enough."

His mouth falls open. "I never *pushed* you, and you *are*—"

"Don't." He made me feel safe, confident. "Don't touch me. Don't follow me." I grit my teeth against a wave of tears. I walk off so fast, I'm nearly trotting. When I'm a few blocks away, and I'm certain he isn't behind me, I lean my shoulder against a brick wall and catch my breath. I'm not going anywhere. I have nobody to run to. Finn is that someone. He's the first someone to care about the real me. The first to *see* me.

I fell in love with him for that.

I should've stopped to think how much it would hurt if he didn't like what he saw.

TWENTY-FOUR

finn

The sun is setting.

I'm likely to crack the kitchen table if I keep slamming my phone down. I wish Halston would answer my texts. She can be mad as long as I know where she is. I almost followed her, but that's what her dad or Rich might've done, and I think I may have treated her that way outside the museum, causing her to take off.

I'm not entirely sure.

I have to be more careful with my words. Her sensitivity spoke to me in those journals, and it's one of the things I love about her. It also means if I hurt her, intentionally or not, the pain starts and ends in her heart.

Although she left in the first place and hasn't returned, I know she'll come back. This isn't over. With Sadie, I often worried our affair could end any moment, as if I were always waiting to have the rug ripped out from under me. Halston, though, feels permanent. I'm a different man than I was when I met her only a couple months ago. I still believe fate brought us together, but I no longer want to leave my relationship in its hands. I want to put it in the work, the time, the effort to keep it healthy. And, I want to be a better photographer. Not just in terms of composition. I have to prove to Hals that I can do this, earn money at it, and support us. No more leaving it up to destiny.

So, I'd better wrap my head around the fucking lingerie. If I'd known when we started this I'd have to share my sweet, sensitive girl with so many people, I might not've suggested it. But here we are. She's happy—truly happy. Her work has been validated by thousands of people. Even if she lets the negative reactions bother her, ninety-nine percent of the response is praise. How can they be wrong?

I'm in charge of the camera. I can make this lingerie thing work, and I will, with her.

I posted an image, a call for her to come home, a signal that Butter Boudoir isn't off the table. I'd planned on keeping the photo for myself. The outer curve of her bare breast is visible and even that feels intimate. But I want her to know I'm willing to try. She was right to remind me this is a partnership. I can't control her, and if I try, I'll be no better than Rich or her dad.

The passage I chose is one of her longest—and it's inspiring more comments than usual, people tagging lost loves or commiserating friends. People lonely on a wintry Sunday afternoon.

You said
When you leave, turn out the lights
Lock the door behind you
Close the gate
How can you not see
When you're gone, there are no lights
The door won't shut
The gate is a cage.
I miss you.

That was three hours ago. I've watched my account like it's a ticking time bomb, deleting any comment or message she might take the wrong way. The last thing I want is for her to see something that might wiggle its way into her head and convince her she's not good enough. If she feels she has nowhere to turn without me, she might fall into a black hole.

A knock on the front door makes me sit up. I gave Halston a key, so my mind jumps to the worst case scenarios: she sent someone for her things; she called Rich to confront me; she's hurt, and the police are here. Holding my breath, I cross the apartment quickly and look through the peephole. Halston sags on the doorstep, weighed down by a backpack I don't recognize.

I yank open the door. She falls into my arms. "Oh, Hals," I murmur, gathering her close. Her nose and cheek ice right through my shirt. "You're freezing, babe. You should've come home. You could've been mad here where it's warm."

She looks up at me with red-rimmed eyes. "Home?"

"You know you belong here with me. Don't you?" For a moment, I'm afraid she doesn't know that, even after I've done my best to make her feel safe here. It's the same feeling I had when my mom would go to her cabinet in the afternoons.

To my relief, she nods. "I forgot my keys."

I bring her inside and sit her at the kitchen table where I just agonized for hours. "What do you want? Coffee, tea, hot chocolate?"

"I want you. I don't care about anything else, not even what we've built." Her eyes water. "You were right. Our relationship is more important."

She looks defeated. That isn't what I want. She shouldn't have to give in just to keep me. That's probably what Rich expected from her. I lean back against the counter. "I've given it some more thought."

"Wait. Before you continue." She puts the backpack on the table and unzips the top. "These are for you."

She pulls out three thick journals in varying shades of brown leather.

"Halston." My chest tightens with anticipation. "Are those . . . full?"

"I didn't bring them all. I started when I was fifteen, in counseling." She picks one up. "This was the first one. It's flowery and juvenile. Hormone central. So, it sucks."

"Can I read it?"

She swaps it for a bigger one. "This one's emotional. Angry, not sexy. It's from when I moved out of the denial stage. Each book has a personality."

"What's that one?" I ask of the third journal.

She looks at me from under her lashes. "It's . . . darker. When the guilt over my mom gets too much, I write in here. It's more explicit than what you've read so far. There isn't much in here, because it's not a place I go very often."

Like a conditioned response, I salivate. My greedy hands tingle. I've devoured what I have, and getting more feels like a gift. "Did you bring them for me to read or just to torture me?"

She takes a breath as if steeling herself. "You can read them. I want you to. This is what I hide from others, but I don't want to hide from you. If it's too weird for you—"

"It won't be."

"You don't know that. If the dark corners of my mind freak you out, I have to know now."

"I mean, what are we talking here? Sex with animals? Incest?"

Her mouth falls open. "*Finn.* God."

I can't help laughing at her reaction. "Well, you're making it sound dire."

She stacks the books on top of each other. "They're just words. Fantasies. It doesn't mean I want all of this, but sometimes it just bubbles up."

"Just because I take photos of a park bench doesn't mean I want to fuck it."

She blushes, looking down. "Before I met you, I would've burned these before I let anyone see them."

"Why, Halston? Don't you understand everyone has fantasies? Everyone has at least one dirty, dark thing they want that they won't even admit to themselves?"

"Yes," she says. "Why do I have to be one of those who admits it, though? And then shares it? Broadcasting it is like stripping in public and asking people to evaluate me."

I did the right thing deleting those comments. I decide here and now to do it with every post so she never questions herself like this again. She's come so far since we met. "I know opening up isn't easy, but you might find it to be a good thing."

She picks up the "flowery" journal. "When I was younger, I got so excited about stuff. I wanted everyone to experience my favorite books, movies, plays the way I did. People made fun of me."

I rub my jaw. This isn't something I can relate to as a man, except that I have a daughter turning nine. Already, I've noticed her feigning disinterest in "uncool" hobbies, like the sticker collection we've been working on since she was four. It reminds me of the eight-year age gap between Halston and me. "Then you should be even more proud of yourself."

"Sometimes I just wonder if being myself is worth the price tag."

Her honesty is brave. I wish she could see that. It's taken a toll on her—the things she said earlier, the way she ran off instead of talking to me, this deep-rooted fear of being abnormal that's stuck with her so long. I'd be lying if I said it didn't concern me, especially with how quickly she weaned herself off her meds. I've bitten my tongue about it, opting instead to monitor her behavior for warning signs that she's not handling it well. Nothing up until today has really worried me. But are there things going on in her head that even I don't see?

I clear my throat. "Have you thought about talking to someone about that stuff from your past?"

"I spent ten years talking to someone about it."

"Not your mom. The other stuff."

"We talked about all of it." She frowns. "Why? You think I need to go back into therapy?"

"No," I say quickly. She's already wary of people telling her what to do after enduring a decade of it with Rich and her dad; it's why I haven't brought this up before. "I just meant you can always talk to me about any of that if you want. No judgment."

She nods distantly and after a few seconds, says, "Maybe I do need to go back. I'm sorry about earlier. I think . . . this isn't easy for me to say, but my moods are a little more extreme now. I don't know if it's still withdrawals or just . . . who I am."

"Withdrawals?" I ask. "You haven't mentioned any before."

She lifts a shoulder. "I've had a few headaches. Nausea."

"Why didn't you tell me?"

"It's nothing major compared to some of the horror stories I've heard."

I want to take her in my arms again, soothe it all away. It doesn't feel like the right moment for touching, though, not while she's working through her feelings. "I still want to know," I say. "Will you tell me when it happens?"

She nods. "This afternoon, I overreacted."

"So did I. I just wish you hadn't run off like that."

"I understand. I'm going to leave these with you." She shows me the journal. "We can talk tomorrow, or whenever you get to them—"

"Whoa, whoa, whoa." I push off the counter. "Nah-uh. You're not going anywhere."

"I can't deal with watching you read them. If you hate them, if you find the behavior 'alarming'—"

"I shouldn't have said that."

Eyes down, she raises her palms. "It's fine. I just need to know now, before I get any deeper with you."

"I don't think you understand just how deep this goes for me. I'm at the fucking bottom here. So don't try and convince me of what I want."

She looks at me finally, small and lonely in her chair, swallowed up by her puffy coat and scarf. She's still wearing her mittens for God's sake, like she's about to make a quick exit.

I pull a chair in front of her and start removing her gloves. "I mean, incestuous fantasies would be an adjustment for me, but it's not enough to scare me off."

She smiles. Her fingertips are cold, so I bring them to my mouth, blowing hot air on them. "If you'll agree to let me control the photo shoot, then my answer is yes."

Her eyebrows meet in the middle of her forehead. She glances at the journals. "Don't you want to read them first?"

"You don't have to hide from me." I don't have to think too hard to figure out what's in the journal. She mentioned her guilt. From the start, Halston has responded to dominance in the bedroom. I'm sure whatever she's ashamed of involves some kind of punishment for her past. I've never been into BDSM, but I'm sure as hell not about to walk away from the possibility of exploring it with her. "I'll never think you're strange for what turns you on." I squeeze her hands in mine. "It's human nature."

"Thank you," she says softly. "I'm sorry we fought."

"I wasn't hearing you. When you brought up money, it got to me because you're right." It's my turn to look away. It's not about the money. I hate that it's been a year, and I still haven't booked any solid, non-commercial work or sold anything off my website. I meet her eyes again. "I want you to know, I'm still doing fine. But I can't live like this forever. I need more money to come in."

"It's not my place to say," she says. "I don't know anything about money. My dad gives it to me when I need it. He pays my rent and most of my bills. I have a 401k and a brokerage account, but his people manage it."

Having been one of the Wall Street guys her dad would hire, I don't like the idea of that. It's just another way to control her. "Get your bank information from your dad," I tell her. "You shouldn't put that in someone else's hands."

"I wouldn't even know where to start."

"I'll teach you everything you need to know about your finances. We'll go through it together. And about Rich . . ." I inhale a breath. On this, I don't want to budge. But when she was out there, being pissed, I promised myself I would try harder to be more understanding. "Tell your dad when you're ready. As long as you and I and Rich know the arrangement, I can live with it a *little* longer."

She smiles. "You're so good at taking care of me."

Fuck fuck fuck. My chest aches. Nobody ever said that to me, not my mom, definitely not Kendra. I'm not even sure Marissa will think of me as a good dad once Kendra's through with her. Halston's hands are nice and warm in mine now. I kiss the place where her palms meet. "We'll do the photo shoot. I need to have final say, though."

"You will."

"There's a right way to do this, I knew there was, I just didn't even want to entertain the idea. I've tried so hard to separate money and art. I don't like them to overlap, because it feels cheap. And the thought of putting you out there like that for other men to look at worries me, but that goes without saying."

"I promise, Finn, nobody gets me but you. I'm yours to share with the world, not the other way around."

"I'm not sharing you. You're mine, and that won't change." I unwrap her scarf from her neck, and her hair frizzes with static. I smooth it down. "I would've gone to look for you, but I didn't know where to start. I don't even know exactly which block your apartment's on."

"I wasn't there long. It doesn't feel like home. I got the journals, then walked around until I ended up here."

"You should give up that apartment." As soon as I say it, I know it's right. I want our lives merged for real. This will be the first step toward showing everyone—exes, parents, children—this is real. "If we fight, if we piss each other off, I want you to come back here. Always. No matter how bad it is. Even if it means I'm banned to the couch."

She doesn't hesitate. "My lease is up in March."

"Do you think it's too soon for us to move in together?"

She answers with a small, goading smile. "Totally."

"March it is, then?"

She stands and floats onto my lap, into my arms, her laugh soft and angelic. "I got your message."

"Which one? I sent like eight."

She kisses my cheek. "You know which one."

I whisper her own words into her ear. "When you're gone, there is no light."

TWENTY-FIVE

I can admit when I'm wrong.

At my desk in the studio, I browse the twenty images I've just edited, chosen from more than a hundred taken yesterday. I may be biased, but my girlfriend wears lingerie like no fucking other.

In one of my favorites, Halston stretches in a doorway, her arms over her head, fingers resting on the doorframe. Her head is turned to the side. A curtain of white-blonde curls covers her face, stopping right above her breasts. The sheer, black leotard—or *bodysuit*, as I was told—has a faint lace design that conceals her nipples and a neckline that dips to her belly button.

I was nothing but professional. I spent the entire session with a hard-on and didn't even touch her.

Halston comes into the studio in head-to-toe sweats, the same pink color of the Mont Blanc I bought her, spooning yogurt into her mouth. She sits on my knee. "They're beautiful, Finn."

I have no better word to describe her. "Yeah."

The black lace is stark against her white skin and colorless hair. The pieces curve smoothly with her hips and breasts. Her nipples point through a nude silk negligee. Her tummy is flat in a baby pink bustier with black garters that connect to matching thigh-highs.

"I'll be honest, some of the stuff they sent looked pretty unattractive in the box, but fuck. Who knew bodysuits could be sexy?"

"I did. That's why I wanted to do this."

I laugh. "Fair enough. Did you also know Butter was sending thongs? They would've shown your entire ass."

She holds out her spoon. "Have some yogurt."

I loop an arm around her waist and pull her deeper into my lap. "Will they let you keep them, even though we didn't shoot them?"

"You can't have it both ways," she says.

I slip a finger into the waistband of her sweats and slide it down her crack. "Can't I?"

She freezes. I don't blame her. We've discussed each journal she laid out on the table last week except the "dark" one. I'm in no rush to get through them, but I'm only human. I've had my nose stuck in one any time she's not around. She probably thinks I have a problem, since my erection's going strong each night she gets home from work.

I give her ass cheek a squeeze and change the subject. "I need to share one of these today. Valentine's is ten days away and we promised ten posts."

"Bodysuit," she says. "Men looking for gifts will need a few days to get used to it."

I slide a pen and notepad in front of her. "Write the caption while I upload the photo to my phone."

"You think I can just snap my fingers and come up with something?" she asks.

"Kind of. You're a pro like that."

"No, I'm not." She pushes the notepad away and tries to get up. "Actually, I'm *really* not, like not at all."

I keep her in my lap. The tautness of her muscles tells me something's wrong, and I can take a pretty good guess what it is. She must've read a comment or message she shouldn't have, which means she's checking our posts faster than I'm able to catch the bad stuff. There's rarely anything negative, but I never know when it'll come. I have to be more vigilant. "What happened?" I ask.

She sets her yogurt on the desk and looks out the window with a sigh. "I don't know. It's not coming as easily as it did."

I tilt my head, trying to see her expression. Maybe this isn't about our photos. "What isn't?

"The words. I used to be able to sit down and let it flow. Even when it was a couple words or lines, writing something down cut the tension in my body like scissors to string."

"And now?"

"Nothing. The blank page stares at me. I can practically hear it laughing."

"But . . ." I put my hand on her shoulder. "We've been doing this for months and you haven't mentioned this."

She shifts toward me. "Because you've gotten almost everything from my journal. What happens when we've used all the passages?"

Now that I think about it, she's right. I almost always turn to her journal, and the few times I've asked her for a caption, it's taken her days to get something to me. "We won't run out," I assure her. "There are hundreds. Plus," I slide my hand inside her sweatshirt, "now I've got even more to work with. I know I haven't mentioned it yet, but I've been reading the other journal."

She shudders but pushes my hand out of her top. "I'm serious, Finn. What if I'm all dried up?"

"You're not, believe me. It's probably just . . ."

She rubs the inside of her elbow. There's a dry patch of skin she absentmindedly scratches when she gets nervous. "What?"

I cover her hand with mine, lacing our fingers together. She got self-conscious about the itching when I brought it up, so I've figured out other ways to help. "Well, things are good between us. You're happy, so maybe it's a little harder to create."

She considers this a few seconds before nodding at the images on the screen. "But you can create. Does that mean you aren't happy?"

"No. It just means I work differently than you. Look, don't worry about the caption. I'll go find one."

"Aren't you getting tired of having to look through my stuff for each photo?"

If I could only put into words how not tired I am. How I could page through her thoughts for hours on end, envisioning how she was before me, then us together, then our future. When I think of her words, I feel as though I could photograph her for weeks and not run out of ideas. Briefly, I wonder if the opposite is true for her. Does *my* work not inspire *her*? Not even a little? I kiss the side of her head. "I'll never grow tired of it."

I get up, and she takes my place at the computer. I find her journals in the kitchen next to yesterday's mail. On the top of the pile is a check from Butter Boudoir. Five grand. Everything I told Halston is true—I don't have to worry about money just yet, but half this payment will cover almost a month of rent, and I earned it doing something I love.

I glance over my shoulder and open the journal she described as explicit. From what I've read, it's mostly what I suspected. There are entries about the sting of a hand on her ass, being bound and helpless to her lover's whims, and even some that walk the line of force. I hadn't expected the anal, though.

Face down, you won't see my shame,
But you'll know with each tight forbidden thrust
By the blush that spreads
Down my spine.

I have to look up at the ceiling a moment to ramp down my arousal. I'm going to whittle her down to nothing if I don't stop fucking her at every turn. I don't have to ask if she's ever tried anal. The tense of her body any time I'm in the area tells me she's not sure she wants it. It's not the only thing in the journal that caught me off guard, though. I flip to the middle, to a passage about several hands and mouths on her at once. I had to read it a few times to process it.

Just tonight, tomorrow we'll go on, but just tonight, I'll be all-loved by lovers all

If I had any question about what I was reading, one line in particular spelled it out for me.

Fucked from both ends, I'm your willing doll.

I hadn't known what to think. Still don't. I got fucking hard, I'm a man after all, but the idea of someone else touching my girlfriend also made my blood boil. She said she didn't necessarily want everything she wrote about in the journal, but I'm not sure how to clarify without upsetting her. If she thinks I'm weirded out by it, she might react again.

I put it away—I'm not able to go there now—and return to my tried and true journal. I can find what I need in here. I pick an entry that describes waiting for her man to come home that'll work for the bodysuit image.

Her phone lights up on the counter, so I take it and the journal back into the studio. "Found what I need in practically no time at all," I say. "I told you it'd be—" Two steps into the room, I stop. Halston's head is blocking most of my view of the picture on the computer screen, but I'd know those tits anywhere. The fan of black hair on the cushion of Kendra's hideous, deceivingly uncomfortable green velvet couch.

Sadie.

Halston doesn't move, but her sweatshirt quivers with each breath. "You told me you never photographed anyone else," she says. "Not like this."

My throat and mouth dry up. As I walk up behind the computer chair, Sadie comes into full view. She stares at the camera with her intoxicating, purple-blue eyes. Her back is arched off the couch, her breasts on full display. Desire is clear in her face. "It's not . . ." I try to explain. "This was something else . . ."

"What was it?"

That afternoon with Sadie hits me in the chest like a slab of concrete. I'd thought I finally had her, but what a fucking fool I'd been. We'd spent the day together, gotten caught in the rain, and sought shelter in my apartment. Her own was across the hall, but she'd come to *mine*. Wet. Cold. Lonely. I'd warmed her up all right, devouring her head to toe.

I can't speak. Halston asked me a question, and I need to answer, or her imagination'll run wild. My silence will hurt her more than I already have. "What?"

Halston only gives me her profile, avoiding my eyes. The cute tip of her nose is bright red, her lips parted. "I asked you what this is."

I set her journal and cell on the desk. "It's Sadie."

"I figured, since the folder's named *Sadie*."

"It was just . . . when we were together, I took these. It wasn't for any other reason than I felt—"

"Inspired?" Her voice breaks.

Fuck. Halston of all people knows what that means. For me to feel moved by someone. She's that to me every day. "She never inspired me the way you do."

"Why should I believe that?"

"It wasn't real. I was looking for something and Sadie came along."

She continues to stare at Sadie, even though I want nothing more than for her to close out of the photo. "What were you looking for?" she asks.

"A way out of my marriage. I didn't think I could do it on my own. I wanted an excuse, a partner to go through it with. I put all that on Sadie's shoulders. I was a coward."

A notification pops up on Halston's phone. She goes to pick it up.

"Leave it." I move it out of her reach. That fucking phone's in her hand more often than it's not. "We're having a discussion."

"But my phone keeps vibrating. Something's happening."

"I don't care. I need your attention on me right now. Please."

"Fine." She returns to the computer and clicks to the next photo in line. And the next. Sadie flips between poses.

I have to look away. "Stop."

"No."

"I never looked at these again, not once after she left," I say.

"It's taken you this long to get over her—if you even are—there's no way you haven't been jerking off to these. Probably even when we were together."

My face warms. I've been nothing but good to Halston. Her accusation is unfounded. "You don't know what you're talking about. She's married. Looking at them never felt right."

"But screwing her was?"

I shake the chair a bit to get her attention. She turns to me, startled. "You don't have to believe me, but it's true," I say. "I never looked at them. I never thought of them when I was with you. I would've deleted them, but I forgot they were there once I met you. I'll delete them now."

She glances at the phone, then Sadie, then me. "She's beautiful. I had no idea she was that pretty. I mean, I guess I figured she was. Is . . . Kendra like this too? Are all your exes like models?"

The way Halston says it, she almost makes it sounds like a contest. Her, versus the other women. I tell her a lot how beautiful and sexy she is. Even if I didn't, she sees herself through my eyes on a daily basis. Will it ever be enough? If I forget to tell her sometimes, will she spiral down, comparing herself to every woman who crosses my path?

"Kendra's . . . cute, I guess." Fuck. *Cute*? How the fuck do I describe my ex-wife and ex-lover without hurting Halston's feelings? "She's spunky. Not beautiful like you."

Halston's shoulders lower a little. "Oh."

"And Sadie, she was attractive, yes, but cold."

Halston shifts against the leather. She unpurses her lips, the lines in her forehead smoothing. With a tilt of her head, she asks, "How so?"

I'd rather drop the subject, but I think Halston needs to hear this. Sadie, the dark beauty on my couch, will eat at Halston if I don't share her flaws. "For the longest time, I didn't see that about her, the way she could so easily detach. I thought she was unhappy, and that she needed someone to make her smile, and I did, but it wasn't enough."

I'm relieved when Halston relaxes, pulling her feet in to sit cross-legged. "I think I can see it in her eyes," she says. "She doesn't look friendly."

I nod. It's working. "She belongs with him—Nathan—her husband—he's right for her, I guess. I think I would've realized after it was too late, that I wasn't."

"Is that how you saw me?" she asks. "Unhappy? Cold? Someone to be rescued?"

"Oh, God. No." I squat and take her face in my hands. "You're the warmest, most loving girl. You know that? You have so much to give, and I just take and take. I'm not even sorry about it."

The corner of her mouth twitches. "I wasn't like that with Rich. Or anyone really. Just you."

"Good. That makes me happy." When she smiles, my heart melts. I never want her to feel inferior or question my feelings for her. I hope her insecurity is only because we're still new, and that one day soon, she'll hear me when I tell her how wonderful she is and stop needing reminders. I lean over her, blocking her view, as I trash the photos. She lets me. Seeing them again makes me feel many things, but mostly just sick to my stomach. I'm not sorry about erasing them for good.

Halston kisses me on the cheek and rolls the chair back to get up. She takes her phone and leaves the room. I think I've diffused the situation, but I'm not entirely sure. Because once in a while, rare as it is, it feels as though the more I get to know Halston, the harder she is to read.

TWENTY-SIX

halston

The afterimage of Sadie's naked body is still burned into my vision when I walk out of Finn's studio. If he photographed me that way, face and all, would I come off as confident as her? By Sadie's expression, she knew she had Finn on the hook. He and I have been together longer than they were. He didn't love her like he does me. I know that's true, but sitting there, faced with her beauty and poise, I couldn't help thinking about all the things I'm not—normal, calm, cheerful, charming. But I am warm, unlike her.

I check my phone. I was only away from it half an hour, but the amount of notifications makes me stop in my tracks. I can't even scroll to the bottom of the lock screen. I type in my passcode and my mouth falls open. "Finn? *Finn.* Come here."

He appears in the hallway. "What?"

I show him the screen. "Look. They keep coming. Like, a lot of them."

"Why? What happened?"

I wrack my brain. The only explanation is that we've been featured by someone big, but when that happens, it's generally *their* account that blows up, not ours. "Did you just post something?" I ask.

"No. I was with you."

The last photo Finn shared has more likes than usual, which doesn't make sense. It's my freshly-manicured, dark-nailed hands cupped together, filled with bobby pins. It was just a filler we threw together since we've been hard at work on the lingerie shoot.

But as I look through our notifications, I realize it's not that one they're interested in. Users are going back to where it all began. Our coffee series, the first three photos, is getting like after like after like. I open each of them.

Finn sees it at the same time as I do, reading upside down. "Does that one have *twenty-one-hundred*?"

I stumble back into the studio and sit on the sofa. Comments are coming in faster than I can track. "Check your e-mail," I tell him as I look through everything we've been tagged in recently. There are more than usual today, a few feature accounts included, each with thousands of followers. Still, I'm not sure why they all chose the same photo. "I can't figure it out," I say. "It's not Butter Boudoir; they don't even have many more followers than we do. I have no idea where this is coming from."

Finn's leather chair creaks when he sits back. "I do."

"You do? Where?"

He massages his jaw, looking at the computer screen. "It's dumb."

"What is it?" I get up and read over his shoulder. "A Buzzfeed article?"

"Yeah. 'Twelve sexy photographers to follow now.'"

"Holy shit. Why is that dumb? Our stuff *is* sexy."

"No. They don't mean it like that. Here's the subtitle: 'These photographers are even sexier than the photos they take.'" He scrolls down to number one on the list, and it's Finn's face. His sun-kissed skin. His butterscotch hair and mossy-green eyes. The photo from the bio section of his website.

Underneath it is the photo of me licking coffee off my forearm and a caption that reads *We'd be drooling too.*

"Sexy photographers," he explains. "As in, every photographer in the article is—well, according to *them* . . ."

"Sexy," I finish.

He moves down the list. A couple other men are included, but most of the accounts featured are women shooting female boudoir—pretty pouts, big eyes, delicate bralettes, smooth-skinned, toned asses.

All the images are embedded on the site, so people can follow with one click. They don't even have to leave the page.

"Someone e-mailed me about this a couple days ago," Finn says, rubbing his temples. "She asked if she could feature us. I didn't think it was a big deal."

"I don't know if it is." I lean over and scroll to the bottom of the article to see if anyone has commented.

"Almost two hundred people," Finn says, reading the screen. "Is that normal for Buzzfeed?"

I stand up again. "It's a lot. Sometimes things like this go viral, so if people are sharing it all over social media, then . . . that must be what happened. Plus, you're number one on the list."

"We're number one."

"That's not my face at the top."

"Hals." His eyebrows draw together, his gorgeous lips turn down into a frown. "Honestly, I didn't know what I was agreeing to. I assumed it was about *our* work."

My caption is included, but that's obviously not what this article's about. Professionally, this is huge for him, yet he looks unhappy. Because he's worried how I'll react to this? He shouldn't be. I want his success probably more than he does. He deserves to have his moment.

"It is about us." I bend down to kiss him. "They wouldn't have picked you if *our* work sucked. And you know what?"

He watches my mouth. "Hmm?"

"I don't need a Buzzfeed article to tell me how sexy you are, but it's still pretty amazing they picked you. And you picked me, so I'm feeling good right now."

He pulls my arm so I fall into his lap. "*You're* amazing."

"You know, there's a lot of pressure on us now. Our next post has to be seriously good. None of that bobby pin bullshit."

He grins. "It's the onesie one."

"The onesie one?"

He gestures over my body. "The leotard thing. That's our next photo."

I instinctively glance at the computer and Sadie pops into my mind. I said I was okay with what I saw, so I need to be. There isn't enough room for both of us to be paranoid about past partners. He has more reason to be distrustful, even though I'd never pick Rich over him. Finn, on the other hand, hasn't ever made me feel insecure about our relationship. "Right. The bodysuit. It's good, but is it good enough as a first post for all those new followers? Let me see which caption you chose."

He pinches my chin. "It'll be perfect. Don't worry."

"But—"

"I'll handle it, babe. I want you to enjoy this moment."

"I am. Remember that day I said I wanted to hit ten thousand followers by mid-January? Before this article, we'd almost doubled it. Now we're closing in on forty, and it's barely February."

"Is this you enjoying the moment?" he asks.

It is. Watching the numbers grow excites me. Knowing all those people are not just reading my words, but relating to them. Feeling them. I hate to admit that the thrill doesn't end there. The article said it, and forty-thousand people agree, so it must be true: the photos are sexy. And they're of me. I can't wait to see what happens when we post the next series of Butter Boudoir images. Just as I'd suspected, they're the most provocative yet. "I think with Valentine's Day around the corner, we can double that number by March."

He looks skeptical. "Eighty thousand?"

"No. A hundred. Pick a day in March. We need a goal to keep us on track."

"Jesus. That's the population of a town."

"We can do it, Finn. This is the kind of thing I was talking about. We can do more with more."

He scratches his chin but nods. "Okay, but . . ." He runs his hand down my thigh. "Can you give me a teensy bit more motivation?"

"If we hit a hundred thousand by the date you pick in March . . . I'll give you blowjobs until my jaw falls off."

His eyes widen. "March first."

I laugh. "Are you sure? Day one? You're going to take that risk?"

With an eye roll and a chuckle, he sits back. "Fine. How about March eleventh? It's my birthday."

A smile warms my face. I had no idea. I'll have to think of something good to surprise him with. "I love March eleventh."

That's just over a month away. With what we've accomplished today, and with what's to come, I just know we can do it. Our own little town.

But then, as is becoming standard since I stopped my antidepressants, it doesn't take long for my high to even out and let doubt in. We can no longer pretend this is a hobby. Now, we have a real following, opportunities to get sponsors, and the ability to charge for advertising. If we play our cards right, this could mean a new life for us—and our art. It also means we have something to lose. And as Finn grows more recognizable, I'll have to share him with the world, watching from the sidelines, hiding behind a mask of my own creation.

TWENTY-SEVEN

Finn squats, examining a box on the floor of my apartment labeled *Books*. "It's all in the knees," he explains. "You have to protect your back." After counting to three, he hoists the box into his arms and stumbles backward a few steps. "What the . . . there's nothing in here."

I can't help laughing. "You can thank Rich. He didn't return any of my paperbacks."

"Maybe next time get a smaller box," he teases. "I think this is the last of what I can fit in the car. We'll have to come back for the rest next weekend."

"That's fine. We've got time."

While he takes the last of today's stuff downstairs, I get out a six-pack I bought for this occasion. I pop the cap from a bottle, and it clatters on the counter, the noise echoing off empty walls. It should be strange to see my place this barren, its eggshell-colored walls looking sad and splotchy, but it hasn't been my home for months. The important things are already at Finn's. We moved some last weekend, some today, and we'll do the rest next Saturday since it's the last weekend before March. That's the way to move.

Finn walks through the front door with a pizza. "I ran into the delivery guy downstairs."

"Perfect timing."

I trade him a beer for a slice, and we stand at the counter to eat.

"When we get home, leave those on," he says, nodding at my outfit.

"What, my overalls?"

He winks. "And the bandana."

"The bandana is to keep sweat out of my hair," I say. "Not to be cute."

"Then definitely wear it, because what I've got in mind will leave you all kinds of sweaty."

"Ew." I toss a piece of crust at him. "Gross."

He laughs and wipes his mouth on his sleeve. "How come you never got roommates?"

"I've never had any."

"*Never*? But that's like a rite of passage into adulthood."

"My dad didn't want me to. He offered to pay for me to live alone, and I'd be an idiot to turn that down."

Finn shakes his head. "It's good to live with people. You learn weird things about yourself, like that you fucking hate the smell of sautéed Brussels sprouts."

I smirk. "Lucky for you, I don't eat Brussels sprouts . . . *roomie*."

"So what'd your dad say when you told him you were giving up your apartment to move in with a smutty photographer?"

I take a long pull from my bottle. Finn looks smug, because he knows I haven't done it yet. Just the thought makes me perspire, so it's good I've got the headscarf. "I'm telling him next week."

"Right. You said that earlier this month, Hals."

"I will." I just need to figure out a way to present it so it doesn't look as though I made this decision rashly, without thinking it through. "I was going to the other day, but he lost another client. I swear, when I finally worked up the nerve to enter his office, his face was purple with rage."

Finn shakes his head, but it's not as if he's guilt-free.

"And what about you?" I ask. "Are you going to tell Marissa I'm the live-in maid next time she comes?"

He crams the last of his pizza into his mouth but continues to be gross by speaking. "You know, you haven't checked your phone in a few hours."

"Smooth topic change."

"I'm just saying, I'm impressed. That's a first."

I pick a pepperoni off and eat it. It's not a *first*. The daily count of new followers is higher than ever thanks to the Buzzfeed feature a couple weeks ago. We're already at seventy-five-thousand followers, and one-hundred's just around the corner. The article's nearly doubled what we had, which is astounding, but we're starting to plateau.

"I spent a lot of time looking through hashtags last night," I admit. "I was trying to find new ones for us to experiment with, maybe tap into a new audience, but . . . I kind of fell down a rabbit hole of sex."

"So that's why you woke me up in the best way possible at two in the morning."

I blush, remembering how it felt to have him come to life in my mouth. "I was excited."

"And now?"

I shake my head at my pizza. "I don't know. Now, in the light of day, I'm . . . not."

Finn puts down his beer. "I told you to stop looking through that shit. What'd you see?"

"It wasn't the comments." I don't have to ask what he means. I ruined our Valentine's Day dinner date earlier this week. While Finn was in the restroom, I checked our account. Someone had commented that busty girls look fat in lingerie, and I read it with a mouthful of chocolate lava cake. I nearly spit it all over my plate. By the time Finn returned to the table, I was convinced that person was right. I was too fat, too gross to be half-nude in such a public forum. Finn threatened to delete the account if I didn't promise to stop reading comments and messages. It didn't matter that all other feedback about our Butter Boudoir shoot was good. Better than good. That comment haunted me for days.

I agreed to Finn's conditions and turned off push notifications. I've still been checking things regularly, just not several times a day like before. "I was looking at accounts similar to ours," I explain. "They post less than we do but have hundreds of thousands of followers."

"We're brand-fucking-spanking new, Hals. What we've done in a few months is incredible."

"I know. I just wonder. What if we posted twice a day for a while?"

"You going to quit your job and pose for me for a living?"

"Maybe."

He gives me a look that warns me not to go down this path, but sometimes, when it comes to this stuff, Finn needs a push. He gets business, but he doesn't always know how to mix it with his art.

I shift my hip against the counter. "We're already getting a few sponsor requests a month. The more followers we have, the more money we can command."

"And is that what this is about for you? Money?"

"You know it isn't."

"So why are you bringing that up?"

"It's a bonus. Imagine if one day, you and I did this for real. As a living. We get a five-thousand-dollar sponsor every month, and that's just to start."

"It's a nice idea," he admits. "I just don't want you getting your hopes up. Things are going well, so let's just keep doing what we're doing."

"Posting twice a day *is* doing what we're doing. It's just doing it more."

He sighs and looks out the window over the sink. Under the harsh kitchen lights, the lines around his eyes are obvious. "It's supposed to be a little warmer this weekend. We should do something. Get out of town."

"Finn."

He turns back to me. "We don't have enough material to post more. As it is, we're shooting every weekend and some weeknights."

"I know. And we're running out of body parts." *And captions.* I tense with the thought. Something has to give. The only thing I've been able to write about lately is Finn, but it's personal, not anything I want to share. Not even with him. It's about my boyfriend, not a faceless sex partner like the fantasy we create for people.

Finn narrows his eyes. "So what do you suggest?"

I've given this a lot of thought. Finn isn't just getting recognition for his work. Since last month, girls have started requesting *him*, the sexy photographer. I know he's seen it, even if he hasn't mentioned anything. "There's only one photo of you. The one in the suit."

He shakes his head. "I'm behind the camera, not in front."

"They want more of you, babe. You're the one bringing in all these people."

"Me?" He laughs. "If you think that, you're even more modest than I thought. This account is all about you. Fuck. You got a marriage proposal the other day."

I try not to smile but fail epically. "I did?"

"It's in the messages."

I've been avoiding those, but now I'm tempted to look. "Well, yes, I have fans too, but they've seen so much of me. All of me. But you? Or even *us*, together? That picture you took while unbuttoning my collar from behind—they love that one." I put my bottle down and go to him, touching the hem of his t-shirt. My fingers are wet from condensation, and they leave a damp spot. "*I* love that one."

"We did that in the heat of the moment. It was a quick, easy shot. I can't do a whole session that way, setting up the camera and then posing for the timer."

"Then let's hire someone."

He slow-blinks. "To take the photos? Are you kidding? I'm the fucking *photographer*. This is *my* work."

"No, no, no." I flatten my hands on his chest and lean into him. "I wasn't saying that at all. I mean we can hire another model. If we don't shoot his face, they won't know it's not you. Or maybe they will, but just having something fresh will revive us."

"*Revive* us? We just had a marathon month."

"You know what I mean."

"Not really."

"He and I would pose together, and you'd direct us. You'd have complete control."

"You want someone else's hands on you," he deadpans.

"It's just business, babe. You can even pick the model, I don't care who he is."

"I'm not going to pick a man to—" His chest expands with a breath. "I don't even . . . is this about yesterday?"

I have the urge to pull away, but I don't. I don't want this to turn into a fight. "What about yesterday?" I ask.

"You *know* what, Halston."

I drop my eyes to his chest. Finn was commissioned, for a lot of money, to shoot a local socialite's boudoir session for her fiancé. If that's not bad enough, she was made famous by stealing that fiancé from her best friend. I would've let him do it, but he accepted without consulting with me. "It's not about that."

"I told you, you have nothing to worry about. I've literally not thought about another woman since I met you." He lifts my chin by his knuckle. "The money I make is ours, not mine. Come to the shoot with me. You can be the director."

"I've heard she's dumb, but I'm sure she's not that dense. She'll know who I am," I point out.

He frowns. "Do you want me to cancel it?"

I'm not worried about her. I'm anxious about what this means for us. Finn's website is getting traffic now. My designer did a great job. It even has a Press section, and there are more than a couple articles in it. Me? I have nothing. Even though Finn mentions me in every interview, there's no website with my name on it.

If Finn starts taking other jobs and shooting less for our account, what does that mean for me? What do I even have, professionally speaking, without this? I never even dared to fantasize that one day, I might write for living, until Finn came along. But the truth is, that dream is smoke and mirrors. I haven't actually written anything in months, nothing worth sharing, at least. What if this is it for me, but for Finn, it's just the beginning?

"Don't cancel it," I say. No matter how low I feel, I would never ask Finn to jeopardize his success for me. "I trust you, and this isn't about her—it's about us."

He rubs his thumb over the corner of my mouth. "Tell me more about that."

"I want more for us. I want to quit my job and be with you all the time." At the beginning of our relationship, I might've been embarrassed to admit that, but now? I know Finn loves hearing my stalker-ish thoughts.

He steps even closer to me, running a hand down to the seat of my overalls. He pulls me against him. "All the time, huh? And you're not worried about the ramifications of hourly sex?"

I arch an eyebrow at him. "The *ram*ifications?"

He shifts, pinning my hips to the counter with his. "You'll have to help me with these overalls . . . unless there's some secret flap down there for easy access."

I get a coat of goosebumps but try to focus on the task at hand. "Imagine it," I tell him. "You don't have to take any more shit jobs photographing spoiled brats. I don't have to leave our bed at seven in the morning." I slip my hand into the waist of his jeans, trailing my finger along his hip. His Adam's apple bobs when he swallows. "We sleep in. We shoot a new photo or two every day. I sit at the window and write while you edit. We cook breakfast . . . for *dinner*."

He groans.

Without bothering to undo his pants, I squeeze my hand into his underwear and take him in my fist. "We make love whenever, wherever. That's our life. If we can build this business even bigger."

Finn assaults my mouth with a hungry kiss.

I have my answer. He wants me, he chooses me—for now. If I can bring new life into our work, I'll buy myself a little more time. As long as our follower count goes up, so does Finn's career. But I'll still be here where I started. If I don't find a way to keep up, I risk getting left behind.

TWENTY-EIGHT

finn

It's not until I've hung up my jacket and emptied my pockets in the foyer that I hear voices. Specifically, one voice. And it's much too deep to be Halston's. I head to the studio.

Halston swivels in my office chair when I enter. She brightens with a smile. "There you are."

I put down my camera bag. "I thought we were doing this at seven."

"No, I told you six." She comes over to me, links an arm around my waist, and gestures to the couch. "Finn, this is Ken."

Ken King—supposedly his real name—sets a steaming mug on the side table and stands to shake my hand. "Nice to meet you. I'm looking forward to this."

Looking forward to touching my girlfriend—I'm sure he is. Halston found him on Facebook, a friend of a friend and a working model with a similar build to mine. He's even got some light brown scruff. I touch my jaw and look down at Halston. "Can I talk to you?"

"Sure." Her breath smells like coffee. She smiles at Ken. "Excuse us."

I lead her out with a hand on her upper back, shooting Ken a glance on the way. I close the studio door once we're in the hallway. "He's been here since six?"

"Just about."

"And you let him in? You should've waited for me."

"He would've been standing in the hall for half an hour."

"I don't care. He's a stranger, and you were alone in the apartment with him. Not just a stranger, but one who knows he's here to take provocative photos with you."

"Finn."

I don't care that he regularly poses for NYU's art department, or that Halston trusts the friend who recommended him. I've been trying, and failing, to wrap my head around this for days. When Halston suggested another model, I wasn't thrilled with the idea, but I'm the one encouraging her to be in control of her life. This project is more important to her than I ever imagined it would be.

Now that he's here, I want to call it off. He's ripped. Handsome, in an obvious sort of way. I guess he would be, since he's a model. I've been trying not to wonder whether bringing a third person into the apartment has anything to do with what I read in her "dark" journal. "I'm serious, Hals. You should've waited for me."

"Finn, he's gay." She arches an eyebrow at me. "He was telling me about a trip to Barcelona with his boyfriend."

It's then that I realize my shoulders are at my ears. I lower them. This night just did a one-eighty. Though I'm relieved, I try to play it cool. "Still. You didn't know that when you let him in."

She half rolls her eyes. "He already signed the release."

"And the NDA?"

She folds her arms behind her back. "Not yet. I thought it felt a little extreme."

"That's why I was supposed to meet him first. Now, he knows who you are without any reason to stay quiet."

"Is that *so* bad?" she asks quietly.

"What about all that stuff with the tabloids? And your dad finding out? You still want to remain anonymous, right?"

She shifts feet. "Yes."

"Then he'll sign it." I return to the studio and pull the slip from underneath the model release. I nod at Ken. "Would you mind signing this too?"

Ken stands from the couch and picks up the paper. "Non-disclosure agreement?" he asks. "For what?"

"Halston explained her situation, right? If you have mutual friends—"

"We talked all about it. I'm going to tell my friend Halston was looking for a model for work." I just look at him until he picks up the pen and adds, "But sure. Not a problem."

I don't even want to think of how Halston would react if her identity were revealed. Now that I know her better, I see why it's important to separate these identities. As long as she's anonymous, there's still a shield between the public and her. If insults about her work hurt now, they'll be even worse if she removes that final barrier.

"Did you get to look through the account?" I ask as I head to set up the equipment. "Get a feel for what we post?"

"I did, and I love it," he says. "I follow a lot of photographers and models because of what I do, but I haven't seen anything like this. Especially with the captions."

"We love it," Halston says. "We're hoping these photos will get us to a hundred-thousand followers. We're not too far, and we still have twelve days left."

"What's in twelve days?" Ken asks.

I've been wondering the same thing. When Halston asked me to pick a date, I indulged her. I hadn't thought she'd be religious about it. Every day she writes our follower count in a journal, biting her lip as she calculates and then announces the difference to our goal.

"Finn's birthday," she answers. "And that's the present I want to give him. One hundred K."

I nod Ken over. "Let me get a few test shots."

He walks in front of the camera, and I direct him around the space. His white button-down is stark against the room's smoky-gray walls. "We're going for sexy, but in a suggestive, subtle way." I turn to Halston, who's standing a couple feet behind me, her thumbnail between her teeth. "Are you ready?"

"Yes." She doesn't move. She has on a black, short-sleeved t-shirt and ripped jeans. I asked her not to dress sexy this time around, promised I'd still make her look good, even if she opted for a Mumu. That's my job. My eyes go to her red and patchy inner elbow.

"Are you sure?" I ask. "We can still call it off."

She covers it when she catches me looking, then passes to get in position. Once they're in front of the camera, I play with the lighting. When I turn around, they both stare at me. "What?"

"What should we do?" Halston asks.

Right. I'm supposed to instruct Ken on how to touch my girlfriend. For a second, I don't think I can do it, even if he is gay. We could switch places.

Nobody would ever have to know I didn't take the picture. Except me. This is my work. My first love, even before Marissa came along. Having another man behind the camera is about as bad as watching him with Halston.

I wipe my forehead on my sleeve. "All right. This photo'll be about domination. Your strength, Ken, versus her fragility."

"Oh. We're jumping right in then," Halston says with a nervous smile.

I stop myself from pointing out that I'm not exactly interested in dragging things out. She's always done what I asked. Made herself vulnerable to me. Allowed me to be a voyeur to her deepest desires. Trusted me. I don't want to lose or betray that trust, especially while there's another man in the room.

I can do this for her.

"Just tell me if we're moving too fast. Halston, turn around. Ken, grab her upper arm."

Once Ken is behind her, he takes her bicep. "How's that?" he asks her.

"Harder," I say. "Enough to demonstrate force, but not enough to hurt her."

He tightens his grip. "Like that?"

"Drop your head back onto his shoulder."

Her hair cascades between them, teasing the top of his hand. She glances at the ceiling, around the room, anywhere she can see, then shudders.

"You're not afraid," I tell her. "You're submitting. You understand that whatever he does to you will be for your pleasure." I snap a couple pictures, but her stiffness shows.

"If you're uncomfortable," Ken says, "try inhaling through your nose and blowing it out your mouth a few times."

"I look that bad?" she asks me.

Ken smiles. "Don't worry. Even professionals get nervous."

Halston waits for me to answer. Just me. I don't even think she's trying to make me feel secure about the situation; she *genuinely* wants me to direct her every move. Ken glances over too. It's a heady feeling having both of them under my direction.

"I could put my hand around her throat," he says. "I saw one like that on your account."

She shifts feet. "I'm not sure that's a good idea."

"I won't do it for real," Ken says.

"It's just that we already did it . . . Finn and I."

I love that she wants to protect our pose. And at the same time, she's the one who wanted this. I was against bringing in a third person, and maybe for that reason, I want to test my authority. "Let's try it," I say. "A familiar pose might loosen you up."

Her throat ripples with a swallow, but she nods. My dick stirs—not just because she's submitting, but because she's submitting *to me*. Not him. While another man touches her, I'm still the one to command her.

Ken splays a hand over her collarbone and pins her back to his front. I know what that soft ass feels like pressed against me. Begging for more. Wearing black and white, they're yin and yang, angel and devil. I take a photo. And another. Ken slides his hand up around her throat.

"Put your finger in her mouth," I say.

He raises his hand to her face. Halston clamps her mouth shut like dropping a gate to keep him out.

I lower my camera. "Hals."

She releases her lip, and Ken sticks the tip of his index finger between her teeth. That's when I realize—as much as I didn't want to do this, domineering Halston never fails to excite me. Only now, I'm dominant with her in front of another man.

How far will she go? How far does she *want* to go? If her journals are any indication, there aren't many boundaries, if any.

"Never mind that," I say. "Doesn't look right."

Ken takes his hand back, wiping it on his jeans. "Might look better if we were facing each other. Or even if . . ."

I adjust the aperture. "If what?"

"She were on her knees."

I glance up just in time to catch him shift feet. Halston looks between us, trembling slightly. Her fear is doing something to me. She's been walking this line for a while by showing me that journal, inviting Ken here, chatting with that stranger on New Year's Eve. But she won't do anything without my permission. Without *my* order. With their silence, their uncertainty as they wait for my answer, my head swims.

"Undo his pants."

Neither of them moves—or objects. If Ken's uncomfortable with it, he can speak up. He doesn't. Halston slowly lifts the edge of his shirt, and he takes it from her, holding it up out of the way. She touches the button of his jeans. It takes her a few tries to get it open. She begins to unzip his fly, then looks at me.

"That's good," I say. "*Now* you can get on your knees."

She freezes. Her eyes are as big and gray as ever.

Ken bites his lip, watching her. He might be gay, but I'm not convinced he'd turn Halston down. Halston senses it too, because her chin trembles.

I need to know that Halston trusts me. Always. That she'll submit because she wants to, and not just to anyone. Only me. "All-loved by lovers all," I tell her.

I can see the words from her "dark" journal entry about the threesome sinking in. Finally, she gets to her knees. I raise my camera and instruct her. I get her hands at his waistband. I take a photo from behind her. Ken threads his hand through her hair and fists it. He isn't pretending. She sucks in a breath. I make sure to capture all of it, and since her face isn't in the shots, she follows me with her eyes.

"Let's try the fingers again," I say.

Ken cups the side of her face. This time, she leans in and licks his thumb. She pulls it into her mouth and begins to suck, keeping her eyes on me.

My heart pumps. I'm both jealous and excited, my erection straining against my zipper.

"My willing doll," I murmur, love and arousal churning through me. Her expression softens. We're speaking another language. *Our* language. There's no one else in the room.

I get closer for my shot. Ken is hard. When a hot, sexy blonde sucks on your thumb, it's inevitable. I've had her hot mouth around my fingers, I know how good it feels.

Halston's breasts jiggle under her t-shirt as she gets more into it. One word from me could end this. He'd take his hand back. I get to decide when and where and how far it can go, and *that's* what's getting me off about this.

I've seen enough. Now I want to act.

"We have what we need," I say without warning.

Halston releases Ken's thumb and sits back on her calves. With one look, I know what she needs. What she'll always need. None of this means anything to her without me.

"What?" Ken asks.

"That's good for tonight." I set my camera on the desk and head for the door. "Come with me, and I'll get you your check."

"But we've barely started," he points out.

I turn back to him. From the corner of my eye, I can see Halston still on her knees, her cheeks bright pink as she practically vibrates. My girl's ready for me, and I'm losing patience. "And?"

"Nothing. Never mind," Ken says when he sees the look on my face. He throws a wave in Halston's direction. "See you."

I open the door, let Ken exit first, then turn back to Halston and point to the couch. "Hands and knees. Now."

I walk Ken out, nabbing the envelope with his check from the kitchen table. He says something along the lines of *next time*, but I'm barely listening. I'm so hard, my ears are ringing. "Yeah, sounds good," I say, nearly shoving him out the door.

When I return to the studio, Halston's in position on the sofa. She looks over her shoulder, tracking me with her eyes. "Is he gone?"

I come up behind her, reach around, and unbutton her pants.

"Finn?"

I yank her jeans and underwear down by their waistbands, just enough to bare her pussy to me. I take out my cock and run it up her wet slit. She must've enjoyed that more than she let on.

"I didn't want it," she says, almost pleads. "What I wrote, I thought maybe . . . *maybe* I might . . . but when his hands were on me, I didn't want him."

I know, baby, I know. "Tell me what you do want."

"Just you."

She nearly drips onto the crown of my dick. I slam into her, and she jolts forward. "Oh, God," she cries. "*Finn.* I only want you to touch me. Only you inside me."

I rear back and thrust again, vaulting her face into the cushion. "Tell me you're mine."

"I'm yours," she says, her cheek pressed against the sofa. "You're all I need."

I mold one hand to the curve of her ass, spreading my fingers over her lower back, and give it to her harder than I ever have. I circle her clit with my two favorite fingers, relishing the way she writhes. I lose myself in her, so much so that I'm not even sure if she comes. I only know I'm not going to wait another second to lay claim to what's mine. To let her know I'm not going anywhere. To leave my mark for any other fucker who might come sniffing around.

I hold her hips in place as I give her a few solid drives and erupt inside her, filling her as deeply and completely as I can. I keep her there while I milk myself, making sure to empty every last drop in her.

She breathes in body-wracking shudders. "You came," she rasps. "You came inside me."

"I know." I stare down at her. "I don't want you ever questioning that you're mine."

TWENTY-NINE

halston

Finn isn't expecting me this early, so I make noise as I enter the apartment. Even though it's officially been over a week, I'm not quite used to living with someone yet. "Finn?" I call as I remove my coat.

"In the bedroom."

I find him in front of the mirror, knotting a thin, black tie. "Hel-*lo*, handsome," I say.

He bends his knees for a kiss. "I thought you were doing happy hour."

"I changed my mind." When I'd asked Benny what she was up to tonight, she hadn't extended an invitation. "I want to come with you instead."

He looks at me in the reflection. "To the rehearsal dinner? But it's a job."

"So?"

"So if you come, they might figure out who you are."

"I thought you said the bride was referred to you by a previous client."

"She was, but still. If she's seen our photos, it wouldn't take much to put it together."

I sit on the edge of the bed. I've been having thoughts about that. Dangerous thoughts, or maybe exciting ones—I haven't decided. The night Ken was here changed some things for me. After he left, Finn and I fucked into dawn, all different ways, until he passed out. I, on the other hand, had never felt more alive, more owned, inside and out. I'd read my darkest desires cover to cover, some of it aloud to myself for the first time. When Finn had recited my words to me with Ken's finger in my mouth, I understood his message—he accepts me as I am, and he'll always take care of me. And I began to wonder—if I'm lucky enough to have that, why do I care what others think? This is a different time than when my mom had her accident, and my name was news. People's names are splashed across the tabloids on a daily basis and forgotten within hours. I'm finally starting to see what Finn's been trying to show me. I'm my own woman. I don't need to be afraid of my dad or anyone else. My talent draws people in.

I want to do this as much for him as myself. "What if they did put it together?"

Finn stops tightening the knot of his tie. "What do you mean?"

"I think I want to reveal my identity."

He turns around. "You think?"

"No—I do."

"That's, uh . . . a big deal."

"I know. I've been toying with the idea for a few weeks."

"It's the first I'm hearing of it, though."

I wasn't aware I had to run it by him. Aside from the rules we laid out that first day, I've never tried to regulate what he posts or how he presents himself on our account. "Do I need your permission?"

"It's something we need to discuss, yes. And take some time to consider."

"Actually, since we're going to hit a hundred-thousand tomorrow, and it's your birthday, I thought maybe we could do it then. A big reveal to celebrate."

He gapes at me. "Just like that? Do you realize . . . I mean, that can't be undone, Hals. Once it's out there, that's it."

I blink in disbelief. Finn's encouraged me for a while to own my sexuality, my weirdness, my words. I would've thought he'd like to see me breaking out of my shell. "Yes, I *realize* that."

He checks his watch. "I have to leave, like, now. We can finish this later, but let's just say it's not happening tomorrow. No way."

I frown, disappointed. This is *our* project, not his. That's exactly it, though. I have to respect his opinion if I want the same from him. I won't let him talk me out of revealing myself, but I can respect that he wants to announce it in his own time. "Okay. I just need to change."

"Hals, it's my *job*. I don't think I'm supposed to bring a date."

It's *his* job. Nothing to do with me, even though I'm half the reason his career is even taking off. "We'll tell them I'm your assistant," I say. "I'll hold your camera, and I won't eat. They sound like stuffy uptowners anyway. I doubt they're up on the latest social media trends."

"All right." He runs a hand through his hair, messing it up after he'd clearly styled it. "You have five minutes."

I pop up off the bed, grinning, and fix his hair. At the closet, I hurriedly browse through my things. Finn gave me half the space, but it's cramped. We had to put our summer things in a bin under the bed. I haven't been to a wedding in ages, but luckily I have no shortage of little black dresses. I pick the simplest one and pair it with heels, jewelry, tights, and a clutch. I come out of the closet a new woman. Well, as new as I can become in five minutes. Okay, eight.

Finn's waiting for me in the entryway.

"Well, well," he says, smiling. "You'll get me in trouble for showing up the bride."

I roll my eyes. No amount of primping could erase a full day at work. "Thanks for letting me come. It means a lot."

He takes my hand. "Don't think I won't put you to work."

It turns out, the bride and groom are over-the-top welcoming and not the least bit old-fashioned. I try to make myself invisible by shadowing Finn, but they insist we sit at the table and partake in grilled salmon and expensive wine. Finn gets up every few minutes to capture speeches and candids. Watching him work in this capacity is like seeing him through new eyes. He's overdressed, and ridiculously handsome, but it's his focus and skill with the camera that keeps my attention.

"What kind of lens is he using?"

I turn to find that Eric, the groom-to-be, has taken the seat next to mine. "Um. I'm not sure."

"I thought you were the assistant."

"I mostly just hold things."

He laughs. "Sounds like my impending position of *husband*."

"I also have to tell him how great he is or he gets cranky."

"Same with Elyse," Eric says. "You're writing my job description right now. More wine?"

I've already had a glass, but tonight, we're celebrating—Eric and Elyse. Finn's birthday and his burgeoning career. My big decision to come out and one-hundred K. I slide my wineglass over for a refill.

Elyse walks up, waving an envelope. "For this weekend," she says, sitting on the other side of me, in Finn's chair. "Your boss won't take it until the job is done, but I just want it gone. All the outgoing envelopes of money are giving me anxiety."

I smile, slipping the check under the table and into his camera bag. "I'll hide it from him until Sunday."

"So do you guys do many weddings?" she asks.

The answer is no. In fact, I think this is Finn's first, but I don't want to ding his credibility. I drink Pinot Noir while thinking of an answer. "I'm new, so no," I say. Not technically a lie. "I've never done one."

"Done one what?" Finn asks, planting his hands on the back of my chair. I look up at him, and he winks.

"Wedding," I answer. "As a photographer's assistant."

"That makes two of us," Finn says.

"Really?" Elyse looks surprised. "I wouldn't have thought so. I guess I should've asked." She laughs. "Luckily, we're easygoing."

"Who was it that recommended you again?" Finn asks. "I didn't catch the name when we were on the phone."

"Oh, well, actually . . ." She lowers her voice, leaning in. "That's not true. I was a little embarrassed to say, but," she and Eric exchange a glance, "we found you because of your *other* photos."

Wait. *Other* photos? Mine?

My jaw drops. I'd wondered fleetingly whether they'd nosed around Finn's website and found the link to our account . . . but this! A *real-life* encounter with our followers.

Finn laughs stiffly. "And your first thought was wedding photographer?"

"We're a little non-traditional if you can't tell," Elyse says. "We were so sick of fake smiles and tears, awkward prom poses. At the last minute, we came across your work and decided to scrap our other photographer. We want something more original."

I look up again, but Finn's stepped back, outside my line of vision. "Wow. I'm glad," he says, although he doesn't sound glad.

Oh my God.

This couple, sitting next to me?

They've seen me half-naked. And they liked what they saw. Enough to hire Finn for the biggest day of their lives.

Did they like what they read too?

I take a fortifying sip of wine. It leaves a film that has me smacking my tongue against the roof of my mouth. "How'd you find the account?" I ask, trying not to sound as eager as I feel.

"I don't even remember. Do you?" Elyse asks Eric. "Was it Sharon?"

"I think so," Eric says. "We have some friends who are obsessed with the latest social media and they're always unearthing these amazing sites. How'd you get started with that, Finn?"

It's making me nervous that I can't see Finn. It could be my imagination—it must be—but I think tension is rolling off his body. "It just kind of happened," he says.

"And how involved is the model really?" he asks. "She can't really be that hot *and* articulate."

Elyse reaches across me to slap Eric's arm. "Hey."

"I just know what a rare combo it is," he backtracks, "since I'm lucky enough to have found it in you. Clearly."

I want to squeal. Kick up my feet. Invite the whole dinner table into our conversation. He's talking about me. *Me.* I'm sitting right in front of them, and they have no idea.

"She's very involved," Finn says. "All the writing is hers."

"Can you give us a hint?" Eric asks. "Is she famous?"

I swipe my clammy palms down the front of my dress, then pick up my wine glass. I can't not speak up. This is a sign—I was right earlier. It's time for me to come out. I stop trying to suppress my smile. "It's me," I blurt. "I'm her."

Both pairs of eyes turn to me. Probably Finn's as well. "Halston," he says under his breath. His hands return to the top of my chair, but I don't look up. I don't care if he's mad. This is my moment. My heart might be racing a mile a minute, the inside of my elbow might be burning, but it's liberating to say the words to someone other than Finn.

"I'm Anonymous," I say.

"No shit?" Eric asks with an open-mouthed laugh. "Seriously? *Anonymous* is coming to our wedding?"

"Well, no," I say. "I wasn't planning—"

"You *have* to come," Elyse says. "My girlfriends will die. They're huge fans of you guys."

"As are my friends," Eric adds with a snicker, then seems to remember Finn is there. "Sorry. I didn't mean to—are you two a couple?"

"They'll go ape shit, my friends," Elyse continues, ignoring her fiancé. "They'll probably want your autograph. Unless—oh, shit. We can't tell them who you are, can we?"

Finally, I turn in my chair to check with Finn. He doesn't look happy. "Unfortunately, no," he says. "And Halston actually can't make it tomorrow night."

My excitement falls. After all the ways I've supported him, and even all the ways he's encouraged me, he's taking this away from me. I turn back to a crestfallen Elyse. "I think I can get out of my plans," I say. "What would it hurt for a few people to know?"

"Halston," Finn says through his teeth. "I need to get some shots of the décor in the front room. Can you help me set them up?"

"She's really your assistant?" Eric asks.

"I admire your willpower," Elyse says. "If I were Instagram famous, I'd be blasting that shit everywhere."

My body thrills from fingertips to toes. *Famous.* Us. Are we? I hadn't even considered we might be, but then again, we're going to hit a *hundred-thousand* followers tomorrow. Last I checked, we were only five hundred away. I've been keeping the sexiest photo we have as our ace in the hole. My pink lips, wrapped around Ken's thumb while his other hand fists my hair. Once I post it, I know we'll hit our goal. We have to.

"Hals? Need your help." Finn puts a hand on my shoulder. "And yes, we're together. She's my girlfriend."

It takes me a second to realize he's talking to Eric.

"Oh." Eric nods. "I figured."

Elyse claps her hands in the following silence. "Go get your shot, then we'll do dessert. The bakery made us something special for tonight, so I want to get a few pictures of it."

"Of course," Finn says. "We'll only be a minute."

Finn helps me scoot out from under the table. I pick up his camera bag, putting it over my shoulder. He waits for me to walk through the glass doors of the dining room and into the restaurant's dim entryway. Tiny tea lights illuminate the area, and Eric and Elyse's guestbook sits open on a pedestal. Other than that, I don't see much decoration.

"What was that?" Finn asks.

"I know. Incredible, right?" It isn't what he means, but he *has* to be excited about this too. Just a little. We've worked hard to get here. I should be able to enjoy our success with him, not from the shadows.

"We decided revealing your identity wasn't a good idea."

I turn my back to the floor-to-ceiling glass looking into the dining room. I don't want to be watching a bunch of happy people while we argue. "*You* decided that. It's only two people."

"And their friends who'll be there tomorrow night. You know Elyse is going to tell—that isn't the point. You did something I asked you not to."

My throat closes. That sounds familiar. Too familiar. My fingertips tingle, like they're trying to warn me. Since when does Finn order me around? Have I made the same mistake with him as I did two years ago with Rich? Do I subconsciously choose my father on purpose? "I've done everything else you've asked," I say. "You wanted my words, I gave them to you. You told me to stay anonymous, I agreed. You wanted *me*, I broke up with my *boyfriend*."

Finn's eyebrows shoot to the middle of his forehead. The shadows on his face make him look angrier than is—or at least, I hope so. "I don't even know where to start with that. How did I tell you to stay anonymous?"

"*You* suggested I keep my identity hidden."

"Only because you wouldn't let me use your journal otherwise."

My last few gulps of wine are kicking in. I don't remember the specifics of that conversation right now, but I do know I never would've gone down this path if not for him. And now he's acting as though

I'm just some model like Eric thought I was. It dawns on me that maybe Finn *wants* me be to that. "Do you not want people knowing who I am?" I ask.

"We've covered this." He glances over my head. "People are looking over. We're making a scene."

I reel back, crossing my arms. "Is it because I'll get the credit I deserve?"

Finn's nostrils flare. "Are you *seriously* suggesting, after months of trying to get you to see your worth, that I don't want you to succeed?"

That's one explanation, but another possibility hits me right in the chest. What if Finn's coaching hasn't been entirely innocent? Maybe he recognized early on that he needed me for this business to work. If I come out, he'll be the one in the shadows, or at least forced to share the spotlight.

Oh God.

I need something, and I need it right now. Anything. Coffee, cigarettes, wine, I don't care. This edge is too sharp for me to balance on without something to dull it.

"This isn't the time for this conversation," Finn says. "But you bet your ass we'll pick it up as soon as we get home."

"Fine." I start to turn. "I'll be outside."

"No. It's cold, and I'm afraid you'll take off. Stay and be mad, but don't go without talking to me first." He squints at me. "And maybe take it easy on the wine, all right? You know I don't care if you drink, but we *are* working."

He goes back inside. That's such a Dad move—tell me what not to do, then walk away before I can argue my point. Is it me? Do I bring out that side of men, turn them into domineering assholes? That's what Dad and Rich and Doctor Lumby have been telling me all along, isn't it? That I need to be on meds for myself and the people who love me?

I'm not even allowed to go outside by myself for fuck's sake. I should leave. It'd serve him right. But that afternoon I ran away from the museum, nothing felt right. I walked for hours, sick over how I'd thrown a tantrum and run away. I needed that alone time, like I do now, but I didn't handle it right.

Taking a lungful of air, I go back into the restaurant. Elyse leads Finn to the kitchen, presumably to photograph a pastry. He glances over his shoulder, and we meet eyes right before he passes through the swinging aluminum doors. I'm glad, because I don't want him to see how I'm unraveling. I head straight for the restaurant's bar. Fortunately, it's off to the side, somewhat separated from the main dining area.

The bartender tosses a coaster in front of me. "What can I get you?"

"Anything. I was drinking Pinto Noir over there."

"You with the wedding party?" he asks, getting a wineglass from the back of the bar.

"Sort of. Photographer's assistant." That's basically all I am to Finn, isn't it? Someone to position and exploit? "Any chance you have a cigarette? I'll pay you for it."

He laughs. "You must be desperate. I'll get you one."

I drink my wine. My mind buzzes from our argument. Finn knew me before he even met me. How many couples can say that? Did we move too fast, thinking we were invincible because we were meant to be? It was exciting, exhilarating—fucking and sharing feelings day in and day out while I led a double life. At work, I was a version of myself, but to Finn, I was just me.

I wonder—who said it was even a good thing to be your true self? To have no boundaries with or secrets from the person you love? Isn't that dangerous? I thought diving in headfirst was romantic. Thrilling. Looking back, I should've been more wary of the red flag, like when Finn threatened to delete the account if I didn't stop going through the messages and comments. And he was so insistent Ken sign a non-disclosure. I thought he was protecting me, but what if he's been monitoring what I see and who sees me?

That's not all.

Even after a few months together, he continues to pretend Marissa doesn't exist in our relationship. I barely know a thing about her. And, he has access to my finances, but I know nothing about his other than what he's told me. He didn't trust me about the birth control until three months into our relationship.

I rationalized all of it. Love is blind, they say, and it's true. Being madly, deeply in love is like allowing the sun to blind you just because it also keeps you warm.

"Another?" the bartender asks. I look up. I've finished my glass. He passes me a cigarette and a book of matches.

I shouldn't. I feel good, though. Angry and hurt, but also lightweight, nice. Blunted like a pencil that's been pressed to the page too hard. "Sure. I'm just going to run out and smoke."

He nods, and I pass back through the dining room to the exit. I don't see Finn, but I'll only be a minute. Outside, cold air nips at me as I light the cigarette. I take my first drag and manage not to cough. I don't like smoking, but sometimes it feels just right, like now, when it goes straight to my head.

I get out my phone. Seeing the numbers rise—followers, likes, comments—it soothes me. It makes me somebody worth listening to and looking at and that's hard evidence nobody can take from me. I was saving our last photo for tomorrow, but I decide to post it now. So we'll hit our goal a day early—even better. It probably won't technically happen until after midnight, and then I can show it to Finn in the morning for his birthday.

The app takes a few seconds to load before it crashes. I open it again, and the login page pops up, even though I never sign out—I haven't even used my own account in months. I type in our username and password, but I get an error message, so I try twice more in case the alcohol's making my fingers fat. It's not that, though. The password's wrong. I haven't had to use it in a while, but I would never forget *halstondecember*.

Did Finn change it?

My hand begins to shake. I try *halstonjanuary*, *halstonfebruary*, and finally *halstonmarch*.

Nothing. I was online in the cab on the way over here, so I know it worked before dinner. Which means . . .

He locked me out—of *our* account.

I'm not sure I really believe Finn doesn't want to share credit with me, but here's my proof. He's gone out of his way to make sure I don't reveal my identity tonight.

Nearly vibrating, I shove my phone in my purse and stamp out the cigarette. Whipping open the door to the restaurant, I head for the dining room. My eyes laser onto Finn near the bar, where he's talking to the bartender. Probably trying to find me so he can tell me how to live my life just like everyone else. But it's far worse when he does it. At least Rich and my dad didn't pretend to be something else to get me to trust them.

"What did you do?" I ask, my heels clicking the wood floor faster and faster.

Finn turns around. "It's just temporary, until—"

"So it's true? You changed the password?"

He glances behind me. "Only to prevent you

from making an irreversible mistake."

"A *mistake*." The word makes me shudder. "Don't you realize that makes you sound just like them?"

His face falls. He doesn't need me to elaborate. He knows the *them* I'm referring to. "I'm not trying to hurt you," he says. "This is for your own protection."

I snort. "My dad thinks I can't take care of myself. Is that what you think too? That I need to be monitored and manipulated and closed out of something *I* built."

"Of course not." His eyes dart over my head. "Please, Hals. They can hear us."

"You know how important this is to me."

He steps forward. "And that's why I'm trying to keep you from ruining it. If you go public, it changes everything. People know who you are and how to find you. People will be looking at *you*."

"Newsflash: they've *been* looking at me. You didn't seem to mind when praise for your work was filling up your inbox."

"That's because right now, you're a fantasy to them," he says, his voice rising, "and if you take that away, you're just you, my girlfriend, *my* Halston, on display. It's not safe, and it's not happening."

"I don't need you to protect me. That didn't work out so well for Rich, did it? Is that what you're doing? Saving me from myself?"

"I'm the *opposite* of them." He sounds strangled. "I've tried to be everything to you they're not, to give you what they can't. I'm not them."

"No. You're worse." Tears fill my eyes, and I steady myself on a barstool. "You pretended to care. You lifted me up to get what you wanted—for what? Your career? Was it even an accident, running into you at the coffee shop that day? Or did you follow me there like you did to the art gallery, so you could convince me to do this with you?"

"I . . . that isn't the reason, but—" He grabs his hair in a fist. "It wasn't an accident. I was waiting for you."

I turn around.

"Not because I wanted your journal . . . I mean, I did, but not for this—" He calls after me. "Where are you going?"

My chest hurts. He was supposed to be my everything. My rock, my soul mate. I trusted him. "Away from you."

"I told—no, I *asked* you not to take off." He follows me through the restaurant. He was right, the guests heard everything. They're silent as we pass through. "I don't know how to reason with you without coming off like your dad," he says. "I've been walking on eggshells since we met, trying not to come off like him, but you know what I think? Maybe you haven't been completely fair to him. You're not being fair to me."

Siding with my dad, just like Rich. I really fucked up, thinking this relationship was any different. Even if Rich tried to keep me in a box, at least he didn't pretend he wasn't doing that.

I want to see him.

The thought surprises me, but it's true. I want to see Rich right now—as a friend. I don't have many of those, and Rich was my closest one for two years. For all his faults, he's always been there when I needed him. My dad lives an hour away and if I show up drunk to his house, he'll never let me live it down.

I exit the building to hail a cab.

"You're going home, right?" Finn asks behind me.

"I don't want to go back to that *fucking* apartment. I feel like I've been cooped up there for months."

"I thought you were happy there." The hurt in his voice is evident, but then he speaks again. "I don't think you should go out. I'm sorry, I know saying this won't make things easier, but you don't need to drink any more tonight."

As a cab pulls over, I whirl on Finn. I want to lock him out the way he did to me, except that I have no control over anything in our business. That's not true for our relationship, though. I want to hurt him. "I'll go home when I feel like it. I'll drink what I want, talk to who I want, *post* what I want." My hands are in two tight fists. "I need you to change the password back."

His tie is crooked, his honey-colored hair disheveled, but he looks nothing less than gorgeous and perfect. "No."

"It's my business too."

"You can't make such a huge decision while you're in this state."

"Change it back. Tonight." I open the door to the cab's backseat. "We're *this close* to our goal—"

"I don't give a shit about that," he cries, taking my elbow to pull me from the car. "Who gives a fuck how many followers we have?"

"I do," I say through a film of tears. "You made me care. You pushed me to do this, and now you're trying to make me feel stupid for wanting it."

"I never pushed you, Hals, and I'm not trying to make you feel stupid. I'm saying that's not important right now—"

"To *you*. Let me go."

"To *us*. And no."

"*You* know what's important to me?" I shove my palms into his chest, and he releases me but doesn't budge. "You think you know better?" I ask.

"No."

I try to take a deep breath, but I can't catch one. "Why don't you just put me back on the fucking drugs? What made me think you'd accept me like this?" I push him again, and he grabs my wrists. "Is this what you signed up for? A crazy person? Is it?"

He spins me around to hug me from behind. "This isn't you," he says, his hands cold and firm as they keep me in place. "You're somewhere else right now. Come back to me, Hals."

My heart pounds a mile a minute. I should've done this months ago, before I fell so hard. I knew deep down—nobody wants someone like me. I'm troubled. I make bad decisions. "This *is* me. Let go."

"No."

"You can't handle me. Nobody can, and maybe I'm better off without any of you. Let *go* of me."

"No. I'm not letting you go. You can fight me all you want, but I love you."

"I'm going to Rich." It just comes out.

After a few tense moments, he releases me all at once, like I've burnt him. "What?"

I stay where I am, back to him as I try to breathe. "I have to process all this—away from you. I'm going to see Rich, my friend, because that's what I need right now."

"If you go there, we're done."

I get in the backseat of the cab and shut the door, but the passenger's side window is open.

"I can forgive you anything," Finn says, "the scene you just made, overdrinking when I warned you not to, telling the people who hired me to do a job something so personal about us. But not this."

I swipe my tears away. On some level, now that the thrill of our relationship is wearing off, I'm sure this is what he wants. But Finn's too softhearted to leave someone who isn't stable, someone who needs him like I do. Someone who's obsessed with him.

Sometimes he needs a push. This is best for both of us.

I give the driver Rich's address.

THIRTY

Rich's doorman looks suspicious as I do my best not to stumble across the apartment building's lobby, but he lets me by with a wave. After all, even if I've been away a few months, I did spend two years coming in and out of this building.

I pound on Rich's door until he yells from the other side, "All right, all right. Jesus. Who is it?"

"Me."

The deadbolt slides open, and Rich peeks out, squinting. He looks less surprised to find me drunk on his doorstep in the middle of the night than I would've guessed. "Come in, Halston."

"I need a place to crash."

"I already said come in." He opens the door wider. "Are you okay?"

"I'm fine, and I'm sleeping on the couch."

He surrenders with both palms up and leads me into the kitchen. "You know where the linens are. I'll get you some water."

"I'm drunk."

"No shit."

"I'm sorry." I steady myself on the kitchen island as he gets a glass from a cupboard. "I know you hate that."

"Actually . . . no. In a way, I'm kind of, I guess, glad."

Did he say *glad*? "Huh?"

He glances up from under his lashes as he pours me filtered water. "I've been waiting for this to happen, and I'd hoped you'd come here when it did. Where you feel safe."

Is that true? Did I come crawling back here knowing the most dangerous feeling I might experience is tedium or Rich's standard-grade condescension? "You're not mad?"

"No." He brings me the glass, stopping for Tylenol from a medicine drawer. "Do you want to talk about it?"

"Not really. I just want to sleep."

"Does it have to do with him? Is it over?"

I gulp down water and pills, looking at Rich over the rim of the glass. It doesn't feel over—how could it be? How could all that love and passion just vanish into thin air? Finn said it, though. If I left, that was it. Defying Finn is less exhilarating now, less righteous, than it was twenty minutes ago.

I wipe my mouth with the back of my hand. Rich doesn't need to know any of that. "Not over."

He sighs on his way to the linen closet. "What's with the bag?"

I almost forgot. I open the flap of Finn's bag, but there's nothing in there. Finn still has his camera. And the account, and anything that means something to me. My chest aches, also empty. "It's his."

"Ah." Rich hands me a pile of folded sheets topped with a pillow and blanket. "I'll let you get some sleep."

I'm surprised he doesn't have more to say, but I'm not about to argue. He follows me into the living room and turns off the lights before leaving me to it. I make up the couch.

While removing my shoes and tights, I topple onto the cushions. I leave my dress on, get under the blanket, and take out my cell. I have the urge to talk to Finn, but what is there to say? I'm still angry. I still don't think he was right to cut me out like that. Does he even want to hear from me?

Instead, I open my camera roll. In here, I keep the photos Finn has sent me that we don't share. The ones that're just for us. Me, sitting up in bed first thing in the morning, the sheet pulled up around my breasts, barely hiding my nipples. My hair is mussed from a night of lovemaking. From Finn. My eyes water.

"Will you be warm enough?" Rich asks from the doorway.

Startled, I put a protective hand over my screen so he doesn't see anything. "Yes."

"Okay." He clears his throat. Tonight's half-moon casts some light into the room. "So he lets you get drunk alone at night in this city?"

"I knew it." *I'll let you get some sleep.* Can't believe I fell for that. "I knew you couldn't resist."

"Sorry that I want you to be safe."

"You just want to say you told me so."

"So I *did* tell you so?" I can just make out the way his eyebrows shoot up. "You're admitting I was right about him?"

"No." I frown until I'm pouting. "That's not what I meant."

"Can I just tell you how things look from my perspective?" he asks. "Then maybe you'll understand my concern. One night, out of the blue, no warning, no valid reason, you dump me. *Over the phone.* Right after you go off antidepressants. Whenever I see you at work, you have dark circles under your eyes or you look like you've been crying. Next thing I know, your bodyguard boyfriend is threatening me to stay away from you. It's like you're brainwashed or something."

"That's *ridiculous.*"

"I don't know what hold he has over you, but something feels off. I'm worried he's encouraging your patterns or worse, he's become one. I don't want you to get involved with something dangerous, something that can't be reversed, because you're blinded by infatuation."

Even in my inebriated state, Rich's words hit close to home. He knows me well—how could he not after two years? What if he sees something I don't? I never recognize a pattern until I'm already in too deep to get out on my own. With coffee, I was excited to find Lait Noir, a place that served it just how I liked it. I hadn't realized anything was different until my dad congratulated me on getting my spending under control again. When had I stopped shopping and started drinking coffee by the gallon?

"You don't need to worry about me," I say.

"I disagree."

"No, I mean . . . you don't *need* to worry about me. I'm not your responsibility anymore. You and my dad are getting on fine without me, you don't need to date me for him to like you."

Crossing his arms, he looks out the window. "I don't know why you so vehemently believe that I loved *around* you. I didn't. I loved *you.* I still do."

Rich doesn't have a romantic bone in his body. Or does he? I didn't think I'd hurt him very badly, or maybe I just didn't think. I was too consumed by my own life. "I do love you, in a way, but I can be selfish. You knew that."

"That's not an excuse. You just left, no explanation, no second chances. Do you have any idea how much that hurt?"

I didn't. Slowly, a thought creeps in. What if, all this time, Rich and my dad really have known what's best for me? What if their protectiveness, and Finn's too, has come out of wanting me to be happy, not a need to subdue me so I can be managed? They've said it, but I've never really *heard* it. I believe the pain in Rich's voice, though, and it makes me think maybe he really was in love with me. More than he let on.

"I'm sorry," I whisper. It's easier to say in the dark, even though the dark won't stand still at the moment.

"You love the drama," he says. "You always have, which is why you wanted to be on antidepressants. Yes, you wanted to, it was just more convenient to blame us than to admit that. You crave the ups and downs, even though they scare you. Or maybe because they do." Rich sighs and pulls the curtains shut, shrouding me in complete darkness. "I'll leave a light on in the bathroom in case you need to throw up."

"I won't. I'm fine."

I close my eyes but immediately open them when the world tilts.

He's such a goddamn know-it-all.

When I'm alone, I unlock my phone and swipe through more photos Finn took of me. He isn't in any of them. Dad, Rich, Finn—they love me, they do. Why is it so hard for me to accept that? Maybe controlling me isn't the best way to show it, but Finn has also supported and encouraged me. He's the reason I've bloomed these past few months.

Isn't he allowed to be protective of what he loves?

I wake at the crack of dawn, and I mean the *crack*. I guess Rich didn't shut the curtains all the way, because one asshole beam of light slices right through the dark and onto my face. I sit up too fast. My body protests almost as hard as my pounding temples. Stumbling to the window, I yank the blinds all the way closed, but with the sun rising fast, it's still not dark.

I'm drudging back to the couch when I see him and nearly fall flat on my face.

George Fox.

He's sleeping in the club chair next to the sofa, his burgundy cashmere sweater wrinkled like he's a bourgeois vagrant. I blink a few times, rubbing my eyes in disbelief. "Dad?"

He shifts. After a moment, he lifts his head, squinting at me. "Banana?"

"What are you doing here?" I sit on the edge of the couch, facing him. "Did Rich call you?"

"He was worried. And before you go off on him, just know he's *been* worried for a long time and kept it all to himself. Until last night." He sits up, grimacing. "I'm too damn rickety to be sleeping on a chair, Halston. Are you trying to send your old man to an early grave?"

I look at the ground, my throat thickening with unshed tears. He drove an hour in the middle of the night to see me. It's becoming clear that I've gone out of my way to hurt all the people who love me. It's been a two-way street, but I've grown a lot the last few months and I can't help wondering if much of my struggle the last ten years was imposed by myself.

"How much did he tell you?"

"You're shacking up with some middle-aged artist?"

I roll my eyes. "He's not middle-aged. He's in his thirties. And we live together."

"You should've told me. What if something had happened? I wouldn't've been able to find you."

"Like what?" I ask. "What else could possibly happen?"

He furrows his eyebrows, then leans his elbows on his knees. "I know you're hurting. I just don't know why you won't let us help you."

"I have to do it on my own, Dad. I want to heal, not numb myself forever. I never properly dealt with my feelings surrounding . . . that."

"Minnie's death."

I inhale back tears. He rarely uses her name. I know it hurts him to even say it. "It felt like when you put me on that stuff, you just wanted to shut me up. Make me move on."

"I wanted to stop the pain for you," he says. "If you were going through even half of what I was—"

"Of course I was. More, because it was my fault."

"Oh, baby." He rubs his face, his hands shaking. "It's not your damn fault."

My chest constricts. I don't know if he realizes he's never said that. "You made me think it was."

He looks up. He's crying. "I'm sorry. I didn't take care of you. I couldn't. Getting you treatment was the only way I could deal with the fact that *I* was falling apart. I was scared to bring you down with me, so I gave you to a professional."

"Then why keep me there for ten years?"

He shakes his head. "I thought you were doing well. Weren't you? You graduated college. Rich was good to you. You've been a productive, creative employee. She'd be so proud of you."

I cover my face to hold in the tears. A blur of the provocative images Finn and I took flash through my mind. "No she wouldn't."

"Yes." He reaches out and pulls one hand away by my wrist. "She is."

After a few stuttering breaths, my sobs break through. Dad moves over to the couch and holds me while I cry. This is what I needed. All I ever needed. To be allowed to be sad, to have regrets, and for my parent to support me through it.

"I've screwed everything up," I say into his chest. "All these years, I resented you when I should've embraced the fact that I still have you."

He rests his cheek on top of my head. "We still have plenty of time, you and me. Time to make the changes we both need to."

"Changes?" I look up at him. "How?"

"I don't know, but I don't want to go back to how things have been. I want to be part of your life, not just at work or during December. How do I do that?"

As soon as he asks, I know the answer. He won't like it, but it might be the best road to repairing our relationship. I swallow through the lump in my throat at the same time a laugh bubbles up. I begin to giggle.

"Are you losing it?" he asks, frowning.

I shake my head. "Therapy. You and me, together. Not with Lumby, but with a new doctor. A fresh start."

"Fuck."

That makes me laugh harder. "It's not so bad. Sometimes it's actually nice to just talk to someone who won't judge you. That's why I write."

"You write?"

"My journals. You've seen them."

"Oh, right. Your diary."

"It's not that," I say carefully. "It's more like . . . poetry, I guess. It makes me happy."

"I didn't know."

How could he? I never told him. "Well, you do now. And one day—" Maybe this is too much for today. I shouldn't push it. But, to my surprise, I want him to know. "I think I want to try and publish it."

He rubs my arm. "That's—I don't know anything about that, but if that's what you want, I'm sure it'll happen."

I grin. It's as good an answer as I'll get for now.

"So what're we going to do about this mess?" he asks. "I assume since you're here, it's over with that photographer and you've got nowhere to live."

My smile vanishes. *Finn.* If I can forgive my dad and Rich and move forward with them, then I can do the same with Finn. Once he understands where I was coming from, and he will now that I feel more equipped to explain, then we can patch up the holes we exposed last night and start on firmer foundation. "I love him," I tell my dad.

"Banana . . ."

"I know. It's soon. It seems irrational." I pull back to look him in the face. "It's not. He's really good to me, Dad. In a roundabout way, he's the reason you and I are having this conversation. I've grown up a lot because he's showed me how to be comfortable in my skin. Well, mostly. I'm working on it."

My dad looks torn, and I don't blame him. It sounds shifty, any way you slice it. "How does he pay the bills?"

"His pictures." *Kind of.* "And he used to work on Wall Street, so I guess he does some trading on the side."

His posture relaxes. "You don't say?"

Now I'm speaking my dad's language. But his question still stands.

What *am* I going to do about this mess?

Because that's what I am—a mess. I'm realizing I'll never have my shit together. And maybe that's okay. Finn fell in love with my mess, and that makes it a little bit magical.

It's become ours.

I ran away, though. I'm still learning to deal with the emotionally-stunted teenager inside me. Will Finn understand that? How can I handle this so I'm tapping into the adult I need to be rather than indulging the adolescent I can't seem to outgrow?

I'm not sure. All I know is, I'm not ready to walk away from him. I'm ready to run back.

THIRTY-ONE

finn

As soon as I hear a key in the door, my eyes open. I didn't shut the blinds last night; the room is bright and cheery. This time, it only takes me a second to realize there's no key. No Halston. I haven't really slept all night, startling awake every time I hear a noise, thinking it's her. I've been too on edge to do much more than shut my eyes, my emotions pinging between worry, anger, and hurt.

She's there.

With *him*.

I gave her a choice, and she didn't choose me.

I told her this would happen. Love can only take you so far. If Rich gave her the kind of stability our relationship may never have, can I blame her for going back to him?

Yeah. I think I can. I let myself fall hard and deep. Now I feel completely fucked.

I didn't handle things the best way last night, but when I saw another empty glass on the bar, I panicked. She was drinking with a big, alluring idea in her head—who knows what she might've done? After months of watching her come apart with even a hint of negative feedback, I wasn't about to let her put herself in front of a firing squad. Not until we'd discussed it thoroughly, and I'd figured out a better way to explain how risky going public would be. She'd have nowhere left to hide. No armor to deflect judgment. Just me, and I'm not sure how much longer I could've gone trying to preempt anything that might've hurt her.

"Finn."

I shoot up in bed, my heart nearly jumping out of my chest. Halston stands with one hand curled around the inside of her dry elbow, still in her dress, tights, and pumps. I look at the clock. 7:49 A.M. She's never up and dressed this early on a weekend. For one selfish moment, I hope she's been wandering around all night, but I know it isn't true. She's been with him.

I sit up against the headboard. "What are you doing here?" I ask, my voice scratchy.

She flinches. "I'm sorry about last night."

"Me too."

The sun highlights the bags under her eyes. The bright red color of her cheeks tells me she's been crying. It's not enough to make me go to her.

She steps into the room, taking off her shoes. "We hit a hundred thousand," she says. "Even without the last photo. Happy birthday."

I clench my teeth together. Again with this shit. I'm so fucking tired of hearing about followers, likes, comments. "Why are you here?" I repeat.

Her chin trembles. "For you. I get it now. I understand it better."

"Yeah? Explain it to me."

"None of us are without our faults or even . . . mistakes. I'm not saying I'll accept being manipulated or controlled, but I'm beginning to see that it's always come from a good place. Even with Rich."

"Stop."

"But—"

"I don't know what this is, but if you're here to justify going back to him, you can turn around and leave."

"That's not what I'm doing. I'll just get to the point. I had a long talk with my dad this morning. He came to Rich's. I've been fighting him for so long, and I'm tired. So is he. We have work to do, but I know he loves me and wants what's best for me. *He's* trying to understand that I'm the one who knows what that is, not him. Ten years ago, he didn't think he had any other option but to get me professional care." She takes a breath. "And now, it's like I've opened my eyes. If I'm not angry at him, I can see you and Rich better. You want to protect me out of love, nothing more. Am I right?"

All I ever did was love her, hard. It's defeating to try and explain that to her. I'm happy she's finally getting there, but I also feel other things about it. Things I don't yet understand. Like will her sentience keep? Was last night just a preview of what's to come down the line? And am I ready for a potential lifetime of that?

The answer is yes. I can handle it. Or, I could have, before she made her decision and got into that cab.

"I want to keep you safe and happy because I love you," I say carefully. "I love you so much, Hals, it hurts. Is it supposed to hurt?"

"A little, I think," she says, her voice breaking. "It never hurt with anyone else, not like this. Doesn't that mean something?"

"It means when you can't handle the pain, you'll go to them. The ones who can't hurt you."

She shakes her head. "That's not true."

"You did it last night."

She swallows. A few tears leak over her cheeks. I want to go to her, take her in my arms, tell her I forgive her for what she did. The one thing—the only thing—I asked her not to ever do. Go back to him. Choose something or someone over me, the way everyone else in my life has. Because there's only one way to describe what that choice did to us.

"Deal breaker," I tell her. "I could've forgiven you anything else. Just not this."

"But nothing happened," she pleads, walking to the bed. "I slept on the couch. I barely even talked to him."

That's probably the least of my worries. After the way she and I have fucked, you don't go back to someone like Rich for sex. "I believe you didn't cheat on me. But it still doesn't matter."

She sits on the mattress edge, close to me, and lifts a hand as if to touch me. I look at it, and she scratches her elbow instead. "I don't love him, either. And I meant it when I said I'd never return to him."

"Sadie, who I thought I loved, chose someone else. My mom chose alcohol. Marissa, she's going to choose Kendra if things keep going as they are. I believed you'd stick with me no matter how hard it got."

"I do. I can. I will."

We stare at each other. She's in my sheets, in my head. She always will be. I don't know what to do. I can't imagine going on without her, but this feels like the worst kind of betrayal. Indecision wars in me.

As she searches my face, her expression eases, and she sits back. "You're right. I have to go."

"What?" I ask. "Where?"

"I have to leave you." Tears fill her eyes again, but she inhales them back and persists. "If I don't, you'll forgive me now and let me stay."

It was true the day she walked into the coffee

shop, and it's true now. I can't walk away. I can't ask her to leave. She's a part of me.

"You shouldn't have locked me out of the account last night. Maybe I would've revealed myself, maybe not—but it was a mistake I needed to make. If I don't make these mistakes, I won't grow up. You're the one who told me that." She sniffs. "I need help, Finn."

I want to help her. So fucking bad. I thought I was doing that all these months, constantly trying to protect her, deleting what I didn't want her to see, watching my words about all things coffee, wine, shopping and smoking so I wouldn't say something to make her feel scolded. She's right, though. I want to kiss her tears away and make it better, but I can't. She has to figure this out on her own, and it's too much for one man, trying to save her from everything. I shouldn't have bitten my tongue about her stopping treatment on her own when I knew it wasn't a good idea. The only way I can help her now is by letting her get the help she needs.

She stands and picks up her shoes. I almost can't take it. Where will she go? She needs me. I need her. "You can stay a few days," I tell her. "While you figure things out."

She looks at me and shakes her head. "If I do, I'll break down into a puddle of tears, and you? You'll pick me up. Dust me off. It's who you are." She takes a deep breath. "I love you, Finn. I love you enough to clean up my own mess."

THIRTY-TWO

All the benches inside the park are taken, even the one semi-hidden by a tree, the one I've declared as *my* bench. Not surprising, since it's a beautiful day. I have to sit on a window ledge across from the park for a few minutes of peace.

Well, peace is pushing it.

When my mind is left to its own devices, it eventually drifts to *her*, and she brings me anything but peace. The memory of her walking out, barefoot in tights, a slump in her shoulders, stings just as sharp now as it did five weeks ago.

I pop the lid off my cup and toss the teabag in a nearby garbage can. I'm not much of a coffee drinker these days. First Sadie, now Halston. It's got an unfortunate amount of involvement in introducing me to bogus soul mates. Some days, I want to say fuck it and go get Halston. It still feels like I'm missing a limb, and it doesn't help that every goddamn square inch of my apartment, with the exception of Marissa's room, is a reminder of her. There's no surface I didn't fuck her on. No corner I didn't kiss her in. No chair she didn't sit in my lap. I might have to give up the place.

I snap the top back in place and take a tentative sip. When I look up and see her coming my way, I nearly spit out my drink but overcorrect and end up dumping burning hot liquid onto my tongue. I use my napkin to mop up the spillage, my gaze trained on her. She hasn't seen me.

Sadie.

My heart hammers in my chest. She walks in my direction. My urges jump between stopping her and bolting, but it looks like I won't be doing either since I'm frozen to the spot. As stealthily as I can, I lower my sunglasses onto my face in hopes she won't see me.

Fuck. In a city this big, I'd hoped I'd never have to see her again. I don't know where she lives now, probably Brooklyn, but she left this neighborhood right after Nathan found out about us.

She looks the same, except that I've never seen her in spring, only winter. I remember her as dark, but she's wearing a pink dress. To my surprise, it suits her. Her face is fuller, her dark hair shorter. A year and a half ago, I would've called her the love of my life, my soul mate, my future. Now I know—she was little more than someone in the right place at the right time. Or the wrong place at the wrong time, depending how you look at it.

Me? Now that I'm completely over her, I can say it was right. I don't miss her. It's a good thing she chose Nathan, because if she hadn't, I never would've met Halston.

Even if just thinking Halston's name is like a knife in my heart, I don't regret a second of my time with her.

As Sadie passes by, the only urge I have left is to thank her for knowing better than I did. I will it to her, hoping she knows on some level that I'm grateful.

And then she stops.

Fuck.

She's a foot past me when she says, without looking back, "I have a baby now. A boy. Nathan, Jr."

I let the news sink in. It could've been me, and I'm glad it wasn't. I respond, sincerely, "I'm happy for you."

"What about you? Have you met her yet?"

"Who?"

"The girl. The soul mate. *The one.*"

"You don't believe in fate."

She tilts her head. "Maybe I changed my mind."

I don't have to think too hard about it. "Yeah. I've met her."

I think she's about to walk off, but then she turns around. She takes off her sunglasses, and so do I. Her eyes are as beautiful as I remember, an intoxicating blend of purple and blue. They're not the cool, calm-before-the-storm gray I want in my life, though.

She comes and sits on the ledge next to me. "And?"

"And what?" My breakup with Halston is on both our shoulders. Just like with Sadie, I put a lot of stock in fate, in meant-to-be. I trusted love was enough, even though I knew better. "I fucked it up. Is that what you expected to hear?"

She sighs, fidgeting with her sunglasses. "Of course not."

"What's wrong with me, Sadie? Why can't I get it right?"

She smiles softly. The baby has made her warmer, I think. "I'm so sorry for how I hurt you. It was brutal. Nathan was my priority, and I didn't have the time to let you down easy. But you know . . . Nate and I, we're so happy now. And we're not."

My body tenses. I don't want to hear this. I don't need to know how content or miserable she is.

"Because that's love, Finn. We work at it every day, still, even though we both understand that the other person isn't going anywhere, even when times are tough."

"What are you saying?"

"Happy endings don't exist. That's your problem. You thought you and I would ride off into the sunset and let fate take the reins." She squints out at the park and shakes her head. "Nope. Fate doesn't stick around for happy endings—it only gives you the opportunity to work for one."

Sadie's been in Halston's shoes. She's had to withstand the pressure of being 'the one.' I know I lay it on thick. I expected to save Halston, and for her to save me. So that I could have my fairytale. And that's not exactly fair.

Sadie slips her sunglasses back on. "I have to get back to work, but I have a feeling you'll be okay. If she's really the one, you'll get her back."

Halston is my soul mate, love of my life, my future. She's a handful and a lot of work, but I've made it this far. Sadie's right. Why would I give it up to fate now, knowing that fucker'll fumble the ball?

She stands and continues down the sidewalk.

"Sadie?"

She looks back at me. "Hmm?"

"Thank you."

The next morning, I admit to myself I don't really like tea. Not every day. Even though it's painful to be there, I miss Lait Noir. It can't be any worse than being at home, so I get my laptop and camera and head down the street to the café for the first time since Halston left.

There's nowhere to sit. It was idiotic to think fate had reserved me a table in a coffee shop or a park in a bench.

Honestly, what the fuck.

I check to see if my secret windowsill is open, so I'll at least have a place to wait for a table to open up.

But what's on the ledge sucks the breath right out of my lungs.

Memories hammer my brain like little metal bullets.

Not again.

I can't go through this a second time.

This is a sick joke.

I walk over slowly, staring at the journal wrapped up in a leather bow. My chest tightens with regret, love, sorrow, longing. I look around, but nobody's nearby. Maybe someone ran to the bathroom and left it to save their spot. Maybe it's an illusion. Maybe fucking aliens beamed it down from outer space. Yeah, that sounds likelier than the other possibility.

It belongs to Halston.

I should walk away.

I pick it up.

Open it.

Like the first time, the opening lines slam me in the chest, but for a different reason.

December 8th

I think I've met the one. Which is strange, because that was supposed to be Rich. I never had this feeling with him, though. This fluttering in my tummy. I'm glad to report (fiiiinally) that butterflies do exist.

I can't do this. I can't be reading this. I continue.

Okay, butterflies are a bad way to describe love. That sounds more like lust. That would be fine too. I've always wanted to know what true lust felt like. I can't possibly love this man I just met one week ago. Oh—Finn. His name is Finn.

I skip ahead.

January 23rd
Rough
Sandpaper kisses as calloused as your hands, as domineering as your fuck, as excruciating as your goodbyes. When you say hello, I can't wait to do it all over again.

February 14th
He's the last Valentine I ever want.

With that entry, there's a rough sketch of us at dinner. All that time, she *was* writing. Just not for anyone else but her, like it was in the beginning. The journal is filled to the last line of the very last page. It's an entry she wrote a few days ago.

April 15th
I still love him. He should have this journal. He knows my heart is this, these pages, these words. And my heart belongs with him, not me.

"Fuck," I mutter.

A woman waiting for her coffee looks at me.

"This is yours," I tell her, hoping she's also in love with some schmuck named Finn. "Right? This is yours."

She shakes her head, inching away from me.

In the top corner of the last page is a drawing of two black and white coffee cups with a heart around them. They each have Lait Noir logos scribbled in. Where it all began.

She's here, I know it. I scan the café until I spot her in line, waiting. She must've been here the whole time, because there are a lot of people behind her, and she's next to order.

I don't hesitate to walk right up behind her. "Is this for me?"

She doesn't turn around. "If you want it."

I don't even try to fight my pull to her. I've missed this, her. The missing her sits like a hole in my chest. "Sit down with me."

"There aren't any tables."

"I know a place."

"Back of the line, man," the guy behind me says. "You think I'm standing here for my health?"

"Two black coffees," I tell the barista. I reach past Halston to put a ten on the counter and get a welcome waft of her shampoo. "Keep the change if you make it fast."

The barista makes quick work of delivering our drinks.

Halston keeps her back to me as she picks up the coffee, inhales quickly enough that nobody'd catch it but me, and heads for the windowsill.

She doesn't look at me once, but I don't remove my eyes from her. "What's wrong?" I ask and let my half-smile rip. "Are you worried I've let myself go?"

"I don't want to look at you until I know what you're going to say," she says.

"*I* don't even know what I'm going to say. Are we going to sit back to back?"

"If we have to."

"I still love you too. How's that for a start?"

She shakes her head. "I already knew that."

I get a sense of satisfaction from hearing that. With all the things said between us, how we hurt each other, sometimes on purpose, how I told her I couldn't let it go that she'd walked out on me, one might think it'd dampen my love for her. Not the case. "Sit," I tell her.

She does and finally looks up. She's wearing blue eyeliner. Little minx. With the sun coming in through the window, the blue makes her gray eyes pop. I take the place across from her. "I thought of you the other day," I say. "Well, I think of you most hours of every day, but, in particular, I thought of calling you."

She looks at her coffee and flicks the edge of the lid. "I had to delete your number or I would've called countless times."

"Why didn't you?"

She lifts one shoulder. "It didn't seem fair. Not until I was ready."

"So this?" I show her the journal. "It means you're ready?"

"It means . . . I didn't want you to forget about me."

"Never."

She fails to suppress a smile. "I moved in with Benny."

I raise my eyebrows. "You have a roommate?"

She nods. "I was nervous to do it, but the alternative was moving to Westchester with Dad or getting my own place again. I bit the bullet and asked if she knew of anyone looking. It turns out her roommate was leaving at the end of the month, and she was actually really excited to have me. I crashed on her couch and officially moved in April first."

I don't want to sound like a condescending asshole, so I don't tell her I'm proud of her, even though I am. "How is it?"

"I don't mind the smell of sautéed Brussels sprouts. Tuna, on the other hand . . ." She laughs. "Benny has these two cats, and they're—I mean, they're just like her friends. Sassy, loud, playful. Her friends are so fun. We meet them after work. We get dinner or drinks or go check out a new neighborhood. Or some of them have side businesses, so we take our laptops to cafés and work side by side. We went to this outdoor movie in a park, where you put a blanket down—"

Her grin fades, probably because I'm staring at her, lapping up every word from her mouth.

"I mean, it's been hard too," she says quietly. "Don't get me wrong. I miss you all the time."

"I want you to be having fun, Hals. It makes me happy. What do *you* work on? On your laptop?"

"Oh, nothing. I don't have a business." She bites her bottom lip with a smile. "Well, I've been doing a little writing. It's starting to flow again. My new therapist says sometimes, you have to force it, you can't wait for inspiration to strike because it might not." A strand of hair falls over her face, and I'm tempted to tuck it behind her ear.

I keep my hands to myself. "New therapist?"

She nods. "Cindy. She got me into journaling in the mornings. It has to be first thing, and it changes my whole day."

"Is that what this is about?"

She looks lovingly at the journal in my hand. "No. I started that when we met. I had a feeling you and I could fill a book, but I was afraid what you'd think if you knew. I obsessed, Finn. You were my coffee, did you know?"

I bring my drink to my mouth, appreciating its warmth. "I think so."

Because you were mine.

"I wrote about you when I wasn't with you. Not all the time, but some days. We only filled it halfway." She frowns. "So when my therapist suggested journaling, I decided to do it in there some days. So I could look back on my transformation."

"Shouldn't you keep it then?"

"Consider it a belated birthday present."

I grip the book. This gift is better than anything she could've bought, and she knows that. It's just one more way to understand, to know her inside out, the love of my life. Maybe her obsession with me has quelled, I'm afraid to ask, but mine with her is strong as ever.

"Speaking of coffee. Are you still drinking it?"

"In moderation." She holds up the cup to make a point. "I still have my urges, but now I try to write about it instead of act on it. It doesn't always work, but it helps. And I'm back on antidepressants, just a different brand and a lower dosage. We're experimenting. Cindy promises it isn't forever."

"Yeah," I nearly whisper. "Can't have my girl losing her fire."

She chews the inside of her cheek, glancing at my lips. "Do you miss it? Us together?"

I make a fist around the leather in my hand. "I thought it couldn't get any worse than when Sadie left, but this feels like sleeping on a bed knives and waking up every morning with re-opened wounds. You know what it's like for me to live where you've slept, eaten, come?"

She blushes. "I wouldn't be able to do it. I'd have moved out."

I can hear the pain in her voice. I didn't think I could be any more miserable, but seeing her miserable too makes it worse. I know going back to therapy was no easier than leaving her stable relationship with Rich. She could've gotten back together with him, gone back to that easy life. Instead, she went outside her comfort zone, made new friends, continued to follow her passion. I tuck the journal under one arm and finally reach out for that lock of hair. It feels like the softest, finest silk between my fingers. I move it behind her ear, grazing the tattoo. "I have Marissa this weekend, but why don't we get dinner next week? See how it is?"

She takes my wrist. It's cold, her hand that isn't holding the coffee, and I want to warm it with my lips. But she pulls my hand away from her face. "No."

No. Did I misread her just now? Did I imagine everything backward these past weeks, assuming she was as broken up about this as I was? I make a fist and put it in my lap. "Why not, Hals?"

"Because I still have work to do on myself. And so do you."

"I know I do. I've been taking on more commercial work, trying to see it in a more positive way. Just because it's not *art*, doesn't mean it's not valuable." I pause. "And just because something's right doesn't mean it'll come together effortlessly. Like with you. We have to work at it."

"You're right, but it's not enough. I need you to let me into all parts of your life. I want to meet

Marissa and maybe even Kendra. If we're going to do this for real."

I try not to look as frightened as I feel hearing that. My relationship with Halston is a breeze compared to the mess that is my other life. Just one mess after another, I suppose. Maybe it's time to meld them all. "I'll work on it," I say. "Not this month, and maybe not next, but I'll start the conversation with Kendra."

She smiles a little and stands. "I have to go, or I'm afraid I'll change my mind. I want to meet you again when I'm a better version of myself—my *real* self."

"How long?" I ask. "Maybe we can just start now, but take it slow."

She kisses the tips of her fingers and presses them to my cheek. "Not yet."

THIRTY-THREE

halston

When I come out of my room, Benny's sprawled out on the couch in front of the TV. "Have you heard of this show, *The Real World*?" she asks.

"Um, yes," I say, "everybody has."

"No, I mean like the real *Real World*, back from the nineties, before reality TV. MTV's doing a special on it. It's so dope, I can't believe I never saw it."

I sigh. "Let's trade places. *Please*."

She sucks Cheetos dust off her index finger. "Nope."

"But I said please."

"You've been looking forward to this for weeks."

"Oh, you mean the pacing, nail-biting, and extra-long bathroom breaks? You took that as anticipation?"

"TMI." She finally glances at me. "You look hot, by the way. Red is a good choice."

"Thanks." I know I do. I *have* to. I spent too much time and money picking out this summer dress, but it'll only be the second time I've seen Finn in two months, and I need everything to go well. If he's changed his mind about me, I'll be forced to find a way to move on, and I'm not sure I can.

Benny pauses the DVR. "Don't be nervous."

I wonder how she can tell. I've been to a dermatologist about my itchy elbow, and she gave me a cream, but recommended I discuss it with my therapist. Cindy and I are working through it. I still get the urge to scratch it, but I'm way better at recognizing and identifying what's behind the impulse.

"He'll lose his shit," Benny says. "Just hope it stays gone long enough for him to forgive you."

I smirk. Benny knows all the dirty details of my relationship with Finn. It's how we bonded the first few nights I stayed with her. It feels really good to have it all out there and accepted. "What if he doesn't show up?" I ask, widening my eyes. "Or worse, what if he's met someone else? Or fallen out of love with me?"

"He hasn't."

"How do you know?"

She hesitates. "I didn't say anything earlier because you've been avoiding it so well, but since you're going to see him, I'll tell you. I follow your guys' Instagram, and girl . . . it's depressing as fuck. That man has no love in his life."

My eyes fill with unexpected tears even as my heart soars. I don't want Finn to be depressed. When he hurts I hurt. But I also don't want him to not love me anymore. "What does he post?"

"Really sad-looking shit, like old churches, park benches, a pile of leaves."

"Me?" I ask.

"Never."

"How many followers do we—does he have?"

She grimaces. "You don't want to know. Let's just say it's less than it was."

I take a deep breath. It's okay. There are more important things than being admired by strangers. I pick up my bag of goodies from the dining room table. "Wish me luck."

"One more thing," she says as I turn to leave.

I look over my shoulder. "What?"

"Tell him about the offer. Even though you're not doing it, I think he'd like to know. That's all. Have fun. If you can't help fucking his brains out tonight, don't bring it back here." She salutes me and returns to her TV show.

I get an Uber to the gallery. There's one detail I've tried hard to overlook, and that's whether or not Finn actually knows we have a date tonight. I have to believe he does. If he read my journal in its entirety, then he would've found the entry dated six days before I gave it to him.

April 12th

I have this idea to show Finn what he means to me, but I'm not sure if it will work. Or if he'll even want me to do it. Or if I have the guts to do it.

Then, I waited. I staked out Lait Noir for days. On the verge of calling it quits, he finally came in. I left the journal on the ledge after scribbling a note in red pen next to the entry.

Vee Gallery, 8pm, May 4th

Three times, I almost e-mailed Finn to cancel. Once, because the gallery owner tried to tell me he could no longer accommodate that date. And twice because those guts I was hoping to have? They went missing.

The car drops me off on the sidewalk in front of Vee Gallery. It looks all wrong. Through the windows, I see nothing but light and white. Too-bright, empty walls. No person should pass by a gallery and see this, and I remind myself to thank the owner again for letting me do this, even if it'll be the fiftieth time.

I let myself in and get to work. I have about an hour before Finn—*hopefully*—arrives. It's a lot to hang on *hopefully*, but he's worth it. When I finish, I dim the lights just a touch so he won't see what's inside before I'm ready to show him. After some debate, I decide to wait for him outside on this perfect May night.

And wait . . . and wait.

Twenty minutes past eight, my nerves have the best of me. He isn't coming. What do I do? If I call him and he saw the note, I'll look desperate. But if he didn't, he'll miss all this. And I don't want that.

I was so sure he'd come.

I inhale and exhale deeply. I've started yoga aimed at people recovering from addiction. The teacher says when we crave something, one of the ways to combat it is to breathe through it. I crave. If I can't have Finn, I crave something to make me forget him.

I close my eyes and breathe.

I'm watching the street, expecting a car. So when I open my eyes and realize someone's standing next to me, I nearly jump out of my skin.

Finn looks down at me. "This dress can only mean one thing," he says. "You brought me here to reconcile. If you break up with me for good in that dress, that's just the cruelest thing I can think of."

My laugh is nervous, but his directness helps break the ice. Right off the bat I understand that he's here to make things work, not let me down easy. Benny was right. The red dress was a good choice.

"Sorry I'm late," he says. "I was going to catch a cab, but it's such a nice night and I needed the extra time to . . . prepare." He squints behind me. "I assumed this was a show or something, so I didn't think I had to be here right at eight."

I take his hand, and he looks back at me. "Is this okay?" I ask.

He tucks some of my hair behind my ear. "You tell me."

I close my eyes a split second to relish the feel of his palm to mine, the brush of his fingers in my hair. Over my feather. "Come on," I say, pulling him behind me into the gallery.

He steps inside and immediately drops my hand. I watch with bated breath as he takes in the scene around him. "What is this?"

I survey the space with him. This in and of itself could be an installation, but it's not. It's just a sketch of one. I've strung Christmas lights along each wall. Taped underneath are small five-by-five prints, ten to a wall. Benny printed them all off for me, and I chose thirty I thought showed Finn's best work.

"It's not much," I say. "I just wanted to show you how it could look."

He walks along the nearest wall, taking in each print. "How what could look?"

"I know the owner through the agency. I wore him down until he finally agreed to look at your work. He loved it, Finn, and I swear, he's a hard ass about these things. It's no favor."

"What isn't? I don't understand."

"He wants you to have your debut show here. I explained to him the kind of following we had, and after seeing your work, he's convinced you're the next big thing. That's why he let me do this tonight. We want to show you how amazing it could be."

He runs a hand through his hair, spun gold sprouting from his fingers. "Are you serious?"

I nod. "He's between shows tonight, so I did some begging to get the space."

"What about you?" Finn asks. "This is your body. Your boyfriend's work. Some people will know it's you."

I take a breath. The thought of having my dad here makes my heart palpitate. But we've been working with Cindy too, and he needs to know this side of me for us to have an honest relationship. He has to meet Finn. "I'm good with it if you are."

"Will he let us put your captions up next to the photos?"

"I want this to be about your work, not me."

"They belong together," he says. "Don't you think?"

I swallow through the lump in my throat. They *do* belong together, yes. "I'm sure it could be arranged, but only your name goes on the promotional material. I have something else going."

He comes over and takes my hand to kiss my knuckle. "Tell me all about it."

"I've put together some of my favorite passages from my journals and submitted them to agents as a book of poetry. It's a long shot, but—"

"No it's not."

"It is." I nod. "But that's okay. Rejection will happen, and it's healthy and normal, Cindy says."

"Have you heard back from any of the agents?"

"No." I take my hand back and wipe my palms on my dress. "Well, kind of."

He brightens up. "Already?"

"I turned it down. One guy said he had a publisher interested, but not in my writing, per se. They wanted our story. Sort of like a memoir, I guess, with a social media spin." I'm no longer looking at Finn, so I can't read his reaction.

"Why'd you turn it down?"

"It's not my story to tell. I'm not even sure I want to try."

"You should."

I look up at him. "It was exposing ourselves that caused problems in the first place. I don't want to put you or myself through that again."

He makes a point of looking around the room, at the myriad photos of me on the wall.

"Touché," I say, "but this is your art."

"And that's yours. Write the memoir, Hals. I'll be by your side through the whole thing. This is who we are, these pictures, your words—isn't it? I don't want to be ashamed of that."

I release a breath I didn't realize I was holding. "Neither do I. I'd like it if we could even . . . keep posting?" It's a bold suggestion after the last six months, but like Finn said—it's who we are.

"Me too," he says, to my relief. "I've tried to maintain the account, but I'm having some trouble finding subjects as interesting as you."

I smile. "I deleted the app from my phone the day I left, but Benny told me. We'll figure it out. Maybe we can try food porn instead?"

He laughs. "We don't have to change the kinds of photos we take. It's how we dealt with stuff that was the problem. I can't protect you from everything. We have to work through the shitty stuff—together—and then move on. No running away."

I nod. "We have to be partners in everything. A team."

"Yeah. We've always made a really good team." He puts an arm around my neck, drawing me in for a kiss. Finally, I get what I really did all this work for—those to-die-for, pillowy lips of his. "I love you," he murmurs. "I don't have a single doubt about that or about us. One day soon, we'll make our team official. If you'll have me."

My cheeks heat. "No doubts here, either. I love you. And I'll have you."

I think Finn just proposed to me in some untraditional, roundabout way.

And I think I just accepted.

Who needs traditional anyway?

#finnandhalston
#TheEnd

TITLES BY JESSICA HAWKINS

LEARN MORE AT JESSICAHAWKINS.NET/BOOKS

SLIP OF THE TONGUE

THE FIRST TASTE

YOURS TO BARE

THE CITYSCAPE SERIES

COME UNDONE
COME ALIVE
COME TOGETHER

EXPLICITLY YOURS SERIES

POSSESSION
DOMINATION
PROVOCATION
OBSESSION

STRICTLY OFF LIMITS

ACKNOWLEDGMENTS

There would be no book to acknowledge without
1) my wonderfully persistent readers
2) my wonderfully patient editor
Elizabeth London: you helped me brainstorm and plot this book when I wasn't sure I wanted to write it. You guided me to the right idea, then through the ins and outs of Finn and Halston's story. Thank you for making Finn happen. Katie from Underline This Editing, you are my safety net. Thank you for always catching what I miss.

Michele Catalano, you dropped everything to bring Finn's cover to life with your brilliant design, and Jade Gabrielle, I just couldn't resist your beautiful images. Thankfully. The *Yours to Bare* cover is life.

Melissa, Nina, Jenn, myriad bloggers and of course, author friends—Suzie, Louise, Staci, Kandi, Lisa, Adriana, Carter, Liv, Rachels, Amy, Brittainy, Lesley, KL, Ruth, the list goes on. Thank you for letting me fret and cry and bitch and moan and cheers and soar while leaning on you.

As always, my number one thanks goes to the readers. This book is 100% for you. My street team, who centers me, and The Penthouse, my reader group, a new venture that has been more fun and uplifting than I could've imagined. Thanks for being excited about Finn.

ABOUT THE AUTHOR

JESSICA HAWKINS grew up between the purple mountains and under the endless sun of Palm Springs, California. She studied international business at Arizona State University and has also lived in Costa Rica and New York City. To her, the most intriguing fiction is forbidden, and that's what you'll find in her stories. Currently, she resides wherever her head lands, which is often the unexpected (but warm) keyboard of her trusty MacBook.

CONNECT WITH JESSICA

Stay updated & join the
JESSICA HAWKINS Mailing List
www.JESSICAHAWKINS.net/mailing-list

www.amazon.com/author/jessicahawkins
www.facebook.com/jessicahawkinsauthor
twitter: @jess_hawk

Made in the USA
Middletown, DE
11 January 2017